# The Twins

## Book four in the Sword Masters' Universe

Selina Rosen

**YARD DOG PRESS**

# Dedication

For Brand Whitlock...
Here's hoping this book sells enough copies we can make
our hike in style; otherwise, it's you and me, a torn up
tarp, an old wool blanket, and a pocketful of dried beans on
the Ozark Trail.

# Chapter 1

*Persius looked down, and* the light from the two full moons was so bright that he could see every blade of grass, every wild flower. The weather was warm, and he was alone in a huge, empty field ringed by a dense forest. He looked into the sky just in time to see the two moons join. It was not an uncommon occurrence; it happened about twice a month, but he couldn't remember ever in his life watching the whole process.

He stood there for what seemed like hours watching as the moons came completely together and then moved apart. Finally he looked around and what had been an empty field was completely filled with huts. It was at that moment that he realized he was naked, but he also knew he had to be dreaming so he didn't care. He looked around at fields of growing grain and pens filled with animals. All around him everyone seemed busy doing something. He could tell by their coloring that they were Kartik, and then he saw her, Tarius the Black, walking through the camp wearing so little clothing she might as well have been as naked as he was. There was a blond-headed toddler holding her hand and she was talking to him though Persius couldn't hear her.

Tarius walked even with Persius without seeing him, but the child turned, looked up at him, and the boy's emerald green eyes burned into him. He didn't speak, just looked at him as if wondering what he was doing there. Suddenly Persius knew exactly where he was; he was standing naked in the middle of the Katabull compound. He woke with a start and sat straight up in bed, his breath coming in gasps.

The room was dark except for the hint of moonlight that slipped through the drapes. In it he could just make out the blond head resting on the pillow beside him. He ran his hands down his face and wished he were alone. That wasn't her fault. She couldn't help that she wasn't Tarius any more than he could help not caring about her sleep or comfort in that moment.

Persius got swiftly to his feet and yelled at the top of his lungs, "Hellibolt!"

**Tarius walked around** the compound with Darian holding her right hand and Pete holding her left. She had tried to change Petrid's name to Tweed for many reasons not the least of which was that Petrid was a horrid name for a Katabull, but he had been four and didn't know who they were talking to so he was Pete because as bad as "Pete the Katabull" sounded, "Petrid" was far worse.

Pete was six now and Darian nearly three; they were mostly inseparable. Since Darian wouldn't let Tarius leave the house without him, and since the minute he went outside he wanted to go see Pete, she usually had both boys as she walked around the Katabull compound seeing and being seen.

"There are too many of us here," Tarius said thoughtfully.

"Yes, too many," Darian echoed. Tarius smiled and looked down at his white head, her son so different from her people and yet so the same.

"What do you mean too many?" Pete asked.

"Even though we limit hunting there aren't enough elk, deer, rabbits and squirrels here anymore. We have to go further and further to find game. We are unable to bring the herds up to what they should be yet everyone wants more meat. Fish are still plentiful."

"Lots of fish," Darian said and made a face. He wasn't fond of fish.

"But the Katabull.... Well we love to hunt and bring down game; it's part of who we are. Because we live so long even though we watch our numbers there are too many of us for this land to sustain us much longer. We will need to separate our people and build a second homeland."

"Where, Madra?" Pete asked. That was another thing about the child that had been a little unnerving. No part of him belonged to Jena or Tarius. His parents had been killed, and he had been adopted by Rimmy and Hared; however, the minute he had become familiar with the terms the cross-paired couples used for their four parents he had started calling her "madra" and Jena "mother." All things considered it now seemed appropriate.

"We shall build it where our people started. We will move

to inhabit the land which should have been ours in the first place," Tarius said. She smiled when she saw Jena walking to join them.

"Ours," Darian said.

"Well I guess that's better than *mine*," Tarius told Pete with a grin.

He grinned back and nodded his head.

She stopped, barely slowing the boys as Jena embraced her. Tarius would have hugged her back if she didn't have her hands full of boys. She kissed Jena's cheek instead. Jena was grinning at her. "What is it?"

"Well first I think it's hysterical how you talk baby talk to them till they are two then immediately switch to talking to them as if they were little old men who understand the very complex subjects you talk to them about."

"It is how they learn. Now if you are going to walk with us get out of our way woman," Tarius said.

"Out of our way woman," Darian echoed.

Jena shook her finger in his face. "That's enough of your mouth, mister."

The boys cracked up.

Jena looked at Tarius, her excitement obvious. "Jestia is here."

A couple of years ago if anyone had told Tarius that Jena would ever have been happy to see Jestia, Tarius would have called them a liar. Much had changed. Tarius smiled at her knowing now why she was so excited. "Why did you not tell Riglid to come get me?"

"I sent him to get Jestia."

"You just couldn't wait, and considering how quickly she got here I'm guessing she couldn't either."

"She was just spotted coming into the compound."

Tarius laughed, "She isn't even really here yet."

"Yes she is.... She will be, by the time we get home she'll be there." Jena moved to take Darian's other hand and he beamed up at her. He loved her with his whole heart, much the way their oldest son did. He wasn't blood related to them, either, but he was theirs, and they'd had him since he was just hours old. They started walking back towards their huts, Jena setting the pace at a near run that the children could hardly keep up with.

"Jena my love I know you think you know, but please I beg you do not set your hopes too high."

**Jestia sat on the Katabull** throne inside Tarius's hut, grinned at Ufalla and said, "You know she will not care."

"I know you should not be sitting on the Katabull throne," Ufalla said, a bit jumpy. "I'm sure there must be some stupid prophecy or something in that book I don't think you should be reading since 'Forbidden' is in the title that starts with, 'When the heir to the Kartik throne sits on the Katabull throne...'."

"It is just a title, the book I mean. Would you please relax? Even if it didn't work this time that doesn't mean it won't ever work, and even if it doesn't work for them that doesn't mean it won't work for us when we're ready which I for one am not," Jestia said. She stood up telling her mate, "You worry too much."

Ufalla shook her head. "That's rich coming from you."

Jestia smiled seductively at Ufalla slid over to her and wrapped herself around her dragging her head down so that she could kiss her. When she moved her mouth away she said, "I wonder if there is some prophecy in the book of forbidden knowledge about a witch making love on the Great Leader's dining table."

"I don't know, but since I have children with me could you just this once not tempt fate?" Tarius said from outside the door.

"Damn! The walls in these things are so thin," Jestia whispered.

"Yes they are," Tarius said.

"And the Katabull's hearing so good," Ufalla added, releasing her as Jestia untangled herself and turned to watch as Jena walked in.

She heard Tarius talking to the boys. "Play in front of the hut, but stay out of the road and do NOT go to the lake or I will beat you."

"Yes, Madra," Pete intoned.

"Spank me and I go to the lake?" Darian asked.

"Child you slay me!" Tarius thundered. "You may NOT go to the lake."

The three of them were all laughing. When Tarius walked

in she looked at them and grinned. "He gets that from his mother."

"Odd, he sounded just like you when he said it." Jestia walked over and embraced Tarius and Tarius hugged her back in that way that was almost too tight that she was used to because it was the same way Ufalla hugged her. What she was sure she was never going to get used to was the transfer of power that ran through her whenever she touched Tarius. It had started right after they had been together at the energy well when all the Katabull had glowed blue—except Tarius, who had glowed white like her. Now whenever they touched there was this energy that passed between them that felt familiar in a way she couldn't explain even to herself but made it hard to let go of Tarius, but she did.

Tarius moved to hug Ufalla, and Ufalla whispered in her ear. "Jestia has been absolutely driving me nuts. We couldn't even stop to talk to my parents and we could see them from the road."

"I can hear you," Jestia said, but couldn't deny it. This was all her idea. Not only did she have selfish reasons for wanting it to work, but she also didn't want to disappoint either Tarius or Jena. "I will need to check you. Can we go in your room Jena?"

Jena nodded and led her through the covered walkway to the room she shared with Tarius.

"Lay down," Jestia said.

Jena did. "Did I send for you too soon, Jestia?"

"Seriously, it's been all I could do to stay away." Jestia dug in her pocket for a crystal pendulum, not that she really needed it. She had just reached that moment when she wanted to know really badly if it had worked, but didn't want to know at all if it wasn't exactly what she wanted it to be. "How have you been feeling?"

"A little tired is all. I went to Yri and he told me it was way too early for him to know." Jena smiled, knowing. "So are you stalling?"

"Yes."

"I think I am, so would you kindly just check to see?"

**Hared came running through** the front door with Rimmy not far behind him. It made Tarius smile because there was no faster Katabull on the planet than Rimmy, so if Hared had beat him it showed he was no calmer than the she, Jena or the witch were.

"I saw... Ufalla... playing... with the boys," he said, out of breath. "Well?"

"We don't know yet. Jestia is checking her now," Tarius said.

"I'm nervous. Are you nervous?" Hared asked.

"Of course she's nervous, dunderhead," Rimmy said with a laugh.

Tarius just nodded. She couldn't speak; she could barely breathe.

Jestia walked out of the room and her expression was hard to read until she smiled and said, "We're pregnant."

Hared grabbed her and hugged her, Tarius rushed past Jestia, grabbed Jena, picked her up and swung her around.

When she put her down Jena just looked at her. "I don't know why you're so surprised; I told you I was."

*A few months ago they* took Darian and went to visit Arvon and Dustan so that they could spend some time with their son and frankly so she and Jena could have a little time alone. She hadn't realized till Arvon and Dustan weren't living with them anymore how nice it was to have someone else to watch the baby every once in a while.

Since Rimmy and Hared had adopted Pete and there were just the two of them they had started trading off. Rimmy and Hared would take Darian, or she and Jena would take Pete. It worked out well because the boys just loved each other, and Darian would only let her and Jena out of his sight if he was with Pete.

At first Darian had thrown a living fit about staying with Arvon and Dustan without them. He loved his fathers but didn't want to be separated from his mothers. After Jena stopped feeling like the worst mother in the world, it was nice to just leave Darian with Arvon and Dustan for a few days and lay around in Jestia and Ufalla's spring. Jena was napping in the sun beside the spring when Jestia caught Tarius's attention. Tarius gave up the comfort of where she was laying and followed Jestia to one of the gardens that surrounded her spa.

"What... and don't ask me again to take your cousin home with me. We can make our own tea thank you," Tarius said.

Jestia smiled and sat at a table under a cherry tree in the back of the garden where—not too surprisingly—there was a fresh pot of tea. Jestia sat down across from her and poured cups for them both.

Tarius took a long drink. "Though he does make really good tea."

"You may never tell Eerin, but I'm only begging you to take him to get on his last nerve. The truth is he gets along well with the guests, does all the gardening and I've actually grown rather fond of him. And Ufalla.... Well, I sometimes think they have grown to be so tight that if he went she'd go with him, though they have very little in common."

"I know you didn't separate me from Jena to talk about your cousin or drink his tea. What is it?"

"I wouldn't dare to go to Jena with this without talking to you first. Tarius, if you could have your heart's desire what would it be?"

Tarius took a deep breath and let it out. "To know in my heart that there was not a single person who prayed to the Amalite gods left alive anywhere in the world. That their hateful beliefs and practices have been forever buried with their bodies"

"I didn't say your pride's desire I said your heart's desire, and I swear if you say world peace I will smack you."

Tarius didn't have to think about it at all. "I wish I'd never put Tragon in Jena's bed."

"You can't change the past, not even I can change the past. If you could have anything..."

Tarius laughed then. "Jestia, why not just tell me what you want me to say?"

"What is the one thing you always wanted that you thought you could never have?"

"I wish that Jena could have her own child."

The witch had smiled and took her hand. "You aren't wishing big enough my friend. You gave Jena half your life. When you did you undid the damage done to her when she miscarried. She can have another child. Now I'm asking you if you could have anything in the world...."

"I'd want Jena to have my baby."

Jestia laughed and said, "I can do that."

# Chapter 2

**"How?" Tarius wanted** to know.

"I found an ancient spell. When the twins converge, when the two become one, you lay between Jena and a suitable male.... And no, neither you nor Jena would have to have sex with him; in fact that would just muddle things. Just as the twins eclipse one another I do the spell, and the male's seed will pass through your body and then into Jena. The child would literally have three blood parents. He would be part of all of you—of course half Jena, but a quarter you and a quarter the male."

"I find that I must eat my words."

"How so?"

"I told your mother that there was no danger of Ufalla fathering your children because you weren't that powerful a witch. But you have found a way."

Jestia could hardly contain her excitement. "But I'm not ready to have children yet for a plethora of reasons. When Jazel told me that she was pretty sure Jena was no longer barren because of the nature of the spell I cast on her, I thought why shouldn't you have this if it's what you both want?"

"And if it works *you* will have to eat *your* words because if you can give Jena and I a baby that is both of ours, then you will take her back to the time when she thought the baby she carried was mine."

**She had immediately** told Jena everything Jestia had said. Jena didn't have even one moment of hesitation before she said yes she wanted to do it. Hared was a natural choice; he was Katabull and he had no blood child of his own. He and Rimmy were already like family, and the four of them were already sharing children.

Now they were going to have a baby in which their blood would run together. Hared and Rimmy and Pete would now officially be their family.

Ufalla came in tugging the boys with her. "Well?" she wanted to know. It was only then that Tarius realized she hadn't let go of Jena, and that she was in fact crying all over her.

For answer Hared looked at Pete and Darian in turn and said, "You're both going to have a new sibling."

Tarius let go of Jena, wiped her eyes on her sleeve, and turned to face the cubs. It was obvious they didn't understand what Hared had said. She looked at Pete and Darian and taking Jena's hand said, "We're having a baby, so now you are real brothers, and we will all live together, and you boys will share the room there." She pointed to the room Darian already lived in the one that had belonged to their grown son Jabone before him.

The boys started hugging each other and excitedly ran off to the room together as if they had never been there before.

Suddenly Tarius realized something; she turned to Jena. "How are we going to tell Jabone?

**It was hard to say** who was more excited: Jestia that her spell had worked, all the prospective parents, or the two boys. By nightfall Rimmy and Hared had moved into Arvon and Dustan's old room and Pete had moved into the room with Darian.

Ufalla and Jestia had gone to visit Ufalla's parent's huts and would spend the night there.

The problem was that the two boys weren't sleeping; Jena could hear them whispering. Katabull homes were a series of round huts connected by short, covered hallways. Theirs had four such rooms, the cubs' room being smack between the fathers' room and the mothers'. The huts were made of small twigs woven together and covered with mud and grass, so they could hear the cubs weren't sleeping but were instead talking.

"Go to sleep, boys!" Tarius boomed.

They got very quiet and then they giggled.

"Don't make me have to come in there!" Rimmy thundered.

The boys giggled again then got quiet.

Tarius held Jena close and whispered, "So how do you feel?"

"I'm a little tired, but.... I have never been this happy in my whole life, Tarius."

"Nor have I. It makes me wonder how I will tell Jabone so that he isn't hurt."

"Maybe we shouldn't tell him."

"I think he's going to notice when you are hugely pregnant."

"Madra, go to sleep!" Darian ordered. Pete started laughing.

Now the truth was that Jena was his Madra and Tarius his mother, but Pete called her Madra and Jena mother, and since Pete was around Darian so much as he learned to talk he had assigned them the same names Pete had. Though they'd tried to teach Darian differently it had never stuck.

Tarius looked at Jena and Jena whispered back. "You got pretty loud."

The boys were giggling and laughing again.

Tarius started to bellow at them, but Jena put a finger over Tarius's lips and whispered, "They are as excited as we all are. They will get tired and then they will fall asleep." She moved her finger and kissed Tarius gently on the lips "And I didn't mean we shouldn't tell Jabone about the pregnancy just maybe we shouldn't tell him that the baby is both of ours."

"While I don't think we should tell the whole of the Katabull Nation or Jestia will never be able to do anything else for the rest of her life, in any family especially ours that is the kind of thing that has a way of coming out and then what will Jabone think that we hid it from him? That we don't love him as much? We do. This is just different, and maybe *that's* what we shouldn't tell him. Hell, Darian has none of our blood running through him, but we love him as if he were our own. Why wouldn't I love the son I bore as much as this baby...? But this is *our* baby, Jena, yours and mine.... Well and Hared's, but mostly yours and mine. It's something I never dreamed we'd have but always wanted, and something you once thought we had but we didn't."

"You're right; the part we shouldn't tell him is that it's different."

**Jabone pulled Kasiria** through the front door.

"Jabone, we should at least knock," Kasiria said.

Jabone laughed at her then kissed the top of her head.

"And I have told you this is my house. I don't have to knock on the door of my house."

"The sun isn't even up yet, and it's obvious everyone is asleep," Kasiria whispered.

"They won't be for long. Hey I could be anyone!" he bellowed.

His Madra walked out of her room pulling her robe around her. "Shush, Jabone. You'll wake the whole house; is something wrong?" Tarius asked.

"I couldn't sleep."

"So you wake your wife and come to wake your mothers?" Tarius rubbed at her eyes, shifting to her Katabull eyes so she could see in the dim light.

"Brother!" Darian came running down the hall and jumped into Jabone's waiting arms. "Pete live with me."

"I know," Jabone rolled his eyes. It had been a few weeks since Rimmy, Hared and Pete had moved in with his mothers and brother, but the baby still had to tell him every time he saw him.

"You can take him with you when you go because I'm going back to bed."

"Don't you even want to know why I couldn't sleep?"

His Madra smiled then walked up, hugged his neck and kissed his cheek and then hugged and kissed his brother as he held him. His brother immediately wanted his Madra, so he handed him off. Jabone knew Darian wasn't going anywhere with him. Until a few months ago he wouldn't even sleep in his own room. He was still sleepy because he lay his head on his Madra's shoulder and started patting her back as she patted his which, was sort of cute.

"So why couldn't you sleep?" his Madra asked.

"Can you wake mother up?"

"Child, you slay me. Your mother needs her sleep."

"I'm already awake." His mother walked into the room walked over and hugged his neck and then kissed his cheek. Then she looked at his Madra. "What's all this then, did he find out?"

His Madra shook her head no.

"We have news," Jabone said. He looked at Kasiria. She blushed and shook her head no. "We're going to have a cub."

"Very funny," his Madra said. "So who told you?"

Jabone was confused. "What? It's not a joke. Yri told Kasiria last night. We are going to have a baby."

His mother hugged his neck and then she hugged Kasiria's. "That is wonderful."

When Jabone looked at his Madra she looked happy but she also looked worried. "Madra, are you not happy for us?"

"Of course I am." She smiled at him. "Of course I am. It's just.... You and I need to talk alone." Darian had gone back to sleep so she carried him towards his room to put him back to bed.

"Is something wrong with Madra?" Jabone asked. His mother just beamed at him hugged him and kissed him again. She backed away and looked up at him.

"Nothing is wrong at all, and this is the best news, but.... She has something she wants to tell you alone is all."

His Madra walked back out walked over and kissed his mother on the cheek and said, "You can tell Kasiria our good news." Tarius took Jabone's hand and pulled him out the door. The sun was just coming up.

**Tarius wished now that** she hadn't been such a chicken shit and had just told him as soon as they knew for sure. She walked far enough away from their hut that Kasiria—who was Katabull—couldn't hear them.

"Son I must admit I am surprised I didn't know you were trying to get pregnant," she said.

"Does it make you unhappy?"

"Not at all, I just didn't know you were trying."

"We weren't but I'm happy. I want cubs and the sooner the better. Kasiria still always changes and so I do because otherwise it's sort of awkward. I had always heard that in your Katabull form you can't get pregnant so I'm happily surprised."

Tarius ran her hands across her face and through her hair. That was what she was afraid of. She wanted a second to process it, but her son wasn't going to give her that and who could blame him? "Madra what's wrong?"

"What did Yri say when you told him you had conceived in your Katabull form?"

"I wasn't there. Kasiria didn't feel well and she'd missed her cycle so she went to him and..."

"She's Jethrik so there is no way she would have told him you were Katabull. Do you know why young Katabull sometimes cat out during sex?"

"Passion."

Tarius looked at him with a certain amount of disgust. "It isn't passion. Do you think I don't have passion for your mother? And though I don't talk about it I have a history of sometimes changing when I don't will it. I have only catted out once during sex by accident and not with your mother. I did it a couple of times with your mother just to do something different, but…"

"I'm sure I didn't need to know that, Madra," Jabone said, making a face.

"My point is young Katabull change during sex because of fear not passion."

"Kasiria doesn't fear me; she certainly doesn't fear sex."

"There are all kinds of fear, Jabone. She was raised in the Jethrik and they have very weird repressed views of sex. For one thing, women aren't supposed to *want* sex. She is still embarrassed about it, afraid of what *wanting* it makes her. She couldn't even tell us she was pregnant as if it is a shameful thing. You are here before the sun comes up; you wanted to tell us last night but she had to process it."

"How did you know…?"

"You're my cub I know you, and your mother was also raised in the Jethrik. I lived there many years; I know their ways and customs."

"We have been together over two years most of the time she starts it and…"

"I'm not sure I needed to know that," Tarius said and grinned. "This is all beside the point. The thing is that eventually she will get more comfortable and she won't change. The more she is able to control when she changes…" Tarius had been working with Kasiria and now Kasiria could bring on a change. It was still work for her, but she could do it. "…the more she won't change without willing it. But…. You conceived this child when you were both Katabull; it is extremely rare."

"Why do I hear worry and not just surprise in your voice?"

"Because I'm not sure you, and especially Kasiria, are prepared for what your child will be."

"Now you're scaring me, Madra."

"There is no reason to be scared, and each child poses different challenges. You know how Waden always wears his Katabull form?" Jabone nodded silently and looked back towards the hut where his wife was. Tarius took a deep breath and let it out. "That is because Katabull and not human is his primary form. I have known only four other Katabull like him. For almost all of us human is our primary form because you see most Katabull cannot conceive while one or both of them are in their Katabull form. Your child was conceived while both you and Kasiria were the Katabull, and that means your child's primary form will be Katabull. He will be born Katabull; we will have to teach him to change into his human form. Just like we normally have to learn to change from human to Katabull, he will have to learn to change from Katabull to human."

Jabone sighed with relief. "Is that all? I thought he was going to be born with two heads or no legs or an imbecile."

She was glad he wasn't destroyed, but she didn't think he realized how his wife was going to take the news. Kasiria was a grown woman before she even knew she was Katabull and her father was the king of a country where the Katabull were barely tolerated. Her grandchild would be different from all but a handful of people.

"Madra, I am only three quarters Katabull, and Kasiria is only a quarter perhaps the baby..."

"The baby will be Katabull, Jabone."

"Can Jestia..."

"Magic can't work against us in our Katabull form. Katabull is the baby's primary form, so magic won't work on it. It is not some curse my son; he will be different that is all. Waden is of our pack, he is brave and funny and beautiful, and his children all have a human primary form because he changed to human to conceive them. If Kasiria is worried you might take her to meet him."

"You are afraid Kasiria will not love our cub."

"I am afraid she will take the news harder than you are. That she may blame herself. I do not believe for a minute that she will not love your cub."

Jabone nodded and smiled. "I'm happy, Madre. If the child was ugly I'd still love it, and he won't be ugly; he will be a beautiful Katabull child."

Tarius hugged him and said, "Of course he will be."

He pushed her to arm's length. "Now what is this news mother was talking about?"

"Your mother is pregnant."

Jabone looked shocked.

"When I gave Jena half my life it cured her womb and well she was young enough and...."

"That is why Hared and Rimmy have moved in with you because Hared is the Fadra?"

"You are *mostly* right."

**"How far along are you?"** Kasiria asked.

"Three months. You?"

Kasiria laughed. "Three months, so if we aren't careful we could have them on the same day. It's sort of weird isn't it? I mean you'll be a grandmother and a new mother."

"The Katabull are very long lived. Look around; it's not all that uncommon here. She never talks about it because they are all dead, but Tarius was not her father's only child. Tarius's father was one hundred and fifty when she was born. He had two children from a previous paring who had grandchildren the same age as Tarius. Many do just what we did have one set of kids early in life and another set later on purposely. And it's not any more unusual to have the second set of cubs with different people."

"But you're not Katabull."

"I might as well be. I have half the life of a Katabull, and I've now lived with them most of my years. My mate is the Great Leader, one of my children is grown, Darian is magic, and this baby I carry is not only going to be Katabull but it will have three parents. You know, nothing really surprises me anymore. Jabone has always loved babies, and he will make a very good father."

"Jena... I'm happy I guess, but I was in no hurry to have children and truthfully I'm scared. My mother died in childbirth."

"So did mine, but surely you have realized by now that the Kartiks have much better midwives and much cleaner methods. It helps a great deal that they don't see women as baby dispensers to be discarded and replaced with another woman when they get the boy child they want."

"I had no idea you harbored such hatred for our homeland."

"I lived through much there that was unpleasant, and all of it was unnecessary. Rules made to put men above and over women instead of putting them on an equal footing. Men and women will always be different, but in the Kartik there are no rules that lift one sex above the other. We are allowed to be different and still want the same things. You have been here for nearly three years; does it seem to you that Kartik men are more or less happy than Jethrik men?"

"Happier, because the women are happy." Kasiria loved the Kartik for many reasons but above all was the equality that all people shared.

She looked at Jabone's mother. Jena was near glowing she was so happy about her pregnancy. Kasiria looked down at the table top. "I think I'm more afraid I won't be a very good mother. I was afraid I was pregnant—not excited, but afraid—and when Yri told me I was my very first thought was that it was going to screw up my sword training and keep me from riding out next time we do a sweep of the coasts—and it was our turn to go. That's not right is it? I'm told I'm going to have a baby with the man I love and my first thought is only of myself and...."

"Jabone was planned and this one I have wanted to have for over twenty-five years, but Darian...." Jena lowered her voice. "Tarius just picked him up and said 'here this is our new baby.' I warmed to the idea right away, but it took me some time to completely fall in love with him. Kasiria, you will have months to warm to this baby, and by the time it gets here you will look into its eyes and be fully in love with it. You'll soon wonder how you ever thought anything could be as important and that having a baby doesn't keep you from doing any of the things you really want to do, it just changes the things you really want to do. Then too soon they are grown and gone."

"And we're Katabull, so we'll just have more," Kasiria made a face.

"Maybe and maybe not. Traditionally, followers of the Nameless God replace themselves then stop having children. There are potions one can take. Of course the two thirds of the Katabull that are queer don't have to worry about that. We aren't likely to have an accident are we?"

Tarius and Jabone came back then and Jabone walked right over bent down and kissed his mother's cheek. "I am so happy for you, mother. You will finally have your baby."

"My dearest love I have already had you and Darian. The only difference is I will carry this one sooner than I did you," Jena said.

Kasiria sighed. *And this is why bards write songs about Jena because she is gracious and filled completely with love. She had every reason to hate me, but she put that away for Jabone and now.... Well I often feel that Jena is the mother I haven't had since I was too young to even remember her. Now I'm to be a mother and not just a mother but the mother of Tarius the Black's grandchild, and I don't feel ready. But maybe no one is ever ready to have another person.*

"Jabone," Tarius said. He swung to look at her. "Your baby and our baby they will each be very different from most, but they will be very much the same. They will have each other and all of us."

"I am not worried, Madra."

*And he isn't, not at all. It is all he ever wanted. He has talked about nothing but having a cub since nearly the moment we coupled and.... Dammit that was what Jena was doing. She was reminding me that this is the Kartik and better than that Jabone is Katabull raised in the Katabull compound. The raising of this baby will not fall to me alone; Jabone will be right there and so will they. They will have their hands full with their own baby and two small children, but they also are not alone there are four of them to take care of their cubs. So now all I really have to worry about is the actual birth and.... That scares me more than any battle I have fought in.* She looked at Tarius since she was the only person in the room who had actually given birth.

"Tarius, about childbirth...."

**Of course the girl had** no idea what to expect. Her mother had died when she was a toddler, and none of her friends had children yet. Jena had at least had the old aunts to teach her about being a woman, but what tutorage had Kasiria had? Kasiria had gone off to the Sword Master's academy when most Jethrik girls were bearing their first child, already having been given away in marriage.

"A person comes into this world between your legs, it hurts, then it doesn't," Tarius said. She didn't know what else to say, so probably she wasn't the one the girl needed to talk to. As if to prove this, Jena looked at her as if she'd grown another head.

"I have midwifed for years, and I was there when Jabone was born." Jena smiled at the memory and at Tarius. "The stoic warlord twice asked Yri to take her sword and cut the baby from her belly. Other than that she just breathed her way through it, and when he was born I caught him. When I handed him to you, you pulled him to you and when he started to feed...."

"I said, this is our son." Tarius smiled at Jena. Now they were going to have another child. She looked at Kasiria. "There is nothing to worry about, Kasiria. It is as natural as walking."

**When Jabone and Kasiria** left a few minutes later, Tarius closed the door turned to Jena and in a whisper so low Jena could hardly hear it said, "The baby is Katabull, so he'll just slide out anyway."

"What?" For answer Tarius took her hand and started pulling her back towards their room.

"In our Katabull form we are very limber. A Katabull baby will be even more limber than a human baby."

"Our baby, too...?"

"No, sorry, but you'll no doubt be screaming to have our child cut from you just like I did. Our child will be born in its human form. Our son's child will be born Katabull."

"I don't understand," Jena said, so Tarius explained it to her and she got very quiet.

"It's really not that big a deal," Tarius said.

"But you are right to worry how Kasiria will take the news. She doesn't really want to be pregnant as it is and has doubts about everything. She needs to settle into the idea, and I don't think she will take this news as well as our son. I think she'll blame herself."

"That is what I was afraid of."

# Chapter 3

**Persius tried to get** Tarius's attention but she didn't see him. Even as he jumped around naked, his balls slapping into his dick and vice versa, he was unable to make any sound. She was instructing a group of workers concerning a section of wall and a guard tower. He couldn't hear her voice at all.

Then the child holding her hand turned to look at Persius, his green eyes shining, and he hissed in a deep voice which didn't match his tiny frame, "Do not leave me to do it alone."

Persius woke screaming, though why the dream so terrified him he didn't understand. This was the first time he'd actually heard anyone speak in the dream.

A different night, another wife, and yet he still didn't give a damn whether he woke her or not.

"Hellibolt!"

His wife woke with a start and he dismissed her without thought, "Leave me."

She seemed only too happy to oblige as smoke and light filled a corner of the room and then Hellibolt walked out of it.

"Is all that really necessary?" Persius asked.

"More so than you waking me in the middle of the night to talk about a dream we have already discussed half a dozen times," Hellibolt answered. He rubbed his eyes and looked with utter disdain at the King of the Jethrik. "What is it you want? I have told you I cannot interpret any dream I have not seen in which no one speaks."

"This time the boy spoke."

"Not Tarius?"

"No. Why does that matter?"

"It doesn't really; it's just interesting," Hellibolt said. He flipped his hand around in the air flamboyantly. "Do go on. I'd like to get back to sleep some time in this millennium."

"The boy spoke...."

"You said that. Try to say it as he did," Hellibolt said.

Persius tried to pull up as deep a voice as the lad had and

couldn't but tried as he said, "Do not leave me to do it alone."

Hellibolt laughed doubling over. "See? I knew that would amuse me."

"Dammit, Hellibolt, this is the sixth time I've had nearly the same dream in as many weeks. It is not some joke to me."

"Wait a minute, was that exactly how the boy sounded?"

"No, his voice was deeper, and there was a humming sound in the background of it and…. Why are you looking like that?"

"That's witch speak. what color are the boy's eyes?"

"Very dark green…."

"You might have told me that before!" Hellibolt hissed. "The boy is clearly a wizard and attached in some way to the Great Leader. You said in the dream the twins converge."

"Yes, it always starts with the moons covering each other."

Hellibolt was silent and thoughtful for a moment. "She's building a wall? What sort of wall?"

"A battlement, obviously for defense," Persius said.

"We know they found the cult in the Kartik two years ago and that they eradicated them and have developed technics to make sure they can't come back both there and in the Kartik-held territories. While we have done nothing here but assume they are all gone as long as we can't see or hear them. Meanwhile there were thousands of them in the ground here for years and we were none the wiser and Tarius the Black had to come from the Kartik to deal with them. The little wizard said, "Don't leave me to do it alone. He's not talking about the wall. I think he's talking about us being more diligent to make sure the Amalite cult isn't here."

"But you aren't sure."

"I am more concerned with a Kartik wizard's prophecy. He wrote, 'When the twins converge on the well of power and shine with the same light and the one bathed twice in blood walks with his royal Katabull brother through the valley of the Katabull and the Great Wall rumbles, those who do not rise against the Amalite gods shall parish by the sword of the Nameless One."

"What does one have to do with the other?"

"I'm sure I don't know. But I think the fact your dream has more than one element from the prophecy in it, since it was the first thing that popped into my head when you told me your dream, and since you didn't know the prophecy existed we'd better pay careful attention to your dreams."

**Tarius had taken Pete** and Darian and headed for the building site. It had been two years since they started building it. This wall was every bit as big and the guard towers every bit as complex as the wall they had built between them and the shore to protect them from attacks from the sea and from sea surge; however, that one had taken three times as long to build.

Harris and the others had found four huge bags of gold when they had closed the pit mine in the territories. While all the gold they'd confiscated from Rorik's and Sedrik's keeps had gone into the kingdom's vaults, Tarius had no trouble at all keeping the four bags of gold the Marching Night had found in the territories for them. After all, the Marching Night was her pack, and they were the ones who found and closed that filthy operation.

While the Katabull were primarily agrarian, growing crops, raising stock and fishing and relied primarily on a barter system, there were more of them than there had once been and that now meant they had to rely more on trade with the Jethrik, the territories and the rest of the island. So they now had their own coins. Having the money made working on the wall go both easier and faster because she had money to pay the workers. More of her people were working on it because there was more money which meant they could afford to. Everyone was happy.

Everyone that is except the Kartik Queen. She thought Tarius should just trust that the kingdom was free of the Amalite scum, that her plan was working. To Hestia the very idea that the Katabull were building a wall to protect them from the Kartiks was an insult.

The wall certainly looked and felt like overkill, but since they could more than afford it, Tarius saw no reason not to build it.

Of course the thing that had made Hestia back down from her whole, "How dare you," stand was Tarius simply telling the truth. "I feel the wall needs to be there. If I do not build the wall and something happens that has me saying, *Damn we would have all been saved if that wall was only standing there*, then I'm going to be kicking my own ass as I die."

This wall was shorter in height than the one against the shore because that one she built in part to protect the compound from storm surge. But this one was longer, so in fact when she ran the calculations it turned out that this shorter wall would take the same amount of work because it was almost exactly the same amount of surface area. When it was finished the whole of the Katabull lands—every piece of farm land every ounce of pasture land—would be walled on three sides with the lake on the fourth side. Both walls started in the lake where the water was nearly eight feet deep, so the lake was an effective moat. When the huge metal-shod wooden gates were closed, it would be a nearly impenetrable fortress.

She put the boys to work mixing cement with Ria and Tarius took up a spot handing stone to one of the masons. When she worked with them they worked faster and with more joy. *Who wants a leader who sits on a throne but never gets their hands dirty? Who would put in power one who wanted to be in power? To lead you must first be willing to stand with the people you lead, do the work they do, eat the food they eat, and live in the place where they live.*

As she handed the stone to Waden he smiled, took it from her and placed it and had the mortar down for the next stone. He worked harder, faster, and better than anyone on the project. Since he was usually Katabull he was stronger, faster and had more stamina. "So to what do I owe the pleasure of having the Great Leader and her sons as my helpers today?"

"I wish to see if I can keep up." She smiled back and handed him the next stone as he had already set the last one. Tarius had them clear the jungle out fifty feet from the wall and they dug a slopping canal around it to catch the water from both the wall and the jungle and channel it towards the sea. Every few feet on the east side of the wall there was a hole at ground level to allow the water that would otherwise have collected on the top of the wall to drain into the channel. The wall was made by constructing two rock and mortar walls ten feet apart and then filling the middle with packed rubble and dirt most of which came from the channel they had dug in front of it.

Since the wall was downhill from the lay of the surrounding land, it was necessary to clear the jungle away and dig the trench: first so that the trees wouldn't allow the walls to be breached in any attack, and second to divert the water that ran down the hillside into the channel so that it didn't dig out the bottom of their wall.

The walkway in the top of the wall which was three feet below the top of the exterior walls would then be planted in strong grasses. As they did with the seawall, they would keep a small herd of sheep on the new wall to keep the grass at a manageable length. She was sure that, like the other wall, very little grass would grow in the middle where the sentries guarding them walked. There were troughs under the eaves of the roofs of the guard towers which both watered the sheep and gave the sentries a place to cool off when they got too hot. Since it rained a little nearly every day the troughs rarely had to be filled.

They had four rock guard towers scattered around the compound that would be used mostly for shelter from storms when the wall and new towers were finished. The huts they lived in were suitable for normal weather, comfortable and easy to maintain, but there was a reason Tarius had built the meeting hall from rock and given it a tile roof, a reason she was continuing to ring the compound with a massive packed-earth double rock wall. When one lived in a house a Katabull could run through you needed some place stronger in case of danger.

"Jena's pregnant," Tarius said conversationally.

"I had heard." Of course he had, word spread fast among the Katabull. "I am very excited for you all."

"My son and his mate are also expecting a baby."

"I had also heard that, what a blessed time for your family."

"My grandchild will be Katabull."

"Both his parents are...."

"The child will be like you, Waden," Tarius said.

Waden laughed and set yet another rock. She could barely keep up with him. "Like me? He should be so lucky."

Tarius laughed too then and shook her head. "Aye, that is what I think, but Kasiria.... She is just now learning our ways and still only speaks Kartik by a spell. I don't know how she will feel. Jabone.... Actually, we are all a little afraid that she might reject her cub."

"So no one has told her," Waden said, knowing.

"It has been a month since I told him, and Jabone still

hasn't told her. Jena says he shouldn't yet because the girl has still not quite warmed to being pregnant. I think the sooner she knows, the sooner she can get used to the idea and...."

"Because to you it doesn't matter, you think it shouldn't matter to anyone else," Waden said, proving how well he knew her.

"Yes, but I also know because I have been a foreigner in a strange land that she can't help it if she doesn't think and see things the way we do. I think if she could meet and talk with you get to know you...."

"That she'd see that it's not such a bad deal?" He smiled and took the rock she handed him and placed it.

Tarius heard the unmistakable, unnerving sound of little boys giggling, and without turning bellowed, "Darian and Pete! Put the mud down and get back to work." Ria laughed out loud, letting Tarius know that she was right about what her sons were doing.

"When you were the only woman, the only Katabull, the only Kartik, in a room full of Jethrik men, how did you feel?"

"Alone."

"There is a reason I made sure my own children would have a human primary form," Waden said. He must have seen the look of dread on Tarius's face because he quickly said, "Let me finish Great Leader. When I was young no one taunted me, no one was cruel. They saw me as a blessing a good omen, but no one was like me and as a young man I thought it a terrible burden to be so different. No longer a rash youth, I would not worry so much one way or the other what my children were. Because I am so different I have done many things others couldn't. Just like because you were so different in the Jethrik you did things no one else could do."

Tarius smiled and nodded, "That is exactly why I want you to talk to Kasiria."

Waden grinned. "Tarius, I have seen that girl in battle and she is all Katabull. It won't be hard for me to convince her— without telling her what her baby is, that should come from Jabone—that she wants her child to be just like me."

"That is all I ask," Tarius said lightly and handed him yet another rock. "You know I think you are building this wall mostly yourself."

Ria grunted as she put a bucket of mud at Waden's feet

and took the empty bucket away. "He certainly keeps me running just to keep him in mud." She walked back to where the boys were mostly getting right in her way as she tried to work.

Tarius moved till her lips were almost touching Waden's ear and said, "The busier we can keep that girl the better."

Waden nodded in agreement and whispered back, "I often think it's redundant to put a hoe in Ria's hand."

Tarius laughed, handed him another rock, and then waved for the fellow whose place she'd taken to take it back. "I'd better take my boys and clean the cement off them before they burn and before they 'help' Ria so much she can't keep up with you. My friend, you can slow down any time you like."

"I can't," he said with a grin. "There is a bet on how many feet of wall I will finish today, and if all of them are wrong I automatically win."

"And how many days a week do you win the bet?"

"Three in six." He laughed. "My woman says on my next break I am to use my winnings to take her to Montero for a vacation."

"If you can make my daughter-in-law want her cub, I will pay for your trip," Tarius said. "Boys, come on, I will have to go dunk you into the lake before mama sees you or she will whip us all."

They ran over and she quickly brushed as much mud off them as she could.

"He started it," Pete said quickly.

Tarius smiled and roughed his hair up. "I have no doubt of that."

"Sorry," Darian said holding his hands up. Tarius gave him a mock snarl and he laughed.

"That's what I thought," Tarius growled. "You aren't sorry at all." She picked him up and put him on her shoulders. He grabbed the braids on either side of her face and hung on and she took Pete's hand and started for the lake. "If you do it again I will not take you with me to the build site again."

"We be good," Darian said and kissed the top of her head.

"Madra, why are we building a wall?" Pete asked.

"The queen asked me the same question though not in such a nice way. I build the wall so that we will be safe. To protect us from storms and any other hazards if they should come."

"When the Great Wall rumbles," Darian said.

Tarius stopped dead in her tracks. "What did you say, Darian?"

Darian laughed and squealed waving his arms so wildly that she found herself scrambling with her free hand to keep him from falling. "Monkey!"

Laz was walking towards them with his pet monkey on his shoulder. He stopped, "Great Leader, cubs." He was Rimmy and Radkin's oldest son, so family. He didn't wait for the request he knew was coming, he just took the monkey and put him on Darian's shoulder. The monkey was tiny, smaller than a squirrel, and both of the boys loved him but Darian was absolutely crazy over him. Tarius took her son off her shoulder and set him on the ground where he and Pete were just petting and talking to the monkey. It seemed more than happy to play with them.

"You can't play with him long because we have to wash the cement off you."

Darian scowled at her and she scowled right back and said, "Maybe next time you will think before you interfere with the wall-building project."

"I hear our family grows on more than one front."

"Aye, soon we will have babies hanging from the rafters," Tarius smiled. "And eventually I will have to get this one a monkey of his own, but though I look every time I hunt I have yet to find an orphan."

No one on the Kartik Island would eat a monkey. In other parts of the world monkeys were hunted for food, but not in the Kartik. Certainly no Katabull living anywhere would ever eat a monkey. Monkeys weren't sacred, but they looked too much like little Katabull to be considered food. However the Kartiks weren't above catching young ones in the wild and raising them for pets. Katabull wouldn't take one unless they found one abandoned which was rare and why there were only two tame monkeys in the whole of the Katabull compound. Of course many monkeys lived or visited there, the wall being no deterrent for them. Most had one or more Katabull families they hit up for food, but they weren't tame by any stretch of the imagination.

"I found Pogo lying in the crook of a tree abandoned after

a rain storm. He was probably only hours old."

"Like me," Darian said not looking up—and continuing to play with the monkey.

Laz looked at Tarius. Laz had been with them when she'd found Darian. She looked at her son curiously. "What do you mean?"

"Madra pick me up," he said, shrugging.

"Who told you that?" Tarius knew they'd have to tell him someday, but they should do it, no one else and not yet.

"I 'member." He just kept playing with the monkey.

Tarius drew in a deep breath and let it out.

Laz smiled at her and said, "Well, he is magic."

"He's also not even three," Tarius whispered back. She took the monkey from the boys who each gave her a look as if she'd beaten them. "I must get you to the lake and clean you up." She handed the monkey back to Laz. "Laz tomorrow come by our house and I will give you a message to bring to your brother in Montero for the queen."

"I could bring it myself...."

"In case you haven't noticed, these days your brother spends more time in Montero than he does here. He is in the process of falling in love. I don't begrudge him that, but I think he forgets he still has a job. It's time he went back to work, and if the boy he is with is worthy of him he shouldn't mind at all going along for the ride," Tarius said.

As she took hold of the boys' hands and resumed their interrupted journey to the lake, she looked down at Darian and asked again, "What did you mean when the Great Wall rumbles?"

**Hestia looked up from** her desk at Riglid and smiled. She got up walked over and hugged him. "Riglid, how good it is to see you, and your mother will be thrilled."

Riglid hugged her back then stepped back from her. "Queen Hestia, the Great Leader asks that you come to the Katabull compound to discuss something of great importance as soon as possible."

"Regarding?"

"That was all she said." He smiled helplessly and shrugged.

"It had better not be about her confounded wall."

There was a young man, small for a Katabull, with Riglid.

He took the young man's hand shyly and pulled him forward. "This is Kaden, Kaden Queen Hestia."

The young man bowed. "It's a pleasure to meet you my queen."

Hestia looked again to be sure that she had read the body language between the two correctly. She was sure they were a couple, but not only was the man small for a Katabull, but he'd bowed to her and all Katabull were followers of the Nameless God. Followers of the Nameless One didn't bow to anyone. When Tarius had first become Great Leader some of the Katabull had worshiped other gods besides the Nameless One. One of the first things Tarius had done as ruler—though Tarius would tell you she wasn't ruler she was leader which was somehow different—was outlaw religion. Yet all Katabull now believed in the precepts of the Nameless God which Tarius assured her was not a religion at all but a way of thinking. This boy bowed to her which meant he wasn't Katabull, and the fact that Riglid didn't immediately smack him or tell him off meant he was smitten with him and hadn't been with him long enough to feel comfortable correcting him.

"It's a pleasure to meet you, Kaden. You are so incredibly lucky that Riglid's mother wasn't here to see you bow to me."

Riglid bent down to whisper in Kaden's ear and he nodded and turned bright red. "I meant no offense your majesty."

"I am not offended, but his mother would be and though he will not tell you, so is he. We will leave with you in the morning, Riglid. There is nothing of any urgency here. I will have a meal prepared for us tonight to be served in my quarters. Till it is ready find your room and rest from your long ride. I will have a bath drawn for you both." She grinned then. "Or you could share if you'd rather."

Riglid knew her, so he just grinned as his man blushed again. "I'd like to see my mother first."

"Of course. I believe she will be in the garden in the middle of the castle."

**"Why didn't you tell me** we were going to the castle to give a message to the queen?" Kaden said, red faced and having to nearly run to keep up with Riglid. "Why didn't you tell me that you are runner to the Katabull's Great Leader?"

"I told you I had to take a message from Tarius the Black

to the queen. I thought it was obvious that we were going to the castle."

"Riglid...." Kaden ran his hands down his face. "I thought you were kidding me, that you just wanted to take me to the capital for some fun. You told me you were a messenger."

"I am. First my father was her runner, and now I am. Well lately my father's been doing it again since I've been so much in Montero with you. Laz said the Great Leader is not pleased by my long absences from my post."

"Why did you not tell me that you had such an important job?"

"Would I not have seemed a horrid braggart if I had said I am the runner for the Great Leader? I am her right hand. You know it isn't easy for me to make small talk, and I wanted you to like me for me."

Kaden looked up at him. "So you work for Tarius the Black?"

Riglid nodded.

"And your mother works for Hestia?"

Riglid shook his head and laughed. "No, no, nothing like that. My mother is Hestia's lover. I don't think she sees that as work at all," Riglid said with a nervous grin.

"Wait, wait, wait!" Kaden grabbed Riglid's arm and stopped, forcing Riglid to stop, too. "Your mother is banging the queen?" Riglid nodded and started walking again, mostly dragging Kaden behind him. "And your mother is?"

Riglid smiled broadly. "Right through this door."

The Katabull woman he saw was easily bigger than Riglid was. Her hair was braided in hundreds of small braids all over her head and then pulled back into a single pony tail that went nearly to her ass. She was sitting on a bench reading a book which seemed about as likely as a horse eating a fish. She was wearing a loincloth and a sleeveless shirt of brilliant blues and greens tied at her waist. Her huge sword was on her back and she wore metal banded vambraces but no shoes. She stood as soon as she saw them, and walked over and embraced her son. she kissed him on the forehead then pushed back from him and looked at Kaden in a way that made him feel naked. She sniffed the air then looked at her son. "So are you here on Tarius's business or did you come only to introduce your boyfriend to your mother?"

"I am here to give a message to the queen from the Great

Leader." He smiled. "I thought it would be a good opportunity for you to meet Kaden and him to meet you."

"Human what do you do for a living?" she roared.

Riglid laughed. "Mother, don't go out of your way to scare him."

She grinned. she was a wild-looking thing, but when she grinned Kaden knew he wasn't about to be killed. "So what is it you do for a living?" she asked again as she walked over to pick up the book she'd been reading.

"I'm a pub bard," he said.

She turned around laughing. "Oh boy welcome to hell, because none of the very private things you will learn about our family may I ever hear you have told in a story, or I will split you."

"She means that," Riglid whispered, his lips nearly touching Kaden's ear.

"Is your mother...?"

"Captain Radkin..." Riglid said proudly, "...like in the stories."

**Kaden couldn't believe** where he was or what he was doing. He and Riglid were in the queen's quarters sitting at her table having dinner with she and Radkin. The most confusing part for Kaden being that until Riglid had taken him to the castle doorstep to introduce him to the queen and his mother he hadn't been sure Riglid was all that interested in him. Kaden had known exactly how he felt about Riglid but wasn't at all sure how Riglid felt about him. Riglid was very quiet and all Katabull which meant he often said things he was obviously quite sure of that made no sense to Kaden at all.

He had met Riglid in a pub he had been working. After he finished telling a story he had walked to the bar to get a drink. The bartender handed him a drink before he'd had a chance to take coin from pocket. Since Kaden didn't get free drinks for working there he looked at the bartender and the man had motioned towards Riglid. Riglid had just nodded his big Katabull head without so much as a smile, but Kaden liked what he saw, and having never been with a Katabull before he was instantly intrigued. He took the drink, went to join Riglid, and found him to be one of the hardest people to talk to he had ever met. That didn't put Kaden off in the least; he liked a challenge. In fact it was a nice change from the men he normally met who talked so much about themselves he often felt like he knew them but they didn't know him at all.

For months after that Riglid would show up, give him a quick tumble, and then take off again. Then he started staying for a couple of days at a time and Kaden now realized that should have told him that the Katabull was interested in a relationship with him. Of course all Riglid told him about his a job was that he was a messenger, so for all Kaden knew Riglid had nothing better to do. If he had known that Riglid was a member of the Marching Night much less the Great Leader's personal runner, the fact that he was spending as much time with him as he was would have told him everything he needed to know about how serious Riglid was about him.

As it was he didn't know at all till he was meeting the Queen of the whole Kartik and Riglid's very famous mother.

"What do you suppose she wants?" Hestia asked Radkin concerning the Great Leader's request.

"I'm sure I don't know, but don't try to pretend that you will be unhappy to go to the compound," Radkin said with a grin.

"I will not be happy to see her confounded wall. I tell you it is a huge testament to the trust she doesn't have in me and...."

"It's a huge testament to the fact that she doesn't trust anyone or anything," Radkin said. "Had you the background she has had you would be at least as paranoid."

"Did she say nothing else, Riglid?" Hestia asked. "Did she send no note?"

"I ah.... I wasn't home. She sent the message through Laz. She sent a note, but Laz lost it; that is all he remembered," Riglid said, not looking up from his plate.

"So..." Radkin looked thoughtful for a moment. "You have mostly forgotten about your position because you've had your head in your pants." Her tone wasn't condemning really, she was just letting him know that she knew what was going on.

Riglid looked at her and held her gaze which Kaden couldn't even imagine he'd ever be able to do. "Since Father and Hared now live with Tarius and Jena, father gave me permission."

"Why are they living with Tarius and Jena? Please tell me your sister has not burned down yet another house!"

"She has not," but Riglid now seemed to be all about looking into his plate.

"What is going on?" Radkin demanded.

"I would probably know, but my head has been in my pants," Riglid said. He looked at Kaden and grinned a sheepish grin.

"Cheeky boy." Radkin laughed and slapped him hard enough he almost fell out of his chair. She looked over at Hestia. "I'm sure we will learn all there is to know as soon as we get to the compound."

"Probably before we get to your huts."

So here he was sitting with Katabull members of the Marching Night and the queen and he realized with a start. *They are just people. At the end of the day they are just the same and.... Well that was one of the things Riglid told me that I couldn't wrap my head around; that everyone is the same. Not only does he believe that because he is a follower of the Nameless One, but he knows it's true because his mother is Radkin his father is Rimmy and he regularly deals with Hestia the warrior queen and Tarius the Black, so he knows they are no different from anyone else. I find that this relationship has caused me to rethink everything I know, and how amazing is that.*

# Chapter 4

**Kasiria walked up to the** campfire in front of her house and noticed they had a visitor. The man was all catted out, and he was talking to Jabone as Jabone was sticking meat in the pot hanging over the fire. Both men fell silent the minute she came into range of their hearing, so as she approached them she asked, "Is something wrong?"

She set the basket of freshly-washed vegetables down on the table near Jabone's elbow. They lived on a tropical island and they were Katabull so while they had a small earthen oven in the house they rarely used it. She looked at the man again. She recognized him; he was part of the Marching Night, and she had fought beside him briefly in the battle at Rorik's keep.

"Nothing at all is wrong, princess," the man said. He called her princess not because she was an actual princess of the Jethrik—which she was but only a handful of people in the Kartik knew that—he called her princess because she was Jabone's wife.

"Just Kasiria is fine," she said with a smile.

"Kasiria, I don't think you have officially met Waden,"

She took his offered hand and touched her elbow to his in the traditional Kartik handshake which still felt so foreign to her.

"A pleasure to meet you almost as much as it was to fight beside you," Waden said with a smile. "I was just telling Jabone that we have had such a blessing as your family. That our oldest cub gave us a grandson at nearly the same time our youngest cub was born. They are as thick as thieves those two girls, and I sometimes forget which is my child and which is my grandchild. My wife and I have been very blessed with both of our children."

Kasiria thought she knew why he was here now. Among the Katabull being a straight couple put them in a minority. *Jabone thinks I need more contact with normal couples.... Well alright the fact that I see us as normal when we aren't among our own people more or less proves that I'm a foreigner still prejudiced by the way I was raised. Now I'm going to have a baby and that baby will most likely be queer because that's normal here, so I need to watch not just what I say but how I think. For weeks now Jabone has been acting strangely like he wants to say something and just can't He knows something is bothering me and he probably thinks what I need is to have some friends that are more like me but.... If nothing is wrong why is Waden Katabull?"*

Her expression must have given her away because Waden said, "Katabull is my primary form."

"What?" Kasiria asked, not understanding.

"For most Katabull human is their primary form, but though it's rare some Katabull are born with their Katabull form as their primary. Waden has a Katabull primary form," Jabone said then added, "It is why he gets so much more done and is never sick."

It was the tone in which Jabone said it that made her knees go weak because it sounded like he was trying to sell her something. She found a chair and sat down.

"Kasiria are you alright?"

Kasiria looked up at the huge Katabull, took in a deep breath let it out and spoke not to her husband but to Waden. "Let me guess, this is why they have all been whispering and stop talking altogether when they see me. And this is what Jabone has been trying to tell me and failing to for weeks— that our baby is going to be like you, no offense meant."

"None taken," Waden said with a reassuring smile.

"Well?" Kasiria asked Waden.

"I promised his Madra I would let him tell you."

"Our baby will be super easy to take care of," Jabone said, smiling at her.

"How do you know our baby will be like him, no offense, Waden."

"None taken." He really had the most brilliant smile.

Jabone was silent. "How do you know?" Kasiria demanded of Jabone.

"Remember I told you Katabull can't conceive while they are in their Katabull form...."

"Which was a bold-faced lie," Kasiria said hotly. It had

taken her weeks to warm to the idea of having a baby and now she had they were telling her what.... What exactly were they telling her?

"It was not a lie. I would not lie to you, Kasiria."

"It is like any other form of birth control; most of the time it works and sometimes it doesn't," Waden said. "When it doesn't the baby born of such a coupling is like me."

"Madra says the baby will be easy to birth," Jabone said.

Kasiria looked at Waden. "There will be nothing else wrong with it?"

"Wrong, child there is nothing at all wrong with me," Waden said with a laugh.

Kasiria put a hand to her growing stomach. *What's the real difference? I have often wished I could spend more time like that and less like this. Were our child to live their life in the Jethrik it would be a horrible curse, but this child will live here in the Katabull compound. Our child will grow up in the Kartik and will be celebrated among the people of the island. Waden obviously is treated the same as everyone else.*

She looked at Jabone and smiled. "If it will really be easier to birth and easier to care for, then it will be just the baby for me."

Jabone walked, over dropped to his knees and hugged her, and she could nearly feel the relief wash over him. She was glad he hadn't told her as soon as he knew. She now loved her baby and if they had claws and fur and cat eyes.... "It won't be born with teeth will it?" she asked Waden.

He grinned back. "No it will not be born with teeth, and I will stay and you may ask me as many questions as you wish until you understand that I am glad I am the way I am and why."

**Jestia had to stop herself** laughing as Radkin made yet another disapproving sound as the young bard tried to work.

"Mother, you are being very rude. Kaden is trying to tell us a story," Riglid said. "Please let him finish."

They were all sitting around on the patio beside their hot spring. It was not as big or glorious a pool as Jazel's but just as therapeutic, and she'd put her spa and her gardens up against Jazel's any day. Jestia's alchemy blew Jazel's away; it was bright and filled with color. No dusty dead stuff hanging around. No in Jestia's alchemy all the dusty dead stuff was in very pretty-colored glass jars.

"He is telling the story ALL wrong," Radkin boomed.

What the boy didn't know was that Radkin was one of the best bards in the Katabull Nation, and the only human bard who could stand toe-to-toe with any Katabull bard was her mate's older brother Tarius who was named for the Great Leader. Then there was the Great Leader, who was the best bard Jestia had ever heard, so poor Kaden had the worst sort of audience. Jestia thought the boy was doing a more than adequate job of telling the story, but Radkin was an amazing bard and she simply could not stand it.

"That is not the way the story goes at all."

"That is the way I learned it," Kaden defended. He was a nice man, and she thought he and Riglid seemed a good match, but he was obviously intimidated by.... Well all of them, and it wasn't helping to have Radkin pick his storytelling apart. Jestia shifted to get more comfortable and Ufalla shoved at her and made a noise because of course Ufalla was laying on one of the huge pillows they had thrown around the pool and Jestia was mostly laying on Ufalla.

"I swear, Jestia, if you don't quit sticking your elbow into my liver every time you move I will push you into the spring."

"I'm just trying to get comfortable," Jestia said.

"Then you might try lying beside instead of on me."

"Oh my dear love," Jestia said, "that isn't ever going to happen."

Her mother laughed from where she sat on a small couch beside Radkin, holding the Katabull's hand.

Radkin turned to Ufalla and grinned. "Hestia thinks it's funny because that is what she does to me, uses me like furniture." She turned back to the young bard. "They did not drown, and they certainly did not die together. You are ruining the story. It is much sadder than that."

"But it is the way I learned the story," Kaden said.

"Mother, it is just a story," Riglid said.

"No, it is not just a story," Radkin boomed. "It is about people who really lived, so to recall their story with no truth insults their lives. For years now I have pilfered the castle library and read most of the books. I have read this story many times; it is a great story which he is mangling."

Her mother kissed Radkin on the cheek and said, "Honey let the boy tell his story. It doesn't matter."

"It does. You and Jestia are kin to these people whose story he is butchering."

Though she'd only been half listening to the story when poor Kaden had been trying to tell it, now that Radkin was reacting so passionately she knew it had to be a really good story.

"Then you tell the story, Radkin," Jestia said.

Radkin didn't have to be told twice; she pulled her hand from Hestia's and stood up. She paced back and forth for a second then stood still. Jestia had watched Radkin tell stories many times and knew the Katabull wouldn't be still very long.

"I tell the tale of the Twins. Long ago there was a king of the Kartik who was filled with the power of magic, a weather wizard like no other whose name was Bentone, and he ruled in fairness and with purpose for over a hundred and fifty years. He had three sons when he was in the end of what would have been a normal human life. His wife died of old age, and his sons also died of old age. He married again and she gave him three sons, and then came the twins. It was a hard delivery and she was very weak, too weak to even name them. Bentone named the boy Tarance and the girl he named Gwen. Their mother could not even feed them, so Bentone hired a Katabull woman who had lost her own cub and her mate in a fire to care for them. She was full of both milk and a great sadness, and she nursed and cared for the twins while their mother fought for her life and they quenched her hot grief.

"The twins' mother struggled, but no matter what potions Bentone gave her or what spells he cast, she continued to grow weaker. She was not meant to live; it was her day to die and she did. The king who had loved her very much thought that being magic he would live only to bury everything he loved, and for a while he barely saw any of his children much less the twins.

"Then one day the Katabull woman ran to find him for she feared there was something wrong with the babies and she loved them as dearly as if they were her own. Now these babies' eyes were the darkest of blue, but at six months their eyes turned emerald green."

Suddenly Jestia's blood ran cold and she took in a deep

breath. Ufalla wrapped her arms more tightly around her.

Radkin smiled, feeling suddenly very smug about her bardic ability, but it wasn't just that Radkin told a good story that made Jestia react. No there was suddenly an uncomfortable familiarity to the story and not because she'd read it. Jestia had never had any interest in any book that wasn't telling her how to make or unmake something; that was what bards were for. No Jestia got the uncomfortable feeling that she was about to get the answer to a question she hadn't asked and didn't really want the answer to.

"When the king realized his twins were magic he knew he would never be alone again and he showered them with love mostly ignoring his other three sons. Hestia's father was being trained to be king, but Bentone was sure he'd long outlive him. He was sure Tarance would be king when he was gone for Tarance was born seconds before Gwen and only his twins would out live him.

"The twins grew and their bond with both their father and the Katabull woman—whose name is not in the records by the way," Radkin added, obviously put out by this omission. "Anyway when Bentone saw how she was with the children, how important they were to her and how important she was to them, he kept her to nanny them. And seeing how gentle and loving she was with his children he developed a fondness for her and she for him and they became lovers."

"Did they really or did you just add that part?" Hestia asked with a knowing smile.

"Woman, do not interrupt my story; as you know your people have always had a thing for my people." She grinned wickedly and then returned to the story. "As the children grew it was obvious that they were completely filled with magic power. Singularly they were each very powerful, but together even Bentone began to worry that they might be too powerful for their own good.

"They were inseparable, and even as teens refused to sleep in separate rooms. It is said that they spoke mostly in each other's heads, never got more than an arm's length apart in their whole lives, that when one was hurt the other felt it. They learned all forms of warfare and how to use every weapon, but mostly their days were spent learning the craft from their father and other wizards. As they got older they started to travel across the Kartik looking for love and adventure as young people will do. They say the twins sang everywhere they rode, that Terrance had a fine voice but that his sister's voice was as magical as she was and that when people heard her sing they felt as if they had been given a special blessing.

"Then came a day, just a normal day, a horrible normal day. The king had no vision; neither Terrance nor Gwen had any vision. They had gone to the sea to comb the shore looking for stones to use in their magic." She stopped, looking at Kaden. "And this is the part you totally mangle in your too-quick telling of the story. Terrance bent to pick up a rock and an Amalite arrow pierced his side. He pushed his sister to the ground and threw a ball of light at the troop of Amalites running down the beach at them. Their guards knew they were too many to fight, so they grabbed the twins and took them as fast as they could back to the palace where their father and nanny were..."

"He died of his wounds, and she died only shortly after though she was not injured at all," Jestia said, rolled in Ufalla's arms and started to sob.

Ufalla held her and patted her back.

"And now you have rushed and ruined my dramatic ending," Radkin said.

Kaden clapped loudly. "You are a far better bard than I will ever be, and I can see why you were so upset by my clumsy telling of the story."

"Kissass," Ufalla whispered in Jestia's ear. Then she must have realized that there was something more going on with Jestia than just that Radkin had told such a tragic story nearly perfectly. "Jestia?"

Jestia could not quit crying nor could she find her voice or stop the tide of memories suddenly flooding her brain. She felt another hand on her back besides Ufalla's and then saw her mother kneeling beside them.

"Jestia, are you alright?"

Jestia shook her head silently.

"Radkin, please get Jestia," Ufalla said. The next thing Jestia knew Radkin had lifted her off of Ufalla, carried her over to lay her down on one of the couches and Ufalla was standing over her checking her vitals.

"Is she alright?" Riglid asked.

"Stand back and give her some air please," Ufalla ordered. "Jestia can you hear me?"

Jestia nodded.

"Is this magic?"

She nodded again.

Then Radkin said, "Riglid, go and get Jazel."

**The moment his mother** spoke Riglid shifted to Katabull form and took off at a dead run. Kaden was left there alone with them not knowing what to do.

"Eerin!" Ufalla yelled. In minutes the guy who had served them their dinner was there. "Eerin, what is wrong with Jestia?"

The guy looked like he felt as helpless as Kaden did. Still he walked to Jestia's side. She took his hand then he went white. He quickly pried out of her grip and stepped away from her.

"Eerin, what the hell?" Ufalla took Jestia's hand and held it tight.

"She is remembering a past life, a close one, her last," Eerin said.

"Is she alright, Eerin?" Hestia demanded.

"She should be, but it is a painful process. Jazel..."

"We sent Riglid for her," Ufalla said.

And then there like the magic it was stood the famed witch Jazel. He had known she lived in Montero but he had never actually seen her. She was wonderful; her long blond hair braided into a long braid that reached the middle of her back, her green eyes like fire. She wasn't very tall maybe five-seven, but she looked bigger. She was slender but also full of curves. She wore a purple dress and carried a staff with odd writing on it. She moved quickly from the smoke she had appeared in to Jestia's side.

"She is seeing her last life," Eerin said quickly.

Jazel nodded. She took Ufalla's hand out of Jestia's, pushed her away and then took Jestia's hand herself and said, "Your sight is my sight. Half your pain I will take. Your soul be free peace to make."

Then both witches were bathed in white light and as quick as he saw it, it was gone and all was still.

*Jazel helped her to sit up* and Ufalla held her up. "I couldn't speak," Jestia said, her voice coming in gasps.

"That must have been horrible for you," Radkin said lightly, and Hestia actually punched Radkin in the shoulder—hard. Radkin made a face and rubbed her shoulder.

"I couldn't even have my own thoughts."

"I know, breathe child you'll be fine. It is the past." She smiled at Jestia then but Jestia could see the pain etched on her features. "It does explain a lot though, doesn't it?"

Jestia nodded. "Only time will tell whether knowing is worth what it cost me and you. Thank you, Jazel."

Jazel just nodded graciously.

Riglid came running in, stopping just short of going ass over tea kettle into the spring in his attempt not to hit Jazel. Jestia guessed that since the sight of the Katabull's skidding and jumping around to keep from going in made her grin she was probably going to live.

"Is she well?" he asked.

"I'm fine," Jestia said, feeling a little embarrassed. It was funny; she didn't mind purposely making a scene at all, but didn't like making one when she didn't intend to.

"What the hell happened?" Ufalla demanded. Normally the magic didn't bother her at all; in fact, over the last few years Ufalla had gotten very good at taking things like magic lights and fish dinners that turned into steak dinners for granted. But one of the things they had in common and doubtlessly the thing that caused most of their fights was that they both liked to think they were in control.

"That's what I'd like to know," her mother said, proving that Jestia came by her need to have control naturally. "Are you sure you're alright?"

"She will be fine. The best thing for her right now is some sleep," Jazel said.

"She is my only living child, Jazel," Hestia said, proving that Jestia came by the dramatics honestly, too. "I'm not sure I'm content with sending her to bed. What if whatever it was happens in her sleep?"

Jazel took a deep breath and let it out, and Jestia smiled because she knew exactly why. Non magic users often got on Jazel's last nerve because they didn't really have the capacity to understand magic but they still wanted to be told how it worked, yet when you told them they still didn't know. So it was a huge waste of time.

"She remembered a past life is all. It's not pleasant but even if I hadn't been here she would have been just fine. Since in this last life she went through a trauma at death it was difficult to remember."

"She is one of the twins," Radkin said in a whisper she barely heard and was sure the human's didn't. "I'm sorry, Jestia."

"I'm not, it was a brilliant story." Jestia turned to Kaden then. "And she was right; you were jacking it all up."

**Of course Jestia didn't go** right to bed because she was Jestia. She waited till Jazel went home and everyone else went to bed then she insisted Ufalla get in the spring with her. Which she did because she didn't want her in it alone and really couldn't think of a good reason to tell her she couldn't go in since as far as Ufalla was concerned there was nothing that could be more relaxing than getting in their hot spring.

"So can you tell me what you saw or is it one of those, 'the world will fall into ruins if you do so' sort of things?" Jestia glided up to her and wrapped herself around her and Ufalla held her then kissed her gently on the lips. "You know you scare the living shit out of me on a fairly regular basis, right?"

"Because you love me."

"You know I do. So can you tell me what happened?"

"Radkin was telling the story and suddenly I was seeing it and then I was Gwen. Remember I told you Tarius told me that she thought my great-grandfather may have made the storms to keep the Amalites from landing on our shores? They say he was mad, and I'll bet if I hadn't had a magic melt down the rest of the story would be...."

"The rest of the story..." Radkin said, slipping into the pool across from them. "I will tell you if you promise not to have yet another little magic melt down." She smiled and said. "I couldn't sleep."

"I'm fine."

"I'm not going to do a big dramatic presentation, first because I am tired just can't sleep, and second because we're all naked and I am easily distracted by swinging boobs especially my own."

**Radkin took a minute to** remember exactly where she had been before all the excitement. "You were right of course because apparently you were there. Tarance died from his injuries and only moments later Gwen died though she had not been injured at all. They say her magic was so strong that she simply willed herself to die being unable to imagine a life without her brother. Then the Katabull woman who had raised them threw herself from the battlements to die on the shore, and the king went mad. His grief became a great storm and he threw it at the coast where his son had been shot. He went back to the capital without even burying his dead, and for a decade every cloud he saw he made a storm in and sent it to the shores all around the island.... Well probably not every cloud, but a lot of them. And he made droughts though he probably didn't do that on purpose because think about it if you send all the rain clouds to the coasts as storms the interior is going to get very dry. Eventually the people rose up and they killed him."

"You know my little brother's name is Terrance," Ufalla said. "Do you know who chose the name?"

"Tarius did, because Tarius was Tarance," Jestia said matter-of-factly.

"And Tarius is third sex," Radkin said. "So it makes sense that she was your brother in your last lives."

"Really? Because none of it makes sense to me," Ufalla said.

Jestia shrugged. "It is just one of the reasons that she can do the things she can do, and I can do the things I can. The magic was so strong that some of that has stayed with Tarius, but most of the magic they both had has come to me alone."

"I have seen her many times do things not even another Katabull could do," Radkin said. Then she got out of the water and started to dry off. "What do you think it means that you didn't come back to the world at the same time?"

"That it wasn't my day to die; that I made it happen, so I sat and waited till it was my time to come to this life. The world needed Tarius the Black when it needed her, and I wasn't needed till later."

Radkin nodded; the answer suited her. "Good night." Radkin didn't bother with a robe just walked naked back to her room. She crawled into bed with Hestia.

**"Well?" Hestia asked.**

"She is fine, and no I did not tell them that the reason I couldn't sleep was because you heard them in the spring and poked me till I woke up and went to spy on them. I was right. Jestia was Gwen in her last life, and Tarius was Tarance."

"My poor child, Radkin. Someone tells a simple story and.... All that power it's too much for her for anyone. It's enough to have to live this life without having to remember another. She and Tarius twins in some other life; I can't even wrap my head around that. In another life if he had lived Tarius would be my uncle. He might be king right now with his sister by his side. It makes my head spin when I think of the many ways everything would have been so different. I'm just going to not think about it anymore; it will be easy for me because for me it's simply a concept. I didn't have to live a past lifetime in a few minutes. Where is Jestia going to put all that? "

"Jestia is very strong maybe because she is attached to the Great Leader. I think witches take for granted things that make our heads spin. And baby, Jestia is crazy, and I'm beginning to understand that crazy is how magic users stay sane."

Hestia chuckled and said, "You are such a Katabull." As if to prove it Radkin jumped on her and started licking her face which just made her laugh more. Then Radkin felt more than just a need to make Hestia feel better. She started kissing her and Hestia eagerly kissed her back. She put her arms around Radkin and pulled her tightly to her and when Radkin pulled her mouth away Hestia caught her eye and said, "I love you." So Radkin kissed her again so that it wouldn't be so obvious that she didn't say anything back.

**Jena was walking with** Tarius on a section of the newly-finished wall, and the two boys were walking along beside them till Darian saw a monkey on the wall and then he took off after it. "Darian leave the monkey alone!"

"Honey, let the boy be."

Jena cut Tarius a look. "It was fine when he wasn't catching them, Tarius but he has caught two in the last week. He is going to get bit or at the very least pummeled."

"No monkey would dare to bite one of my sons," Tarius boomed, and beside her Pete laughed. "Well they wouldn't," Tarius said right in Pete's face, which just made him laugh more. Jena smiled. All kids and horses loved Tarius.

"I agree with Pete. Tarius!" Jena pointed to where Darian was about to snag the monkey's tail. He missed and fell head first into one of the watering troughs.

Tarius dropped Jean's hand and covered the distance in three long strides. She grabbed her son and pulled him out; he took in a deep breath and started to cry. She hugged him and patted his back. "There, there son you're fine."

Jena took off at a run, but Tarius had him long before she got there. Jena pushed the wet hair out of his face making sure he wasn't bleeding, "Are you alright, Darian?"

"I swear sometimes I think you could tell the story of our lives by just saying 'are you alright' and sometimes even as the words are leaving my own mouth.... Well it's obvious that if they were alright you wouldn't be asking. Why don't we say what we really mean? Is anything broken? Are you about to die? Is your blood pouring out of you?" Tarius mumbled.

Jena smiled, and Darian was still just bawling.

"Darian, you're alright," Jena said, trying to sooth him

"My monkey got away," Darian cried.

"Child you slay me." Jena stopped petting him. "For the love of the Nameless One! Tarius, you have got to do something about his monkey obsession before he gets hurt."

"I have been looking for a monkey...."

"How about you try telling him no instead of just giving him everything he wants?" Jena suddenly stopped and took in a breath. "Oh."

"What?" Tarius asked, looking at her in panic.

Jena couldn't help it; tears started to well up in her eyes. She took hold of the hand Tarius was patting Darian's back with, and stuck it on her stomach. "Tarius, our baby is moving." At four and half months it wasn't a lot but she could feel it and soon Tarius could too. Tarius beamed a great smile at her and just kept her hand on Jena's stomach.

Their moment was interrupted by angry monkey screams. When she turned to look at where it came from, Pete was in

Katabull form and was trying to keep hold of the monkey he had caught.

"I caught a monkey," Pete called out triumphantly. Tarius neither put their son down nor took her hand off Jena's stomach.

"Son, let that monkey go."

"But Madra," Pete said as the monkey was basically pummeling him. "Darian wants a monkey."

"Can you not see that monkey will trounce him?" Tarius laughed, leaned down and kissed Jena on the cheek.

"Not let monkey go," Darian begged Pete.

"Yes, he is beating your brother to pieces," Tarius said. She gave Pete a hard look. "Let the monkey go, Pete."

Reluctantly Pete released the monkey then he looked at her proudly. "Look, Madra, I changed."

"I saw that; very good, Pete."

Darian quit crying he looked at Pete and clapped. "Brother's pretty." He wanted down so Tarius put him down and then moved to put both of her hands on Jena's stomach. Jena looked over and Darian was giggling as he petted Pete's hands and arms. Pete just grinned proudly.

"Great," Jena sighed. "I wish you hadn't taught him to change so soon. I think you have forgotten how much trouble Jabone got into because of it and those two get into enough trouble without one of them being able to shift. No monkey in this compound will be safe now."

Tarius looked at her and kissed her gently on the lips, Jena kissed her back. Tarius moved her lips till they were nearly touching Jena's ear and whispered, "Our baby is moving, Jena. Moving on the day Pete shifted for the first time. What a wonderful day this is."

"Not for the monkeys," Jena laughed.

Tarius finally took her hands off Jena's stomach and turned towards the boys. "Pete, take your brother and go and find your fathers as they will be very excited to see you have learned to shift."

"By ourselves?" Pete asked.

"Of course, you are the Katabull now."

"I don't think...." Jena started.

Tarius leaned over and whispered in her ear. "From here we can see all the way to the huts. They will be fine and I can see that Rimmy and Hared have come back from hunting and are even now at our campfire starting lunch. If we stay gone long enough all we will have to do is show up to eat." Jena nodded and Tarius straightened and looked at the boys who were now standing at her feet waiting.

"Now go and do not I beg of you molest any monkeys on the way. You are the Katabull now, Pete, and with that comes great responsibility."

Pete nodded took Darian's hand and started down the wall towards the stairs in the guard tower. Seeing the worry on Jena's face Tarius smiled and took her hand. "They will be fine."

They turned to look over the wall and soon saw the boys running towards their huts. "Look how Pete slows down and keeps pace with Darian," Tarius said.

Jena looked at her and could see the pride and love she had for them.

"He is a very good big brother," Jena said.

Tarius draped an arm across her shoulders as they watched the boys. To Jena they were little more than specks she could hardly make out, but she knew Tarius could see them clearly. As if to prove it she hollered as loud as she could. "I said leave the monkeys alone!"

A bird with blue plumage landed on Tarius's shoulder and she let go of Jena, took hold of the bird and removed the note from its leg. She opened it and smiled, "Hestia and Radkin are coming and Jestia and Ufalla are with them. What a great day this is."

**They left fairly early in** the morning mostly because Jestia held a lot of secrets that she couldn't tell, so when there was one that wasn't going to cause mountains to move and rivers to run dry she wasn't the greatest at keeping them. Not telling Radkin and her mother about Tarius and Jena's baby was nearly killing her. However she didn't cast any sort of spell to make the horses go faster because the truth was she loved to ride and didn't often get the chance. Between her studies and running their spa she was pretty busy all day most days.

It wasn't unusual these days for her mother to leave the castle and travel alone with Radkin to Montero or to the Katabull compound. At first the queen's personal guard and her advisors had tried to tell her it wasn't safe, but they all knew that was crap. Her mother was more than capable of taking care of herself and as long as Radkin was beside her no one else could touch her. It wasn't like this was the Jethrik; there weren't bandits lining every road. In a country where most of the population had been in military service and everyone carried a weapon only a fool would try to rob anyone much less the legendary warrior queen and her huge Katabull bodyguard.

Hestia tried not to rub her Katabull lover in the kingdom royals' faces, but she was mad in love with Radkin so any form of pretense was a tough act for her. Any excuse she could come up with to leave the castle and go off with Radkin was a welcome one. Unlike Jestia who preferred comforts, Hestia liked roughing it. It reminded the queen of her glory days in the Great War so it seemed to Jestia that her mother preferred the mud huts of the Katabull compound above everything else.

When Jestia's brother Katan died, it caused a wave of events none of them had been prepared for. It had changed the course of all of their lives but none more than her mother's. The death of her son and everything that happened because of it made Hestia have a huge epiphany which resulted in her totally embracing her true self. Because of that Jestia finally had the mother she'd always wanted and no father at all because Jestia had disowned him.

If she hadn't disowned him before, she would have done it after the scene he threw at her and Ufalla's wedding. *That drunken bastard, he was so lucky Radkin was in such a good mood or she wouldn't have just beaten him to a pulp she would have killed him. Otherwise it was a lovely day and come to think of it having him show his entire ass and then watching as he got it kicked was really one of the highlights. At least it's the thing people are still talking about. I was wearing a gorgeous gown; Ufalla was beautiful in her armor all shiny and dark. The whole of the Marching Night were in attendance, and a good chunk of the royal family. We had great music and dancing and the food was out of this world, and what does everyone remember first? That my father showed up drunk as a goat with a whore in tow and tried to pick a fight with my mother.*

**He had not been invited** to her wedding. She had disowned him with good reason; it was his fault her brother was dead, a fact only her father, she and Ufalla knew. If anyone else knew they'd kill him, and while Jestia thought he was a worthless turd she didn't think he actually deserved to die, not for something that was really just a tragic accident.

Tarius had performed the wedding ceremony, Hestia stood with Jestia, and Jabone stood with Ufalla. Eerin had made sure there was no rain, and the weather in Montero had never been more perfect. Everything was just as she had planned and pictured it and when it wasn't she tweaked it a bit with magic until it was.

They were just about to start when her father showed up so drunk the whore with him was all that was standing between him and the ground. Then he proceeded to yell not at her, but at her mother about her.

"Hestia!" he yelled, walking down the aisle towards them. "How dare you allow this marriage? My daughter is the heir apparent. She must marry a royal, a man."

And why was he so pissed off? Because since her mother had divorced him Jestia was not the only one who had disowned Dirk. He had lost his station, and his own family—seeing that he was always drunk and in the company of unsavory women—had abandoned him in an attempt to save face among the other royals.

Ufalla told her later that she saw Radkin look at Tarius, that Tarius had nodded, and Radkin had gotten right up and started for him.

"And why do you suddenly think it is alright for our daughter to marry a common woman, Hestia? Only because you roll around with this Katabull thug like a common whore...."

She'd never know what her father was going to say after that because Radkin punched him in the stomach with such force that she knocked both him and his whore to the ground. Then she picked one up in one hand and one in the other, dragged them a few feet past the wedding guests and proceeded to beat Dirk to a bloody pulp. Then she straightened her clothes and her armor and returned to her seat between Jena and Rimmy. Tarius started the ceremony again as if nothing had happened.

***What a great day that*** had been. She smiled.

Radkin had ridden up beside her. "So what were you thinking?" Radkin asked.

"I was remembering my wedding."

"No one calls my woman a whore," Radkin mumbled.

Jestia looked at Radkin knowingly. "So what is on your mind?"

Radkin looked quickly back over her shoulder to where Ufalla was riding beside her mother talking about gardening of all things. Behind them Riglid was riding with Kaden.... Jestia wondered briefly what was going through the human's head. Radkin looked back at her. "The spell you did on Jena and that I'm sure you did on Ufalla. I want you to give half my years to Hestia."

"That is not some simple spell, nor should it be. In order for it to work you have to love her, and not just because you don't want to be alone or because she is a good lover or companion. You have to love her, really love her. Can you imagine how dangerous this spell would be if it didn't hinge on something one cannot create? Every witch and wizard who knows the spell would have to guard against evil people who would hold them hostage and take half of everyone's lives. And the spell is very difficult; I will not even try it unless you love her because it won't work and I will have wasted my time and energy."

"It will work; just do it," Radkin said.

"Because you love my mother?" Jestia asked.

"Jestia.... Why must you always be you? Just know it will work." Radkin snarled at her. "It's in your best interest, Jestia. It means it will be at least a hundred and twenty more years before you will have to take the throne."

"Very tempting, but it will only work if you love her."

"It will work."

Jestia sighed. "Why can you not say it, Radkin?"

"Why must I? Is it not enough to show her?" Radkin snapped back.

"How many times has she told you she loves you?"

"Hundreds," Radkin mumbled, and it was hard to tell whether she was guilty or pissed off about it, but Jestia guessed it was probably a little of both.

"I will do the spell on two conditions. First mother must agree. Tarius didn't tell Jena, we did it, and Jena would hardly speak to me for years. Then I didn't ask Ufalla, I just did it, and she let me sweat for a year and half pretending she didn't know just to get me back for not asking. I selfishly did it for myself without fully realizing what I was doing to her or to me. It isn't like giving your lover a trinket, and it doesn't mean that they can't die; it just means they will age with you and you will only live half as long as you would have...."

"I don't care. I don't want to be alone, and I don't want to live without her."

"My second condition is that you must tell mother that you love her."

"Dammit, Jestia, doesn't the fact that I'm willing to do this prove that I do?"

"Why can you not just say it?"

"Because if I do I will feel like I'm cheating on my wife," Radkin spat out quickly.

Jestia laughed then. "Yet shagging mother rotten two and three times a day for years now doesn't make you feel bad at all."

"We don't do it that often... anymore."

"Irvana is dead, Radkin. You didn't wish it so, you didn't want it...."

"You are wrong, Jestia. When she was so sick and in so much pain and my life became nothing but caring for her and watching her die I did wish her dead Jestia, many times."

Jestia took a deep breath and nodded. Now it made a certain amount of sense. "But Radkin, do you think that Irvana wanted to live like that?"

Radkin shrugged.

"She died, Radkin. You did not. You were a good mate to her...."

"I wasn't; I almost cheated on her once," Radkin admitted.

"Almost and did aren't the same thing at all Radkin, you know that."

"Yes, but the person I almost cheated with was Hestia."

Jestia was more than a little shocked. "Oh this has got to be a great story so come on, tell."

"I'm not proud of what I did, Jestia. I loved Irvana, but your mother is and always has been a very beautiful, sensual woman. During the Great War Irvana was here and I was across the sea in the Amalite for months without sex, which isn't an excuse it is just the truth. Your mother and I became good friends; she was easy to talk to I enjoyed her company and her attention. One day we sacked and laid waste to a bunch of Amalite priests and soldiers holed up in a temple. It was a close battle mostly inside, so we were more than bloody, we were gory."

Jestia knew what she meant close-in fighting like that you didn't just get splattered with blood you wound up with gut, bowel, and brain matter all over you. The smell was awful.

"We found a creek and we all went to bathe. I looked up and there was your mother naked and fantastic. I realized we were alone—the last ones there. I can't remember, and won't lie, but I might have waited till the others left because I had been thinking about her and after a battle the Katabull get very randy. Again that's not an excuse for what I did, but it is the truth."

"Hell, I'm not Katabull and after a battle all I want to do is couple," Jestia said.

Radkin smiled. "You're like your mother; just looking for any excuse. Once again you are interrupting my story."

"Sorry."

"Anyway there was your mother drying off and I just walked right up to her, took her in my arms and kissed her. She kissed me back, and if Tarius hadn't called me then I would have cheated on Irvana because I wouldn't have stopped. I also know, because she has told me, that Hestia would not have stopped me. After that your mother mostly steered clear of me and I for sure steered clear of her. I loved my wife, Jestia. Irvana was my life, but I never had the passion for her that I have for your mother, nor did she have the passion for me that Hestia does. When Hestia tells me she loves me and I start to tell her the same I feel worse than I did that day I held and kissed her by that stream. I feel like Irvana's death has allowed me to have a private dream."

"Radkin, who can be more faithful to anyone than someone who comes so close and has such a longing and yet does not act on it? How much must you have loved Irvana to walk away from your desire? She died, but you didn't show up at the castle and knock on mother's door the next day. You grieved for years. You tried to kill yourself; I saw you do it myself. Do you think that's what Irvana would want for you, for you to give up altogether, or live alone and hate your life and never love again? I thought you thought more of her than that. How could you have ever loved anyone who was such a selfish hateful bitch?"

Radkin's head turned quickly to look at her.

"You know in your heart, Radkin that none of that is true. She was a wonderful person. She'd want you to be happy." Jestia knew Radkin; she was blunt and honest almost to a fault. "You told her what almost happened, didn't you?"

"Yes, but not how I felt."

"We can't help how we feel, Radkin. Did she damn you and kick you out of the house?" Jestia asked.

"No," Radkin grinned. "She said if she had the chance to bed Hestia the warrior queen and I was across the sea that she would have and Tarius could have screamed herself hoarse, and she still wouldn't have quit what she was doing."

"Somewhere the part of Irvana that cannot die is running around as a small child wondering why her heart jumps a little every time a long-legged Katabull walks by. She is not judging you or the love she had for you; she is too busy having another life. My mother loves you. If you really want to give her half your life and if she agrees, I will do it, but you have to tell her how you feel."

# Chapter 5

**Tarius sat on the** Katabull throne outside her hut keeping an eye on the boys and watching the road. "Ah, there they are. Look boys they are almost here. Jestia and Ufalla, your brother and his new boy toy, and cousin Hestia and her sex slave."

Jena threw a piece of carrot she was putting into the pot at Tarius and hit her in the head. "Tarius, Darian repeats everything you say, you know that."

"I'm pretty sure that's why she's doing it," Rimmy said with a grin. He dumped all the meat he had just butchered into their huge kettle. Most days this was how they cooked—throw some water and herbs in the kettle and then just throw in whatever they had that smelled like it went together.

Tarius laughed stood up walked over and kissed Jena on the cheek. "I'm going to walk to meet them. That way maybe Hestia will be done bitching about our wall by the time they get here."

"Bitchin' about that wall," Darian said, nodding.

"See what I mean Tarius?" Jena scolded.

"You boys stay here," Tarius said.

"I've got them," Hared offered.

Tarius took off at a run and she heard Jena laugh. "That's not walking, honey."

Tarius met up with them shortly after they had passed the guard tower on the south side of where the gate—which was still under construction—was going to be. To her surprise Jestia jumped off her horse, ran over and hugged her. Tarius hugged her happily and tried to ignore the little tingling of power that transferred between them.

Jestia didn't seem like she was in any hurry to let go, so she just held the girl and patted her back.

Getting off her horse Radkin said to Tarius, "Jestia found out that you and she were brother and sister in your last life. It's a long story but don't ask him to tell it." She hooked a thumb towards a human Tarius didn't know, so assumed he was Riglid's boyfriend. One sniff told her she was right.

Radkin peeled Jestia off Tarius. "Quit hogging the Great Leader." Radkin hugged her and she hugged her back.

"Your wall is nearly finished. I hope it's done before there is some horrid squirrel invasion," Hestia taunted.

Tarius laughed, released Radkin and looked up at her huge friend. "Can you not control your woman?"

Radkin walked over to help Hestia off her horse. "My dear you would feel very silly if squirrels should break through Kartik defenses and make way for the Katabull compound."

Which meant Radkin, while she didn't see the wall as a huge insult to queen and country, did think it was unnecessary. Radkin didn't put up a hand to help Hestia. No in true Radkin style she just put a hand on each of Hestia's hips picked her up and set her on the ground in front of her.

Hestia smiled up at Radkin then turned to look at Tarius. "Look at it, Tarius," she waved a hand flamboyantly at the wall. "Do you really think all this is necessary to separate your people from mine?"

"I do *not* do it to separate your people from mine. You know that to me we are all the same people. I do this to protect my people from whatever might come. Quit thinking of it as an insult to you or the country and just think of it as my madness." She grinned.

Hestia grinned back reached up and patted Tarius's cheek with her palm and said, "That I can do."

"Riglid, could you please attend our guests' horses and take your mother and Hestia's things to your mother's house, and Ufalla and Jestia's things to Harris and Elise's?" Looking with meaning at Kaden she added, "And don't be late for dinner."

Riglid nodded got off his horse and started to gather the horse's reins.

Tarius looked up at the human boy who still hadn't dismounted. "You boy, what is your name?"

"His name is Kaden, Great Leader," Riglid said.

"Is he a mute?" Tarius asked, and they all laughed except Riglid and Kaden.

"Do you know anything about horses except how to ride them?" Tarius asked. Kaden nodded. "Then get off your horse and help Riglid, please. Jabone!" In seconds he was there. She gave him a second to say hello to everyone then said, "Jabone can you help Riglid and his boy toy to take care of the horses and put everyone's things in their huts?" She was already tired of all this. She wanted Radkin and Hestia to see that she and Jena were pregnant.

Jabone slid up to Riglid and whispered in his ear though all the Katabull could still hear him, "You should hear what she calls your mother."

"I'll help you," Ufalla said and kissed Jestia on the cheek. She looked up at Kaden, "Well?"

Kaden got off his horse and as he did he took his palm and slammed it into his forehead. Tarius laughed and moved to pat the boy on the back.

"You know, boy, I think you're going to work out just fine here."

**Kaden followed them as** they led the horses with their packs towards Riglid's house.

Jabone slid up to him and the huge Katabull slapped him on the back. "Don't let any of them get to you, Kaden. My mother is human and my Madra is the Great Leader. They are just testing your metal."

"My mother could test his metal a bit less, she all but growled at him within moments of meeting him just to make him jump," Riglid said.

Then Jabone grabbed Ufalla in a headlock and dragged her along like a ragdoll, "I mean look, Ufalla still has her head and she married the heir apparent."

"And you married Persius's daughter," Ufalla reminded and with a swift twist broke right out of the head hold Jabone had her in, then shoved him for good measure.

Kaden nearly tripped as he realized exactly what Ufalla had just said. "You married the daughter of the man who shot your mother through with an arrow?"

"No, he shot my madra through with an arrow," Jabone corrected. "And we don't speak of Kasiria's father outside the family."

"Madra means the mother of his birth," Riglid told Kaden. "So see? No one is going to kill you. No one disapproves of you." Riglid looked at Jabone. "He thinks none of you will like him."

Ufalla laughed and looked at Jabone. "He should only know what we do to people when we don't like them."

Jabone laughed loudly and popped the girl on the back with enough force to have bowled most people right over. "So, have you seen my fathers lately?"

"I have. I've actually started working with them helping train their more advanced students. Though you and I will have to practice while I'm here because fighting always with people who aren't as good as I am I will get rusty. When your fathers heard we were coming to the compound they decided to come, too but they had scheduled sword classes all day today and will ride in tomorrow."

Kaden tried to relax. He looked around the compound. There were thousands of huts and in the distance everywhere he looked was the massive wall the queen was so peeved about. The huts were simple but pretty with thatched roofs with massive overhangs to keep the rain off the mud and stick walls. On the top of most of the walls there were huge shutters that could be opened or closed depending on the weather. It was very warm today so nearly all were open; a latticework made of bamboo kept animals and birds out of their huts. Every hut had a garden filled with a mixture of flowers and vegetables. There were animal pens in a few yards, but Riglid had told him the bulk of the livestock, like the horses, were kept in huge fenced pastures on the west side of the compound bordering the lake. Everything was very neat and very clean, and then Riglid opened the door to his two-roomed hut and it looked as if a skirmish had taken place inside.

"Have you been robbed?" Kaden asked.

"Rea!" Riglid hissed. They wound up leaving their things in the mess. Riglid was hot and mumbling. "I never said she could stay in my house."

"How do you know your sister did it? Maybe you've been robbed," Kaden said.

"The Katabull do not rob each other, and I think I know what my sister smells like," Riglid said looking at Kaden as if he had a cat crawling out of his mouth.

For reasons Kaden could only guess, Ufalla elbowed Jabone in the ribs and said, "Everyone knows what his sister smells like." Then they both cracked up.

When they got to his mother's huts and opened the door. If anything it looked worse than Riglid's house, and Riglid exclaimed, "Why did my mother have to have that horrid girl? The queen can't be expected to sleep in this mess, and my mother will skin us all if she sees our home in this condition. He deposited their things then stepped out the door and bellowed. "Rea!"

In seconds a female Katabull was standing in front of Riglid. She was smaller than he was and very pretty, but also very unkempt. She looked from Riglid to the interior of the hut and back.

"What the hell were you thinking?" Riglid demanded.

Apparently she knew she couldn't claim she didn't do it. "I was living with Laz sharing Fadra and Hared's old house when Fadra let Laz kick me out."

"No doubt because you trashed out his house as well. So.... What? You moved into Mother's house till it was too dirty and then you moved into mine...."

She smiled at him. "Well she doesn't live here and you were hardly using yours." She looked Kaden up and down, and then sniffed him. "...and I can see why."

"He is mine, Rea, mine! Keep your hands and everything else off of him. Clean up mother's huts and then clean mine," Riglid ordered.

"I will not. You are all entirely too worried about tidiness." She waved at Jabone then winked and said, "Hello Jabone." Then the girl actually reached out and rubbed her hand on Ufalla's shoulder. "So good to see you, Ufalla."

"You know Jestia would have turned you into ash if she'd seen you so much as look at me," Ufalla said matter-of-factly.

"And Rea just because my wife is pregnant don't think she will not cut your head off and crap in the hole," Jabone said.

"Kasiria is pregnant!" Ufalla exclaimed and then she was hugging Jabone's neck and Jabone was gushing about how happy he was even as Riglid reached over and shoved his sister hard enough to rock her on her feet.

"You *will* clean mother's house and then you will clean mine and sleep with the dogs and monkeys for all I care."

His sister shoved him right back and then they were growling at each other. Then without further warning Riglid jumped on his sister and they were wrestling.

"What, what should we do?" Kaden said.

"We?" Ufalla asked.

"What should I do?"

"Stay out of their way and hope Riglid wins or you will have to help him clean the houses," Jabone said. "Come on, Ufalla, let's go deliver your things to your parent's house and put these horses up. This..." he said, pointing at the fighting siblings, "...is going to take a while. Nice meeting you, Kaden."

"Same here," he said, jumping quickly out of the way to stop from being mowed down by the wrestling siblings.

**It said something about** the size of their extended family that in order to all eat together they had to go to the Great Hall. It didn't matter; she was the Great Leader she could have a family meal in the Great Hall if she wanted to. Of course dinner started with Tarius and Hared trying for the fifth time that day to get Pete to drink the vile of blood and change back to his human form.

"But he's pretty," Darian said, "like a big monkey."

"You aren't helping, Darian," Jena said. She took his hand and walked away with him.

Pete looked at the blood in the vile shut his mouth tight and made a face shaking his head. He wasn't having any part of it.

"Come on Pete," Hared begged "Dinner is getting cold."

"I can eat like this," Pete said.

Tarius looked at Pete. The problem was that the longer he stayed in his Katabull form at this age the more unreasonable he was going to become. It wasn't good for someone so young to stay Katabull so long. She gave up being nice and in spite of Hared's protests grabbed hold of Pete, forced his mouth open, poured the blood in his mouth then forced his mouth closed. She whispered in his ear, "Now put him back where he goes, put him away."

In seconds Pete was his human self again he started to get mad then licked his lips and smiled at her.

"Not bad at all, right?"

He nodded.

**Jena sat beside Radkin** pulling Darian into her ever-shrinking lap. "She shouldn't teach your cubs to change so young,"

Radkin said.

"Don't tell me; tell her. Well, she isn't doing it to this one," Jena said, patting her stomach. Tarius sat down and set Pete between them. Jena looked at Pete. "Aren't you sorry you made such a fuss now?"

"Yes mama," he said.

Rea showed up late and looking like she'd been in a fight which Jena found out later she had been.

"So tell me again about this magic baby," Radkin said.

"I'm three," Darian answered.

Radkin laughed. "Not talking about your baby that is magic, talking about your baby that was made with magic."

"It is mine of course and a quarter Hared's and a quarter Tarius's." She moved till her lips were almost touching Radkin's ear. "So mostly it is mine and Tarius's baby." Radkin chuckled as Jena moved away from her.

"That's amazing. I couldn't be happier for you," Radkin said.

"That being the case may I ask why on occasion today you look like someone is making you chew glass?" Jena asked.

Now it was Radkin who moved to whisper in her ear in a voice so low she could hardly hear her. "Jestia has ordered me to tell Hestia that I love her."

Jena laughed and shook her head. "I'm sure you will live through it."

"Hey you two," Tarius said jokingly, "Don't think I have forgotten that cuddling episode."

**Kaden was stuffed. The** meal had been really good, a thick, rich stew filled with meat and vegetables and seasoned to perfection, plates of cut fruit and flat fried bread. And boiled lobster served with goat butter.

He looked at Riglid. "I'm never going to be able to keep up. You are related to ALL these people?" Kaden asked looking around.

"In some way, yes. My father's mate Hared is the Fadra of the baby Jena is carrying. Tarius is Jena's mate. Jabone is Tarius's and Jena's son—his fathers live in Montero—Kasiria is Jabone's wife. Pete is Hared and father's adopted son. Pete is Hestia's dead cousin's son, so royal but half Katabull which is why he is with us. Darian is Jena and Tarius's son—he has the same fathers as Jabone—he is human. My mother as you know is Hestia's mate Jestia is Hestia's daughter, and Ufalla is Jestia's wife and Harris is Jena's brother and he and Elise are Ufalla's parents. Laz and I have the same birth parents both of our birth parents are dead now. Jaden and, may the Nameless One help us all, Rea are our mother and father's children. I think that covers it."

Kaden worked that all out in his head and realized that the only person Riglid was blood related to was his brother Laz. But it was pretty obvious that to Riglid every one of these people were family and.... Well he was just never going to be able to remember all their names let alone be able to remember who belonged to who and how.

"Come on just let me tell you the sex of the babies," Jestia begged from where she sat across from the Great Leader.

"Jestia," Tarius laughed, "Kasiria and Jena have both said they don't want to know."

"So.... It's some stupid Jethrik thing," Jestia scoffed and looked at Tarius. "Did you know what sex Jabone was before he was born?"

"Of course," Tarius said.

"And he has all his legs and arms and toes and only the one very handsome head."

"Jestia let it go," Jabone said with a laugh. But then he turned his head and put up his hand and mouthed, "Tell me later."

Jestia nodded covertly.

Darian walked up to Kaden and said, "Pick me up."

"Excuse me?"

"Pick me up."

Kaden looked at Riglid and Riglid smiled. "He wants you to pick him up."

"Move your plate and set him on the table; that's what he wants," Tarius said.

Riglid moved his plate and Kaden picked the child up and sat him on the table in front of him. Darian looked right at him. "Laz is going to get Pogo. Do you like monkeys?"

"Oh for the love of the Nameless One not the monkey thing again," Jena said rolling her eyes.

"I do," Kaden answered the boy.

"Who are you?"

Riglid once again answered for him as if he were a mute, "He's Kaden, Darian, he's my...."

"Boy toy," Darian said, and grinned even as everyone else cracked up. Kaden noticed Radkin was laughing louder than the rest.

Jena turned to look at her, "If you think that's funny you should hear what Tarius has been trying to get him to call you."

"What would that be?" Radkin asked still laughing.

"Darian," Tarius prompted. "What do we call auntie Radkin?"

Darian turned looked at Radkin looked thoughtful and then smiled and said, "Hestia's sex slave." If anything this made Radkin laugh even harder. Hestia smiled, so obviously she had a good sense of humor.

"Don't encourage her; she teaches them awful things," Jena said.

"I don't know if I can stay here with you, Riglid," Kaden whispered.

"Why not?" Riglid asked, a hint of hurt in his voice. "They are only teasing you."

"It's ok boy toy," Darian said and patted Kaden's face. "You stay here and you'll be safe when the Great Wall rumbles."

The Great Leader apparently heard the boy because she asked, "Darian what does that mean when the Great Wall rumbles?"

The boy didn't answer because Laz walked in then with a monkey on his shoulder and the boy nearly jumped off the table and took off. "Monkey!"

"Dammit all!" Tarius boomed.

Riglid looked at Kaden and almost pleading said, "Don't you want to be safe when the Great Wall rumbles?"

Kaden smiled and shook his head, "He's just a boy."

Tarius looked around Riglid at him and cut him a look that would have curdled milk. "He is not just a boy; he is my son and he is filled completely with magic." She looked across the table at Jestia. "This is not the first time he has said that, do you know what it means?"

Jestia appeared to be very busy feeling up her wife, and she just looked at the Great Leader and shrugged, "I'm sure I don't know," but it was obvious the witch wasn't concerned though that could have been because she'd had more than a little to drink and was pretty busy. Whatever the reason, her calm dismissal of the matter seemed to calm the Great Leader right down as if the witch had cast a spell on her.

"Tell a story, Madra," Jabone said.

"Yes, Tarius," Hestia said, "tell us a story."

Tarius the Black stood up and then just as Radkin had done the night before she started pacing. She stopped and looked at Pete smiled and said, "I tell the tale of Yorik and Shadra..."

"That was Pete's mother and father," Riglid whispered in his ear.

And then Tarius the Black was telling a story of love and treachery and great bravery. And Kaden laughed and he cried and when she had finished telling the story he decided he would take up sheep shearing.

**Hestia was helping Radkin** to make up the bed. "I'm so sorry, Hestia. That girl is going to come back and finish cleaning this place tomorrow," Radkin said.

"It's not that bad." Of course it never was when it was someone else's kid doing it

"There is no excuse for the things she does," Radkin said with a sigh. "I swear I didn't fall or drink while I was pregnant with her. No one dropped her on her head. No one beat her..." She smiled wickedly. "...though maybe thinking back we should have."

"I'm just happy to be home." Hestia flopped onto the bed and Radkin looked at her and smiled.

"Is this place really home to you, Hestia?"

"I have three villas and a castle where servants take care of my every need and I am never as comfortable in any of them as I am here alone with you," Hestia said. Mostly she admitted only to herself that the fact Radkin would bring her to the house she had shared with her beloved Irvana—even though they always slept in what had once been Tweed and Rimmy's room—meant she must care for her a great deal. It was stupid to be jealous of a dead woman, and so she refused to do so.

Radkin lay down beside her and started to untie the robe Hestia was wearing. She opened the robe slowly then started to run her hand up the outside of Hestia's leg across her buttocks and up her side. Then she pulled her towards her so that they were facing each other and she kissed her and Hestia kissed her back. When Radkin removed her mouth from hers and she could feel her own pulse racing with her desire Hestia said it, that thing she kept telling herself she was never going to say again but always did. "I love you."

"I know!" Radkin said and flopped on her back to look at the ceiling.

*Well that was different.* Hestia quickly moved to wrap herself around Radkin. She kissed the side of her face. "What's wrong?"

"I need you to do something for me, Hestia." Radkin spoke as if the words were being ripped from her.

Hestia stiffened. "Radkin, I will do anything for you but leave you. I can't and don't ask me to...."

Radkin stuck a finger over Hestia's lips, laughed and Hestia relaxed a little. "Woman, that isn't even close to what I want and I wonder if you know me at all. Do I have to say it? Don't you know how I feel?" She removed her finger from Hestia's lips and ran it down her body between her breasts in a way that made Hestia quiver.

"Sometimes I think I do."

"I need you to take half my life. I need you to take half my life because I can't bear the thought that you are going to die before me. I have lived through that kind of loss once before; I can't do it again. Jestia said she would do the spell on two conditions the first being that you agree to it."

"What is the second?" Hestia asked cautiously.

"That I tell you that I love you, but since the spell will only work if I do I don't understand why I have to say it."

"Because I need to hear it, Radkin," Hestia whispered. "I need to hear you say it. I know that may sound stupid to you, but I love you with every fiber of my being and I just need to hear you say it. I would like to know that you love me, too, and until you say it I will never be sure."

"To my shame, Hestia, part of me has loved you since the very first time I kissed you."

Hestia jumped on top of Radkin and looked into her black eyes. "And I have always loved you, always; I just didn't know it."

**"Do you really not want** to live with me Kaden?" Riglid asked even as he climbed off of him.

Kaden was trying to catch his breath he laughed. "It's hardly fair at all to ask me anything when you have made love to me like that."

Riglid took him into his arms and held him. "I love you, Kaden."

"And I love you, but...."

"I know I am asking you to leave everything you know, but until Petrid turns thirteen I am to take my father's place at the elbow of the Great Leader. It isn't a duty I take lightly.... Well, I have been but I shouldn't and I don't want to."

Riglid was serious it was only one of the many things Kaden loved about him. He wasn't like so many of the human men Kaden had known who seemed to have no interests past getting drunk and banging each other. Of course as a pub bard where did he meet men.... In a pub where men were looking to get drunk and have sex.

"This is going so fast Riglid," Kaden said. After all they had met only three short months ago.

"You can't go too fast, Kaden. My fadra died in battle a very young man; if he had wasted time he would have had less than no time with my father and he never would have had us. My madra, she also died young of a wasting sickness, and with her death I was sure I would lose my mother as well. Were it not for Kasiria and my brother Laz she would be dead. Wasting time is a crime against the Nameless One. Stay with me. I am the Great Leader's runner. I travel with her you will see great things and meet amazing people and be safe when the Great Wall rumbles."

Kaden laughed and stroked Riglid's arm where it held him. "Are you really going to try to woo me with the prophecy of a three year old?"

"Are you going to stay?"

Kaden thought about where he was and what staying here might mean. "Yes, I will stay."

**Before daybreak she and** Hestia walked out into the yard to do their morning set of Simbala. As they silently went through the motions and the breathing Radkin felt a lightness of spirit she hadn't felt since she was a youth.

*Because finally I am completely over Irvana's death and I*

*wonder if the little witch knew that all I needed to reach through the last door of my grief was to tell Hestia how I really feel.* She glanced sideways at where Hestia was going through the motions all expression washed from her flawless face. *We're not supposed to be thinking as we do our set. We're supposed to clear our mind of chatter. I will do that tomorrow morning. This morning the air smells sweeter and my limbs lighter and.... Irvana would absolutely crap if she could see the mess her garden is in. And when I think of her today even in this place there is no pain.*

Radkin quit her work out grabbed Hestia and lifted her up so that Radkin then had to look up to meet Hestia's eyes which were smiling down at her. "You know this is not the way to do a set right."

"I know we are done with this set," Radkin said, threw Hestia the rest of the way over her shoulder and carried her back in the house.

**Rea watched her madra** carry her lover back into their huts with a sigh. She brushed the dog hair off her shirt and pants. There weren't many dogs in the Katabull compound but apparently every one of them decided to sleep on the bottom floor of the guard tower she chose to sleep in and it had been a warm night so she certainly didn't need them.

Her madra's house was still a mess and she knew if she didn't get it cleaned back exactly as she had found it she'd get a much worse beating from her madra than she'd gotten from her brother. Her mother's gardens were a mess; she decided to work on them while she waited for her madra to finish doing the queen.

**When Radkin walked** out of the house, Hestia's hand in hers, she was surprised to see her daughter pulling weeds from the forgotten beds around the house.

"Go on to Tarius's I need to talk to my daughter," Radkin said.

"Don't be too hard on her, Radkin."

"I am in such a good mood if I saw an Amalite priest I would kiss him before I killed him." She kissed Hestia than popped her on the ass as she walked away. Hestia was so used to it she didn't even turn around. Radkin walked over to loom over her only female child. "So, doing a little guilt gardening."

"I came to clean the house but you were obviously busy servicing the queen."

It wasn't what she said but the way she said it. "Watch your mouth girl."

Rea was silent.

Radkin took a deep breath walked over to a bench she had made long ago at Irvana's request and sat down. She looked at where the girl on her knees was now mostly only pretending to pull weeds. "Why Rea, why?"

Rea looked up at her. "What?"

"Why any of it, Rea? You aren't stupid. You are beautiful and I know there is goodness in you. In our hour of need you were there and helped your brother to put Tarius in a cell which saved us all untold grief and the gods alone know how many lives. I have seen you in battle and you are as good as any and better than most. They tell me you are a very good worker when you aren't hung over or drunk." She pointed towards her house. "Why do you constantly make messes that others have to clean up?" From the look on Rea's face she knew Radkin wasn't just talking about the house. "How many times must your fadra and his mate or your brothers go to Montero to fetch you from some bar till it has gotten to the point that the bartenders in the entire city quake whenever they hear you are in town? What on earth is wrong with you?"

Rea quit pretending to work and stood up. "I'm sure I don't know," and there was defiance in every feature of her face.

Radkin let out a low throaty growl. "Child, what is it you think we have done that you punish our family and no one more than yourself?"

"I have no one," Rea said, now seeming to be close to tears. "No one cares about me; everyone hates me."

"Child, don't you dare cry. That will not work with me; you are going to clean my house. Everyone loves you they just can't stand you because you have no respect for anyone or anything. You bed people indiscriminately and I'm sure even you don't know if you prefer women or men or both or neither. The proof of how absolutely self-destructive you are is demonstrated every time you flirt with either Jabone or Ufalla because Jestia is an extremely powerful very jealous witch and Kasiria.... Well I sometimes wonder if she's not crazier than Jestia is. Hell, your brother told me last night that you even made a pass at his new boyfriend. You can't do those things, you can't take a stick and stir people up and then expect to have friends. You are purposely pushing people away as fast as you can and have been ever since your mother died. You cannot continue to use her death as a reason to fail at life."

Now Rea started to cry, and these tears were real so Radkin got up walked over and embraced her. Rea put her head on Radkin's shoulder and Radkin patted her back till the girl's teeth rattled. "That's what I did, Rea," Radkin whispered in her ear. "When we all went to fight in the Great War Riglid was barely seven, Laz was five, Jared was nearly three and you my sweet girl were only six months old. We all went and fought the Great War and your mother stayed here with all of you alone for nearly a year. Tweed died and you never really knew him but my how he loved you. Rea when you were born he yelled out, *I finally have my girl,* and from the time you were born till we got on that boat if any of us wanted to hold or care for you we had to near pry you from your father's fingers.

We came home after the war and as you know war changes people for the better or the worse. But it always changes you. Your fadra especially, but I as well had been so changed by the war that it was a while before we functioned in normal Katabull society. Your mother was always so strong and she carried us all through that time. And though you were my own cub you bonded completely to Irvana because you were so little when we left and we were no good to anyone when we came back."

"I miss her, Madra. I miss her so much."

"We all do, and the way she died took a lot out of all of us. But it's been five years, Rea. It is time to quit crying over it. Quit punishing us all because we aren't your mother. You are only alone now because you have pushed everyone away, and are frankly such a shithead no one can stand you. It's the way you've been acting but it isn't who you are."

"But no one's ever going to forgive me...."

"That is no excuse to continue to make a mess of your life and drill a hole in everyone else's. When someone messes up the way you have it takes a long time for everyone to trust much less forgive them. It's the price that is paid for bad behavior that you have to behave much longer than you showed your ass before people forgive you." She pushed Rea away from her and put her finger under her chin and lifted till she had to look at her. "But Rea, unless you bring a charm-wearing member of the Amalite cult and sit him at our dinner table your family will always love you. I love you. I'd forgotten that sometimes people need to hear that." She kissed her on the top of her head. "Now.... Get busy and clean my house."

"Yes Madra."

**"Do you think it will do** any good?" Tarius asked. They were gathered around her camp fire eating breakfast.

"I don't know, but I had to try," Radkin said. "I think she wants to do better, but that may be wishful thinking. Time will tell, right?"

"She's not a bad kid, Radkin, just a stupid one. We're all stupid when we're young," Tarius said. Hestia walked over with a bowl of sweetened gruel—which was what they were all having for breakfast—in her hand.

"While I'm thrilled to hear all your news and I'd rather be here than in the castle, I'm sure you didn't call us here just so you could tell us you're expecting a new baby and your first grandchild or so that we could have a vacation." Hestia smiled a knowing smile. "Because you are Tarius the Black and you rarely doing anything for only one reason."

"I want some money...."

"Tarius, I swear if you expect the kingdom to pay for that monstrosity you are building...."

"I do not." Tarius laughed.

She had finished her bowl and Jena walked over and took it from her. "Be still," she told Jena. Jena was still and Tarius put her now empty hands on Jena's stomach. She left them there till she felt the baby move then kissed Jena and let go of her.

Jena looked at Hestia, rolled her eyes and walked away and Tarius pretended not to notice.

Tarius looked at Hestia again. "Look around you, what do you see?"

"A great huge wall blocking my view of the landscape,"

Hestia said and showed why she liked being at the Katabull compound so much when she put her bowl down and just wrapped herself all around Radkin and sort of hung there relaxed.

"There are thousands of us here, Hestia. Our tides bring in much driftwood, but the woods all around us are getting bare of deadfall, and we've had to start cutting trees to fill our wood needs. We ration hunting, and yet there is still not really enough game to make the Katabull happy. We have plenty of fish...."

"Yuk fish," Darian said, walking by sticking out his tongue.

"As you know Hestia the Amalite was the original homeland of the Katabull, or so the story goes. In the raids on Rorik's keep, Finias's palace and Sedrik's keep we found much gold. The Katabull did their part to fight the Great War. I think we have the right to homestead the territories...."

"Of course the Katabull have a right to homestead the territories; there was never any question of that, and if you also want a share of the gold even if it's for your stinking wall..."

"It is not. I don't want to just send my people to homestead. I want to send a third of my people to build another compound in the territories. Right now most of the Katabull in the world are right here in the Kartik. If something were to happen to the island my people would probably die out altogether, and I could not imagine a world without Katabull."

"Nor could I," the queen said.

"By splitting them into two groups I double our chances of surviving any catastrophe."

"You don't have to sell me on the idea," Hestia said. "Let us not forget that it was my idea to split the Amalite between us and the Jethrik and move to inhabit the land."

Tarius nodded. "Dwellings there will have to be more substantial than what we live in here because of the cold weather and therefor more costly. There would be much they would need and...."

"Tarius were it not for you and all you suffered none of that gold would be in the kingdom's possession. Whatever you need you have but to ask it. My trust in you is now, always has been, and always will be complete."

Tarius grinned. "Yet you hate my wall."

Hestia grinned back. "Yes I do because to me it says that you do not yet trust me."

"But you know I do or I would not have let you have my sister." Tarius smiled. "My plan is to send many of the very young—twenty to forty years—who are easily bored. My wall project is about to be over probably before our baby is born. That will leave many of my people without the steady work they have now and young Katabull when there are no wars to fight or no steady work to do want to spend all their time hunting or fighting. The fighting gets tiresome and as I said if we hunted all we wanted there would not be enough game on this side of the island to sustain us. But the territories are filled with game...."

"And poisonous snakes, and predators. Lions, wolves and bears," Jena said, walking over and handing Tarius a cup of hot tea.

"Thanks love," Tarius said of the tea. "Katabull are not afraid of predators, of lions or bears and certainly we aren't afraid of wolves."

"What about poisonous snakes, Tarius?" Jena asked with a smile.

Tarius shivered at the thought and made a face. Radkin and Hestia laughed at her and she grinned back and said to Radkin, "Would you like me to tell your woman how you ran screaming like a little girl from a tiny rattlesnake?"

Radkin just grinned back. "I think you just did. At least I didn't wet my armor."

Tarius grinned broadly back. "I told you I was sweating."

"We had gone on a scouting expedition. Harris just matter-of-factly points down and says, 'watch out for that rattlesnake,' These two came completely undone," Rimmy told Hestia, "And this one," he poked his thumb towards Jena, "walks right over, grabs the thing by its tail, pops it's head on a rock and goes right on walking."

"I don't want to hear it from you, Rimmy," Radkin said, "as I recall you went up a tree."

He laughed loudly. "Yes, but I neither pissed myself nor screamed like a girl."

"What's all this screaming like a girl crap? You sound like a bunch of straight Jethrik men," Jena said. "Girls don't scream any more or worse than boys do."

"I hope your baby is a boy because if not in another couple of years you're going to be sitting down to a big ole bowl of wish-I-never-said-that soup," Radkin said.

Hestia nodded.

"From the age of three through seventeen I'm sure you could have heard Jestia throwing a fit here," Hestia said. "And some things never change."

"To get back to the subject.... I plan to send a bunch of our youngsters and as many if not more of our elderly," Tarius said.

"Why your elderly?" Hestia asked curiously.

"Two reasons really: first, they have all the skills and life experiences a bunch of youngsters don't; and second, the Katabull detest dying of old age," Tarius said.

Hestia looked at Radkin for confirmation which meant she mostly just had to move her head and look up because she was still draped all over her.

"It's true; we all want to die in battle, in some horrid hunting accident, or having sex," Radkin said.

"I'm sure if Hestia just keeps using you as she does we all know how you will die my friend," Tarius said. "The thing is they can teach all these youngsters everything they need to know to build a successful colony in the territories then they can go off into the woods and have hunting accidents...."

"Wait, wait, wait...." Hestia finally moved away from Radkin she turned to Tarius. "That seems so wrong."

"Do you want to die of old age by itself?" Tarius asked.

"What do you mean by itself?" Hestia asked.

"If you understand what's about to come out of her mouth, please explain it to me," Jena pleaded.

Tarius ignored her. "Wouldn't you rather live to an old age and die being attacked by a bear or a huge tree fall on you or while you're having sex than to just have them find you lying in your bed having just died from being old?"

"I'd rather not die at all," Hestia said with a smile.

"But that's not an option," Tarius said.

Hestia looked at Jena then back at Tarius took a breath and said, "Let me see if I've got this right. You want to send a bunch of your old people to the territories so that they might go hunting and die in bear attacks instead of just dying."

Tarius nodded. "Well, that is what would make them

happy."

**It had just been she and** Tarius, Rimmy and Hared, and Hestia and Radkin and the two boys till Jabone and Kasiria got there. Kasiria was a horrid shade of green and Jabone was walking beside her, his hand on her elbow.

"Is Jestia not here?" Jabone asked with concern. He helped Kasiria sit down.

"It's nothing, Jabone," Kasiria said. "We don't need to send for Jestia." She looked at Tarius, "I just feel sick to my stomach. Yri gave me something to take. I took it a few minutes ago; it just takes a minute to work."

"Mother, you're not sick at all," Jabone said to Jena.

The tone he said it to her in had her smiling and saying, "Well I'm sorry son."

"I was sick with you a few times," Tarius said.

"I wasn't sick at all with Jaden, but sick every day for three months with Rea, go figure," Radkin said.

"And I was never sick with Jestia but always sick with Katan," Hestia added.

"While I have never been sick with any of my children," Rimmy said. Radkin hit him hard enough he had to catch himself.

Jena watched as Kasiria's color improved though it was hard to say whether her relief came from whatever herb Yri had given her to take or just knowing that these three women had all had healthy children and none of them had died doing so. Jena wondered why she wasn't scared at all. After all her mother had died having her and she'd had a horrible miscarriage, she'd been far enough along that they knew what sex he was. Yet she wasn't scared at all. She looked over at Tarius and knew why *I am with her this time and will be for the whole time and she would never let anything happen to me or our baby. As absurd as it may seem I just know that I'm safe as long as I'm with her.*

Jestia and Ufalla showed up and Harris was with them. He walked right up and hugged her as Jabone immediately grabbed Jestia.

"Could you please look at Kasiria and make sure she's alright?"

Jestia looked at Kasiria and screamed loud enough to wake

the dead and make Jena rethink her argument. "She's Jethrik!" Ufalla shoved Jestia then caught her when she nearly fell. "She's fine; do you know the baby has a Katabull primary?"

"Yes we do," Jabone said, and the look he gave Jestia clearly said "what if we didn't big mouth."

Hestia whispered something in Radkin's ear and Radkin whispered something in hers and Hestia nodded.

"And I could easily tell you what sex the babies are," Jestia offered again.

"Jestia you are like a dog with a bone," Harris said with a sigh, so Jena guessed he'd had to listen to her going on about it the whole time they'd been at his house.

"I just don't get the big deal," Jestia said.

"If it's not a big deal then shut up!" Ufalla said and shook Jestia which just made her laugh.

Jabone took off running and when Jena looked up she could see why. Arvon and Dustan had just come into view.

"Darian!" Tarius called and he ran over to her.

"I wasn't doin' anything," he said.

Tarius laughed. "I didn't say you were." She got down on his level and pointed up the road. "Look who's here."

"My fathers!" Darian took off running, and Dustan met him somewhere in the middle, picked him up and hugged him.

Jena smiled. "We are nearly even now," Jena said to Kasiria.

"If we take Ufalla out of the mix then we are even and since she is half Jethrik...." Kasiria trailed off.

Arvon was limping a little but not badly, time in Montero in the springs had helped him. Jazel weaning him off the powders he'd been abusing hadn't hurt either. Within a couple of months of living in Montero he was more himself than he had been in years.

As Arvon got closer he stopped, blinked a couple of times, looked again, and his whole face lit up, his smile going all the way to his eyes. "Kasiria, am I about to be a grandfather?" Kasiria nodded silently. Then he just walked up to Jena and hugged her and she hugged him back. He whispered in her ear. "Sister, am I seeing a miracle?"

"More than that my brother, more than that."

**Riglid had a series of duties** he had to perform, and Kaden had followed him. Riglid had to go to the dock and make sure all ships that were supposed to have sailed had and all that were supposed to be back at port were and then he had to make sure the sentries in all the guard towers hadn't seen anything suspicious. That the gates to the beach had been opened properly—it was closed every night—and that work on the wall was progressing as planned.

It was a lot of walking, but Kaden wasn't sorry he'd gone with Riglid. It was a beautiful day the piece of ocean they were on was fantastic and the Katabull port nearly as impressive as their wall.

"Riglid, why do you not use a horse to make these rounds?" Kaden asked as they headed for the Great Leader's huts.

"Unless we are hauling something or there is an emergency we do not ride the horses around the compound proper, there are many children who play in the roads and too many horses in amongst them is just asking for trouble. Plus we are Katabull; we don't tire easily and the truth is I usually run when I'm doing this."

"But you knew I couldn't keep up," Kaden said.

"And I know the Great Leader is so busy with her guests that she will not care if I'm a little later than usual making my report."

He saw his sister walk out of his house. "What is she doing now?"

"Rea!"

"Relax," Rea said holding up her hands. "I just finished cleaning up the mess and I'm sorry." Riglid looked shocked and was silent; his sister punched him in the shoulder. "I know shocking, right?"

She started walking away and Riglid tapped her on the shoulder. "Rea if you really have nowhere to stay...."

"Then I will have to go and beg Laz to let me stay with him; you have someone now."

She walked away and Riglid started walking slowly back the direction he'd been going. He looked at Kaden and smiled, "Who was that odd person?"

When the Great Leader's huts came into view he could see nearly as many blond heads as there were dark ones. He said something about it to Riglid and Riglid explained. "Kasiria, Jena, Harris, Arvon and Dustan are all Jethrik."

"Captain Arvon? From the stories?"

"He is Jabone's Fadra."

"Dustan, the page Tarius turned into a great warrior?"

"You would not think him such a great warrior if you'd seen him whining over what was basically a flesh wound a few years ago when the Marching Night fought the battle for Rorik's keep."

"I was there doing the end of my two year stint in the military. I was with the Kartik army on the other side of the keep. Though I tried I never got even a glimpse of either Jestia or Tarius the Black but," he snapped his fingers, "That is where I know Kasiria from. I was with my unit in the keep doing a sweep of the rooms and we ran into a blond Katabull alone. She near attacked us before she realized we weren't the enemy."

"There is no other blond Katabull except Arvon on the whole of the island, and no other blond Katabull woman. Crazy Kasiria, she broke ranks and went into the keep before the rest of her troop had regrouped. Come to think of it she probably caused Dustan's injury."

"Wait, wait wait..." He stopped and grabbed Riglid's arm, forcing him to stop. "Kasiria is king Persius's daughter. How can she be Katabull?"

"Well she had a mother didn't she?" Riglid said.

"Your mother was right. This is bard hell."

**That evening they were** all eating in the Great Hall again and Kaden still wasn't very comfortable. Tonight he found himself sitting right next to Arvon. They had just finished eating and Darian was sitting on the table in front of Arvon holding Pogo in his lap. Kaden had just finished telling Arvon that he was sure he was never going to remember who was who when Darian announced he knew who everyone was and it was easy.

"So you know who everyone is do you," Arvon asked Darian.

"Yes, get me down and I'll show you."

Arvon picked him up and sat him on the floor and the monkey climbed on his shoulder.

Darian pointed at Arvon. "Father." Then he walked to Dustan's chair and pointed. "Fadra." Then he walked behind Jabone's chair. "My brother," then Kasiria, "my brother's wife," then Tarius, "my Madra."

"Your mother," Dustan corrected.

"No," Darian said and walked to Jena who sat beside Tarius. "Mother."

"No that's your Madra."

"No," Darian said.

"Give it up, Dustan, you will not win that argument," Tarius said with a smile.

Darian walked to Pete. "My brother." Then Rimmy, "My uncle." Then Hared, "My uncle." Then Harris, "My godfather." Then Elise, "My godmother." Then Hestia, "Pete's cousin." Then he stopped at Radkin's chair and grinned a huge smile. "Hestia's sex slave." The whole room started laughing except Dustan.

"Who taught you that, wicked child?" Dustan scolded.

Riglid whispered in Kaden's ear. "Raised in the Jethrik.... Still thinks people should kiss the ass of royalty."

"Who do you think taught it to him?" Jena asked.

Darian walked up to Jestia and kissed her on the cheek. "My teacher."

Beside him Riglid took in a breath. Kaden looked at him and Riglid whispered in his ear. "They plan for her to teach him magic, but he should not know that."

Then Darian touched Ufalla's back. "My Ufalla."

Then Rea. "My stepsister."

Then Laz. "My stepbrother."

Then Riglid. "My stepbrother."

Finally he reached Kaden; he grinned big and said, "Boy toy."

"Tarius, for the love of the gods," Dustan said, and laughed in spite of himself.

"Oh," Darian said. He walked over and handed the monkey to Laz.

"Well that's got to be a first. He put the monkey down," Jena mumbled.

Darian trotted over to Kasiria and put his hand on her stomach. He looked thoughtful then smiled. "My nephew." There was silence around the table as he then walked over and put his hand on his mother's stomach. He looked at her, smiled the most brilliant smile and said, "My sister."

There was silence then Jabone near exploded, "I'm going

to have a son!"

Radkin looked at Jena and said, "Three boys and then a girl. Oh, Jena, I am so very sorry."

"Hey!" Rea protested.

Jestia then jumped to her feet and yelled. "Oh I get it! It's cute when the baby does it!"

# Chapter 6

**"So what should we name** her?" Jena asked Tarius as she crawled into bed and curled herself around her.

"You know he could be wrong."

"I think you know he's not. So what should we name her?"

"I was thinking Shadra for my mother and then I thought that was also Pete's mother's name and that would be so confusing for him. Even if it wasn't, my mother died in an honorable but horrible way very young, and Pete's mother also died in an honorable but horrid way, and I don't want to do that to our little girl. What was your mother's name?"

"Vera, you know Tarius.... She also died in a horrible way giving birth to me and I don't really have any idea what sort of person she was. I just know what other people said about her and you know how it is when someone dies people often give them attributes they didn't have in life. What could be worse than making a life you never get to share?" Jena was thoughtful. "I read a story when I was a girl. I don't remember much of the story, but there was a character who had a name I liked so much I wished it were my name. Diana."

"Diana," Tarius said. "Diana. Yes, I think I like that. Wait.... Diana the Katabull." She smiled. "Yes, that works fine. No wait.... Pete, Darian, Diana leave those monkeys alone and get over here or I will beat you." Jena laughed and Tarius said, "Yes, it is a perfect name."

"I think Arvon was more excited for us than he was about his own grandson."

"Yes, and I was worried he might be angry or worse hurt."

"Because we have moved on with our lives without him and Dustan?" Jena asked.

"Yes, and because I was afraid he wouldn't want me to have a child with anyone but him. He has this weird thing where he thinks our coupling when we made Jabone was something beautiful." She made a face. "I would never tell him because I love him and I wouldn't want to ruin a cherished memory for him, but the whole time I was mostly thinking, *Are you done yet? Get off of me.*"

Jena laughed and suddenly she understood exactly what the Katabull meant when they talked about a third sex. "Don't you see, Tarius? Arvon is a queer man. When he thought you were male he had a crush on you he never even tried to hide. You have maleness about you, so for him it was like being with a man and not just any man but someone he loves and admires someone he found attractive. There is nothing the least bit feminine about Arvon; he is all male. You however are a lover of women, so it was very uncomfortable for you."

Tarius nodded. That made perfect sense. She put her hands on Jena's stomach. "Our baby girl. Are you disappointed our son told us?"

"I sort of already knew." Jena leaned over and kissed her.

**The Great Leader had** called every Katabull from the entire nation not to the Great Hall—which Riglid had told Kaden would no longer hold even half of them—but to the last section of the wall that had just been finished. Kaden didn't really know what to expect, but he was glad she would be speaking from the top of the wall because though at six foot one he was well within average height for a Kartik man he felt rather short amongst the Katabull. Even in their human form they were just bigger in every way.

Riglid had been busy all day yesterday and today making sure that every Katabull who wasn't giving birth or dying was in attendance. It had already rained that day, so unless the clouds above them decided to drop yet more rain they should all stay dry.

Kasiria and Hared joined him, Darian and Pete in tow. Kasiria's belly was huge and obviously she was not in that moment comfortable. She looked at him smiled and said, "I think my son is standing on my backbone with his hands pushing against my stomach."

Hared elbowed him hard enough to rock him. "Someone needs to tell him that is not the way out."

The Jethrik girl blushed scarlet and Kaden smiled. In the few months he'd lived there Kasiria had become his best friend. She was Katabull but because of her history she was just learning their ways, so she could easily relate to the fact that he often had no idea what was going on or what they were saying. Once he had told her where he had first seen her and she remembered nearly killing his whole troop before she realized they weren't the enemy, they became fast friends. Having seen her that day he didn't even have to ask why the whole of the Marching Night referred to her as crazy Kasiria, but to him she was the sanest one of them. At least she was the easiest for him to understand.

Well she and Jena, so he'd spent most of the last few months in the company of two pregnant women each of which was having completely different pregnancy experiences. Jena was ecstatic and felt great. Kasiria felt horrible and was worried about the entire process. Of course Jena was twenty-seven years older than Kasiria though they were physically nearly the exact same age.

That was another thing that was a little unnerving; they all just sort of took even the most amazing feats of magic completely in stride. For instance Jena's baby physically had three parents and they were like so what. A toddler stands up at a dinner party and announces the sex of both babies and no one even pretended like he wasn't right. Hell, Jena and Tarius had already named their baby.

Kasiria had introduced him to Ufalla's brother Tarius— named for the Great Leader what a great story he had—as soon as he and his wife returned with their Marching Night troop after a sweep of the coast. His wife Eric had a fascinating story; like Kasiria she was of the Jethrik and trained at the same Sword Masters academy the Great Leader had attended, and she also had hid as a man. This Tarius was blond and small and the only human bard he had ever seen who could hold a candle to the Katabull storytellers and he was more than happy to share stories and teach Kaden tricks he'd learned about grabbing and holding an audience.

Kaden had started writing all the stories down. Not just the new ones he was learning, but all the ones he was seeing happen every day and all the ones Radkin had warned him never to tell. It was annoying that all the best stories he had fell into that category, and writing them down helped him vent his frustration.

The Great Leader walked out of the guard tower followed

by Rimmy and Riglid, Jena, Harris and Jabone.

Kaden put his lips nearly against Kasiria's ear and she smiled. He knew why; she had told him that this close whispering was a Kartik thing. He whispered anyway, "Do you suppose Jabone will be Great Leader someday?"

Darian looked up at him and said, "No, Madra says he thinks too much with his heart."

Kaden shook; sometimes the little wizard creeped him right out.

"He's right. Jabone almost got us all killed in the Jethrik territories because he wouldn't listen to Jestia," Kasiria said.

Pete yanked on Hared's pant leg. "Fadra, I can't see."

Hared picked him up and lifted him even with his head.

"Me too," Darian said and looked expectantly at Kaden. Kaden shook his head and picked him up.

"You know it's not nice to listen to other people's conversations," Kaden told him.

Darian looked at him like he was eating a live frog.

"Don't talk so loud," Darian said.

"He has better hearing than the Katabull," Hared told Kaden.

The crowd was loud, so loud Kaden wondered how the Great Leader expected to be heard until she cleared her throat and the whole group was so silent it was eerie.

"My people," she started, apparently she had walked onto the wall with the highest ranking members of her pack her wife and her oldest son and that was what equaled pomp and circumstance for the Katabull. "Look around and what do you see? That we have returned to our former glory, that there are now thousands of us, that there are too many of us in this place. There is not enough wood, not enough game to let us continue to grow here. I have talked to Hestia, and the Katabull have been given a huge chunk of the Kartik-held territories of the Amalite. Hestia has promised to give us enough gold to build a new homeland there—a Katabull colony. This is a new land, a very dangerous land filled with predators. There is also much game and fertile lands to till and plant.

"This will be no easy task. Only those Katabull between twenty and forty and over two-hundred and twenty-five without children under twenty will be allowed to establish the colony. When it has been firmly established anyone who wants to go may go. So if you are not chosen to go now know that you will have a chance to go later if you so choose. Our presence there will be a return of our people to our native lands. Our presence there will make sure that no one who follows the Amalite gods," as a nation they all spit, "will live to infect the land and further secure the Kartik. I need a third of the nation to volunteer. Those who are chosen to go will have the next three months to prepare to leave. Even now shipments are coming from the interior of the Kartik, supplies we will need to build a new homeland there. Those who fall into the proper age groups and who wish to be considered to go need to make a line starting at my huts. Only a third of you will be sent. First come; first serve...." As many of them started moving immediately she added quickly and loudly. "Those caught fighting in the line will NOT be considered. I will be going home now do not stop me on my way, that is all."

Kaden realized he had just seen history made and he smiled. *That is why they are all such excellent bards because they are regularly a part of the stories they tell, and now I am part of it. I should have known that. What story did I tell in pubs that was always the best received? The story of cleaning Rorik's keep and running into a blond Katabull who almost killed us.*

**Tarius sat on her throne.** She had been tired of it before it started, but she had known it would be just like it was—talking to hundreds, thousands of her people day in and day out, making some very happy and some sad. And as she had thought she had more that wanted to go than she was willing to send, and more of the old who wanted to go than the young—though she had too many of both.

She was coming to the end of her third day and was close to having all she would send when she looked up and saw Rea standing before her. "Did you want something child?"

"I want to go to the territories, Great Leader," she said.

Tarius was some taken aback. "Have you talked to your fadra, your madra?"

"I have not talked to my fadra and how could I have talked to my madra? I am grown; they don't govern me."

"You cannot go," she heard Riglid say where he stood at her shoulder.

"That is not for you to say," Tarius said. "Go and get your father."

Riglid cut his sister a look and then took off running to go and find Rimmy.

Tarius looked at the girl carefully; she was serious. "Can you tell me why you want to go, Rea?"

"Because I need to. Tarius, I am just what you need there. I'm a good fighter, a good hunter, and Waden has taught me all he knows about masonry. I'm a good worker, and mostly.... I want a chance to start over again. I've made a mess of my life here. I want to make my family proud of me. I want to be proud of myself again."

Rimmy showed up with Riglid. Tarius did not turn to look at him, just kept looking at Rea. "Rimmy, your daughter wishes to go to the territories. The members of the Marching Night that are going will need leadership; I wish to make Rea their captain and send her to the colonies with the rest of the Marching Night that are going on the first ships that sail out. But since you are my brother and she is your daughter, I will only do it if you agree."

Rimmy looked from Tarius to his daughter. "Rea, is this what you really want?"

"Yes, Fadra."

Rimmy looked at Tarius. "She is a grown woman, Tarius. If she wants to go and you want to send her, I will not stand in her way."

"Do you understand what I am handing you, girl?"

"I think so."

"Thinking so is not good enough. Fifty of the Marching Night are going, and you will be in command."

The girl straightened up and looked at her. "Surely one of the others would be better suited. I have not been the most stable..."

"They are all either young or old. The young lack your experience in battle, and the old are too old to be put in command and will have more important things to do. Besides none of them, not one is of my own household. So if you go you will be the captain of the Marching Night there, or you can stay here."

"I will go. I will do it and make my family proud," Rea said.

Tarius stood up walked over and hugged the girl. Her lips

almost on her ear she said, "I was proud of you when I looked up and saw you standing there."

**Jena had enjoyed being** pregnant she really had, but now she was a week overdue according to Jestia's calculations, big as a barn, and she just wanted to have her baby. She wanted to see her and hold her, and quit carrying her on the front of her body.

Tarius and Hared were also driving her crazy, acting like she was purposely not having the baby just to confound them. She looked across the table at Jestia. "Can you not do something so she will come?"

"I can't and what did Elise say?" Jestia asked with a knowing grin.

"That babies come when they want to," Jena said. She started to get up and she didn't remember making a single noise, but the door opened Tarius ran in and helped her to stand. She smiled at her. Tarius was a nervous wreck. She said she wasn't but she was. She hadn't been like this with Jabone. When it was Tarius's own pregnancy she had kept on doing nearly everything she normally did and would growl if they tried to help her. On the day Jabone was born she'd gone hunting that morning, but Jena apparently was a fragile invalid incapable of even the simplest task.

Of course right at that moment Jena sort of felt like an invalid, so she had quit complaining about Tarius doing everything but cutting her meat for her a couple of days ago. "I have to go to the privy again."

"No problem," Tarius looked at Jestia. "Is it going to be soon?"

"What's Darian say?" Jestia said lightly. "Elise is right the baby will come when she is ready to come."

But Jestia and Ufalla had arrived the day before and Jena was pretty sure that meant she expected the baby to come soon.

Tarius helped her to the privy. Jena thought she had to go, but she didn't and when she walked out of the privy she looked at Tarius. She had a little pain and she was sure she knew what that meant. "You know Tarius, I think I might be in labor."

Tarius scooped her up ran towards the house kicked the

door open and announced. "The baby's coming," as she ran Jena into their room and lay her on the bed.

"Tarius, I said I think I'm in labor. It could be hours or I may not be in labor at all and it could be days."

"Or weeks," Jestia said with a sadistic grin.

Hared came running in the house. "Is it time?!"

"Oh for the love of the Nameless One," Jena sighed. "I said I could be...." Another pain cut her off. "I'm in labor."

"Jestia, get Elise," Tarius ordered.

There was a popping sound, and the next thing Jena knew a very startled Elise was standing at the foot of her bed with a practice sword in her hand. "Dammit all, Jestia," she said without even turning to see if the witch was in the room.

"You're welcome," Jestia said.

"How many contractions have you had?" Elise asked looking down at Jena.

"Two well maybe three. I thought I had to go to the bathroom and I didn't, so maybe more."

"How far apart?" Elise asked.

"I don't know," Tarius said as if she'd failed at life.

"I wasn't asking you," Elise said with a smile.

"I don't know either." Jena had another pain. "They are close."

Ufalla and Harris came running through the front door and right into the bedroom. "Is Jena having the baby?" Harris asked. Since they both still had practice swords in their hands it wasn't hard to figure out what they'd been doing when Elise vanished which was a dead giveaway that she was in fact having the baby, and for some reason Jena found the need to yell at him.

"Yes! I'm having the baby! Does your wife just vanish on a regular basis?" Jena had yet another pain and realized she'd probably been in labor all day and didn't realize it for what it was till she was having actual pain.

Jabone ran in, "Is mother...."

"Yes, I'm having the baby!" Jena yelled, and suddenly she was having all the fears she hadn't had for her whole pregnancy. And then Tarius was beside her holding her hand. "Oh Tarius, I can't have a huge Katabull baby."

"She won't be huge like our son that I bore," Tarius said in a soothing voice.

"It's not a competition!" Jena yelled.

Tarius brushed the hair out of Jena's eyes. "My love you are the bravest woman I have ever known, and when you look back you will know that this is your finest hour and I'm going to be with you through it all. Just like you were there for me and when it's over we're going to have the most perfect baby girl that is part of you and me.... Well and Hared."

"I am always an afterthought," Hared told Jabone.

"My fadra said the same thing," Jabone said. "And I am a full half of him."

It was true, Jena had always seen Jabone as theirs—hers and Tarius's—but this baby was, and she just couldn't stand it if anything happened. "I'm scared; I wasn't and now I am and it hurts so much."

"Just breathe Jena, breathe with me. You know all about this. How many babies have you helped birth over the years, our son included? The only person in this compound who is a better midwife is Elise, and she's right here with you."

"It's really no big deal," Elise said, and Elise was quite calm and not excited at all because Elise rarely was and her demeanor helped to calm Jena in a way Tarius's words really didn't.

Till she remembered the only time she'd ever seen Elise lose it completely was when her son Tarius was born dead and Jena's Tarius brought him to life breathing her own air into him. Then Jena felt another wave of panic and then she remembered that tiny baby was now a tiny man very much alive and well and she calmed again and then she had another contraction and yelled out, "This was a really bad idea!"

"Ufalla, get me the supplies I need. Everyone who isn't one of the parents get out. And someone go and get Yri. We will need him to check the baby when she gets here," Elise said. "We need room. I told you we should do this in the Great Hall where there is so much more room." Which was of course why most Katabull babies were born in the Great Hall.

"And I told you I wanted to have her here because I don't want the whole compound to watch me give birth. Where are the boys, Hared?" Jena asked.

"Rimmy has them in the main room," Hared said, "I can't believe even now you are worried about the boys. What a good Madra you will be."

Jena ignored him and looked at Tarius. "I don't want the boys in here with me while I'm giving birth."

"She will still be the best Madra," Tarius told Hared with a crooked grin.

"I don't want them in here at all, Tarius, I mean it. I don't want everybody and their brother." She cried then as she had another pain. "I just want you, Tarius."

"It will just be you and me and Hared, Elise and Jestia and Ufalla. Alright?"

"That's still a lot of people!" The contraction passed and Jena calmed. "Alright, but could you move Hared to the head of the bed instead of the foot," she whispered. "I don't want him to see my.... Well everything."

Hared smiled and moved to the head of the bed. Jestia had moved up to Tarius's back she stood on her tiptoes and whispered something in Tarius's ear and Tarius nodded. She was too busy trying not to push to have the inclination to worry about what covert things were transpiring between the witch and her mate, but seconds later Jestia left the room.

"What's wrong? Why did she leave?" Jena asked because the witch did nothing without some reason.

"Nothing, she cannot stand your pain is all. She is right here if we need her for anything."

Ufalla walked in with clean towels and Montero spring water—which was antiseptic—in a bottle. She poured the water over her mother's hands and then her own. She looked at Jena and smiled. "Tarius is lying. Jestia just told me she couldn't stay because Tarius's anxiety is making her sick."

Tarius glared at Ufalla as Elise laughed and started taking Jena's underwear off. She threw her wet drawers on the floor. "Well obviously your water has broken. After the next contraction I'll check you."

"I'm not anxious," Tarius told Jena, "just excited."

Jena looked at her and smiled. "You are such a liar."

"I love you, Jena, that has never been a lie, and if I could have these pains for you I would," Tarius whispered in her ear. As she had the next contraction she really wished there was some way that Tarius could have her pain. When the contraction ended Elise checked her.

She washed her hands again and smiled at Jena. "You should be able to start pushing after just a few more contractions."

Which was good because the next three just about killed her.

**Kasiria sat at the table** in the main room like everyone else. Jabone was cringing and doubling over every time Jena screamed, and it certainly wasn't making Kasiria feel any less anxious about her own child's upcoming birth.

*Look at him, and this isn't even our child. He's going to be useless. And all this time I kept thinking, I hope Jena has her baby first so that I'll know what to expect and....*

Jena screamed so loud they might have heard her in the capital. "Damn you, Tarius and Jestia and your bright ideas!"

Jabone groaned and doubled over again.

*I so wish I'd had my baby first now. All this time they've all been saying it's beautiful and natural and.... That does not sound like anything I want to do.... Why are you kicking me now?* Kasiria moved to put her hand over where she was pretty sure her little furry bundle of joy was about to try to kick a hole right through her belly. She pushed back where she could nearly make out his foot, and he seemed to calm right down. *My poor little guy, he's going to be different from almost everyone else and.... He's Katabull, so he's probably kicking around like this because he can't stand the noise.*

She got up.

"Where are you going?" Jabone asked, his face a mask of pain.

She smiled at him. "You do realize you aren't having the baby, right?" Everyone laughed at him; he obviously wasn't amused. "I am going to go sit outside. There are too many people in here, and our baby doesn't like the noise." She walked out and sat down at the fire. She was some surprised when Jestia joined her sitting next to her on the bench. She didn't look much better than Jabone did.

"What's wrong with you Jestia?"

"Tarius is scared witless and she's making me sick," Jestia said. "I left the room and it didn't stop and...." She took a deep breath and her color seemed to come back. "I can block her out here."

"Tarius isn't afraid of anything," Kasiria scoffed.

"I think I know my own brother.... Used to be brother...."

Whatever, and oh my gods." She looked at Kasiria. "That's why I never got close to Katan, why I never let him get close. Because Tarance died and it literally killed me and I never wanted to get that close to anyone else especially not another brother. And Katan did die and maybe part of me knew he would and...."

"Jestia, I wonder what it must be like inside your head," Kasiria said in confusion.

"Oh..." Jestia smiled. "It's a mess up in there."

**As soon as Elise told her** she could push Jena seemed to calm right down and so did Tarius, but Hared didn't do so well.

"How's Hared?" Tarius asked.

"Alright just out cold," Ufalla said with a smile as she straightened having just checked Hared out where he lay prone on their floor.

Jena was between contractions.

"I don't know for sure, but as much as they do it I think Katabull men consider it a matter of pride to pass out at the birth of their babies," Elise said.

"As you know Arvon wouldn't even walk into the Great Hall when I was having Jabone," Tarius said. "Dustan was there; he did just fine, but he's not Katabull."

Elise looked, "The baby is crowning, Jena, just a couple of more pushes."

Jena had another contraction and she pushed for all she was worth.

"One more ought to do it," Elise said.

"I'm so tired," Jena cried, looking at Tarius.

Tarius let go of her hand and moved to look between Jena's legs. She looked up and smiled. "She has black hair." She moved back and took Jena's hand. Jena's next contraction came hard and she squeezed Tarius's hand. "You've got this, Jena, come on."

"Almost Jena, one more push," Elise prompted.

"I can't, I...." Tarius pulled her hand out of Jena's, put her hands on Jena's stomach and pushed hard as Jena bore down, and Diana was born so quickly Elise barely had time to catch her. Elsie scooped the goop out of the baby's mouth and she cried. Tarius grabbed the baby, goop and all, out of Elise's arms. Elise cut her a look. "What? It works on goats."

Ufalla walked over with towels, but Tarius had already put the baby in Jena's arms. She took the towels from Ufalla and started drying the baby off as Jena held her.

"Oh, Tarius, she's perfect," Jena said. The baby cried.

"Hush little one," Tarius said, wiping her face clean. "Oh Jena you did such a good job." She kissed Jena on the lips.

"I realize you have taken over," Elise said with a laugh at Tarius's expense, "...but at some point we will need to tie off that cord and cut it."

"Jestia!" Tarius hollered. And there was the witch.

"Do you ever just walk anywhere anymore?" Elise asked with a grin.

"You know I do, mother. Yuk what a mess," Jestia said. She moved to get a look at the baby and tripped on the baby's Fadra. She shook her head leaned down and touched him, and he came to. "Get up dunderhead, the baby is here."

Hared jumped up took one look at the baby in Jena's arms and started to cry. "She's so beautiful."

"How can you tell? She's all covered in goo," Jestia said, and then she wasn't because Jestia didn't want her to be.

Hared lay his massive hand on the baby's tiny head and looked at Tarius. "I could not be more honored than to share this baby with you and Jena, Great Leader."

"And we are honored to share our child with you. Jestia, we want you to cut Diana's cord," Tarius said.

"That's some Katabull thing." Jestia made a face. "Do I have to?"

"Yes," Tarius said. "Were it not for you we wouldn't have this baby."

"So I'm being punished?" Jestia asked.

Tarius laughed. "Honored."

Elise tied off the baby's cord and showed Jestia where to cut it and there was a bright light and the cord was gone.

"Well that was different," Elise said. "Jestia could you go out and tell everyone the baby is here and Jena is fine? Jestia nodded and left.

**The baby was crying, so** Jena put her to her breast. She didn't latch on right away so for reasons known only to Tarius, she took Jena's nipple and stuck it in the cub's mouth. Jena started to protest, but then the baby started suckling.

"There's our girl." Tarius got a small blanket and covered the baby up on Jena's chest.

As the baby nursed, Jena felt another contraction starting and knew she was losing the afterbirth.

"Ah...." Hared started for the door. "I'm just going to go tell Rimmy."

"Because of course Jestia hasn't already told everyone in the complex," Ufalla said.

Elise finished cleaning Jena up then covered her. Elise and Ufalla cleaned up all the mess from having the baby and put it in a bucket. "We'll let you guys be alone and go plant the tree."

It was Katabull tradition to plant a tree on top of the placenta every time a baby was born.

Elise came over, kissed Jena's cheek and whispered in her ear, "My sister she is perfect. Well worth the wait."

"Thank you, Elise, for everything," Jena said.

"Yes thank you, Elise," Tarius said.

"Someday, Tarius, you will have to teach me that goat trick." Elise laughed and left the room.

"How do you feel?" Tarius asked Jena.

"Incredibly happy, incredibly tired," Jena said. "Could you...." She didn't have to finish the sentence; Tarius helped move the baby to her other breast. And then once again she put Jena's nipple in the baby's mouth. Jena smiled and shook her head.

"What?" Tarius asked with a smile.

"Let's see, she's only minutes old and already you have pushed her from my womb and put each of my nipples in her mouth. I'm thinking this child will never do anything on her own."

"This child...." Tarius's voice broke and she laid her head on Jena's stomach and didn't say another word, just started crying. Jena held the baby with one arm and put her other hand on Tarius's head.

"Everything you ever wanted?" Jena said knowing, Tarius nodded against her. "You were scared to death?" Tarius nodded again. "Happy so happy that the baby's here and I'm fine and she's perfect." Tarius nodded again. "That is exactly how I felt when you had Jabone."

***Kasiria walked back*** into the house when the noise level was such that she knew the baby had been born and everyone was healthy. She got there just in time for Jestia to say to Jabone, "You can quit having labor pains now, your mother has had her baby." Rimmy was telling Hared as he patted him on the back, "That's alright, honey, Tweed passed out at the births of all four of our children." Then Ufalla and Elise walked out with what looked like a bucket of guts and the next thing she knew everyone was going off to plant a tree. Kasiria didn't feel like planting a tree, so she just sat there.

Her baby was kicking up a storm and it was quiet now, so it might be something she ate. She got up and walked around. She knew Jena and Tarius wanted to be alone with their baby, but she really wanted to see her and see that Jena was really alright.

"Kasiria, you can come see the baby," Tarius said.

Kasiria didn't have to ask how she knew it was her, Tarius no doubt heard her moving around and she knew her scent.

She walked down the hall opened the door and walked in quietly. When she saw Jena really did look fine, and the baby was eating she suddenly felt like having a baby was no big deal. *I'm tougher than Jena; if she can do this I can. Quit kicking me you little shit.* She smiled and pushed on him again where he was pushing on her. She walked over and looked down at the baby and when she did the baby finished eating and she could see her face and.... "Oh Jena she's beautiful. Can I touch her?"

"Of course," Jena said. Kasiria reached out and touched the baby's tiny hand. "It just dawned on me. Have you ever actually taken care of a baby, Kasiria?"

Kasiria shook her head. "No. I've seen them. I didn't even play with Darian till he was old enough to be interesting"

"Child, why didn't you say something? You're about to have a cub of your own," Tarius said.

"Jabone said he knows what to do."

"He does," Jena told not her but Tarius. Tarius nodded and gently took the baby from Jena, put her on her shoulder and patted her back.

"Tarius, please don't pound our baby."

"I'm not Madra, look I'm being very careful." The baby

burped and Tarius caught and held Kasiria's eyes. "Do you want to hold her?"

Kasiria shook her head. "I couldn't..."

"Sure you can," Jena said. "It's really not all that scary."

Tarius handed her the baby and Kasiria took her and let Tarius position her properly. She was tiny, she had a shock of black hair that was still wet, her eyes were bluish grey, and she was just the most perfect thing Kasiria had ever seen.

"We named her Diana," Jena said.

"From the story book." Kasiria looked at Jena and smiled. "I see both of you in her face." Kasiria frowned. "I don't suppose our baby will look like either of us."

"Of course he will, Kasiria," Tarius said. She bent down and kissed the baby's head. "He will just look like you both when you are in your Katabull form is all." Tarius took the baby back and held her.

"Sorry, Kasiria, I'd like to tell you differently but that is probably as long as you'll ever get to hold her, and if you aren't careful you'll never get to hold your son much more than that. Tarius is a baby hog."

"I tell you, I don't know what has gotten into him." Kasiria pushed on her stomach again where it felt like her baby was trying to get out. "He is just kicking up a storm."

"He wants to play with Diana doesn't he, oh yes he does, he does." Tarius said to the baby.

"And so it starts," Jena said with a sigh, rolling her eyes.

Suddenly Kasiria felt a searing pain in her abdomen, and then there was a rush of water between her legs that covered the floor. "I.... I'm so sorry."

Tarius handed the baby back to Jena and Jena took her. Before Kasiria had time to wonder what was happening Tarius had scooped her up and was running with her towards Rimmy and Hared's room. Jena screamed after them, "Your water just broke; you're in labor."

Tarius laid her on the bed in the room then yelled out, "Jestia!"

Jestia popped into the room, took one look and the next thing Kasiria knew there was Elise.

"Dammit, Jestia!" She looked down at Kasiria and grinned at her. "And poor Jabone has just gotten over his mother's labor pains."

"I've only had one pain," Kasiria was in a panic now. "I'm not ready I don't want him to come yet. I'm just not ready."

"That's not the way it works honey," Elise said.

Jabone came running into the room, ran over and took her hand. Tarius walked over kissed him on the cheek and whispered in his ear, and he nodded. "You will be fine, Kasiria," the Great Leader told her, and then she started to leave no doubt to be with Jena and their new baby. She stopped on the way out and whispered something in Jestia's ear that Kasiria couldn't hear, and the witch nodded.

"I'm not having another pain, so I'm not in labor right? I don't have to have him now right?" Kasiria said.

"You're water broke; the baby will be here soon."

"Elise," It was Jabone. "...have you ever delivered a Katabull primary baby before?"

"No," Elise said honestly. "But a baby is a baby and all come out the same place."

Kasiria had another pain. She squeezed Jabone's hand and he doubled over, so obviously he was going to go through her labor with her just like he had his mother's. To her surprise, Jestia moved to her other shoulder. She took Kasiria's other hand and said, "Don't think of it as him letting you down when you need him the most, think of it as the fuel you can throw on the fire every time you argue with him for the rest of your lives." Kasiria's pain started to subside.

"I am right here, Jestia," Jabone protested.

"You have not even had a chance to see your sister yet and now your wife is having your baby and they will have the same birthday. What kind of mess is that going to be? You should have planned better but no with you two it is always the most indiscriminant coupling," Jestia said.

"Us Jestia?" Jabone said, straightening and glaring at her. "No one does it as much or as indiscriminately as you and Ufalla."

"Yes, but we're queers we will decide when and if we get pregnant," Jestia said. "You straight people.... Well I pity you really, what a mess your life is. Not to mention the ugliness of your coupling." She made a face.

"You didn't think it was so ugly when you were screwing every man who walked near you." Ufalla had arrived with all the necessary supplies and they were doing things Kasiria didn't want to know about. She had another pain and it wasn't all that bad.

Jabone neither grimaced nor doubled over he held her hand and said, "Breath through it Kasiria," and she did.

"I'm pretty sure I did," Jestia continued, "and just did it anyway because it seemed like what I should be doing at that time." Jestia seemed to think about it for a minute then grinned wickedly. "Nope now I think about it I most likely did it totally because I shouldn't have been doing it. That's beside the point. I don't even know how a woman could ever look at a man without a total air of disgust. And men are so aggressive during coupling it's no wonder your baby is going to be born Katabull all the ugly rutting and rolling around you two do."

"Jestia, of all the horrid things you have said...."

"And done," Jestia added.

"This has got to be the worst," Jabone hissed.

Kasiria had another pain. Jabone just looked into her eyes and now he was the Jabone she knew; strong and with her protecting her, loving her.

"Breathe, Kasiria, breathe," and she listened and was calm because he would never let anything happen to her.

"My madra said, don't listen to a word Jestia says, so she must have known you were going to say such hateful things and why now of all times Jestia?" Jabone said.

"Because your madra asked her to," Kasiria said, knowing.

"You can thank me later, Jabone," Jestia said.

**Rimmy and Hared showed** up with the boys only moments after Tarius got back to the room.

"Come here and meet your sister," Tarius said. Darian ran right over to her and she picked him up even as Hared lifted Pete up so he could see Diana where she lay asleep in Jena's arms.

Pete just smiled and nodded approvingly.

"Was I that little when you picked me up?" Darian asked. She didn't pretend she didn't know what he meant. He knew. He was magic and he knew.

"Yes." she thought about it for a minute how much Diana weighed in her arms how much Darian had smiled and said, "Actually I think she is exactly the same size you were when I picked you up."

"She looks like mother, so pretty," Darian said. She sat him on the bed and he crawled over and sat next to Jena so that he could see the baby better. He started to pet her head. Tarius moved to stop him, but Jena looked at her and shook her head. He was being very careful, very gentle. He quit petting her and crawled around till he could kiss her on her forehead. The baby opened her eyes and looked at him. "Baby has blue eyes," he said.

"They will probably turn brown like Madra's and Hared's," Jena said.

"No, they will just get bluer." He kissed her again. "I love you," he told her. "Pete, come see our sister."

Hared brought Pete over and gently sat him on the bed on Jena's other side. Pete looked at her, smiled, and then reached over and took Diana's hand. The baby wrapped her hand around one of his fingers and Pete looked at Jena and smiled brilliantly and said nothing. Of course he didn't really have to because Darian as always was doing enough talking for both of them.

"Look! Sister holds brother's hand." He took her other hand and the baby grabbed one of his fingers, too. "Now we all hold hands, mother, all your babies except Jabone."

"Where is Jabone?" Rimmy asked. "Has he even seen the cub yet?"

"I thought you knew; Kasiria is having her baby," Tarius said.

Rimmy made a face, no doubt finally putting a cause with the sound. "Need I ask where?"

Tarius just smiled and shrugged. "It was the closest place."

"Don't be such a wanker, Rimmy, it will clean," Hared said.

"So says the man who passed out at the birth of his own child," Rimmy teased.

"May I hold her?" Hared asked.

"Hared, she is your child, too," Tarius said. "You don't have to ask permission to hold her."

Hared very carefully pried little boy's fingers out of the baby's hands and then picked her up. Rimmy looked over Hared's shoulder at the baby. "Look at this bright girl, yes, look at her. You have your mother's blue eyes and your fadra's chin and the Great Leader's scowl, yes what a bright pretty girl you are what a...."

"Why did no one warn me that Rimmy does the idiotic baby talk thing, too?" Jena said in mock distress.

Tarius laughed bent over and kissed her on the lips.

"I am going to go see if we are grandparents yet," Jena nodded.

As Tarius started for the door she turned in time to see Jena hug each of the boys in turn then get Darian to lay beside her so she could just hold him. "I will be back in a minute."

**As far as Jestia was** concerned the fact that Tarius walked in at the exact moment the baby slid out only proved that she'd brought more of the magic from her past life than she knew she had.

After she had pissed Jabone off so bad he wanted to kill her he had been an amazing coach for his wife, and Kasiria in true Kasiria fashion had made having a baby look like taking a walk around the lake on a clear day.

Jabone wanted Ufalla to catch the baby and so she did, and then he wanted his Madra to cut the baby's cord because he was sure that the fact she had showed up at the instant he was born meant that it was meant to be. The baby was a little blond furry Katabull and while not beautiful like Tarius and Jena's baby, possibly the cutest thing Jestia had ever seen.

*He reminds me of one of the stuffed animals I used to have when I was a kid and I just want to hug him and squeeze him and.... I probably shouldn't be around babies.*

"Jestia, did you hear what Kasiria said?" Ufalla said, and she was obviously excited.

Jestia just shrugged. "Nope, wasn't listening."

"We," Jabone started, "want you and Ufalla to be our cub's godparents."

Jestia suddenly felt like someone had knocked all the air from her, and she felt a ball of tears welling up in her throat. The next thing she knew Tarius was hanging onto her arm holding her up and worried, so worried. "I'm alright; I had no vision," Jestia said, and noticed as everyone in the room sighed with relief. "I'm just, this has been a hell of a day." Jestia started to cry and Tarius patted her on the back hard enough to rock her whole body. She looked at Ufalla.

"You know my answer," Ufalla said.

"Then yes we will be his godparents, and I promise not to squeeze him too tight. What are you going to name him?"

"Arvon, after my fadra," Jabone said.

"Jabone, you know it isn't the Kartik much less the Katabull way to name after the living; it causes much confusion," Tarius said. She looked at Ufalla and added, "Look at all the trouble we have with Tarius. Every time we talk of him or me we have to add some word to the name to make sure others know who we are talking about, and I for one have never warmed to 'old' Tarius."

Jabone laughed at Tarius. "Madra three of my parents are Jethrik, and it is their custom to name for the living. It will bring my fadra great joy."

"Yes, I'm sure he will love being called 'old' Arvon," Tarius mumbled.

And then Jestia did have a vision; one that she didn't tell them.

**Jena was exhausted,** but she could sleep later. She just wanted to hold this moment; her little boys lying on the bed on either side of her Tarius holding Diana as the baby slept.

Hared and Rimmy had gone to make dinner for everyone.

*And this is my life. Had Tarius never gone to the Jethrik. If I hadn't lost my other baby or come here I never would have had this.*

As if the moment wasn't already perfect, Jabone walked in carrying a bundle which she knew was her grandson. For reasons she would find out later he looked at his madra and said, "Thank you for Jestia." Then Tarius was holding Diana up so that he could see her and he beamed an even bigger smile. He looked at Jena unshed tears in his eyes and said, "Oh mother she is beautiful just like you."

Jena tried to untangle herself from little boys so she could sit up better.

"Boys, get off your mother now. She needs some rest and she wants to see your brother's cub." Begrudgingly the boys untangled themselves from their mother and dragged themselves off the bed. Jena sat up better and Jabone walked over and carefully laid the baby in her arms. His belly was round so he'd already eaten. His eyes were the same blue-grey color as Diana's that they were all sure meant they were going to be blue, and she wasn't sure at all. He was a little Katabull no doubt about it, his fingernails were claws, his eyes had an elongated pupil, his brow was thick, and he was covered in blond fur. "He's beautiful, Jabone."

Darian walked over and tugged on Jabone's pants leg, Jabone looked down at him. "Brother, I want to see your baby."

Jabone nodded and picked him up. Darian squealed with delight. "I finally have a monkey!" Jabone's face crumbled, and for a minute it looked like Jabone was going to drop his brother on the floor, but then Darian said, "He is my favorite! Much prettier than sister." He looked over at Pete. "He will be our best friend, Pete."

Pete trotted over to the side of the bed and Jena held the baby so that Pete could see him and their usually quiet child looked at Darian and shouted, "He will be the most fun yet!"

# Chapter 7

**When Tarius led Radkin** and Hestia into their bedroom to meet their baby and Hestia looked twenty-five, Jena didn't say a word just smiled and acted like it was the sort of thing that happened all the time.

Diana was two weeks old and Jena was feeling pretty good, but Tarius still wouldn't let her do a thing. And while she had pounded their poor sons like she was tenderizing meat she was so gentle with this baby it was almost funny.

Jena had just fed her, Diana was asleep, and Jena was holding her mostly because she could. Radkin walked right over and pushed the blankets off the baby and then said. "Gods and spiders what an ugly baby!"

"Radkin, you jackass!" Tarius boomed, making the baby jump in her sleep but she didn't wake up.

Hestia smacked Radkin but said to Jena, "I tried to tell her all the way here that it wasn't funny." Hestia didn't just look younger she sounded younger as well and Jena realized that she probably had too and just didn't hear it in herself. Hestia pushed Radkin out of the way and took a look at their little girl she smiled. "Oh Jena, she's perfect."

"She is," Radkin told Tarius, "but that's not in the least bit funny."

Radkin flopped on their bed then grabbed Hestia and pulled her into her lap. Hestia made some play at trying to get away but they all knew it was just play. She didn't want to get away at all.

"Any idea where Jestia is?" Hestia asked.

"She and Ufalla are staying with Jabone and Kasiria for a few weeks to help with their cub. They are the godparents."

"You mean Ufalla is taking care of the baby," Hestia said.

"Actually," Tarius said, "it's all we can do to pry him from Jestia's hands. The only one who's worse about wanting him so much his mother barely gets a chance to feed him is our youngest son, Darian. Yesterday Darian got up before the rest of us, snuck out of the house, went to Jabone and Kasiria's, got Arvon out of his cradle—without waking anyone in their house mind you—then he brought him all the way home. I woke up to the sound of the boys laughing and I went to see why and.... Well there they were playing with the cub like he was a toy. Fortunately he was fine and I got him back to his house before anyone noticed he was missing, but Jabone and I had to put a lock on their door."

"Neither of them are as interested in their sister, and I'm sort of relieved," Jena said.

"The rest of the compound is more interested in Arvon, too. It has been a long time since there has been a Katabull primary cub born. Apparently he is a good omen," Tarius said.

"Go ahead and ask them Tarius," Jena prompted.

"We want you to be Diana's godparents."

The queen looked truly humbled, "We'd be honored...."

"Are you kidding me!" Radkin cut Hestia off. "Are you forgetting your daughter or worse yet mine? You do understand that being her godparents means that if Tarius and Jena go off and get themselves stupidly killed we will be stuck with her, and...." Radkin smiled broadly at Tarius and Jena. "Of course we will be your baby's godparents though it will be a huge pain in the ass."

Hestia looked at Tarius. "You're right; she is a jack ass."

**"This is huge, Tarius,"** Radkin said looking at the docks and the shore filled with supplies being loaded on every boat in the Katabull fleet—twenty ships in all.

"And this is just the first of three such armadas. Two thousand of our people in all are going. It's a lot of people to move and a lot of supplies needed. Fortunately they all have their own belongings and gear, so that cuts the cost considerably. Still it's a lot of food and building supplies and tools—everything they will need and then some because they will have to change the way they do everything. Crops that grow well here will not grow at all there. When we plant, what and how are all different there; here *every* season is the growing season, but there is only a short window in which to grow and raise food there. The terrain is different, the hunting. Things they think they know they will have to learn to do differently. So I must send enough to make sure they can survive through the learning process."

"Sort of makes me wish I was going," Radkin said. "Sounds like a grand adventure."

"Oh aye, I have thought that myself. Of course I lived overseas for many years and I love no place as much as the Kartik." Tarius smiled. "I may go there to die. Have you talked to Rimmy yet?"

"No, but if you are going to complain about him talking like an idiot to your baby I'd say you two deserve each other. I do feel sorry for Jena and Hared." Radkin laughed and slapped Tarius on the back.

"Rea is leaving with this group, Radkin. She wanted to go and I agreed to let her. This is the first group going. They will have to set up a base camp. I am sending all of the Marching Night that is going first so that they can secure the area, and I have put Rea in charge of the Marching Night there."

"Which means you're mostly putting her in charge of the whole thing. Tarius are you sure you know what you're doing? I love my daughter, but she is possibly the most irresponsible person I have ever known." Radkin couldn't believe what she was hearing.

"In battle I would trust her at my back. She is a good worker, and since you had your talk I have seen a change in her. She says she wants a chance to start over again. Both you and I have been right there; sometimes you need a change in order to make a change." Radkin nodded. "And here's the thing, the Marching Night is there, and in our pack we have never let rank stop us from telling someone they are wrong. If she can't do it they will help her or just take over. I think she deserves this chance."

Radkin didn't quite know how she felt about one of her children moving overseas then she remembered, *Tarius the Black is my best friend and my lover is the queen both have ships and would do anything I asked them within reason. Anytime I would want to go see Rea all I'd have to do is say so. It wouldn't be a much bigger deal than it is to ride here.* She nodded, "You know I only bothered talking to her because I sensed she might be ready to listen. She didn't take her mother's death well and I was too busy licking my own wounds to realize she was in serious trouble till it was way too late to turn the tide. She had to want to do better and understand that just wanting something will not make it happen."

"I think this proves she understand now." Tarius put her arm around Radkin turned her around and started leading her back up the dock and towards the compound her palm in the middle of her back. "So what did your mate say about the wall?"

Radkin grinned. "That she wasn't going to say any more about it because she thinks you derive great pleasure from how much it annoys her."

Tarius laughed. "She does know me so well."

"Seriously, Tarius, what's it really for? The guard tower on the south side of the gate is four stories tall; what is that for?" Radkin would never really question Tarius, but she didn't understand the need for a massive wall. The Katabull liked to be free, and to her the huge wall was almost like they were being closed in.

"From the top of the tower I can see Montero with a spyglass," Tarius said.

"And why is that important?" Radkin asked. Tarius shrugged and Radkin laughed. "You really have no idea why you've built it except that you think it may someday be needed. Meanwhile in the nearly twenty years it has been since you built the wall between us and the sea we have only needed to close the gates twice and only once did the wall ever even get wet."

"But it did get wet once, and I have my babies here," Tarius said, as if that was all the explanation she needed to give.

"You spent the gods alone know how much gold and had the entire compound working for years to build something to make you less anxious about your babies?"

Tarius looked up at her and grinned. "Well when you say it like that it just sounds crazy." Radkin laughed and Tarius removed her hand and just walked beside her as they moved through the massive gates that opened onto the sea. "Look there is a reason why I have to send so many of our people away and a reason why I didn't do it till the wall was done. There are way too many of us here. We have run out of jobs for everyone. Harris and Jestia found four bags of gold when they closed that mine in the territories. The people had jobs; they got paid. It made work for everyone, and we got a wall that may or may not protect us at some time. It certainly isn't hurting anything."

Radkin decided not to tell Tarius that she wasn't a big fan of her wall. *After all no matter what I say they aren't going to take it down now. I probably only dislike it anyway because I have let Hestia get into my head.... And other places.* She grinned. and then she saw Rea walking towards them carrying a huge bag, a look of purpose on her face. When Rea saw her she nearly dropped the bag. Then came running up to her, put the bag down, and embraced her. Radkin hugged her child to her and held her.

"Mother, you came to see me off!"

Radkin thought about it for just a second and then said as if she hadn't just learned it a few minutes ago, "I would not let you leave on such a grand adventure without saying goodbye. I am so very proud of you, Rea." There was suddenly a little catch in her throat.

"The ships leave port in an hour. Your madra and fadra, your brothers and I will be sure to come and see you off," Tarius said.

Radkin let Rea go, pushed her to arm's length and nodded. Rea smiled at her pulled out of her grip and punched her in the arm. "Are you getting soft on me now?"

"That will never happen." She smacked Rea hard enough to rock her on her feet.

**Hestia had wrapped** herself around Radkin's back where she lay on her bed. "How do you really feel?"

"Right now fantastic."

"I meant what we were just talking about," Hestia said, and bit Radkin on the back between her shoulder blades.

Radkin shook and said truthfully, "There will be no more talking tonight if you do that again; I will just be all over you."

Hestia laughed. "How do you really feel about Rea going to the colony?"

"A few months ago I would have just been glad to have her out of my hair. I'm not worried about her going there, she can take care of herself and if I find I miss her enough I must see her I will simply get on a boat and go...."

"Can I go with you?"

"Hestia, of all the stupid things.... If I'm going anywhere

you WILL go with me even if you don't want to. To the Kartiks you are the queen, but to me you are my mate which is a much more important position." Hestia bit her again, and this time she held on. "Woman what did I tell you?" She chuckled.

Hestia turned her lose and said slyly, "That you'd be all over me. And I'm going to hold you to it."

**Tarius was sitting on the** throne outside her hut holding Diana watching her little boys play with twigs in the dirt outside their hut. Well actually it wasn't so much dirt as squishy mud. They'd had slightly more than their normal rainfall, but their house like most Katabull houses was built on mounds of dirt that drained the water away. There was a big puddle of mud for them to play in because one of them—neither would either confess or blame his brother—had turned on the spigot to one of their many rain barrels and emptied the contents onto the ground to make a river for their "town."

"I swear, Tarius, the woman is aroused by the oddest things," Radkin said, and then she was filling Tarius in on what she and Hestia had done the night before. "... and she just kept biting me which...."

"Radkin! If she were not aroused by odd things, you and she together would be a huge mistake," Tarius said laughing. "Jena has just given birth; we have not made love in weeks, and it will be weeks more before we can, so please spare me your naughty, naughty queen stories."

Radkin laughed. "I'm sorry, Tarius."

"Have you seen my grandson yet?"

"I did and you were right; Jestia is completely enthralled with him. Weird," Radkin said. "Though I have to say he is just the cutest thing ever."

"My little monkey," Darian said lovingly, not looking up from the mud and stick replica of their house he and Pete were making.

"Dammit, Darian, I have told you a dozen times now, your nephew is not a monkey," Tarius said. Radkin cracked up. "You! Do not encourage him."

"I told him he wasn't, too," Pete said.

"I don't want to hear it from you, Pete, he went and got him by himself, but you didn't come and tell us; you just played with him, too. Arvon is a tiny cub and he could have gotten hurt. You boys are never to touch him again without his parent's permission, do you understand me?"

"Yes Madra," Pete said, and couldn't hold her eyes.

Darian however stood right up put his fists on his hips—mimicking the way she often stood and looked at the compound—looked her right in the eyes and said, "I would never hurt my little monkey. He likes to play with us, he didn't cry. I was very careful...."

"He is not a toy or a pet; he is your brother's cub."

"But I love him." The toddler's eyes started to fill with tears. "I love him, Madra."

"You can love him all you want, but if you ever touch him without his parent's permission again I will beat you."

He turned around sat back down and started playing in the mud again. He looked at Pete and said in what he thought was a whisper, "I don't know why they would get us a monkey and then not let us play with it." Pete nodded silently.

Radkin lost it. Tarius looked at her and gave her a crooked grin. "You are not helping."

**Kasiria handed him his** grandson, and he forced a smile. They had told him and he'd tried to prepare himself and after all he was Katabull and the cub was attractive in his own way but it was hard to see him as a baby. Among the Katabull they spoke of their young swapping the word baby and cub around pretty evenly, but when you looked at his son's child the word "cub" was a much better fit.

"He's very big isn't he," Arvon said, that being the only thing he could think of to say.

"He is," Jabone said, "much bigger than my mother's baby, and Kasiria just pushed him right out." There was an anxious note to his son's voice no doubt because he feared Arvon and Dustan would look at his baby and see a freak. "We named him Arvon for you."

"I am honored," Arvon said quickly, and he was. His son named his first child after him; that was huge. It went against Kartik and Katabull tradition which meant his son particularly did this to please him.

"He is very cute," Dustan said, looking over Arvon's shoulder.

Dustan was right he was cute, but not like a baby. *Like an animal. He will spend most of his life in his Katabull form just like I spend most of mine in my human one. What's the difference really? When I'm Katabull I'm still me—a little wilder me, but still me. And Waden has been one of my best friends; there isn't a better man anywhere. The look on Jabone's face near screams that he is afraid I won't love his son because of what he is, and Kasiria....* He looked at her and was pleasantly surprised. She didn't care what anyone else thought. He was her son, she loved him, and she had completely embraced his differentness. *She doesn't care what we think because in her mind she has already accepted that Persius, and all the people she knew before she knew what she was and moved here would take one look at him and think him a freak. So she's going to love him more for all of those who won't and.... I will not be one of those. I cannot be, dammit this is my grandson and he's cute, strange but cute, and what does Tarius always say? Quit worrying about what you want and embrace what you have.* And then he really saw him. *That damn Tarius she has marked this child just as she has marked Jabone. He looks like them when they are catted out but he is colored like his mother.... And like me. He is only blond because of me.*

"He looks just like us," Arvon said, choking back tears. He picked the cub up and kissed his forehead.

"And what does your little brother think of him?" Dustan asked.

Jabone took a deep breath let it out and looked at the floor, but Kasiria just said, "He thinks he's the prettiest monkey he has ever seen. Considering how much he loves monkeys I choose to consider it the greatest of compliments."

"We have to watch Pete and Darian very closely or they take off with him," Jabone said.

"They just want to play with him. Jestia isn't much better," Kasiria said with a grin.

"At least she doesn't call him her little monkey," Jabone mumbled.

Arvon decided to change the subject. "We ran into them as we were leaving town and I have to say I was a bit shocked when the witch just started gushing about your cub." It was true, too. She had gone on and on about him as if he was not just any baby but an extraordinary one. The witch obviously wasn't bothered by his appearance at all. Considering that

Arvon had always thought Jestia rather shallow he just became even more determined to be alright with what his grandson was.

Arvon had twisted his bad leg the very day the babies were born. He'd been feeling so good he'd forgotten he had a bad leg. He'd gone hunting, slipped on a wet rock while climbing up hill and was reminded. So Jestia and Ufalla, who had stayed with Jabone and Kasiria for weeks helping them with the baby, were just getting back to Montero as they were leaving.

Riglid and his man had showed up at their door in Montero to tell them that the babies had been born. Arvon couldn't lie—at least not to himself—he had hoped that they were wrong and that his grandson was just a "normal" Katabull. When he asked Riglid whether the cub was human looking or not and Riglid said he was Katabull Arvon was glad he had to wait for his leg to heal. It meant he'd had two weeks to wrap his head around it all and he was glad he'd had the chance to talk to Jestia and Ufalla before they got there, too. He'd hate to think how badly he would have botched this if he hadn't had time to process it.

Tarius and Jena walked through the door. He was not at all surprised to see that Tarius was carrying their baby, Tarius loved babies, all babies, and especially her own. The look on Jena's face was pure joy. She had always been a good mother, but now she had her own cub and not just any cub but a baby that was part hers and part Tarius's.... and Hared's. All those years ago on that darkest night when he'd washed not just her blood but Tragon's off of her, when he delivered and then buried her dead baby, this was what he hoped for her, that someday she would have a baby. Then she couldn't get pregnant and Tarius gave her Jabone, and then later she handed her Darian and that never really fulfilled his wish for her. It was close, and Jena was happy, but now she had exactly what she wanted, what she deserved.

Tarius walked right up to him and said, "Trade me, Grandfadra."

They traded babies, and Arvon looked into the baby's eyes—as blue as her nephew's eyes were. Born on the same day; what were the odds of that?

Tarius started to chuff at their grandson, and to Arvon's astonishment not Jabone's cub but Jena's started to chuff right back. Arvon laughed out loud. *They are both half Katabull. They don't look it, but they are the same. Both carry a quarter of Tarius's blood. This tiny baby is my huge son's sister and.... Neither of them would be here were it not for the witch Jestia. This baby I hold is here because of not one but many of her spells, and were it not for the spell Jestia used to save Kasiria's life my son's child could not have been born. Of course maybe if he hadn't married crazy Kasiria my grandson would be a normal Katabull....*

*How absurd. Am I a normal Katabull? I who was raised a human among humans and in the Jethrik no less. He is as normal as any Katabull.*

**The servant had opened** the drapes at his request, yet now as the grayness of the day trickled through the window he wondered why he'd bothered. He threw his covers off and moved to sit on the edge of his bed. Persius was glad that he was alone.

He'd had the dream again. It had been exactly the same, so nothing more for the wizard to analyze. Perhaps the only thing more troubling than the dream itself was the crazy prophecy Hellibolt was sure it was attached to.

Especially considering what they had found only a week ago. One of his advisors had shown up very agitated and excited carrying a simple clay pedant on a leather thong.

"This was given to me by a man who owns a pub here in town. One of his employees found it while cleaning after hours."

One look at the clay article told him everything he needed to know about why the man thought Persius needed to see it.

The design was one he knew only too well. Five parallel lines connected in the middle to five horizontal lines. Tarius had explained the meaning to him all those years ago. The five horizontal lines represented the five Amalite gods whose names meant vengeance, ambivalence, competition, apathy, and deceit, the lines coming down from them had two meanings blessings for their followers death to the nonbelievers.

Persius had thrown the thing on the floor and crushed it with his heel. The thing was a blessing for Amalites so a curse to him. But he did not forget what it meant. There were still people who worshiped the Amalite gods in the Jethrik, and he had to deal with it.

But he had no idea how, and now he'd had the dream again and it was obviously a warning, but what was he to do? It told him he needed to do something but not what he was supposed to do.

There was a knock on his door. "Come in."

One of his pages walked in. He smiled at the king and announced, "I have a letter from princess Kasiria. It came in by boat yesterday and was delivered by rider only moments ago." He walked over and handed it to the king.

Persius took the note, his hand shaking. "Thank you. You may go."

The boy left, though obviously he wanted to stay and see what was in that message. The wax seal that bore the insignia of the Katabull Nation hadn't been broken, so he couldn't know. The boy left and Persius looked at the scroll in his hand. It said "For Persius, king of the Jethrik from the princess Kasiria," but it wasn't in her hand. He hadn't heard one word from her—though he'd heard many about her—since they had parted before she went to fight the battle in the cave.

*Tarius the Black the Marching Night and the Kartik army that is where my daughter is and why? Because I have never been able to stop the bloody Amalites from invading my country and always the Katabull have to come and save me. And Hestia sent word to warn me there had been an Amalite uprising in the Kartik and what did I do? Nothing. Once again I thought it could not happen here. And this is not Kasiria's hand writing so what is this, who is it from, and am I about to learn that I have lost Kasiria?*

He ran his hand over the wax seal. It was the same design as the one Tarius the Black wore on her signet ring. This might indeed be made with that very ring after all his daughter was married to Tarius's own son. He popped the seal and began to read.

> *Since I still only read and speak Kartik by a spell that turned my knowledge of Jethrik language into Kartik I cannot write in Jethrik, so my friend Eric writes this for me. Much has happened here. I have fought many battles. Jabone and I have our own home in the Katabull*

*compound. We are all well.*
   *I write you to announce that Jabone and I*
*have a son, his name is Arvon...*

Persius took in a deep breath. He smiled and breathed again. Kasiria had borne a son. He had a grandchild whose blood was shared with Tarius the Black. He didn't even get his feelings hurt that the child was named for Jabone's father instead of him. What Katabull child could bear the name Persius? After all Persius was the villain in the Katabull's favorite story.

He read on.

   *...and he is strong and healthy and grows*
   *daily. He looks at everything with such wonder*
   *that I find I see the world with new eyes. He*
   *will be two months old tomorrow. I didn't think*
   *I would be a good mother. It was not something*
   *I thought I wanted to do and now I can't imagine*
   *a day without him in it.*
   *I hope my missive finds you well.*

   *Love,*
   *Kasiria*

Persius did the math in his head including the time it took the note to reach him and then he got up went to the wall and looked at the calendar. According to his calendar, the boy had been born on the seventh of Dulan.

Suddenly Hellibolt in his usual smoke and light show appeared in his room. "Dress quickly, Persius, and have your servants pack for a long trip."

"What?"

"We must go to the Kartik at once and talk to the Kartik queen."

"What?" Persius asked again.

Hellibolt pointed to the open scroll in Persius's hand. "Come on dunderhead, a Katabull royal born on a night when the twins converge."

"Dunderhead?! Now see here wizard.... How did you...."

"What sort of wizard would I be if I couldn't read an unopen scroll? Now come on chop, chop."

"Why must we go to the Kartik?"

"Do you have any answers about what to do to stop the Amalite menace from once more invading your country?"

"No but...."

"The Kartik queen does. She has installed a protocol which makes sure her country is clean of the curse of the Amalite gods. We must learn what she has done and copy her but mostly.... Don't you want to see Kasiria and Jabone's baby?"

Persius sighed. "I do, but they are in the Katabull compound and for me to go there would be suicide."

"Do you not think the queen could summon Kasiria and Jabone to the capital? Come on, Persius, don't think; just do. Get dressed have your servants pack. Pick who is to be in charge while you are away. I plan on leaving before noon. Will you be on the boat with me or not?"

# Chapter 8

**Persius couldn't remember** the last time he'd been at sea. Hellibolt had given him a potion to keep him from getting seasick. It had tasted like bilge water mixed with horse crap, but he wasn't sick, and what he remembered about being at sea before was that he had gotten sick.

As he stood at the bow looking out at the ocean before him he wondered why it had been so long. It was exhilarating the sea breeze in his face the spray of the ocean occasionally hitting him, blue as far as the eye could see the sway of the ship beneath him. Hellibolt strode up to him.

"I should have done this long ago," Persius said. "Go to the Kartik to meet with their queen. How far did you say the port is from the capital?"

"A day's ride," Hellibolt said.

"And how many days at sea?"

"Three if the weather remains clear and the wind good."

"So four days' travel time." The tone of the wizard's voice was not one that put Persius at ease, but his silence was worse. "What is it?"

"It will take us much longer than that to get to the capital."

When he turned to question him further the wizard was gone. Persius frowned and looked out at the water. "And I was having such a good time, too."

**Tarius stood on the dock** her cub in the crook of her right arm as she held the eyeglass to her eye with her left. "And that's it; they are out of sight."

"I don't understand why you were in such a rush. Why send them today instead of tomorrow as was intended?" Jena said. She looked over at the beach at where the two boys were playing in the sand, occasionally walking into the surf.

"They were ready, all the supplies were here, the weather is good, why waste a good day?" Tarius asked. She put her eyeglass away, resituated the baby, took Jena's hand and walked her to the beach where the boys were. It was spring now, warm and the boys like their Madra were wearing blue cotton loincloths and nothing else…. Well Tarius was wearing a piece of blue fabric she said was a top. Jena swore the strap on Tarius's sword's scabbard covered almost as much. Of course if it wasn't for the baby Tarius probably wouldn't have bothered with a shirt at all, however babies tended to see any nipple as a feeding opportunity and while trotting around mostly naked didn't bother the Great Leader at all, having the baby latch onto her dry nipple did.

Jena had given up years ago trying to make Tarius wear more clothes. She'd even gotten used to her running around with no shirt in front of the entire compound. After all Tarius wasn't the only Katabull female who stripped her shirt off the minute the days got hot, and the truth was most had so little breast you had to look twice to see whether they were female or male. But she herself had never gotten comfortable with so little clothing.

She'd felt down right scandalous the first time she'd worn one of the wrap-around dresses that came to just above her knees. After nursing three babies she was comfortable feeding in front of people she knew, but not those she didn't. Kasiria still took Arvon in another room alone to nurse him. Jena made a face. Tarius was right; it was uncomfortable to name babies after the living.

Jena had started out being shy about feeding Jabone, but by six months she was just feeding him whenever, wherever, and Kasiria would, too. About the hundredth time she had to leave a conversation get up and take a screaming infant somewhere else to feed him and come back only to realize she now had no idea what had been said or decided, modesty would take a back seat to convenience.

Tarius was about to find a piece of driftwood and sit down when two men walked up carrying the Katabull throne. She sighed but thanked them and sat down. Jena sat beside her.

Darian ran over. "Look what I got you." He handed her a shell.

"It's very pretty," Jena said.

"Can sister play in the sand?" Darian looked at Diana who was awake and just looking up at the palm trees that shaded the beach. The breeze was blowing and the leaves floated back and forth looking like green birds. She was chuffing and her hands played with the air like she was trying to grab them.

To Jena's dismay Tarius moved as if she was going to lay the baby in the sand. Jena grabbed Tarius's arm.

"No, the cub cannot play in the sand." She didn't know who looked more incredulous the child or the warlord. "She will put sand in her mouth," Jena said. Tarius nodded, but Darian was not to be put off so easy.

"So, I eat sand and I'm okay."

"He does eat sand," Pete said, shaking his head as he continued to dig a big hole in the sand to watch it fill with water.

"Quit eating the sand," Tarius scolded Darian. He nodded and then crawled up in Tarius's lap and started petting Diana, getting sand all in her hair. Tarius looked at Jena and smiled. "It will wash off Madra."

Darian twisted his head so that he could see what the baby was looking at. Then he leaned down to her, his lips almost touching her ear and said, "Don't worry, Diana, trees grow back."

Then he climbed off Tarius, crawled into Jena's lap and kissed her cheek. "We will all be alright you know, mother."

Jena hugged him and kissed his head. She looked at Tarius and she shrugged. Darian got off her lap and went back to play with Pete. "He is starting to worry me."

"I think as long as he is saying we will all be alright we should just take him at his word and not worry," Tarius said. She stood up then and handed Jena the baby. She took her sword off and leaned it against the throne. Then she went to take the baby. Jena held her close.

"What do you think you are doing?"

"Taking our baby girl for a swim."

"I don't know, Tarius."

"Come on, Madra, it is very warm and both our sons had already felt the ocean water by now," Tarius kissed her on the forehead. "You can come with us."

Jena nodded and let Tarius have the baby. They walked into the ocean and the water was more than warm enough. The baby grabbed the braids on either side of Tarius's face in her hands and held them tight, but she didn't look the least bit afraid and in fact as the waves started to hit her splashing her face she seemed completely content.

*Diana like me and the boys knows that Tarius would never let anything happen to us. Nothing that she could stop. She wouldn't take her into the water unless she thought it was warm enough and calm enough.*

Jena put her hand on the baby's back. "So what do you think my bright-eyed girl?" And her eyes were bright and every bit as blue as Jena's were. It hadn't surprised her at all that Arvon's eyes had stayed blue, after all he was three-quarters Jethrik, but her baby was only half, and both Hared and Tarius's eyes were so dark brown they looked black. Tarius sensed as she often did that Jena wanted to hold the cub, and so she handed Diana to her but stayed close.

Everything was perfect and then Riglid came running up to the edge of the surf. "Great Leader!"

Tarius took the baby from her and started out of the water and Jena followed. "What is it, Riglid?"

"There is something wrong with the water coming into the compound," Riglid said.

"What?" Tarius asked.

Riglid shrugged.

"Boys come on," Tarius said, they got up and ran over without a moment's hesitation because the tone of her voice told them they'd better. She handed the baby to Jena and grabbed Darian up and started walking so fast Jena couldn't keep up and Pete had to run to do so. It was almost funny when the two Katabull carrying the throne passed her. "Take that to my house." They were going through the gates when Tarius stopped and put Darian down. She waited for Jena to catch up. "Honey, take our cubs and go back to the house."

Jena nodded, but didn't understand how dirty water or a plugged pipe rated the level of urgency her mate was exhibiting. But Jena didn't balk, and the boys beat her back to the house. She dried the baby off dressed her then lay her in her cradle and started to dry herself off when she noticed both boys had followed her and were standing there watching her, quiet and obviously worried.

She went ahead and got dressed because they were her sons and well Darian had never let her have a moment's privacy since they'd gotten him and Pete wasn't much better. "Nothing's wrong, boys. Madra has to check the water system that is all. Why don't you go play in your room and I'll make lunch?"

They nodded but didn't leave. She picked the cradle up with the baby in it and went to the main room to make some lunch. The boys followed. She would have run them into their room or outside to play and told them not to worry, but suddenly she felt like she did right before she went into a battle, and she wasn't about to let any of her cubs out of her sight. The fact that they seemed eager to stay right with her did nothing to ease her mind. She started making lunch and gave them each jobs to do and within seconds that uneasy feeling left her, but her magic child kept looking over his shoulder and that couldn't be good.

***There was a spring in the*** foothills which was just inside the northernmost portion of the wall. It was a good spring and they had dug it out, built a stone and mortar reservoir, and put a roof over it. They had made pipes of timber bamboo and run them to six different places spaced throughout the compound so that it was easy for everyone to bring their containers and get clean drinking water.

Tarius walked to the spigot closest to her own hut. When she opened it the water looked white. She put a finger in it put it her mouth and tasted it she made a face, it had on odd taste. It could be something that had formed in the pipes. "Are they all like this Riglid?"

"Yes."

Tarius called on the night so Riglid did automatically. He was her runner and he couldn't very well keep up with her if she was Katabull and he was not.

"Rimmy!" Tarius called, and Rimmy was there in seconds. He was in his human form, but when he saw that his son and Tarius had both changed so did he.

"What's wrong?"

"There is something wrong with the water supply. Riglid and I will go check the source. I want you to put the word out, till further notice everyone is to get their water from the lake and boil it. Rimmy nodded and took off even as she and Riglid started running. It was at the furthest end of the compound and mostly straight uphill, so Tarius was glad she was Katabull.

When they got to the spring house it looked unmolested, but when they opened the access door the water was white.

"It looks like someone dumped powders in it and stirred," Riglid said.

"But the only smell of anything living is you and I and monkey." Tarius was thoughtful. She looked up at the Great Wall. From the top of it you might be able to nock an arrow and reach the spring house, but only a Katabull could do it, and the spring house like the Great Hall had a tile roof and no openings save the door which had been closed till they opened it. Tarius reached into the spring and scooped up a handful of water and put it into her mouth.

"Great Leader!"

Tarius put up a hand. She swished the water around in her mouth; it had a taste but not a bad one. She swallowed. Riglid looked at her as if she'd lost her mind and he was soon going to have to announce that she was dead. "The water is fine, just filled with minerals I think. It doesn't taste much different than the water in Montero. I think it is fine." She laughed at the look on Riglid's face. "If I don't die by morning we will tell everyone it is safe to drink."

Riglid mumbled something even she couldn't hear.

"What's that, Riglid?"

"I said," and it was obvious by the look on his face that he was not pleased with what he considered to be her rather cavalier attitude, "I am glad that you are not my mate."

Tarius smiled. "Because I would always be on top?"

"Because I wonder at times if you care at all for your own life, and it must be very hard to love you the way she does knowing you always risk yourself first," he said. Tarius hugged him and patted the side of his face.

"You are far too serious, Riglid. I have much to live for and would not have drunk the water if I thought it would kill me. You are so like Tweed." She smiled at a distant memory. "Sober Tweed." She started walking down the hill at a Katabull march, and he followed. "This is nothing, some rain we did not get here but high in the mountains has loosened some mineral deposits is all."

Then she stumbled and fell and lay prone and still on the ground. Riglid ran to her side in a panic. He rolled her to her back and started shaking her, "Great Leader, Great Leader!"

Tarius opened her eyes a crack looked at him and said. "Seriously, Riglid you have got to lighten up." She cracked up, and he looked as if she had smacked him. He jumped up and started down the hill in a huff. She jumped up and went after him.

"That was not funny!" he yelled back at her.

"Ah come on, Riglid, it was just a little joke. Riglid..." She laughed again. "Come on, it was funny."

"No it was not!"

He was still mad when Rimmy met them as they walked back into the complex proper. He looked at Riglid, "What's wrong, son?"

"The Great Leader is an ass," he said, throwing his hands in the air as he walked past his father.

"We all know that son," Rimmy said lightly. He looked at Tarius. "So what did you do to break my poor boy?"

She told him as they walked back towards their huts, and Rimmy laughed. "What I didn't tell him was that I was sure it was fine because I saw a monkey drinking from the overflow and I didn't see dead monkeys anywhere. By morning it may be running clear and even if it isn't, it's safe. To err on the side of caution we'll let the lake water and boil order stand till I can test it again tomorrow."

"By you drinking it?"

"Or you could do it; it doesn't have to be me," Tarius said lightly.

Rimmy shook his head. "So.... All kidding aside you want to tell me what's got you rattled?"

Tarius took a deep breath and let it out. "Bad feeling in my belly, mostly my little wizard will not stop saying strange things."

**"Riglid calm down,"** Kaden said. He had been at Kasiria's playing with Arvon when Riglid showed up—because he said he could smell Kaden was there—fit to be tied. "What on earth is wrong with you?" Because of course he was in his Katabull form and pacing back and forth and breathing hard enough he could hear it, and Riglid was normally very calm.

Riglid stopped and looked from him to Kasiria and back and said, "She is an ass!"

"Kasiria?"

"No, not Kasiria."

"Who then?" Kaden asked.

"The Great Leader."

"Everyone knows that," Kasiria said with a smile.

Arvon started to fuss and Kasiria came and got him. He absolutely did not sound like a human baby when he cried, but then to his ears neither did Diana although she was closer. Arvon sounded like someone had stepped on a box full of kittens when he was unhappy—which he hardly ever was. Arvon laid his head on Kasiria's shoulder and seemed to calm right down. "Well hurry up, tell us what she did. He's going to want to eat in a second and I don't want to miss the story."

Kasiria wouldn't feed her baby in front of anyone.

Riglid started his story. "We went up to the source to check the reservoir and..." He told his story and when he finished it was all Kaden could do to keep from laughing, and Kasiria didn't even try. Her laughing made Kaden laugh and then Riglid was even madder. "Maybe you didn't hear me right our leader drank what very well could have been poison water." This just made them laugh louder and made Riglid even madder, "Kaden! I expect crazy Kasiria to laugh but not you!" Then he turned on his heel and stomped out of the house, slamming the door and making the baby jump and then start crying.

"Well now I'm not laughing," Kasiria said, rocking the baby but she was still laughing.

Kaden worked to stop. "He's such a tight ass, I mean come on when I tell that story, and I will, everyone is going to laugh. Well, I better go after him."

"And I'd better feed this one. Though I don't know who was crying louder, him or Riglid."

Kaden left almost running into Rimmy. "Did you see...?" Rimmy pointed with a knowing smile. "Thanks." Kaden took off at a run knowing it was the only way he'd catch Riglid, if he even could. When he did he didn't touch him. After all Riglid was a huge Katabull and mad right now. "I'm sorry, Riglid. I shouldn't have laughed."

Riglid turned and stopped so quickly Kaden had to catch himself to keep from running into him. "No that's alright!" he boomed, then lowered his voice to a whisper, "the Great Leader is dead; that's hysterical. I don't know why I'm being such a tight ass." Kaden cringed. He had forgotten that in his Katabull form his mate could hear a gnat fart.

"No, that wouldn't be funny, Riglid, and it's one of those things that if she had done it to us it wouldn't have been funny at all."

"But it's funny if she does it to me?" Riglid said. "I thought she was dead. I thought I was going to have to tell everyone that I love that she had died. Your people are all alive; you don't know what it's like to lose someone."

"You are right, Riglid," Kaden took his hand and looked into his eyes. "I'm sorry." Riglid seemed to calm down. "Do you have to check in or do anything else?" Riglid shook his huge Katabull head. "Then let's go home."

"There is something wrong, Kaden... something. And I know Tarius feels it. She made a stupid joke because there is something not right. I think that's why I'm so mad because I'm scared, and I don't know what of."

# Chapter 9

***They were a day and a*** half out when the Captain called for him. He was about to dress the man down for summoning him when beside him Hellibolt pointed, and on the horizon were not one, not two, but an entire fleet of Kartik ships coming at them.

"They are not Kartik," Hellibolt said at his shoulder as if he were reading his mind. "Those are Katabull sails and flags."

"So many of them, why? What could have possibly gone wrong?" Persius couldn't for the life of him think of a reason for so many of them to be at sea at once grouped together going towards the Jethrik.

"I'm sure I don't know," Hellibolt said, and then he was gone and Persius was left with the captain to sweat—and he was, too—the closer they got to the Kartik the hotter it got.

"What do you want me to do, sire?" the captain asked.

"What can we do, imbecile? Steer the boat around them. That is the Katabull fleet, and we are one ship. If they mean to take us out we will soon be in the bottom of the ocean."

Then Hellibolt was back. He had a stick covered with cooked pieces of fruit and fish in his hand.

"Well?" Persius demanded.

"It's quite good, sublime really, well spiced and...."

"What is the Katabull fleet doing in the middle of the ocean heading for the Jethrik?" Persius asked, tugging at what was left of his hair.

"Oh that? Well first off they aren't in the middle of the ocean that would be days that way." He pointed, and Persius didn't pretend to know what direction it was. "Second they are not headed for the Jethrik. They are headed for the Kartik-held territories of the Amalite." Then the blasted thing just kept eating his snack.

"Why?"

"Tarius the Black has sent a third of her people there to

start a Katabull colony." Hellibolt said.

"Why?" Persius asked.

"You have a library full of books, have you read none of them?" Hellibolt scoffed and finishing his meal and threw the stick in the ocean. "You know it's odd Katabull are always using wood yet stab one of them with it and they nearly die. I wonder what the difference is. Gets into the blood stream I guess or..."

"Just tell me!"

"I just said I don't really know why they can eat off of it with no ill effects but if it stabs them..."

"Not that. Why are the Katabull building a colony in the territories?"

"The Amalite is the Katabull's native land."

"Are they going to attack us?" Persius asked.

"Now why would they do that?"

"Because they hate me."

Hellibolt laughed. "Oh that's right they do. They don't know that you are on this ship though. They can't read your flags or sails and see that they are even of the royal fleet. They only know the meaning of flags and sails they normally see."

"What did they think about you popping in?"

"Unlike Jethriks, Kartiks—and particularly Katabull Kartiks—have no fear of magic. They are quite used to both Jazel and Jestia popping in and out."

"I meant did they not recognize you?" Persius said.

Hellibolt shrugged. "I didn't see anyone I knew. These were mostly youngsters between twenty and forty."

Persius laughed then. "Maybe forty is a youngster to you, old man...."

"Your ignorance never ceases to amaze me. The average Katabull lives three hundred years," Hellibolt said.

"Is it wrong of me to expect a little respect from you?" Persius hissed.

"Wrong no; deluded is more like it." Then he was gone again, and he didn't come back till the Katabull ships had sailed past them and continued on their way. When he popped back up in front of him it was with the usual flashy—and Persius knew unnecessary—smoke and light show. He patted his belly, and there was a sauce stain on his purple robe. "The Katabull certainly know how to eat."

Persius found his sense of humor probably because he wasn't afraid that he was about to be drawn and quartered by an armada of angry Katabull. "So did you bring me nothing to eat?"

Hellibolt laughed and clapped his hands together. He reached in his sleeve and pulled out one of the fish and fruit skewers. The fish had been smoked and Hellibolt wasn't lying; it was sublime. He nodded his head in appreciation.

"They were talking about your grandson. Apparently he is the darling of the entire Katabull compound; they count him a good omen."

Persius smiled and nodded then asked, "What of my daughter?"

Hellibolt smiled. "They call her crazy Kasiria. Apparently she earned that mantle in battle. They say she tries to do things only Tarius the Black can do and that Jabone has had to save her many times."

"And of Tarius?" Persius asked.

"Oh Persius, you are like a dog with a bone." He plucked what was left of the skewer from Persius's hand and then he was gone again.

"With every other trick that he does he has to say the most horrid incantation, but this one he just does without warning. No doubt because this is the one I'd like most to be warned about."

**Arvon and Dustan had** risen before the first light, saddled up and headed up the Great Mountain. It had no other name; it was called the Great Mountain because it was the tallest mountain on all of the island. Arvon had always been amused by the simplicity of the way that the Kartiks named things.

They'd tethered their horses and sat in a jungle thicket waiting, bows at the ready. When they had been up here a couple of weeks ago they'd seen a huge buck deer that they had both missed because he had been just out of their range. They were in a better, closer spot, and if he used the same trail this time they'd get him.

Arvon smiled. His leg didn't hurt at all. He'd just injured it badly not three months ago, and now he felt fine. Even the walk up the side of the mountain hadn't left him with any more than mild discomfort.

Dustan nudged him and pointed and together they nocked their bows. Arvon let the arrow fly. He would shot first and if he missed or didn't get a good solid hit Dustan would fire. Why? Because it was his turn to fire first. Arvon got a bead on the deer and let his arrow fly. He got a good hit but the deer still ran, so Dustan let his arrow fly and when his arrow hit the buck went down. They were about to celebrate their kill when the ground beneath them moved, and then there was a massive booming sound.

He looked at Dustan, Dustan looked at him, and then they started running.

***Jestia had been uneasy*** for days, and when she spoke about it to Jazel she had said she was as well. Eerin said he was too but he might have just said that to be like them. Ufalla said they were all crazy.

Jestia had been sound asleep and then she sat bolt upright and the ground was shaking. When she looked at her Ufalla was still sound asleep, so she smacked her.

"Wake up," Jestia ordered. She got out of bed and she was instantly dressed by some spell she didn't cast. Ufalla had barely gotten to her feet when there was a boom so loud it shook the entire house. She covered her ears, but they were still ringing.

"What the hell is that?" Ufalla asked in terror.

"I think we're about to find out why Tarius built a Great Wall. Come on, we have to grab Eerin and get to Jazel."

***Hellibolt had been asleep*** in the belly of the ship when he felt a shift in The Everything that had him out of his bunk in a single movement. He looked over at the king who was still asleep. He shook him awake.

"Something is wrong," Hellibolt said.

"What?" Persius asked sleepily.

"Get up and dress at once; something is wrong."

They had just walked on to the deck when a huge flock of birds in many different colors came over their port side and then there was a sound like nothing he'd ever heard before.

"What in hell's name was that?" Persius shouted holding his ears.

Hellibolt ran to the helmsman. "Turn the boat and follow

those birds."

"What?"

"Follow the birds."

"But that is off our course."

"Do you not think those birds have run from something?" Hellibolt asked.

"Do what he says," Persius ordered.

The helmsman started to turn the ship, but Hellibolt was pretty sure they weren't going to outrun it, whatever it was.

**Tarius was awakened by** a small hand on her arm. She looked up; the light was just starting to come in the open shutters. She adjusted to the light and saw Darian standing there. "What is it, son?"

"The Great Wall rumbles."

Then she felt the whole earth quake and she heard it. It sounded like someone had picked the whole wall up and then set it back down. Darian covered his ears. "We'll be alright, Darian." Diana was sleeping between she and Jena, and she reached over and covered the baby's ears with her hands. "Jena, wake up and cover your ears."

"What?"

"Cover your ears."

Jena had just done it when there was a boom so loud it shook the whole of the Katabull compound again.

"Rimmy!" Both Hared and Rimmy skidded into their room. Rimmy had Pete.

"Rimmy, go sound the alarm." Rimmy put Pete down, called on the night and was gone. Tarius threw on a pair of puffy pants and a shirt and grabbed her sword even as Jena did the same. Tarius threw Hared one of her loincloths as he was buck naked and he quickly put it on. They were all out of the hut in moments. Jabone and Kasiria met them just outside. The cub was screaming and clinging to his mother, so Tarius knew he'd taken the full impact of the noise.

"Madra, what is going on?" Jabone asked.

"Come with me. Kasiria, go with Hared and Jena; take the cubs to the Great Hall," Tarius said and started for the tower on the south side of the gate.

**Arvon found himself** trapped under a huge tree that had

fallen when the top of the mountain appeared to blow off. The smell was foul like rotten eggs, and the mud was hot. The mud had missed him by a couple of dozen feet; however, one of the many trees it had laid down like grass in a gale did not. He'd been in Katabull form when it hit, had in fact been mostly dragging Dustan after him. When he'd seen the tree coming down he'd thrown Dustan as far as he could.

He wasn't Katabull now, and he knew what that meant. The pain that went from his belly to his back meant one of the limbs of the tree was sticking through him. *Stupid belly wound. You never die quick from a belly wound.*

"Arvon! Arvon!" he heard Dustan yelling.

"Over here!" he yelled back.

In seconds Dustan was standing above him. He was bruised up and cut up, but still mobile.

"Get out of here, Dustan, the gods alone know what will happen next."

"No." Dustan shook his head. He looked around found a big limb and tried to pry the tree off of Arvon.

"Honey, you look ridiculous." Arvon forced a laugh. "This tree is as big around as the both of us you will not move it. You have to go."

"I will not leave you," Dustan said. "I will never leave you." He kept pushing on the lever till it broke.

"Dustan, please go. Look, go to town, get one of the witches, and come back. Only magic can move this tree," Arvon pleaded. But Dustan looked up the mountain and he could see things the tree kept from Arvon's sight.

"There isn't time. We rode for most of two hours, and I have no idea where we are now. There isn't time." There was a quiet resolve about him as he said it.

"Just run away from it, Dustan. There is time to save your life. I have lived a full and happy life. I should have died all those years ago when Tarius saved me and I have cheated death many times since then. I've had you, and my son. I even saw my grandson, he's a furry little beast but he's mine and he's named for me. Don't you want to see him grow up?"

"I will stay with you." Dustan sat down on the ground and moved till he could put Arvon's head in his lap. "We will die together, isn't that considered some sort of Katabull blessing?"

"But I wasn't raised with them, my love, and you aren't

Katabull at all. I would rather you live."

"But I won't live without you, Arvon, I will only exist. I stayed with you even when you were nearly impossible to bear and why do you think I put up with you like that? Because I can't imagine my life without you. Like you I have had a full life and had two sons because I count Darian even though I know you don't, and I have a little furry grandson and I have all of those things because of you." He stroked Arvon's head. "I nearly lost you; we nearly lost each other when you were eating powder. I lived for years with only part of you, and it was hell. I can't imagine living without any part of you. I'm not afraid of dying."

"You charlatan! There is not an ounce of fear in you. You were faking when you got injured. You great liar."

Dustan smiled. "I was not faking at first. At first I really was that freaked out, I kept it up because I realized the only way to get you to stop fighting was for me to stop because Tarius would never separate us."

"Please Dustan go while there is still time."

"Don't waste even a moment more of the little time we have left asking me to go. I will not go, my love."

"It was a wonderful day till the mountain exploded. You and I together doing what we love. We brought down that deer together. We almost lost each other, Dustan. I almost ruined us, and we found our way back to each other and these last few years have been some of the best of my life. I know you think, have always thought that I loved Brakston more than I ever did you. And I have told you a dozen times it wasn't true, but it only took me telling you that I did once when I was very angry to make you doubt my feelings for you. There was never anyone I loved like I have loved you, and in our next life I will look for you until I find you and spend another life with you."

"And I will look for you and happily spend another with you."

Dustan's tears touched his face, and then everything was quiet.

**Jestia stood between** Ufalla and Jazel looking up at what was left of the mountain. It looked like someone had taken a knife and cut the top off, and now it was spewing ash and steam. They only had seconds to assess the situation and act. And not too surprisingly it was Jazel who took charge.

They were not alone; it looked like most of Montero had awoken and were in the street.

"Eerin!" Jazel shouted. He ran to her side. He was white as a sheet and obviously petrified. Without warning Jazel slapped him. He looked shocked and jumped back. "Snap out of it, boy."

"But.... I didn't say or do anything," he protested rubbing his face.

"Preemptive strike," Jazel said. "I need you to make a wind to blow the ash and steam out over the ocean and drop it there away from the populace."

He nodded lifted his arms and said, "Wind blow west...."

"Southeast knuckle head!" Jazel roared, "West is the Katabull compound."

Eerin nodded and started again, "Winds blow southeast, send this ash and dust away from us out to sea out to sea; oh horrid cloud let us all be."

Jestia watched as a strong wind seemed to whip up from the wizard's hands and catch in the tops of the trees before it raced quickly for the ash cloud. Then he just kept playing with his hands till the wind had caught the cloud and was blowing it towards the sea.

A red ugliness started to ooze from the top of the mountain. "Jestia, I need you to build a trench from the mountain around the west side of Montero to pull the lava flow away from the town."

"I don't think I have enough power to do that, not as quickly as it must be done," Jestia said.

"And that would point it right at the Katabull compound," Ufalla protested.

"There is a mountain range to the east of the city; the volcano is part of that range. The mountains get smaller as they go to the west, so there is no other way. Right now that lava wants to flow right through Montero and every town between us and the sea. There is nothing to the west of Montero but jungle and the compound. We will just have to hope that the Great Leader's wall will hold," Jazel said.

"That mountain is miles away from here; it could take hours for the lava to get here. We can evacuate all of Montero."

Ufalla said.

"To where? And what of the other villages between here and the sea? We don't have hours; we have minutes. Unless we channel it that will run all over this side of the Kartik from those mountains to the Great Wall and nothing will be left alive. We have to build a trench, and there is only one place we can do that. Either way it would still hit the wall." But she wasn't talking to Ufalla anymore, she was talking to Jestia. "I cannot do that trenching spell, Jestia I don't have that kind of power and it is your spell."

Ufalla looked at Jestia and Jestia said. "She is right; it will hit the wall either way. But I don't know, I have only used the spell once at Rorik's keep and it was slow with a fraction of the amount of dirt to move. We will have to move a thousand times that much dirt in seconds."

"I will seed every cloud overhead with rain and point them from the mountain to the Katabull compound. If everything is saturated it won't catch fire as easily," Eerin said. He looked at Jazel for confirmation and Jazel nodded. Even Eerin seemed to be thinking, but Jestia couldn't wrap her head around any of it.

"I will go with you and add my power to yours," Jazel said, "If you have a better idea...."

"I do not," Jestia said. She grabbed Ufalla and kissed her even as Jazel hugged Helen and then as Eerin was shouting his ugly-assed incantations at the poor unsuspecting clouds, Jestia looked at Ufalla and said, "I love you; please don't get yourself stupidly killed while I am gone." There was a look of pure panic on Ufalla's face as Jestia and Jazel popped out of there to stand at the base of the mountain.

**Ufalla looked at the** empty space where Jestia and Jazel had been standing only moments before. She hadn't even had enough time to tell Jestia she loved her, nothing and.... Well were they all about to die in the most horrible way, or was this going to be yet another story riddled with "then Jestia did this spell or that one while Ufalla sat around like a boil on a goat's ass and did nothing."

Eerin was just spitting out the ugliest excuses for incantations she'd ever heard, but at least he was doing something of value, and what was she supposed to do?

She looked at Helen. "So, what should we do?"

"Over the years I've gotten really good at staying out of Jazel's way...." Helen said with a shrug.

That wasn't really going to work for Ufalla; she needed to be doing something. And then she knew what. She started towards the stable.

"Ufalla, where are you going?"

"I'm going to the compound to warn my people," Ufalla said, and she started running.

***"Great!" Helen mumbled.*** She looked around at the panicked town's people. "I wasn't finished talking, and now I have to do the rest myself." Helen sighed deeply, walked to the middle of the street held up her hands and clapped them as loudly as she could.

The Kartiks fell silent and Helen thought, *Ufalla would have commanded so much more attention than I will. I know I'd listen to her. I'm of the Jethrik of course they all know me, but few know my name most of them just call be Jazel's woman if they think of me at all and.... Oh I should probably say something while they are all looking at me.*

"Good people of Montero fear not. The witches will take care of everything." The people cheered and she hoped she hadn't just lied to them all.

***They were trying to sail*** back the way they had come as fast as the ship could go with Hellibolt adding wind to the sails, but the minute he saw it he knew they couldn't get around it, and they sure couldn't punch through.

"Turn the ship around turn it around!" Hellibolt ordered.

"Are you kidding me...? Oh shit!" The helmsman turned the ship as quickly as he dared, and Hellibolt put as much wind into the sails as he could going the other way. It didn't matter the tidal wave hit them anyway.

***Jena watched as Tarius*** called on the night, took two steps and vanished.

"Dammit, Jestia!" Jena yelled.

Jabone looked at her, a lost and confused look on his face and yelled, "What do we do now?"

Jena handed Diana to Hared. "Hared and Kasiria, take the

children and get to the Great Hall at once." Kasiria had changed as soon as Tarius vanished, and Hared changed as well now for the strength and speed no doubt. Kasiria grabbed Darian up in her free arm and Hared grabbed Pete in his and they took off running.

"Rimmy, run and make sure the sea gates are closed and the barricades in place."

Rimmy took off and she and Jabone headed for the tower just as Riglid ran up.

"Riglid, run ahead and make sure the gates into the compound are being closed and barricaded." Because of course she wasn't Katabull, and she was going to slow Jabone down and for selfish reasons she wanted her son with her.

Harris ran up to her. "Jena, what the hell is going on?"

"I don't know for sure, but whatever it is it is happening in Montero."

"Mother how do you know that?" Jabone asked.

"Because your madra does not just vanish in the course of a normal day, and there is only one witch I know who could do that. Jestia took her, and she wouldn't have done that in the middle of whatever this is if she didn't need her which means they are in more trouble than we are right now. Tarius said she built the tower four stories tall on the south side of the gate because from it she could see Montero with a spyglass."

"Do you have a spyglass?" Riglid asked at her shoulder. She jumped. She hadn't seen him come back.

"Are the gates...?"

"They are being closed now," Riglid said. "Do you have a spy glass?"

"No, but Tarius's is on the table by our be...."

Riglid was already gone.

As they reached the main gates to the compound the last of the barricades were being fixed into the last notch in the door. There were two notches in each door. Four footings had been poured thirty feet out from the door and on each was a pole with a huge metal pin that fit into holes in the concrete on either side at the base and anchored the pole. The poles were twenty inches in diameter and forty feet long. Normally they lay on the ground in their hinge pointing towards the compound. But when the gates were closed, four Katabull on each pole picked up the poles, levered them up, and then let them drop into their notches on the back of the massive gates. The gates were four-inch thick wooden planks shod in metal on the outside. When these doors were barricaded like this, nothing but the Katabull could open them.

Jena started running up the tower taking the steps two at a time. They met a Katabull coming down and he stepped aside then fell in behind them. "The sheep are going nuts atop the wall. The Great Wall rumbled."

"What did you say?" she asked, but she didn't quit running up the stairs.

"The Great Wall rumbled."

"That's what I thought you said." They were at the top of the guard tower. The sun was still not quite up and suddenly it started to rain.

"Here." Riglid handed her the spyglass and she looked at him in disbelief.

"I believe you are even faster than your father." She handed the spyglass to Jabone. He looked at her in confusion. "Your Madra said SHE could see Montero with a spy glass from here. I am not the Katabull."

Jabone nodded. He looked through the eye glass for only a moment and then he jerked it away. "What is it, boy?" Harris demanded.

"The top of the mountain is gone, and it is on fire." He handed the eyeglass to Riglid who took a look and then nodded.

She grabbed the arm of the man who had met them and then followed them up. "Sound the gongs again, make sure everyone knows.... What the hell?" A wave of monkeys and squirrels started climbing up the walls and into the compound. "That couldn't be good. Sound the gongs and keep sounding them. We want everyone in the Great Hall or the guard towers; we don't know what's going to happen next."

"Mother, the rain is magic," Jabone said. She looked at Riglid and he nodded, confirming it.

"Everyone is doing all they can do then. I'm sure Jestia had a good reason for taking Tarius." Jabone gasped and pointed towards the ocean which she could clearly see from atop the tower now that the sun was mostly up. It was a wall, a giant wall of water. "Everyone down, get down." Jena said, and they started running back down. They hadn't all made it to ground level when the wave hit, and the wall barely shook.

They all watched as water splashed over the top of it. But only splash came over; there were no breaches, and the wall of water didn't come in. The sea wall was just tall enough.

There was another huge impact, a splash, and when they walked back up and looked the water was starting to rush back out to sea taking several trees with it. The water was still well over the docks, so she had no way of knowing whether they had survived the hit or not.

"If our ships had been here, not one of them would be anything but sticks." It was Rimmy who said it, and she hadn't seen him get there. "They had just opened the gates for the day; we barely got the sea gates closed in time."

Jabone looked at Jena. "Oh how I wish Madra could have been here to see this. Had the wall not been there we all would have been dead."

Jena sighed. "I am just hoping we will not need this one." she looked at the rain now coming down in buckets. "You know there is some reason they are doing this to us."

**Kaden had found Kasiria** and Arvon with Hared and Diana. Both Pete and Darian were under the Great Table; Darian was holding his ears, rocking back and forth and crying. Arvon was just screaming, and Kasiria couldn't seem to console him. Kaden was scared but around him the Katabull were panicking which did nothing at all to calm him. He said as much to Kasiria.

"We are mighty warriors, Kaden. Give us an enemy to fight and we will be right there. Put a sword in our hands and point us towards two thousand men wanting to kill and eat us, and we will have no fear. But being attacked by the very earth itself, not knowing what is going on, whether there is anything at all we can do, and having it happen here where we live with our cubs this is not a fight for Katabull. And the Great Leader has vanished."

"What do you mean she has vanished?"

"She just disappeared. Jena said Jestia took her."

Jabone walked in and made his way towards them, and suddenly Kaden became aware of something that made the hair stand up on the back of his head. Tarius had just a few days ago sent off the last of a third of her people. They would in fact probably be docking in the territories in only a few hours. And.... Well they were packed in pretty tight, and he was sure the guard towers were just as full. If she hadn't sent a third of them away there would not have been room for all of them.

Jabone whispered something in Kasiria's ear, and she looked grim and nodded. Jabone took off and the people if anything became more restless and frightened. Jabone was the Great Leader's son; they doubtless thought he was going to tell them something but he hadn't, and now they were more worried than ever. Kasiria looked at her screaming baby then bent over where Pete and Darian were huddled under the table. She spoke to them. He couldn't hear what she said, but both boys seemed to calm down and then she handed her cub to Darian who took him started rocking and singing to him, and amazingly the cub stopped screaming.

Kasiria jumped onto the table top and paced back and forth, reminding Kaden of how the Katabull storytellers started all their stories, and then she stopped and addressed the now quiet group.

"My people, a tidal wave just hit the Great Wall that borders the sea. The wall held, and though water came over the top twice we are in no danger of flooding. Yes it is true that the Great Leader vanished, but that is because the top has come off the Great Mountain and the jungle is on fire. Jestia took the leader because whatever is happening in Montero must be stopped before it hits us, and she needs the Great Leader to do that. Jena, Harris and Rimmy are in charge, and they ask that we all stay put here where we are safe till we know what is happening. I do not feel that it is our day to die, but if we die, we die."

As a whole the people calmed down. He didn't find that last bit comforting in the least, but apparently they did.

"While we wait Tarius will tell us a story." Tarius helped Kasiria down off the table and then she helped him up. She went over and sat in the floor under the table with the children, and Kaden joined her.

Tarius launched into his story, but Kaden couldn't even bother to listen. When he looked over at Kasiria she looked at him took a deep breath and let it out.

"You did a good job," he said.

"Did I?" She started to take Arvon from Darian and then

seeing both were perfectly happy she left them alone.

"Really I was sort of surprised he asked you to do it instead of doing it himself," Kaden said.

"He didn't ask me to do it. He just told me what was happening because he wanted me to know then he had to run right back and help his mother. And you heard them; they were even louder after he left and I thought.... Well I felt better knowing than guessing, and maybe everyone else would too, so then I just told them."

"And having Tarius tell stories?"

"When we were all in the territories there was a time when we were camped outside a village that had been gutted and the inhabitants eaten by the Amalite scum. We all felt pretty sick and scared and Tarius told stories. It made everyone feel better. If we are all about to die in some horrible catastrophe clinging to each other and our babies, is it better to be petrified or entertained?"

"If we die we die?"

Kasiria smiled. "Don't ask me. It's a Katabull thing; they find it comforting."

**One minute Tarius was** trying to line the compound out and the next she was being flung through something that was hard to explain and then *poof!* she was standing in front of Jestia.

"Dammit, Jestia!"

"Last time I looked I only had one name. Shut up and look." Jestia pointed at a river of lava pouring out of the mountain heading straight for them.

"The Great Mountain is...."

"A volcano, yes we have figured that out," Jazel said. "We are going to have to use Jestia's trenching spell and make a trench around Montero and funnel it all out to the sea or this whole side of the island will be destroyed. Oh, and we only have minutes to do it and...."

"That will send the lava right at the compound," Tarius breathed.

"You will have to trust your wall," Jazel said.

"I need to be with my family, my people, they need me."

"There are many leaders among your people and all know what to do," Jestia said. "I can't do this spell without you."

"I'm not a witch, Jestia."

"Minutes," Jazel reminded.

Jestia grabbed Tarius's hand and Tarius heard Jestia's voice in her head. *When we stepped on the energy well and we both glowed white we tapped into the power of everything and by using that power I can do the spell and blast a trench in minutes around the city but I have to have you. We will use the energy of the volcano to beat the volcano. I only have that sort of power when I am linked to you, my brother."*

Jazel lifted her and Jestia into the air with some spell, and then Jestia was blasting a trench into the earth five feet deep, twenty feet wide and all the way around the city of Montero. It seemed that she was not going to be able to keep ahead of the lava, but every time it was about to run out of trench more trench appeared. And the rain kept falling which kept the jungle—not from burning—but from igniting into a fire no one could contain.

Tarius could feel the power of The Everything coursing through her body and into Jestia. At times tiring at times exhilarating always unreal and terrifying. It was like being a visitor in her own nightmare or dream depending on how she was feeling at any given moment.

**Ufalla ran the horse full** out the whole way and turned a half-day ride into a couple of hours.

When she got to the compound the gates were closed which was no surprise at all. She got off her horse and slapped his ass trusting that he would be smart enough to get to high ground. The rain made it hard to see anything.

"Hey!" she yelled, "Hey!"

"Ufalla!" a familiar voice cried out from the top of the tower.

"Jabone, could you throw me a rope?"

"I'm coming, Ufalla." Jabone yelled back and then even through the rain she could hear him clunking down the stairs. She could just make him out on the top of the wall and seconds later there was a rope. She started to climb it and was having trouble finding her footing because the wall was so slick from the rain. Next thing she knew she was being hauled up the side of the wall and then her huge Katabull friend was hugging her. Then her father was taking her from Jabone. She pushed away from him and looked at Jena.

Before she could speak Jena said. "Let's get out of the rain." They walked into the tower.

"What happened?" Jena asked.

"The top came off the Great Mountain and it is a volcano and the lava is heading this way. Jestia and Jazel think the wall will hold it."

"Have you seen Tarius?" Jena asked.

"I haven't but Jazel and Jestia popped off the way they do and I wouldn't be a bit surprised if Jestia took Tarius because.... Well its complicated." Ufalla temporarily felt like she'd been gut punched as she realized something. *She used to use me to ground her I used to be enough and now Tarius is who she needs and what am I?* She shook the unwanted thoughts from her head; there wasn't time for that kind of crap. "I have no idea at what place on this side of the wall the lava will hit, but...."

"If it hits the gate, it might melt the metal but it would surely burn the wood," Jena said.

"I was thinking a bucket brigade," Ufalla suggested.

"Ufalla, water will not stop lava. If it would just the rain would be enough," Harris said. "The channel outside the wall might be enough."

"I don't like might," Jena said.

"I wasn't thinking water," Ufalla said. "I was thinking dirt, well mud. Mud will neither turn to steam or burn."

"If we pour enough mud in front of the gates the lava will never touch them.... And we removed a mountain of mud when we dug out the bottom of the lake to put in the Great Wall," Harris said.

Tarius had wanted to use the silt they dredged from the bottom of the lake in the wall as fill Waden had said it wouldn't work that there was more of plant than dirt in it and it wouldn't pack. So they had just stacked it up and when anyone needed dirt for their garden they went and got some. But it was huge and drew flies, and now there was a use for it.

Jena nodded. "We set up a bucket brigade from the mud mountain to the wall over the gates. Our people would rather work to protect us than sit and wait to see what will happen. Let's give them something to do."

**When Jena and the others** walked into the Great Hall, young

Tarius was standing on the Great Table telling a story and all were quiet till they saw her and Jabone, Harris and Rimmy. Then Tarius was silent. When Ufalla walked in behind them with Riglid they started to roar, no doubt because they thought Ufalla's presence meant the witch was there and she'd save them from this great unknown enemy.

Jena put up her hand and shouted. "Jestia is not here; this is what's going on...." Then she told them and then she told them the plan. "Riglid I want you to go to the guard towers send the children and people with babies in arms to the Great Hall." Riglid took off. Jena walked over took her fussy baby from Hared, flopped her tit out and started to nurse her without stopping talking or pacing. "This is NOT our day to die. In Montero Tarius, Jestia, Jazel, and Eerin are all working to save us; now is our time to take action. I need twenty volunteers to get to work in the kitchen in the Great Hall to make food for us; we still all have to eat. Parents with babies will watch the other kids here. Kaden...."

Kaden stood up some surprised to be called by name, "Yes?"

"You will take young Tarius's place telling stories to the children."

He nodded silently.

"Tarius and Eric I want you to captain the bucket brigade."

"Yri, gather all medics and go to the guard tower that is closest to the middle of the compound and set up a surgery there just in case we need it." Jena switched Diana from one breast to the other.

"Kasiria, you take care of things here. Make sure the kids get food as soon as it's ready, and make sure Kaden does a good job."

Kasiria nodded.

She wound up with only ten volunteers to cook because most of them wanted to move mud. But there were enough people with infants that said they could do both—cook and take care of their cubs to fill in the holes.

Her cub went to sleep still nursing and she removed her and started to hand her back to Hared. "Jena, you could stay and I...."

"No Hared." She stuck Diana in his arms and whispered, "You are Katabull. You can better protect our cubs if something goes wrong here and if something should happen out there to Tarius…" She pushed down the panic she'd been feeling ever since Tarius had vanished. "…she will need a Katabull parent more than a human one." She kissed her cub on the head then reached down and picked Darian up hugged and kissed him, and then she hugged Pete and then she left before any of them could see her cry.

***They had traveled quite*** some distance past Montero, and Tarius was convinced that Jestia was going to be able to blast a trench all the way to the sea and the lava could be diverted away from the compound. She felt mostly useless but just kept willing the trench to be built and the wall to hold. She kept remembering the power that had coursed through her at the energy well. She still felt like she was doing nothing, but at least she was trying. One minute light was streaming from Jestia's empty hands, hitting the earth and tearing a trench in it. The next they were landing on the ground on the east side of the lava flow. Jestia's hand started to go limp in hers, and Tarius found herself willing her strength into Jestia. Then the light was gone and everything was black.

***Persius found himself*** adrift clinging to a piece of mast. He looked around and all he could see was what was left of his once proud ship and a couple of his men who were also clinging to debris. One of them he recognized as his helmsman. He kicked his way towards him.

"You there man, any idea where we are?"

"None at all, sire."

He heard something behind him and a sudden panic filled him. He was probably about to be eaten by sharks. He turned quickly and the bow of the lifeboat nearly hit him, then two stout men were lifting him into the boat. Then they grabbed the other two men. When Persius looked up there stood Hellibolt.

"I have never been so happy to see anyone in the whole of my life," Persius said. Then remembering why he was at sea in the first place shouted, "This is all your fault!"

"Funny, I seem to remember a catastrophic explosion followed by a huge tidal wave neither of which I made. I suppose if you were to go to the latrine and lighting struck it that also would be my fault," Hellibolt said. "And whose fault is it that you were rescued…. Oh that was mine as well."

Persius looked around the small boat at the men who had lived. There were only eight of them counting him and Hellibolt. There had been fifteen sailors on the ship, he and Hellibolt, and ten of his personal guard—all sword masters. Only six of the crew had made it; not one of the sword masters had.

"Is anyone else alive?" Persius asked knowing the wizard would know. The wizard shook his head. "You saved me nearly last," Persius accused.

"You're welcome," Hellibolt said.

"I should have been your first concern."

"Huh, *I* am always my first concern, Persius. I found the boat over there, and I picked up survivors along my way. Would you have had me row past them to get to you?"

Persius found the eyes of six wet sailors looking at him waiting for his answer even as he noticed the oars rowing the boat seemed to be doing so of their own accord. Persius looked at his feet. "No of course not; you're right. Do you have any idea where we are?"

"I know the closest land is that way; after that I know nothing. Considering we have no water or food and there is a nasty looking cloud to the east, I'm thinking we row towards the closest land that will put us the furthest distance from the cloud—though it looks like no matter where we go we will run into rain."

"Shouldn't we look for some port? As you say we have no supplies, no water…."

"It is a tropical island; fruit should be everywhere, and as I said it is raining there now."

"So we are closer to the Kartik than home?" the helmsman asked, leaving Persius with less than no hope for their survival. The helmsman was supposed to be a man with knowledge of the sea, and even Persius knew they would have to be closer to the Kartik than home. They were nearly to the Kartik when they tried to run backwards, and they hadn't done that long when that wave hit them propelling them in pieces back towards the Kartik. *If Hellibolt hadn't sent us back the way we'd come we'd have been slammed into the island itself, and if he hadn't turned us before the wave hit there would be none of us who would have lived.* And what could it mean that when he tried to go to the Kartik to gain knowledge of how to fight the Amalite's cult in his kingdom his ship was hit by a massive tidal wave? Surely it could only mean that he was angering the Amalite gods.

**There was almost exactly** the right number of them to run the bucket brigade. It's not that there weren't enough; there were a few too many, so those stayed handy and took over from anyone who looked like they were getting tired.

They just kept taking Jena out of the line, and Jena kept getting right back in because though she was exhausted and covered in mud from head to toe, keeping busy kept her from worrying about Tarius. She just had the most awful feeling that she was never going to see her again, so she just kept working trying not to think.

From the top of the wall above the gate Jabone cried down, "The lava comes!"

As a people they all put their buckets down, and then Jena wasn't the only one trying to make her way up one of the towers to get to the top of the wall. When she finally made it to the top, her huge Katabull son put his arm around her shoulder and pointed. It was coming fast. She looked at the giant mound of mud that now covered the gates nearly to the top. Katabull crowded onto the wall and watched to see if the wall and their fix on the gate would save them or if this amazing and terrifying sight was the last thing they would see—a river of lava.

It hit the wall first at what would have been the middle of the gates and scalding hot steam rose off the mud, forcing them to stand back. Then the lava started to run down the length of the channel barely even touching the wall. They were all holding their breath, but when it became clear that everything was going to work they roared and cheered as the rain came down in such sheets it washed them clean.

The rain came off in waves of steam when it hit the lava and it hissed, but nothing like when the lava hit the sea. The wall stopped on the eastern side where a steep cliff led to the beach. They could hear the lava falling and then they heard the ocean popping, hissing and bubbling as the lava hit the water. Billowing clouds of steam mixed with the rain to reduce visibility to a few feet at best.

But Tarius did not come popping back, and somewhere in her Jena felt a growing despair she tried to ignore. Tarius was fine; she had to be. Fate would not be so cruel as to give Jena everything she wanted and then take away the only thing she couldn't live without. Tarius had built a wall that saved them all. She just couldn't die because she was on the wrong side of it; that would be a horrible story.

Jena forced a smile and looked at Jabone. "I'm going to go check on your sister. Tell me or send Riglid if anything changes, please."

He nodded.

She was soaking dripping wet—though all the mud was gone—so she went to her hut first. She went to her and Tarius's room, stripped then dried herself off and started to dress. She ran a comb through her hair then grabbed her cloak. When she started to put it on she realized it was Tarius's, but put it on anyway then sat down on their bed and started to cry. Tarius was alright; she had to be. Jena stood up and dried her tears.

When Jena walked into the Great Hall Kaden was telling a child-appropriate story, and from the look of him he was about worn out. He started to stop, but she waved her hand in the air, so he continued. Darian ran up to her and immediately started crying and wanted to be held, so she picked him up and held him. To her surprise she found Kasiria sitting on the Katabull throne in front of the gods and everyone nursing not just her cub but Jena's as well.

"She was throwing a wall-eyed fit," Kasiria explained. "You want her?"

"I better take care of this cub right now," Jena said. "You seem to be doing just fine with that one."

"You are so lucky," Kasiria said. "She doesn't bite."

"Darian was a biter."

"So what's happening?"

"Kaden, could you give me a second?"

He nodded, looking happy to have a break.

She cleared her throat and said in a voice they could all hear, "The lava hit in the middle of the gate, but the mud protected the gate and the gate and wall are keeping the lava out of the compound at this time. If that changes, we will all go to the sea wall, go up the guard towers and stand on the top of the wall; that should protect us from the lava."

Young Tarius walked in the front door whipping off his cloak. He was dry and dressed and more than happy to take Kaden's place on the table telling stories. Jena looked at Kasiria who smiled and scooted over. Jena sat down with Darian who had quit crying and was playing with her hair.

Hared joined them, and he and Kasiria exchanged a look.

Jena sighed. "You want to go see the lava flow?"

They both nodded. Jena sat Darian down beside her and took the cubs Kasiria handed her. Only after Kasiria had finished settling the cubs did she bother with fixing her shirt and covering her breasts. Jena smiled and thought, *and just like that modesty has been averted.*

Pete walked over and crawled up on the throne next to Darian. He held Darian's hand though it was hard to tell if he was trying to comfort Darian or just needed to be comforted.

"Are you alright, Pete?" Jena asked, and then wanted to kick herself. What was Tarius always saying? *That we could tell the story of our lives by just saying are you alright?*

Pete looked ashamed then looked down at his hands and whispered, "I peed myself."

"Oh, honey, I'm sure a lot of us peed ourselves today; it's alright," Jena said. Diana was sleeping peacefully and very still, but Jabone's cub was thrashing around and growling.

"He's having a dream," Darian said and petted the cub's head.

Jena took a deep breath. She shouldn't do it; she shouldn't even think about doing it, but she couldn't help herself. "Darian, can you see Madra? Is she alright?"

"She is tired very tired and not here or there. She would never leave us." Then he frowned and started to cry again. "But my fathers are dead."

**Radkin had woken her** up spitting out what she at the time thought was some insane thing about the world rattling, but as she came fully awake she could feel it and she could hear things falling off of other things all through the castle. Then there was an ear-piercing sound that made everything shake again and then everything was still except her heart.

She held Radkin and Radkin held her and didn't let her go yet still found a way to get out of bed.

"That came from the direction of Montero." Radkin pushed her to arm's length. "We have to go now."

But there was absolutely nothing they could do because a river of lava went across the road and blocked the way to Montero. She and Radkin and the fifty soldiers they had brought with them had wound up having to backtrack to avoid being hit with hot ash and pieces of lava the volcano was spitting out. Steam rolled through the air and the rain was coming down in sheets and she was glad because it was keeping the jungle from catching on fire.

Radkin had taken her Katabull form even as they were dressing. "There is magic in the rain."

"Then Jestia must be alright."

"Eerin is a weather wizard," Radkin reminded. "Still if he is doing spells you know Jestia must be fine."

One of her scouts came running back to her. "My queen, a trench has been dug around the west side of Montero. It looks like the lava is heading straight for the Katabull compound."

Hestia took in a deep, horrified breath. She grabbed Radkin's arm figuring her next step would have to be to hang on her lover and beg her not to throw her life away trying to beat a river of lava to the compound. But when she looked up the Katabull was just smiling down at her.

"There is really nothing I can think of to do," Hestia said, thinking maybe Radkin was about to snap.

Radkin bent down and kissed her on the forehead, oblivious to the many soldiers that were possibly watching. "My love, you do realize you're going to have to take back all those nasty things you said about the Great Leader's wall, don't you?"

Hestia sighed with relief. "I would love to."

# Chapter 10

**Tarius looked down at** her hands and they didn't look right. They were nice enough hands, but they weren't hers. They were clean and pristine; no sword callouses no sword scars, just hands. She looked around her and realized that the place wasn't real nor did it pretend to be. Everything was bluish, haloed in white light, and there was nothing she was seeing that she couldn't see through.

She saw a mirror hanging on nothing. It was a big, gaudy-looking thing. She walked over to it and was only a little surprised to see a man's face staring back. He was nearly as tall as she was in her Katabull form and every bit as dark with short, jet-black hair and a neatly-trimmed beard and mustache. His eyes were as green as Jestia's. She stroked the unfamiliar beard.

"I'm not Katabull, and I could not have been full Kartik," she said out loud.

"That is what I thought. Kartik men don't have beards, or if they do it's certainly not one so thick and fine. And you're bigger-boned than a normal Kartik, broader shouldered," Jestia said. When Tarius turned she was not so surprised to see that Gwen didn't look much different than Jestia did. She was a little shorter and she didn't have Jestia's really great rack or hips, but other than that there wasn't much difference. "I looked it up; their parents had a trade marriage..." Which meant royals married for the sake of trade. "Except the story goes that he really loved her. She was a royal of the court of a nation that no longer exists. It was called Triad. Turns out the Amalites wiped out their entire race and took their country. It makes me wonder if the hateful bastards didn't target the royal family simply because they were the last of the Triad's blood line."

"That's very interesting, Jestia but...." Tarius played with the beard a little longer. "Where are we?"

"As close as I can tell, Nowhere."

"I can't be Nowhere, Jestia. I have to get back to Jena and my children, my people."

"Well it wasn't the plan to end up Nowhere, Tarius." Jestia hugged her and she hugged her back though she could feel it but couldn't. "I am just so excited to see this you."

"Are we dead?"

"I don't think so."

"Jazel will be able to find us...."

"She'll find our bodies if she's alright, but she can't find us here. We have to get out of this ourselves if we can."

"How did we wind up Nowhere?" Tarius asked.

"Oh, good idea!" Jestia looked up at her or was it him, but she didn't let them go. "If we can figure out what happened, it may be as simple as undoing it."

Tarius smiled suddenly and really looked at Jestia's face. There was a familiar difference to it. "I find that I am happy to see this you, too."

"You know I don't miss being her; I don't think she was anywhere near as brilliant as I am. Do you miss being him?"

Tarius grabbed her crotch and grinned. "I miss writing my name in the sand, standing to pee."

Jestia laughed and pushed away from her. "Do you miss being him? Being my brother?"

"No, because I am still him, and you will always be my little sister."

**Montero was safe;** Jazel didn't have the strength or power to find out if the compound was. She couldn't feel either Jestia or Tarius, but she was so depleted she couldn't be sure her finding spell just didn't have enough energy to run. The mountain was still spewing lava though it was drastically slowing now.

Jazel had gone back to Montero as soon as she had done the spell that allowed Jestia and Tarius to levitate and basically all but fly along the line where the trench needed to be dug.

She'd found Eerin and Helen sitting in her alchemy drinking tea of all things.

"Where is Jestia?" Eerin asked in a panic.

"She called Tarius the Black and together they are building a trench. Where is Ufalla?"

"She took off towards the compound to warn the Katabull," Helen answered.

"Helen you moron! Do you have any idea what Jestia will do to us if anything happens to her woman?"

"In her defense, have you ever tried to tell Ufalla to do or not do anything?" Eerin asked.

He was worried and depleted, but then worried and depleted was the theme for the day. Jazel sat there trying to rebuild herself and waiting to see if they were all going to burn alive in a river of lava. When they didn't she knew that Jestia must have been successful.

Now she couldn't find them. They had been flying by virtue of a spell that had drained Jazel's well of power dry, and she just didn't have the power to find them. Somewhere out there in all that mess was the Katabull's Great Leader and the heir apparent to the Kartik throne, Hestia's only living child. They had saved Montero. If they had saved the Katabull compound as well they would have done the impossible, and in Jazel's experience a high price was usually exacted for doing the impossible.

**Riglid wrote a quick note** which he was able to slip into Kaden's pocket without him noticing. Then he ran back to his house, packed a backpack, and ran to the gates where he climbed the right tower and walked out on the wall. It was way too close to the lava, so he kept walking north till he had more than enough room. He was Katabull, so he simply jumped from the wall to the ground where he took off at a run beside the lava towards its source.

*I am the Great Leader's runner; I should be by her side. My last words to her were to call her an ass, to tell her that I was glad I wasn't her mate and that I felt sorry for Jena. To me she is not just the Great Leader; she is my family, my mentor. Jena has been so brave, but when she told me she was worried.... If Jena is worried something horrible has happened to the Great Leader and I must find her.*

Jestia took her, Riglid was sure to deal with the volcano. He knew Tarius was probably on the other side of this lava, but every time he tried to get closer to the flow the heat was so intense he was driven back. Even with the rain and him being drenched it was too hot. He didn't know what was harder:

to see through the rain or to see through the steam from where the rain hit the lava.

*She would have been doing something about this. If I follow it up I should find her, if she is on this side it should be easy....
But the heat is so intense that I can hardly see across the lava flow. But I can. I can and I must.*

**"What were we doing**, Tarius?" Jestia asked. If they were walking Jestia wasn't aware of it, yet every time she looked around the scenery had changed. It was still nothing, but it was a different nothing. Places she assumed the twins had been, the jungle, the beach, inside elaborately-decorated homes and palaces and an alchemy filled with everything a witch could ever ask for, but still not as nice as hers.

"When?" Tarius asked.

"This morning; what were we doing exactly?"

"Don't you remember?"

"I know what I remember, dumbass, I need to know what you remember."

Tarius looked at her and smiled with Terrance's face, and for a moment she could clearly see Tarius in the man's features. "Words can wound as deeply as a sword you know."

"What were we doing?" Jestia laughed and shook her head.

"*We* weren't doing anything. *You* were blasting a huge trench in the earth. All I was doing was holding your hand. I have felt more useless in my life, but I can't recall when right off. Jazel put a spell on us, so we were flying." She—or was it he—shrugged.

"What happened just before there was nothing?

Tarius looked thoughtful then troubled. "We landed and your hand went limp in mine."

"Then what happened, Tarius?"

"Nothing."

"You weren't doing *nothing* all morning. What were you doing?"

"I.... I was thinking of the energy well. of the power I felt there. and willing the trench to be built.... So nothing. I did nothing."

Jestia grabbed Tarius and shook her. "Don't you understand?" The mirror appeared again and so Jestia pulled Tarius to it and made her look inside. "You are him. This dead connection came back to life when you and I stepped onto that energy well together. *He* is magic. When you and I are together I can feel his magic in you. Now, what did you do?"

"When your hand went limp, I felt like I was being shredded, so I willed my strength into you."

Jestia hugged Tarius even though she couldn't really feel her—or was it him—she could almost feel something. Tarius hugged her back and patted the back of her head, bouncing it off the chest that wasn't quite Tarius and that she couldn't quite feel. She pushed back from her and looked up.

"Tarius, I remember that I was sure I was dead and then we were here. I was using the energy of the volcano, using my body and yours as a conduit to channel the energy. You are Katabull so it didn't kill you, but though I'm a witch I'm still just human; it was too much for me, but you sent what you had left to me."

"Are we alive, Jestia?" Tarius asked sadly.

"You would never leave your family, Tarius. You may have willed your strength to me, but the biggest part of you belongs to Jena, and that strength would never leave you."

The tears came into the green eyes of the man she was looking at. "But you, Jestia, are you alive?"

"If I wasn't alive I wouldn't be Nowhere doing nothing; I'd be Somewhere doing something."

"How do we leave here, and if I get back first what should I do with you?"

Jestia smiled at Tarius. "I have no doubt you will get back before me, and when you do simply take me to the place that healed you."

**It was nearly dark, and** his eyes were burning from constantly looking across the lava and all the smoke and steam. Something—Riglid would never know exactly what—made him take another look and through the steam and rain and near dark he could just make them out lying on the ground on the other side of the lava field. He took off running and someone tackled him, taking him all the way to the ground. When he looked up his brother Laz was sitting on him.

"What the hell are you doing?"

"The Great Leader and Jestia are on the other side hurt and...."

"You were going to sling yourself into lava. How would that help?" Laz got off of him and then put down a hand to help him up. Riglid took the offered hand.

"I am the Katabull. I was going to jump...."

Laz pointed at the river of lava nearly twenty feet wide.

"No Katabull could jump over that; that is a river of death. We must think of something else. That is how the Great Leader wins, because she thinks first."

Riglid nodded then looked at Laz, "How did..."

"I get here in time to save you from a fiery death? Kaden found your note. He was crying and whaling and.... Well really, Riglid, what do you see in him? I went after you."

"But... why?"

"Why? Because you are my brother, Riglid. I love our mother and our father, Jaden, and even our puke of a sister Rea, but they are all my non-blood kin. Our madra's pack was killed by the Amalites, our fadra's pack was the same as the Great Leader's, so all dead, and our madra and fadra are both dead. In all the world you are the only person I share blood with. So we will help the Great Leader if we can, but I will not let you throw your life away to do so nor will I toss mine out. It isn't what Tarius would want and you know it."

"I said terrible things to her, Laz."

"Do you think that someone who would play a joke like the one she pulled on you would hold a grudge over what someone said about it? That is not Tarius."

"The day our madra died I told her I wish she would just die and get it over with," Riglid said, looking at his feet and feeling all the shame he'd felt when he was told she was dead.

"Just like the Great Leader will not hold you accountable for things you said when she played a dirty trick on you, our madra would not hold a grudge for that. Riglid, our madra didn't die in battle or having sex, or in a horrible hunting accident. She had been in a coma for four days when she finally gave us all a break and died. Why do you think we were all wrecks for so long? We all loved her, and we all wished she would have died quicker, so we all have guilt. Killing yourself trying to save Tarius will not bring our madra back."

Riglid nodded then snapped his fingers, took his pack off and pulled the axe from it. "We will chop a tree and fall it over the lava."

"My brother, it will burn in minutes," Laz said.

"Aye, but I will only need seconds. You will chop the tree as soon as it falls I will run across. You will stay here...."

"I should go and you should stay. You have a whiny human boy...."

"Man."

"All I have is a monkey."

"I will go. I am the Great Leader's runner, and you I will not risk because you are *my* only blood kin."

**Tarius felt something wet** and warm slap her face. The Nowhere was gone, but Jestia hadn't told her what to do.

"Gre... L... der...." A voice, small and disjointed, but she was sure it was real. "Great Leader!" Louder. Water, so much water.... Rain. It was raining on her, and Jestia was in trouble. She opened her eyes and there was Riglid. She jumped to her feet in one movement, looked around found Jestia ran to her and lifted her into her arms.

She stopped just long enough to look from Riglid to the river of lava and back. "Is the compound...?"

"Safe all are safe."

"How did you...?"

"Laz is on the other side. We dropped a tree I ran across. It burned," Riglid said quickly.

"Laz!" Tarius yelled across the lava. "Go back to the compound. Tell them I am well and that Montero has been saved."

"What about Jestia?" The rain and the hiss of it hitting the lava were such that she could hardly hear him.

"Tell them Jestia is fine." And then Tarius took off running in the direction of Montero.

"She does not look fine," Riglid said, finally reaching her side.

"The last thing I need is Ufalla, Harris, and half the compound coming to try to save Jestia. Only I can save her."

"How?"

"All she said was that I must take her to the place that healed me. Since I don't think she meant between Jena's breasts, I'm taking her to Jazel's spring."

**Riglid watched as Tarius** took off with a burst of speed he simply could not match, and he ran after her in shock. She jumped downed trees and rocks as the rain pounded on her. The ground was slick yet she was sure-footed, and then he realized she was barefoot. He kicked his boots off, caught them in the air and found he still couldn't catch her. So it turned out that it was neither he nor his father who was the fastest Katabull in the world; it turned out the Great Leader was faster.

He slid—literally because the rocks were so slick in his bare feet he could get no traction—into the area around the spring just in time to hear Jazel tell Tarius the spring was too hot.

Tarius didn't listen; she just jumped in with the limp girl. Riglid quickly put his foot into the water and found that it was uncomfortably hot but not immediately dangerously so.

"It's bearable," he told Jazel.

Eerin and Jazel were hovering around the pool in the rain. No one was saying anything as Tarius kept whispering things to the girl that not even he could hear.

"She's...." Jazel stopped and looked puzzled. "She's speaking an incantation."

Tarius then put one hand on Jestia's rear, the other under her shoulders, and lifted her above her head. Then she just dropped Jestia in the water and white light enveloped both the little witch and the Great Leader. Then there was a loud popping sound, they were all sprayed with the hot water from the pool, and Jestia broke the surface of the water gasping for breath. The light was gone as suddenly as it came, and Tarius grabbed Jestia and left the water as quickly as she could. She held Jestia and rocked her like she was a tiny baby.

Jestia coughed and spat water out then she wrapped her arms around the Great Leader's neck and started to weep.

**Tarius carried her inside** and plopped in the first chair she found. So did Jazel and Eerin. Jestia had buried her face in Tarius's shoulder and was sound asleep. Tarius wasn't aware she was rocking her till she heard the squeaking of her chair against the floor.

"I thought for sure you were going to cook," Jazel said, shaking her head.

"A few more seconds and I think we would have. I think I

will never know what it means to be cold again."

Tarius looked at Riglid. He didn't look much better than the rest of them did. She shook her head. "You...." Her voice caught in her throat and she swallowed hard. "I owe you a debt I can never repay." She smiled then. "Still, I think I will always regret that I didn't jump to my feet and yell *gotcha!*"

Riglid shook his head and laughed.

**Jena sat on the Katabull** throne with her sleeping baby in her lap; her boys, including her grown son, were sleeping on pallets under the Great Table. Jabone's cub was curled up in his arm. Laz's monkey was sleeping between Pete and Darian. She hadn't known why Pete and Darian had stayed under the table most of the day till Jabone told her that Tarius had told him when he was little that the safest place in the compound was in the Great Hall under the Great Table. No doubt she had told their little boys that as well. The fact that Jabone chose to sleep there now with his own cub said everything about how much trust he still put in his madra.

She hadn't told him what Darian said and she wouldn't. Darian didn't tell him and she was glad. If Arvon and Dustan were gone she could deal with that later, not now. Not when she had no idea where Tarius was, when she just had the most horrible feeling that something was terribly wrong.

It almost seemed foolish for them to stay there or in the guard towers instead of in their own homes in comfortable beds, but there was still a river of lava flowing outside the wall and no one would be going home till they were sure it was safe. The mood in the camp was near celebratory. The river of lava was visibly shrinking, the constant rain had kept the jungle from burning unchecked, and any ash that flew up from what did burn found nothing but wet to fall on. Inside the compound walls everything was exactly the same except that now the huge, ugly mountain of mud the wall project had left behind was out of the compound.

Ufalla walked over to her and whispered, "We could all be dead. They are all happy because they all worked on that wall and it saved them and we moved mud and that saved us, so they all feel like they had a hand in saving the day. They have all been touching me the way they do when we come back from battle as if I had killed our enemies and it will rub off on them, and I have seen them doing it to you. It's all I can do not to slap the smiles off their faces, and when I look at you I see that you feel the same way."

Jena nodded then answered, also in a whisper, "There is nothing, no word from them. If they were well they would have found a way to tell us. They would never leave us in this kind of hell where they are not with us. All of this has happened and they know we are not like them and can never know for certain whether they are alive or dead till we see them."

"There was nothing I could do in Montero of any worth, and I just had to do something and now.... I should have stayed there."

"Ufalla had you not come.... I don't want to think about what might have happened. You want to hear something really scary?"

"No."

Jena smiled. "I will tell you anyway. Waden just told me today that Tarius wanted to put the gate thirty feet to the right. She wanted to move the road, but she couldn't think of a good reason so she let them talk her out of it because let's face it moving it would have been a huge pain in the ass. The road itself would have been bad enough, but huts would have had to be moved, and.... If the gate had been thirty feet to the right the lava would have been nowhere near it. But it wasn't, so if you hadn't come, Ufalla, and told us what was happening, had you not thought of the gate, the lava still would have gotten in here and the wall would have been mostly some place for us to stand in the pouring rain while we watched the compound burn."

"I cannot take credit. When we came here last Jestia told me she thought the gate was in the wrong place," Ufalla said. "And that's what they do, isn't it? They say absurd things you don't dare not pay attention to because they always turn out to be right. It's infuriating and.... Oh gods, Jena, what are we going to do if we never see them again and.... I, too, have the most awful feeling."

Jena said nothing. She couldn't; if she had she would have started crying and then every Katabull in the compound would have known she was worried. If she was worried something must have happened to the Great Leader, and in the face of all of this they would panic. Perhaps the only person who looked more miserable than she and Ufalla was Kaden. He sat slumped against the wall soaking wet not caring just staring at nothing. She looked from him to Ufalla. "Poor boy, he is alone here, a human among Katabull like you and I. But you were raised here, and as we know now you are more of them than us. I am the mate of the Great Leader, and I have given birth to a Katabull child, but he is new here and new to this. New to being in love and he isn't just in love with anyone. No, like you and I, his heart is bound to someone who will always run in where others will not go."

"Honestly Jena I was a little shocked when Kaden read that note. It's not what I would have expected of Riglid; Laz yes, but not Riglid. If I were Katabull I would go, but I'm not and if I get myself stupidly killed after Jestia told me not to.... well if she is alright she will find some way to make me pay even in my death."

Jena watched as Kasiria brought Kaden a warm mug of something and pressed it into his hands. Kasiria knelt down and talked to him then she pushed on the bottom of his mug till it was to his lips. Jena shook her head and thought, *Jabone's the one he ought to be talking to. After all Kasiria's the one who just runs into battle trying to get herself killed... but not today.* Kasiria like most of them had been in her Katabull form most of the day. She had been helping serve food and clean up all day and usually with a cub in one arm. *She didn't do anything crazy because there was no enemy to fight and she had her cub to think of. Even now she doesn't go even a few minutes without looking over to check on him and yet she knows he is safe and asleep with his father.* She looked down at Diana sound asleep. She could put her down but she wouldn't. When and if she could stop worrying about Tarius or just couldn't stay awake anymore, she would make a pallet and lay down with her sons under the table her baby in her arms.

The door burst open and Laz rushed in soaking wet yet still covered with soot. Her heart stopped and then he said the most beautiful words she had ever heard. "Riglid has saved the Great Leader. They yelled across the river of fire that they are fine and Montero has been saved. My brother is a hero." He looked around till he found Kaden. "A very much alive hero!"

# Chapter 11

**Riglid woke; he was sure** it was from the grumbling in his stomach. They had all been exhausted, so when Jazel pointed out a room they could stay in they just took their wet clothes off, put on the dry ones Helen brought them, and fell into bed. He literally couldn't remember the last time he'd eaten, and now he was starving.

The bed was comfortable, and though he was hungry he found himself rolling over instead of getting up. When he looked over at the other bed in the room, he saw that Jestia had wrapped herself all around Tarius and Tarius was just holding her. Neither was awake.

Jestia had been completely out and the rest of them weren't far behind her. Only Helen had the energy to get Jestia's wet clothes off and put some dry ones on. Though Jestia wasn't awake and not coherent, it became obvious that Jestia would *not* be separated from Tarius; in fact, the hardest part of undressing and redressing Jestia was having to work around the fact that any time Helen removed the witch's hand from Tarius it went right back.

So now they were in bed together and they were holding each other. A stranger might come in and assume they were lovers, but Riglid knew they were not. Nor were they just friends and they had been through something.... Something that saved all of them and nearly killed them both, and they were the only ones who knew what that was.

He thought of Kaden and felt alone. He wondered how long Kaden was going to be mad at him. Riglid had never been in a relationship before, but he had seen his elders and their relationships. What he knew without a doubt was that when one partner put themselves in harm's way without asking the other one, the one who didn't take the risk always wanted to strangle the one that did as soon as they learned they hadn't died.

His madra once didn't talk to his mother for a week because she dove from the bow of a ship into the ocean just for the fun. His mother kept bringing her flowers and apologizing, and his madra just gave her the cold shoulder. When he asked his madra why she was so mad she told him, "I love her and she loves me, and when she goes off to battle every time she does she chooses what needs to be done over me. That I signed on for, so that I can live with. But when she risks her life doing some stupid-assed thing just so she can say she did it; that is not part of our deal. That is an unnecessary risk of her life. When you bind yourself to another part of their life becomes yours and part of yours becomes theirs. She has no right to risk my life, the life that I have with her, for bragging rights."

From that he understood that Kaden would be mad at him and knew why, but Kaden was human and he didn't know whether he would accept what Riglid did because.... *I didn't really tell him what I do or what I might have to do till he was living with me and even then I didn't really explain it and.... This isn't really what he signed up for at all.*

He didn't want to think about it. He knew it was foolish to worry till he knew how mad Kaden was. Who knew maybe he wasn't mad at all. He got up, retied the string of the loincloth they had given him to wear, and tiptoed out of the room going in search of food.

When he got to the dining room he wasn't too surprised to see that the only people there were Helen and people who were guests. The witches were all wiped out.

He found a seat and sat down though he supposed it was sort of stupid to think everything would be business as usual. He felt less foolish when Helen put a cup of tea in front of him. "The mountain stopped breathing fire in the middle of the night and looks quiet."

"That is very good news," Riglid said.

"I bet you're starving; I'll bring you some food."

*Is it really that easy? Everything fell completely apart and we all might have died, yet today we sit and eat breakfast and yesterday's near catastrophe becomes today's topic of conversation and.... Life goes on because three witches and a warlord did the impossible, and I don't know that any of them even know how they did it.*

***Hestia and Radkin and*** the soldiers with them had made camp. Hestia had the soldiers watch the lava flow in shifts. She and Radkin went to their tent and went to sleep. She knew that at least the next few days and probably several weeks were going to be hectic and filled with trying to fix this, that, or the other thing, and she would do all that when she was sure her child and her friends were safe.

She sent a rider back to the capital to take to the street and shout out what they knew. He would go to the castle, take to his bed, and another would come back in his place.

In the middle of the night one of the soldiers woke her to report that the lava had stopped flowing. Hestia had told her to report if there were any further changes, and then she'd gone right back to sleep. She noticed Radkin hadn't even woken up and that she had taken her human form again. Radkin obviously trusted completely that the wall had held and the compound was safe. The rain outside was horrible and Hestia was starting to worry that their next disaster might just be a flood. The tent was dry, but her head was still wet. She fell back to sleep hearing the cracking sound of the lava as it cooled in the rain.

Now she stood and watched as Radkin poked the lava with a stick. "It is hard," she announced. She knelt down and stretched out her hand.

"No don't!"

Radkin stopped and looked at her. "I am not stupid. I will not touch it if I sense it is too hot."

Hestia nodded. Of course she wouldn't.

Radkin let her hand hoover over it closer and closer. Finally she touched it; she held her hand on it for a while and then withdrew it. "It is still hot but not unbearable. I am more concerned that it may be only a thin crust over still-molten rock and that if we walk on it we may crash through."

Because of course for all her wildness Radkin was insanely well read and had some knowledge of nearly everything. She told Hestia last night that she recently read a book about volcanos and lava and their relation to earthquakes. Radkin looked around then walked over to a huge rock and pointed at three soldiers in turn.

"You, you, and you help me lift this rock and throw it into

the middle."

Hestia watched as Radkin and three of the soldiers lifted the rock and carried it to the edge of the lava field.

"On three," Radkin said. "One, two, *three!*" They hurled the huge boulder into the middle. It made a sound like breaking glass but stayed on top; it didn't crash through.

Radkin started to walk out on it and Hestia grabbed her arm. Radkin looked at Hestia's hand on her arm then into her eyes.

Hestia moved her head till her lips nearly touched Radkin's ear. "If you walk out on that I am going with you. If you don't think it's safe for me to walk on it, then it isn't safe for you, either. I will not be left behind."

Radkin shook her hand off in a dismissive way and Hestia took immediate offense. She set her chin and ran across the lava field. When she reached the dirt of the other side her feet were hot but not unbearable. She turned and looked at Radkin who now looked as mad as Hestia had been just moments before. Radkin took the distance across the lava in a handful of strides, grabbed Hestia by the shoulders and lifted her till their eyes were even, and though Radkin had not changed her eyes had.

"Woman!" she thundered. "If you ever do anything like that again I will...."

"Nothing! You will do nothing!" Hestia was not afraid of Radkin, "You belong to me and I belong to you, and if you are at risk then I will be at risk, and if I die I die!" Hestia said in a harsh whisper.

Radkin put her down.

"I'm pretty sure that the fact that you accosted me and not one of them came to my rescue means they are either too afraid to run across the lava field or stand toe to toe with you to save me, in which case who cares what they think? It's more likely they know exactly what we mean to each other and have no desire to get between us in a fight. Either way, go ahead and kiss me." She wrapped her arms around Radkin's neck and Radkin kissed her and all her people pretended not to notice.

Radkin mumbled something under her breath.

"What?"

"I said.... You are not easy to love."

Hestia's breath caught for moment. She knew the Katabull and knew what it meant that Radkin said that. Hestia kissed her again quickly then said, "You are not easy to love, either."

She separated herself from Radkin then turned to look at her troops on the other side of the channel of cooling lava. She noticed there was no longer steam coming from the lava and was sure it hadn't been for hours. It was still raining so hard it was hard to see anything or notice anything except your cloak couldn't shed water fast enough and you were wet and miserable. She called across the lava, "We will leave the horses here. Two of you will stay to watch them. The rest come with me double time."

The two of them started at a run down the road towards Montero while the troops crossed the lava flow behind them and tried to catch up.

**Tarius woke up, and for** just a second thought she had dreamt the whole thing. Then she smelled not Jena but Jestia and knew it had all been real, even the part that hadn't felt real at all.

She didn't let go of Jestia or push her off her. She knew Jestia still needed her, yet didn't really know why or how. However so soon after being him and feeling so clearly his connection with his sister, the love he had for her, and after almost losing her again she had no desire to let go of Jestia anyway.

She looked over and saw Jazel walk into the room.

"Do you feel any better than you look?" she asked Tarius.

"Probably not. What about you my dear friend?" Tarius asked.

"Actually I'm pretty sure I feel worse than I look right now which since I have seen a mirror this morning is saying a lot. The mountain has stopped spewing and the lava is cooling."

"Good. Do you think that Eerin is strong enough to push the rain into the sea and quit drenching Montero and my people?"

"I hadn't thought of that. It's doing more harm than good at this point. It's a simple spell; I'm sure he can. I'll go get him and have him do that." Jazel started to leave then turned back. "Tarius.... How is Jestia?"

"Exhausted and in deep mourning...."

"Deep mourning?"

"She could explain it to you better than I can. I mean I can tell a story, but I don't understand magic and I'm not really sure what happened to us, except I was him and she was her and Jestia is more tied to that life than I am. His death killed her once and she still misses the connection she shared with him."

"What about you?"

"I feel a connection to Jestia and the connection I have to her is enough for me, but in this life I am Katabull and because that life trails mine there is more magic in me than other Katabull, but I am not magic. The twins understood each other; their magic came from the same well, and they spoke a language only they understood. There was no wondering what the other thought because they dwelt in each other's heads. That is what Jestia is mourning. I'm mostly raw because I almost lost her in this life. She is raw because she lost me in that one and she knows I was, but will never be him...."

Jazel held up her hand and smiled. "You are right; I'm sure she can explain it better. I will go get the boy to make the rain stop."

**When they got up in** the morning, the sheep on the wall were calm, the monkeys had gone back to the jungle, the sea was calm, the lava appeared to have stopped flowing and to be cooling, and Jena hit the top of the tower just in time to see Ufalla had climbed outside the wall and caught her horse. She watched in horror as the girl ran across the lava field.

"Ufalla, what the hell!" Jena yelled down at her.

"I have to get to Jestia. I don't care what Laz said; there is something wrong." Ufalla had her horse on a long tether. She had taken the end of it with her and she was yanking on the horse trying to get him to walk across the lava field. The fact the horse was fighting her proved in Jena's opinion that the horse was smarter than the girl.

"What do I tell your parents?" In that very instant the clouds parted, the rain stopped, and the sun came out.

Ufalla finally wrestled the horse into putting one foot on the lava and then he ran quickly across because she was yanking him and he didn't want to be on that stuff. She jumped on her horse, looked up at Jena and shouted, "Tell them the lava will hold a horse, and it looks like it's going to be a beautiful day."

"Ufalla when you see Tarius tell her I love her and that all is well here. You will see Jestia is fine, too."

Ufalla nodded spurred her horse and took off.

Jena sighed. She wished she could jump on her horse and go to Tarius, but she had two little boys and a nursing baby and.... There was a huge pile of mud that kept them from even thinking of getting the gates open. The rain had stopped; the lava was hard enough to run a horse over it. The lake was up a foot above normal, the compound was already starting to drain, and if the sun stayed out by mid-day the mud would start turning back into dirt. Their soil was very sandy, and the compound had been built in such a way that no water pooled in the streets and it ultimately ran into the lake. She walked back down the tower and slogged through the mud towards the Great Hall. She was almost there when one of the sentries on the wall was yelling, trying to get her attention. She looked up at him and seeing he had succeeded he shouted, "Great Leader's wife!" She smiled. They all knew her name but because their Great Leader was gone all but those who knew her best had been calling her Great Leader's wife as if it were a title.

"There is a huge whale stuck on our beach."

"I am going to the Great Hall. We will open the gates to the sea and see if we can help the beast back into the water,"

"Aye, aye."

Jena started walking again. "And if we can't or if it is already too late then we will eat it because that's what the Katabull do," Jena muttered. Feeling a sudden urgency, she started running for the Great Hall.

Once in she announced in rapid succession, "The lava has stopped flowing. I need people to now move the mud from the front of the gate. There is a whale stuck on the beach, so I need the sea gate crew to pull off the barricades and open the gates. Then I need as many of you as can to go to the beach and push the whale back in the water. The worst is over, so everyone who is neither moving mud nor whales or has any other task to do, go home."

They all cheered. There was no need to delegate further. There was a group of people whose job it was to repair things that broke; they would all go work at getting their gates operational again so that they could go inland which they couldn't do right now unless they went down the wall on a rope and then walked. Everyone would clean up their own mess when they left the Great Hall, and the crew whose job it was to clean up would stay and do that.

Hared walked over and handed her Diana and the boys walked up to her.

"Why don't you take the baby and the boys down to see the whale?" Hared said. "Rimmy and I will gather up all our things and bring them back to our huts."

She watched as Jabone shook Kasiria awake. She had taken her human form back and finally lay down to sleep only when Jabone had more or less forced her to.

There was still a lot to do. "I don't know...."

"We will meet you there, mother," Jabone said. He took Arvon from Kasiria stood up then put his hand down and helped his wife to stand. "It will be good for all of us."

*Unless the poor thing is dead in which case my children will get to see how the Katabull butcher a whale.* The Katabull revered whales and dolphins. They would never hurt them or hunt them for food, but if they were dead, hadn't been dead more than a few hours, and hadn't died of a disease they were fair game as were most things.

"Let's go," Darian said. "See whale."

She nodded and started walking. Her cub chuffed at her and she tried to make the sound back. She couldn't but it was close, and the half-smile Pete gave her told her he enjoyed her effort. They all thought it would do her good to go to the beach. What they were all forgetting was that a huge tidal wave had slammed their beach hard enough to leave a whale. And while the boys and everyone going to hopefully save the whale acted like they were just going for a fun day on the beach, part of her did not want to see what had become of their beautiful little paradise much less their harbor and docks.

The barricades were down and the gates open before most of them got there. That's how efficient the Katabull were. As she walked through she could see the seas off the coast were still very rough. The docks had taken a beating but were more than repairable. A bunch of seaweed and massive amounts of driftwood covered the beach. They'd lost a few palm trees;

others were damaged and would have to be cut down. All the small boats that had been lashed to the docks were either completely trashed, slung against the wall, or on the beach in varying states of disrepair. It was going to take a lot of cleaning, but.... She smiled. *The loss of all the row boats is the worst of it, and many of those can be fixed. The docks can be salvaged, most of our trees are fine, and the Katabull will just see all this wood as building material and firewood they don't have to go to the woods to get. In a few weeks anyone who hadn't seen it before would notice no difference at all.*

"Mother look," Pete said, excitedly pointing down the beach.

She'd been so busy assessing the damage that she had missed the giant mammal stranded on the sand. It was a huge blue whale. Hundreds of Katabull were walking down the beach. She had thought it was overkill, but looking at the size of the thing they needed all of them. As they got close she could see it was still breathing, and all the rain had kept it from drying out. They all started moving any debris between the whale and the water. There was no doubt in her mind that her people could put the animal back into the sea and save it.

*My people, I have lived here so long they have become my people. I see no difference between them and myself, and yet I am still in awe of them.*

"We have to work quickly," Yri addressed the group even as he threw a piece of tree out of the way. "The animal is large and used to being supported in the water. Too long out of it and he will start to collapse in on himself." And just like that they were working twice as fast.

She looked down at her sons, both mesmerized and frightened by the size of it. "Come on let's go pet him." She walked forward and they seemed reluctant. She walked up and started to pet its sleek head. In a second the boys joined her but seemed afraid to actually touch it. She took Diana's hand and rubbed it against the side of the whale, and shortly after that first Darian and then Pete were petting the whale. They were not the only ones petting him. *Because none of us has ever been able to do this, and we will very likely never get the chance again. Someday when we have our little girl out on a ship Tarius will see a whale.... Because she always spots them when no one else does.... And she will put the glass up to Diana's eye and point, Diana will see it, and I will tell her that she has touched one. Last night I was just sure Tarius was dead and now I know she's not. My kids are petting a whale, and my people will save it.*

They dug three trenches in the sand under the animal then threaded rope through them and then a bunch of them grabbed the ropes in the front and a bunch more pushed on the whale's back, and in minutes it was back in the shallow ocean water. They just kept pushing and pulling until the animal was in enough water that it could move to free itself. Then they just got out of the way and they all sat on the beach and watched as the whale flopped and flopped till it was in deep enough and then they watched as it swam away.

The Katabull cheered.

Then Darian pulled at her pants leg, pointed and said, "Dead man."

Right where the whale's tail had been was a body.

"When I tell her about petting the whale, I will leave out the dead man," Jena mumbled and started to herd the boys back towards home.

**The rain hit with a** vengeance and the seas were rough. They were catching rain water to drink in the same pot they were using to bail out the boat till Hellibolt pointed out that they could just drink the water they were bailing as it was all rain water. Now normally the king would have protested drinking water that was running off men and their clothes and gathering in a dirty boat, but they'd all been in the sea long enough to wash off any really bad stuff and this rain was coming down in sheets. Besides he had to keep drinking water because he just kept throwing up.

"Can you do nothing?" Persius begged of Hellibolt.

"I am rowing the boat. I am plotting the course. Magic is not a bottomless well from which a wizard can pull. I am used up, spent. We were hit full force by a gigantic tsunami. Have you any idea how many spells I had to cast to save any of us?" Hellibolt spat back.

"The Amalite gods are going to smite me. I have brought the anger...." To Persius's disbelief it was not Hellibolt but one of the sailors who cut him off.

"I cannot.... *Will* not hear this again! If we are all to die I will not die from swallowing my own tongue!" he bellowed at

Persius. "I thought you a bit of a poof, full of yourself and made arrogant by the power given you that you didn't earn, but I didn't think you were actually an idiot until on this lifeboat you started to scream that the Amalite gods have cursed you. Really? Men died. *Thousands* of men died needlessly because you didn't listen to Tarius the Black, yet you never took a single bad wound because she saved you. You have had a dozen wives and a hundred children; never have you been hungry. The many men who died because of your short sightedness, do you think any of them praised the Amalite gods as they lay dying?"

"I did not praise them!" Persius gasped.

"To say they have cursed you is to say they have power. To say they have power, that they even *exist,* is to praise them," Hellibolt hissed. "The man is right; you are an idiot. Do you not think a real 'god'—if such a thing exists—couldn't have smote you long ago? Do you think they would do such a half-ass job of killing you now? We are not going to die. We are going to reach the shore by the end of this day. We are on one of the greatest adventures of our lives. Others were on that boat with us. They died, not because of the Amalite gods but because of something natural. Sometimes nature does that. The planet we live on is alive, Persius; you humans don't understand that. It is alive, and every once in a while it smacks us for all the many things we do to it."

Persius started to yell. He was the king! How dare they speak to him in such a way? Then he took a deep breath and really heard what they had said. He looked down, unable to look any of them in the eye in that moment. When he raised his head he looked at the sailor who had told him off. "I am sorry, you are right. When I think about it I know the Amalites have no gods. If they did Tarius the Black would have died on my arrow and we all know she didn't. I apologize for I had thought myself a man and have found myself acting like a woman." Hellibolt looked at him, shook his head and sighed.

"What?"

"You were doing so good right up till that last little bit. We are getting ready to land on an island where all people are different but equal. If you should say something like that in the presence of any of these people they will think you more stupid than this sailor does. Should you say to the queen who rules this island what you just said to us, she will probably have your head removed from your shoulders."

# Chapter 12

**They had barely entered** town when a youth going the same direction they were ran past them.

"Snag him," Hestia told Radkin.

She did, nearly tripping the lad in the process. He looked at the Katabull and Radkin looked back at Hestia as if to say, "alright I have him why did you want him?"

So Hestia answered, "After a disaster like this one anyone running.... It's probably bad news. So lad?"

"My queen," he said, even as Radkin released him. "Master Arvon and Dustan are missing. Their horses were found saddled outside their house, but they are not home. I am one of their students. They said they were going hunting on the Great Mountain yesterday morning early." He pointed to what was left of the Great Mountain. "No one has seen them since the night before last."

And just like that without a word Radkin took control. "You, you and you go with the queen." She kissed Hestia quickly on the cheek and then slapped her on the ass, her way of dismissing her. "The rest of you with me. You too, boy, show us the trail that is usually used to go up the mountain."

Hestia started to tell Radkin everything that was wrong with what had just happened but.... Well there really wasn't anything at all wrong with it. Arvon and Dustan were missing; they needed to search for them. Hestia needed to get to Jestia. Radkin was a captain in the Marching Night. She was one of the few people Tarius went to when there were problems to solve or battles to plan. She knew what to do in a crisis situation. Everything Radkin had said made perfect sense under the circumstances.

So Hestia took off again in the direction of the spas, running double time.

When she came even with Jazel's she stopped. *Would they be at Jazel's or Jestia's, and....* Suddenly it registered.

*Arvon and Dustan are missing.* She looked up at where the mountain had lost its top, at where the debris had slid down and covered the top part of what was left in muddy ash so deep there were no trees to be seen. *They are dead if they are not here. If they were up there, then they are dead.* For a moment she couldn't move, couldn't even breathe. She had liked Dustan, but Arvon had been a dear friend someone she loved and admired, but in that moment all she could think was, *A million things could have gone wrong. Jestia was in the big middle of all of this and my daughter could be as dead as I'm sure Arvon is. I could have lost her and I have just found her. And if she is well is she at Jazel's or is she at her home?*

She had already reached Jazel's and Jestia's was very near the other end of town so she decided to check Jazel's first. She took a deep breath and started walking. One of her people opened the door for her, and she walked in. As she entered the dining room everyone in the room stood and bowed except Riglid who sat at a back table and didn't even stand, and Jazel who looked up at her and managed a smile which screamed of exhaustion.

Hestia looked at the bowing people and she just lost it. "Stand up! What is wrong with you? The whole island has fallen apart. People are dead. I don't know what has happened to my child. And now I know why this display so annoys the Katabull and why I prefer to be with them than anywhere else. How useless it is to lower yourselves to me. I am no different from you; I am only a woman who is afraid to ask...." she turned to Jazel as tears streamed down her face. "My dear friend, do you know what has happened to Jestia?"

"She is alive and she is not going to die, but she isn't well," Jazel answered and pointed to the hall.

Riglid stood up. "I will take you to her." He smiled at her, walked forward and took hold of her arm. He had never done more than tolerate her and make it clear that he barely approved of her as a mate for his mother. "She is still sleeping and...." He stopped suddenly and panic entered his voice. "Where is my mother?"

"She took the troop and went to check for some missing people." She turned to her soldiers who were still following her. "Kindly leave me be." They nodded and walked back towards the dining room.

Riglid grinned. He pointed to an open door and started to let go of her arm, but she quickly put her hand on his to stop him.

"Please stay with me Riglid, I find I am suddenly terrified. Is she going to be alright?"

He nodded and started leading her again. "I think she will be fine, but she has a death grip on the Great Leader."

"Tarius is here?"

"Aye, Jestia took her by spell from the compound even as the earth had hardly stopped quaking and the Great Wall rumbled," Riglid said.

"Why?"

"I'm not sure anyone knows save maybe Jestia. Something to do with them having been twins once is all I've managed to get out of it all. When I found them at the end of the trench I thought they were both dead and.... Well it is a long story that someone else will tell better." He stopped at the open doorway.

Riglid wasn't exaggerating. Tarius was propped up in bed and Jestia was wrapped all around her sound asleep. Tarius's eyes were closed. Hestia walked forward quietly. Where Jestia's right hand gripped Tarius's left forearm her knuckles were white and Tarius's flesh was blue.

Hestia pulled up a chair and sat down next to the bed. She dried her face quickly on her sleeve which did little good. She realized she was still so wet she was making a puddle on the floor. "Tarius," she said softly.

Tarius's eye opened a crack and she looked at her. "Hestia, how...?"

"We walked across the lava." She turned to Riglid and gave him a smile. "It is a long story that someone else will tell better."

Tarius's eyes opened the rest of the way and she took a deep breath and let it out. "Where is Radkin?"

"There are some townsfolk missing, and she and the troop I brought with me have gone to look for them. How are you?"

"I will be fine and so will she." Tarius nodded towards Jestia.

Hestia started to touch Jestia's hand and realized again that she was soaked. She started to cry and Riglid started pounding on her back.

"Hestia, get out of your wet clothes and put on dry ones

then take my place here. I need to get up for many reasons, and Jestia needs you."

"Me?" Hestia cried. "Why would she need me?

"Because every child wants their mother when they are sick. Now go," Tarius ordered. "Riglid stay with me."

**"Riglid I have to piss so** bad I can taste it, and I am too weak to untangle myself from Jestia without help."

Riglid nodded and moved forward to help; it was no easy task. When he had finally managed to pry Jestia off her, it was all Tarius could do to stand.

"Now get into bed with Jestia and stay there till her mother returns."

"What?"

Tarius was hanging onto the back of the chair for support. She grinned at him. "I'm pretty sure you not only heard but understood me. Get in bed with her." Riglid made a face. "Come on; it will not make you straight though if it could that one there would be the one to do it."

Riglid realized the Great Leader wasn't kidding, and when he got into bed with her Jestia immediately attached herself to him like a squid on an oyster. The Great Leader looked at him and said with a mock pout, "And now I don't feel special at all."

"She is…. She is making me tingle," Riglid said, some afraid.

Tarius grinned gleefully at him. "Perhaps she is changing you…."

"I am not tingling *there*," Riglid said as his face went red. "All over."

"That is the magic, Riglid. It will not hurt you." She let go of the chair, started to walk and almost fell.

"Great Leader!" He tried to get up but couldn't.

"Stay still boy." She wound up having to sit in the chair. She took in a deep breath and let it out. Hestia returned in dry clothes, and Tarius looked up at her. "I have not pissed myself since I was an infant, but I am near it now. Hestia, could you please help me to the outhouse?" Hestia helped her up without hesitation and put an arm around her and started walking out with her. Riglid smiled and looked down at the girl in his arms.

"You know Jestia, your mother is alright. I think just today

I've seen why my mother loves her so."

Jestia didn't make a sound. All of that and she hadn't woken up. He became worried suddenly that she might not wake at all.

**As they walked through** the dining hall her people moved to take Tarius from her, but she waved them away impatiently. Long before they reached the privy Hestia was wishing she had allowed them to at least help. Tarius was no light weight, and she could hardly move and couldn't hold her own weight, so Hestia found herself mostly carrying Tarius.

She had to help Tarius to sit and to stand again and then they were walking back and Tarius seemed to be having less trouble but she was still leaning heavily on Hestia.

"Tarius are you really alright?"

"I will be and so will she," she said again. "But we.... We shouldn't have lived, Hestia. Jestia channeled the power of The Everything through us. The power didn't come from us but it passed through us and it sort of hollowed us out. Leave me in the dining room and go and be with Jestia."

After she and Riglid managed to remove Jestia from him she climbed into bed with her and soon found Jestia wrapped all around her. She held her and started to sing softly to her. She wondered what Tarius meant that they'd been hollowed out. What did it mean that they had moved Jestia all around several times now and she showed no sign that she was going to wake up any time soon? What was really wrong with her?

Jazel walked in walked over and sat in the chair Hestia had moved to the side of the bed. "Even in the state she is in Tarius bosses people around though being Katabull she must be *asked* to do anything."

"I believe she assumes people will feel as if they have been asked and not told," Hestia said.

"In that case she has 'asked' me to assure you that Jestia will be fine. And it's true she will be, but it will take time. What she did.... She shouldn't have been able to do at all, and she nearly killed both she and Tarius."

"Tarius said they were hallowed out by The Everything?"

Jazel smiled and sighed. "And after she got done speaking you knew less than you did before. Go figure you must have been talking to a Katabull, though I think you understand them better than any human I know. We witches aren't really any better. We're magic; they're magic, and being magic we take for granted things humans spend lifetime's trying to figure out." Jazel seemed to think for a minute then got up. "Give me a second."

It took considerably longer than a second. When she came back she had an empty cup, a cup of sand, and a funnel. She held the funnel up and Hestia could see that the walls of the funnel were coated with something glowing and green, but the funnel still looked functional.

"Think of the funnel as Jestia, and the magic goop...."

"Magic goop?" Hestia asked.

"Yes, magic goop, think of that as Jestia's personal energy, her power if you will." She held the funnel over the empty cup and picked up the cup of sand. "Now the sand in this cup represents the power of The Everything, and the empty cup is the spell a witch is trying to do. If I put only a little sand through the magic goop it doesn't budge; there is no change at all. But if I pour all the sand through...." Jazel poured all of the rest in and Hestia watched as the sand ran through now obviously taking the magic goop with it till the cup ran over and it spilled onto the floor. "You get a huge mess on the floor that I wasn't counting on and that I hope someone else will clean up. Or a channel is dug to take lava away from towns and to a low area where it can flow to the sea doing as little damage as possible." She turned the funnel up so that Hestia could see that all the magic goop was gone. "...and the witch is empty. In this case the witch and the kingdom's warlord are both empty."

**Radkin was the best** tracker in the Marching Night, which meant she was possibly the best tracker in the world. It was not a boast; it was simply the truth. But Arvon and Dustan's trail was beyond cold. There was still a hint of sulfur in the air and the rain had wiped out any other scent she might have been able to pick up as well as any tracks.

They had reached the edge of the ash and mud that used to be the top of the mountain. If the two men were anywhere under that they were dead. The lava had run down from the top in a mile-wide strip that burned everything in its path till it hit a trench only powerful magic could have built.

They were looking for Arvon and Dustan, not idiot children, but seasoned fighters. Were they alive they would have immediately come down to help. If nothing else they wouldn't stay in the jungle knowing people would come looking for them. If they were just hurt she would have heard them or smelled them. Radkin swallowed hard. They were either under the ash and mud or under the lava, but either way they were dead and no one would find their bones.

"Well?" one of the soldiers asked at her shoulder.

"Keep looking. I am going to go into town and check on the queen and Jestia."

"Yes captain."

Radkin started the long hike back to town. She was Katabull, but still she didn't run. She was still looking, but she knew in her gut she wouldn't find her friends. *They died together in the most horrible of hunting accidents, and I must console myself with that. I will miss them whenever I am someplace they should be. I will miss their smiles and their laughter. Dustan was such a fine bard... for a human. All those stories he had will never be told in the same way again. How many times did I take one flank and Arvon the other? How many times did we hold each other's lives in our hands? Now he has been killed by a mountain. What a great story.*

When she got to the town everything appeared to be going along as if it were a normal day. As she walked past Arvon and Dustan's house where they had their sword school she stopped and looked at the sign over the gate. A sword school was important. All joined the military it was true, and all were trained by the kingdom, but a school like this taught those who were born for the sword. It didn't turn out competent fighters; it turned out excellent ones. Arvon was obviously an excellent teacher because he had helped to train Tarius the Black, her children, even herself. Her eyes filled with tears she refused to shed. She became increasingly angry at the citizens of Montero who were just going on with their lives. Did they not know how close they came to dying, how they were only saved by magic and barely so at that? And people were dead. She didn't know how many but she knew it wasn't just Arvon and Dustan; there were bound to be more.

As she passed Jazel's on her way to Jestia's she sniffed and found many familiar scents, two of which shocked her.

She walked quickly into the dining room at Jazel's and there sat her son and Tarius. Her son ran to greet her with a hug, but Tarius didn't even get up and Radkin could tell her friend was in pain. She held her son and patted his back. "What are you doing here?" she asked not her son but Tarius.

"It's a long story, but the only reason I am alive at all is because your boys saved me."

"Is Jestia...?"

"Alright? No, but she will live," Tarius said. "Hestia is with her now. Did you find who you were looking for?"

"We did not, the soldiers are still looking," Radkin said quickly. It was clear Hestia hadn't told them they were looking for Arvon and Dustan and why would she? It was obvious looking at Tarius that she had been through some horrid ordeal. She needed no other worries and dead people could take care of themselves. "My son, are you well?" Riglid nodded. "And the compound?"

"All are safe. The wall stopped the lava and the tidal wave."

"Tidal wave?" Radkin asked. She released her son and went to sit at the table with Tarius suddenly feeling the hours of hunting up and down the mountain on wet ground.

"Yes a tidal wave." Riglid sat back in the chair he'd been sitting in. "It was so big it splashed over but didn't breach the wall. Tarius had vanished and Jena took her place leading...."

"Jena, my Jena?" Tarius asked with a laugh. "Not Rimmy or my huge Katabull son, but my little human woman took command in my place. I wish I could say I'm surprised, but she's been running my life for years."

Helen brought Radkin a cup and she happily poured herself some tea from the pot in the middle of the table. She was no longer dripping wet, but she was damp all over and wanted some dry clothes, but for the time being warm tea was good. She threw off her cloak letting it drape over the back of the chair.

"We felt the earth quake; it knocked stuff over all through the castle. Then we heard the explosion and we came as quickly as we could with fifty soldiers but were stuck on the other side of the lava till this morning," She frowned then smiled at the memory of it. "That confounded woman! I started to walk out on the lava to make sure it was safe to go across. She grabbed my arm to stop me, whispered some speech in my ear about how she owned me and I owned her and if I was going she was going and if we die we die. Well I gave her a look which clearly said, *You don't tell me what to do woman, you will stay here and like it,* and I threw her hand right off and started across anyway. Hestia then looks right at me, gives me the most magnificent *You can go to hell look* and then runs across the lava field just to show me who's boss. Well I run right after her and when I catch her I'm so pissed off I grab her and lift her right up till our faces are even and I didn't change but my eyes did that's how mad I was. She is not the least bit afraid of me and then she orders me to kiss her and I do and.... She is very difficult to love."

Riglid clapped, grinned and said, "She said someone else could tell it better."

Radkin drank her tea and poured another cup. She looked at Tarius who looked like she'd been through more than a battle. Her eyes were sunken into her head and ringed in dark circles. She looked gaunt, as if she'd been off her feed for weeks. What could have happened to do that?

Tarius started to stand and sat back down hard.

"Tarius, what the hell...?"

"I am very weak. I would like to check on Jestia and we will have to tell Hestia about the tidal wave."

"Why...?"

"Because like it or not, Radkin, your mate is the queen and it has just now dawned on me that we have no idea how much of the coast will have been affected by the wave. There are many villages on the shore that don't have walls to protect them. Hestia will need to figure out which villages were hit and which need kingdom aid."

"My friend you are right, but I was asking why you are so weak?"

"She helped Jestia dig the trench," Riglid explained.

"With what, a really big shovel?"

**Hestia watched as Radkin** walked in nearly carrying Tarius. Hestia caught her eyes and Radkin silently shook her head no. Hestia nodded that she understood. Radkin sat Tarius in the chair.

"Tarius, you should relax and gloat about your wall a bit," Radkin said, giving Hestia a wicked grin.

"Oh you mean that horrible monstrosity that is completely unnecessary for the safety of my people and so very much infuriates the queen?" Tarius said lightly.

Hestia saw a glimmer of a twinkle in her friend's eye, and in that moment she looked more like Tarius than she had yet that day. "I happily sharpen my knife in preparation of eating a huge plate of crow concerning your beautiful, very necessary wall."

Tarius laughed then sniffed the air. She looked at Radkin then looked back at Hestia and smiled. "I'm afraid you're about to lose your spot my queen."

Ufalla came running into the room, panting for breath. She ran around them without so much as a nod towards their existence and without taking her boots off jumped onto the bed and crawled up to Jestia's back and hugged her. Hestia wasn't even surprised when Jestia released her, turned around and grabbed onto Ufalla. Ufalla winced a bit and Hestia knew why; she held up her arm to show her where Jestia had grabbed her and then Tarius and Riglid did, too.

Ufalla pulled Jestia tightly to her ignoring the pain. She looked at Tarius. "Is she going to die?" Ufalla asked.

"So, someone listens to me." Tarius laughed and shook her head. Ufalla's panic just seemed to melt away from her.

Feeling suddenly foolish Hestia got out of the bed and looked down at them. "I think she'll be fine now you're here."

"Where were you?" Radkin asked Ufalla.

"She went to the compound," Riglid said, "to warn us about the lava. She is a hero."

Ufalla looked up at him, tears in her eyes, and said, "You're the hero. Laz told us what you did. I owe you a debt I cannot pay."

"How did you get here?" Radkin asked Ufalla.

"I rode."

"You can take a horse across the lava field?"

"At the compound it is much wider but not as deep. It would have cooled more quickly," Riglid explained.

Hestia couldn't read Radkin's face but knew she had something in mind.

Tarius fell asleep sitting up and almost fell over. Radkin caught her then picked her up like a baby. "Radkin! For the love of the Nameless One," Tarius protested, but Radkin just carried her over and lay her on the other bed in the room.

"You are so weak you can't shift or you'd be home already," Radkin said gently. "I have known you most of our lives, and I have never seen you this weak. Jena and your babies are fine because of your wall and whatever you and Jestia did. We can take care of things. If this were a battle and you were in this kind of shape who would be in command? Me and Hestia and Harris and Rimmy...."

"And Arvon," Tarius said.

Hestia saw Radkin hesitate and then go on. "We are here and they are there, and we can take care of it. So shut up and go to sleep."

Tarius closed her eyes and she was out.

Hestia was a little shocked. Not a lot because she knew Tarius trusted Radkin's judgement, but a little. Radkin walked over to her, took her arm gently and nodded towards the door.

"Riglid come with us. Tarius is asleep and Ufalla will care for Jestia." Radkin led them all the way out of Jazel's and explained, "I didn't want to take any chance that the witches or Tarius might hear us. "Hestia, Riglid has just told me that a tidal wave has hit the coast. It was bad enough it splashed over the Great Wall. Tarius said there are many towns...."

"I will send runners to each of the towns along the coast and when we know which towns need what we will send troops with supplies, provisions and medics," Hestia said. "What else?"

Radkin turned to her son. "The people we are looking for are Arvon and Dustan." She gave him a moment to process the information. "They had gone up there," she pointed to what was left of the mountain. "...to hunt. No one has seen them since, and I looked and nearly fifty soldiers are still looking. Are you my son well enough to ride?"

He nodded.

"I want you to go to the compound and get Jabone. I do not in my heart believe there is any chance they are alive...."

"But if it were my fathers I would not believe it unless I had looked myself," Riglid said understanding. "Ufalla rode a horse over it, so I will take one of Jazel's and go at once. What should I tell Jena about Tarius?"

"Tell her the truth, that Tarius will be fine but she is in

bad shape. Do not let her come here with her babies. Jena could stand to see Tarius like that—it would be hard but she could do it because Jena is a strong woman—but Darian couldn't stand it because of what he is, not what is wrong with Tarius or Jestia or even Jazel and Eerin. Their magic has been drained from them. Tell Jena that the very minute Tarius tells me she can leave this place we will bring her home. Tell her that I am personally taking care of Tarius." He started to go and she grabbed his arm. "You, Riglid, make me more proud every day to call you son. Go and be careful." Radkin kissed him and he took off like the wind.

Hestia looked at Radkin and sighed. "I keep hoping we will wake up from this nightmare but.... We have no idea how far this tidal wave might have reached on either side of the compound." She should go back to the capital. There would be troops to arrange and dispatch and damages to assess, a million things she needed to do that could better be done from the capital. After all there was a reason it was smack in the middle of the island.

"You will do what you said. You will send runners to every town that might have been hit. You will send those three soldiers in Jazel's back to the capital with a scroll lining out what you want done and leave those whose job it already is to take care of the actual doing of it. If it was a battle you would go and run things from the front. This side of the island is the front of this battle, my love. Your place is here with your daughter. To the rest of the country you are the queen, but to Jestia you are her mother, and that is a more important position."

**"Jestia, can you hear me?"** Ufalla brushed the hair out of Jestia's face and then was almost sorry she had. Jestia looked colorless and lifeless. "Come on, baby, come on, I know I did this to you once, but you don't *always* have to try to get one up on me. Sometimes you could let me win."

Ever since they had all stepped on the energy well together Ufalla had been able to feel the hum of Jestia's magic even when she wasn't casting. She could feel it now, but it was vibrating all wrong. It made sense that Jestia was weak; she had blasted a giant trench around a city in hours. What didn't make any sense was that Tarius didn't seem to be in any better shape. *You told me you needed me that I grounded you, that you could pull power from me, but not this time. No, this time you grabbed Tarius because I wasn't enough. I shouldn't have left, but you did and if I hadn't.... And what could I have done here? Nothing, because if I could have helped, you would have taken me and left Tarius alone. You wouldn't have taken her if you didn't need her and that being the case why do you need me at all?*

It wasn't the time for self-doubt or self-pity. Maybe Jestia needed her right now, and if nothing else she needed Jestia. "I love you, Jestia, I always have and I always will...."

"If I didn't know that I wouldn't be here at all," Jestia mumbled.

"Baby, can you hear me?" There was no answer. She looked around covertly then shook Jestia as much as she could; the only result was that Jestia's nails bit deeper into her flesh and Ufalla's arm started to bleed. "So what's this then, Jestia, the minute I'm gone you just take anyone into bed with you?" Ufalla was surprised at how much calmer she felt since Jestia had spoken to her. Ufalla remembered that they'd all taken turns talking to Kasiria when she was in her magic-induced coma, and was this really any different? She decided to just keep talking to Jestia. "So, you probably already know everything that's been going on but let me tell you about the adventure I've been on...."

**Jena hadn't gotten far** when Kasiria shouted at her back. "Jena! You'd better see this."

Jena turned and saw her son's head bobbing up and down urgently. She looked around. "Yri, could you please take the boys back to our huts for me?"

"Of course, come on boys."

Pete just took his hand, but Darian looked at her with near panic and shook his head. "No mama, no with you."

"Go with Pete and Yri, Darian. I will be home as soon as I can."

Yri started to sing a song about a whale. Darian's entire demeanor changed, and he just went with Yri. It reminded Jena of something she often forgot; the Katabull were also magic.

Jena walked up to where Kasiria was looking down at the

dead man, Arvon sitting on her hip. It was a good thing he had a good grip because he was still too little to really be on a hip. His little head was just sort of hanging out in space over the dead body. *That poor baby. It's a good thing he is a Katabull primary or he would never make it through Kasiria's mothering.*

She was about to be a bit pissy because she just wanted to go home sit down for a while and relax. Then she saw the blond head, the blue and white tabard, and the chain mail. "He is a Jethrikian Sword Master," Jena said in disbelief. "How in the hell did he get there?"

"Great Leader's wife!" A Katabull called from down the beach.

Kasiria smiled at her and Jena shrugged.

"There is another one here!"

"Perhaps they were on a trade ship heading for another port," Jabone suggested.

"Son, you don't understand. He is...was a Sword Master." She looked at the body again and shook her head. "Your madra always hated the chain shirts and never fought in them. She said they were clunky and noisy and much too heavy." Kasiria nodded in agreement. "Wearing them at sea was just ignorant. They wouldn't have had a chance. Once they were in the water they might as well have been tied to the anchor." Jena had grown up the daughter of the head master of the Jethrikian Sword Master's academy. Kasiria had attended the academy and had been a Sword Master herself.

"Sword Masters work for the king, they work for the country, they don't leave they don't ship out, they don't sail," Kasiria told Jabone.

"We found another one!" Yet another Katabull shouted from down the beach.

"Are they all wearing what this one is?" Jena yelled back.

"Yes, Great Leader's wife."

Jena looked at her son and rolled her eyes. "That is getting old quick. I am ready for your madra to be home for a whole list of reasons, but that right there is on the top of the list."

"Could the wave have brought them from the Jethrik?" Jabone asked.

"If it did, I don't think even your madra's wall could have stopped it."

"What should we do with them?" Jabone asked.

"Strip them and bury them." Jena shrugged. "It's curious, but we have way too many things to do and worry about to add dead strangers to the list. I'm taking my cub and going home."

**Jabone watched his** mother walk away.

Kasiria straightened and looked up at him making a face. "She didn't mean *we* should strip them and bury them, did she?"

"No, but I should help. Do you know him, Kasiria?" His mother hadn't been at the academy since she was a youth, but Kasiria had left there just three short years ago.

"Not this one, but I should go see if I know the others." She started to take off.

"Give me the cub Kasiria." She handed him Arvon and took off at a run.

Jabone smiled and tucked the baby into the crook of his arm and walked away from the body. Already a crew was working on the docks doing repairs. After all the whole of the armada would be back in less than two weeks, and the ships would need to have some place to dock.

"I'm sorry, son. She is as rough as my madra was with me and Darian, and you for that matter. My madra is as gentle with my sister as she is with my mother, yet if anyone was to say there is a difference between men and women she would be the first one to growl in their face." He looked quickly around to see if anyone was close then grinned at Arvon. "Such a good boy, such a little man oh yes you are. Someday you will be a great, huge Katabull, and you'll roar and roar and...."

"I told you not to do that to our son," Kasiria said with a laugh at his shoulder.

"My mother did it to me. It is a tradition. Did you know them?"

"One looked familiar, but it was hard to tell because his head had been smashed open on something and there was a lot of well yukky stuff."

"What do you think it means? They had to be at sea. Why?"

"I'm sure I don't know." It was clear she also didn't care when Kasiria said, "I'm starved; let's go eat."

**Hestia looked in the door** and saw Ufalla holding Jestia and talking to her so softly Hestia couldn't hear her. *To think that is the union I tried so hard to break. Thank the Nameless One that I did not get my way.*

Ufalla must have seen her standing there because she said, "Hestia do you know what is wrong with her? With both of them?"

Hestia walked in sat down in the chair and stuck her hand on Jestia's back. "Ufalla, what they did should have been impossible, and it is not just them. Jazel and Eerin aren't in much better shape. It took Jazel a bunch of props to explain it to me but..." She smiled. "...you are the Great Leader's goddaughter and you have lived with Jestia for years so I have a feeling that you will understand Tarius's explanation in a way I didn't till Jazel put on her magic show for me. Jestia channeled the power of The Everything through she and Tarius. It wasn't their power but it flowed through them and hollowed them out."

Ufalla nodded then sighed. "So all she has to do is rebuild her power?"

"No." Jazel walked in the door at her back and Hestia turned. "That is not all. She is deeply grieved over the death of her brother."

"Katan?" Hestia asked. Jestia had hardly any reaction at all to her brother's death as far as Hestia knew. Jestia was like her and could hide her feelings but why would she fall apart years after his death? Of course thinking of her dead son as her other child just lay there lifeless did nothing to squelch Hestia's fear.

"No, Tarance," Jazel said in a voice that said she thought they were both imbeciles.

From the look on Ufalla's face she didn't understand any better than Hestia did. "But.... That was another life not this one and if Tarius used to be Tarance and Tarius is fine...."

"Tarius is not fine! She can't shift. She can hardly move, and she can't walk or stand without help." Jazel was angry no doubt because she was also drained. "They are tied to that life. Last night I saw Tarius do a spell, and not just any spell but a powerful one I didn't recognize, yet she is not a witch. She told me that Jestia has a much stronger connection to that life than she does yet Tarius did a spell. A Katabull did a spell and Tarius said Jestia's tie is stronger, and Jestia is mourning her brother. You have a lot of work to do." She walked out and Ufalla looked back at Jestia with new panic.

"They tell me to sleep and then they will not shut up!" Tarius boomed from her bed. Hestia grinned at Ufalla.

"Tell me what I need to do, Tarius. Tell me," Ufalla said.

"You are doing it, little sister. Just love her," Tarius said, "She and I are the same, and what do I need most in this world?"

Ufalla didn't even hesitate. "Jena."

"And all Jestia needs is you." Hestia started to get up and leave but then Tarius rolled over caught her eye and held it. "All she needs is you, but her mother is also here and she will not leave her side except to pee."

And so Hestia stayed right where she was.

**Jena had put the baby** and Darian down for a nap, left Hared to watch them, and then she'd gone back to the wall and climbed up the tower. She looked through Tarius's spyglass and she couldn't see Montero. Hell she could barely make out the Great Mountain. However with the glass she could clearly see it had no top. She sighed and took the glass away from her eye. Below her the Katabull were moving the mud away from the gate. Waden was in charge of the operation. He had come to her with the idea of using the mud to cover the lava field where the road should be.

"The lava has cooled but is as slick as glass. No horse will step foot on it."

"Unless pulled by a very determined girl," Jena mumbled.

"What?"

"Nothing, go on," Jena said.

"I was thinking to pull the mud over the lava. There is enough of it to cover the flow thick enough that it should repair the road," Waden said.

"That's a brilliant idea. You know how much Tarius adores doing one task to complete two."

He put his hand on her arm. "She will be fine Jena."

"But she's not fine now. If she was she would be here already. I should be with her."

"When we fix the road and get the gates open maybe you

should take your cubs and go to Montero."

And it looked like she wouldn't have long to wait. The gates were nearly cleared and they were using a huge log with ropes on each end pulled by Katabull power to smooth the mud out over the road.

Then she saw a vague shape on the horizon. She put the glass to her eye and could just make out a horse and rider coming fast. Her heart stopped, and she forced herself to calm. *It doesn't have to be bad news; it could be good news, or just news.* As he got closer she could see who it was. *It's Riglid and he's coming in hot. Still it doesn't have to be bad news. He's her runner; he is probably just bringing me a message to tell me not to worry.*

The last of the mud was moved and the gates were opened. Jena ran down the guard tower just in time to see Riglid run his horse across the freshly-covered lava field and through the gates, getting a dirty look from Waden because they had just gotten the mud all smoothed out.

"Sorry!" Riglid yelled back in Waden's direction.

Riglid looked at Jena and said quickly. "Tarius is going to be fine, but she is very weak. Jestia is in worse shape but will also live. The worst news is Arvon..."

"Arvon and Dustan are dead," Jena said so matter-of-factly that she felt guilt. They were more than friends; they were family, yet she'd already gotten used to the idea that they were gone.

"I was going to say missing. Mother thinks they are dead. How did you...."

"Darian told me. I hoped he was wrong but.... How bad is Tarius?"

"She is too weak to shift, she can hardly stand, and she can't walk without help," Riglid said.

"Go and tell my son about his fathers, I cannot bear it and you know he will have to go and look for them himself. I will pack for myself and my cubs and get a wagon.... Why are you shaking your head?"

"Mother says you could stand to see her like that because you are very strong, but that Darian couldn't stand it, that because of what he is he couldn't be around any of them; their magic has been drained..."

"Then I will leave Darian with Rimmy, Hared and Pete...."

"The same Darian who woke up screaming for his mother, and won't be consoled?" Rimmy had appeared seemingly out of nowhere and handed her a sobbing Darian.

His little body was just shaking, and he buried his face in her hair.

"Oh, baby, calm down now." She rocked him and looked at Rimmy. "He would be fine, Rimmy." She started crying. "Tarius needs me. She needs me and I'm never with her when she really needs me. I need to go."

"Mother said they will send her the minute she says she can go. Jena, there is nothing you can do now; she is just sleeping."

"What did Tarius say, Riglid? I don't care what Radkin said what did Tarius say?"

Riglid took a deep breath let it out and said. "Tarius is well enough to tell bad jokes. She is fine you should stay here with your cubs. Mother is taking care of Tarius."

"What did Tarius say?"

"Jena, she is fine or she will be. It doesn't make sense for you to go to her," Rimmy said.

"I don't care what makes sense, Rimmy. I'm tired and scared and.... I stood and watched him put an arrow in her. I turned my back on her. She was clinging to life and what was I doing? I was feeling sorry for myself." She was crying uncontrollably and Darian was still crying but he was patting her back now trying to calm her. "And when her mind cracked I could do nothing with her. I had to ask Jestia for help and then Harris."

"What she needed you to do you did, Jena. You ran the compound, you took care of your cubs," Rimmy reminded her.

"Don't you get it? I *want* to take care of Tarius. I *want* to. Just once I want her to know that she comes first."

**Jabone had been** helping to bury the bodies when he heard the sound of his mother in distress. He couldn't make out what she was saying, but could tell she was beyond upset. He threw down the shovel he was using and took off running. She was all the way down by the gate and he'd been near the shore yet he was there in minutes.

He skidded to a stop in front of her. "Mother?"

"Your Madra isn't well and they won't let me go to her.

They say I must stay here."

Jabone looked at Darian in her arms just crying, reached over and took him from her and held him on one hip as he wrapped his other arm around his mother. "Is that true?"

"My mother said Darian should not be there," Riglid said.

"Darian can stay with Kasiria and I. You will stay with us won't you brother?"

Darian nodded.

Jena took a deep breath and let it out. "And only now do I see what a selfish ass I am being. I'm not thinking about anyone's needs but my own. Tarius doesn't need me; I need her. My cubs need me here. I'm sorry," she said to Rimmy and Riglid. She dried her eyes on her sleeve and looked up at Jabone, but couldn't hold his eyes.

"I can...." Riglid started.

Jena stuck out her hand and put it on Riglid's arm. "No. I've got this. Jabone..." Her voice broke on a sob and she took another deep breath. "Your fathers are missing. You must go to Montero and look for them. You must go and take care of your Madra."

"My fathers are missing?"

"They went up the Great Mountain to hunt and no one has seen them since," Riglid said.

"But.... The top of the mountain is gone," Jabone said, and then Darian was crying harder and hugging his neck. Jabone swallowed hard and patted the toddler's back. "Calm brother, I will go look for them." He peeled Darian off of him, kissed his cheek and handed him to their mother. He fought his own tears. "Mother, I will go to Montero, search for my fathers, and I will bring Madra home to you." He ran to get his horse.

**When he got back to** the gate his uncle Harris and Rimmy were saddled up and waiting for him.

"Riglid needs rest," Rimmy said.

Jabone nodded jumped on his horse and looked at Harris.

"I will go to look for my brothers, and I will help you bring Tarius home to Jena."

Jabone nodded and they all took off. He was glad they were going with him. If Harris was his Madra's right hand, then Rimmy was her left. They were also very close to his fathers. But mostly they were constants in his life, and if his madra was sick and his fathers gone he wasn't so proud to say—at least to himself—that he needed their support. They were riding too fast to talk, but his mind was going a mile a minute. *If my Madra wasn't in very bad shape she would have come home to my mother and her cubs. What has happened exactly? Riglid would know, but I didn't have time to talk to him, and it's no wonder Rimmy made him stay behind he looked wrecked. My fathers were hunting on the mountain. The mountain is missing its top and no one has seen them, but that doesn't mean they're dead except.... Darian was just crying and crying. And my fathers are fighters. They think, and they would have known after what happened if people didn't find them at home they would have gone looking for them. They would have come right back if they could, which means they can't come back and they are probably dead. That's why Darian is crying because he knows we have no fathers. I must not think that, not yet, I don't have all the facts. The lava flow might have blocked them coming back to town. They might be trapped somewhere. Why did I not take the time to question Riglid?*

Jabone went back over what Riglid had said. It wasn't much, but what did his Madra carefully teach him? *To hear also what is not said. Riglid said that Darian should not be there. Why? Not because of our fathers, he would feel no less sad there than he does at home. It is because of Madra, because of what is wrong with her. He loves her more than anything in our world; he could not stand it if she is in pain or worse.* He spurred his horse on faster. *No, Riglid wouldn't lie about her condition, and if Mother thought Madra was dying an army could not keep her in the compound no matter what.* He slowed his horse some. *No! Riglid said his mother said Darian should not be there.*

He reined his horse to a stop and started to cry. Rimmy and Harris slowed their horses and came back to him.

"What's wrong Jabone?" Harris asked.

"Radkin is in Montero, she is the best of the Marching Night trackers. She loves my fathers. If she didn't find them they are dead," Jabone said. Neither Rimmy nor Harris said a thing. "You know I'm right."

"We will look anyway," Harris said. "We will look for them

ourselves and when we have turned over every rock and looked behind every tree then and only then will we accept it. We will accept it and then we will bring your madra home."

"We will check on Madra first, because if Radkin doesn't think Darian should be around her then she is in worse shape than Riglid is telling us." Jabone started his horse going again and soon had him running as fast as he could go. He let himself have a good cry hoping to do it and have it over with before he saw his madra.

# Chapter 13

**"Sit down, you're going to** tip the boat over!" Persius yelled at Hellibolt.

"He will not tip the boat over unless he tries!" the man named Thomas roared. He was a big man with just a hint of a belly, a sailor by trade and the same man who had already told him off once and acted like he had more he wished he'd said.

They had slept on the boat; it had been terrifying. It had been darker than he'd ever seen in his life. He asked Hellibolt to make a light but Hellibolt said it was all he could do to keep rowing the boat and that if they stopped rowing they'd wind up in the very middle of the ocean and no one would find them and they'd die a horrible death. Which was apparently the old wizard's way of calming them all down.

The rain hadn't stopped and the waves just kept tossing them around and he was cold, wet, and sick all night. They took turns bailing the water out of the boat, and he doubted any of them had slept any more than he had which was not at all.

The rain hadn't stopped so much as they'd finally rowed through it. Now the skies were clear and with the sunshine everything seemed less terrifying. He didn't consider himself a sissy; he was a man filled with vigor and strength. He considered himself brave when he was up against an enemy he could fight. However tested against the elements he found himself completely lacking.

*Even in battle, on the front I had people with me who did everything but fight for me and wipe my ass. Left to my own devises in nature I would die.*

"I see land," Hellibolt said. He sat down and the oars rowed faster.

The men all looked in the direction Hellibolt pointed as did Persius, and when he saw what Hellibolt was pointing at he didn't have to wonder why the sailors all cheered. He could see what was clearly a huge island not that far in the distance. As they got closer he realized the island was much bigger than he had thought because what he'd first seen were only the tops of mountains in the far distance. And he could not now see around it to be sure it was an island at all.

**Riglid wasn't surprised** when he found Kaden sitting with Kasiria, Jena and Hared around the fire pit in front of the Great Leader's huts. Darian and Pete were playing in the mud with sticks on the ground right in front of Jena. Jena was holding Diana just looking at her and rocking her, and the baby was chuffing. She was a very happy baby. For some reason the Great Leader's baby chuffing made Riglid feel better about not going back with the others, like she was saying, "It's okay. You are more needed here right now."

Jena saw him first. She smiled, got Kaden's attention and tossed her head towards Riglid. Kaden turned saw him, jumped to his feet and ran to him. Riglid grabbed him hugged him and then while he had fully expected Kaden would be overwhelmed by his emotion Riglid found that he was the one who held Kaden and just started crying on his shoulder, mumbling incoherent things. Kaden gathered him up and lead him away from everyone else knowing Riglid wouldn't want them to see his belly.

"What's wrong Riglid?"

"I am so tired and now I know why Father made me stay. He could tell.... I am just done in. Arvon and Dustan are no doubt dead. Tarius can hardly move, and Jestia might as well be in a comma and.... Are you going to leave me because this isn't what you signed up for?"

"Signed up for?" Kaden laughed and shook his head. "I was so mad at you when I found that note, but then I read it again. I didn't know at first but over the last few months it has become quite obvious that you are exactly the kind of man who would climb the Great Wall, jump off it, and run into the night to look for the Great Leader. I was scared to death I'd never see you again. Jena said when I saw you I should tell you that you are very difficult to love."

Riglid cried even harder and croaked out. "Thank you."

**The springs had resumed** their pre-volcanic eruption temperature. Tarius told Ufalla to take Jestia to the pool and she went herself. She wouldn't let Radkin carry her, but once she was in the pool she admitted that it probably would have been easier for Radkin if she had.

She was weak and it was all she could do to hold herself up against the side of the pool, but the longer she stood there the better she felt. She was glad when Ufalla showed up carrying Jestia. Ufalla walked into the pool with her and you could tell the instant the water started to bear more of Jestia's weight than Ufalla was because the look of concentration left Ufalla's face to be replaced by relief. She had heard Ufalla turn down Radkin's offer of help.

*Clearly that child is my goddaughter because she is every bit as hard-headed and stupidly proud as I am. She is a strong girl and Jestia is much smaller than she is, but Jestia is no china doll and too big a load for Ufalla. But just like I made Radkin work harder so that I could pretend that any part of me can walk, Ufalla must carry Jestia because.... There is really nothing else she can do for her and she just wants so much to help. I hope being in the spring helps Jestia. It is helping me, but I am Katabull.*

Jestia had spoken only a handful of times that morning, and so far it wasn't clear that she was awake even one of those times. That she had ever really woken up.

*Last night this was so hot it nearly cooked me and I thought I'd never again want in here. Today I am chilling and the water feels good. The sky is clear, the air smells sweet again, and if I could not see the scar on the Great Mountain and feel the pain in my bones I could believe that it was yesterday morning and nothing had happened yet.*

She walked towards Ufalla and Jestia. Jestia seemed to have less than no reaction to being put into the pool.

"Jestia!" Tarius barked at her. "Can you not wake up for even a minute so that we can moronically ask if you are alright and you can tell us how stupid we are and then we will know you are still with us?"

She was almost shocked when Jestia opened one eye a crack. Then she closed it.

It was then that Ufalla lost all ability to be strong and

brave and just completely lost it. "She's burned up inside! She's gone! She's gone! Do something. Why don't you do something? You are always asking her to do things she shouldn't do, and now she is what? What is she?"

Tarius let the girl have her fit, Ufalla deserved it. When Jena and Darian had been kidnapped she'd said much worse things to whoever was in firing range of her frustration and fear. This wasn't Tarius's fault; it wasn't even her idea. Jestia had done this to Tarius not the other way round, but after all Tarius had in the past asked Jestia to do a spell that left her in a similar state though not for this long.

"As near as I can tell she is asleep and...." Tarius then knew what was wrong with Jestia. Maybe it was clear now because she was starting to feel better herself. "Give her to me."

"You...? You can hardly hold yourself up."

"Give her to me, give her to me," Tarius said excitedly. "Give her here please." No doubt because Ufalla had grown up doing what Tarius told her to do she handed Tarius Jestia. "The pool wasn't for her; it was for me."

"I don't understand," Ufalla said.

"Last night I was the wizard, and what did Jestia tell us? That she only has the one healing spell, and so would he. This is a version of healing sleep—the same spell Jestia did to Kasiria. I didn't recognize it because the words were just fed into my brain and Jestia did the spell without speaking because that's what Jestia does. The spell reacts differently because Jestia is a witch and because I am—was—a different wizard with a different spell. Don't you see, Ufalla? Jestia is just going to sleep until she heals, and what is wrong with her? She has been used up. She channeled the power through us but didn't keep any for *us*. If we can give her just a little bit of her magic back, she will wake up."

"You can't even shift how can you give her any magic when you don't have enough for yourself?" Ufalla was looking at her like she thought maybe Tarius had finally taken one too many hits in the head and hissed, "So what are you really doing besides cradling my naked wife?"

"She is very beautiful, but I think you know that I could never have lust for Jestia any more than I could for you, little sister. I healed in this pool. I was here for weeks, and since that time I have come back hundreds of times and soaked and Jazel uses this pool nearly every day. This pool is full of energy and part of that energy is mine. We were spent last night and she knew I'd need the magic of this pool to do the spell. That spell did to me nearly exactly what it did to Jestia when she cast it on Kasiria. It takes a piece of the caster, but that piece is still in this pool because this pool is magic."

She put her lips against Jestia's ear and whispered, "You must leave the past in the past, Jestia. We are where we should be and who we should be. Grab the energy and pull it into yourself." In her mind she made an image of the energy in the pool as threads of white light all running into Jestia. Then Tarius dropped Jestia into the water where she proceeded to drop like a stone.

Tarius began to think maybe Ufalla was right about her and she'd just gone nuts. After all she was a Katabull not a wizard, and at the moment a Katabull stuck in human form.

Ufalla dove in after Jestia, but Jestia beat Ufalla to the surface. She took in a deep, shuddering breath. Ufalla came up out of the water and before she could see Jestia was standing on her own palmed Tarius on the shoulder. Tarius fell in and had a little trouble getting back on her feet again.

When Tarius's face broke the surface of the water, Ufalla was looking into Jestia's eyes then she grabbed her and hugged her and Jestia asked, "Who the hell are you?"

"What?" Ufalla asked.

"Who the hell are you?" Jestia asked. Ufalla pushed her away a bit and looked into her face.

"I am your mate," Ufalla said slowly.

Tarius smiled, wiped the water off her face and moved back to the side of the pool to give them some room.

"Oh no, no that couldn't be true," Jestia said shaking her head wildly.

"We were married right here in Montero," Ufalla assured her.

"Now how did that make you feel?" Jestia demanded.

"What?" Ufalla asked in confusion.

"I wake up from some magic-induced coma and I don't know you and how does that make you feel?" Jestia asked with a wicked grin.

"Not great and...." Ufalla started to cry then grabbed Jestia and just held her. "I love you so much and.... I don't even care that you are vindictive or hold a grudge forever as long as you're alive."

She looked over at Tarius. "I am so sorry. Tarius for every...."

"Don't be sorry." Jestia looked at Tarius, too, and grinned at her. "She had no idea whether that would work or not."

"That is all I have done for most of two days now. Guess a lot and do things without knowing whether they will work or not. How do you feel?" Tarius asked.

"How do you feel?"

"When you ride in formation if the horse in the front shits by the time all the other horses have tread over it those horse turds are so trampled they don't even look like turds anymore. Then the last horse shits on them and they are under them. I feel like the pummeled horseshit under the fresh stuff," Tarius said.

"In that case I feel like the dirt the first horse shit fell on."

"So, much better than last night?" Tarius asked with a grin.

"Yes, a world better than last night. Ufalla, you are holding me so tight I can hardly breathe.... Well I didn't tell you to stop."

**Hestia had been on her** way to the spring when she heard talking. She couldn't tell what they were saying but they were loud, so she took off running. When she saw Jestia was awake she walked the rest of the way into the pool area, flopped in a chair and started to cry.

Jestia looked up at her. "Mother when did you get here?"

"She has been here since early this morning," Tarius said. "She has not left your side except to go to the privy."

It was true, too. The minute Tarius said it she knew that's what she should do, and she had in fact been coming back from the privy when she heard them.

"Mother," Jestia said softly. "I'm alright."

"As mean as ever," Tarius said looking up at Hestia. "She's seconds out of her comma and she says to Ufalla, *Who the hell are you?* Just to get even with her."

"At least I didn't say *My finger is in my sword,*" Jestia said, making a face.

"That wouldn't have made any sense; your finger isn't in

your sword," Ufalla mumbled. She was holding Jestia so tightly.

Hestia tried to quit crying and failed.

"Mother, I'm going to be alright," Jestia said.

"No you won't," Hestia cried. She stood up and looked down at Jestia. "This power has cursed our family for generations, and it is because of me that you are a witch. I love you and I can protect you from nothing."

She didn't know where she came from, but the next thing Hestia knew Radkin was holding her and patting her back with enough force to knock most of the air out of her lungs.

"Hestia, you can never protect your children," Tarius said. "All you can do is love them. Jestia, tell your mother the truth. If you could choose anything else, you'd still be a witch."

"I love being a witch. If I didn't have this power Montero would be gone," Jestia said.

Hestia nodded and pushed away from Radkin before she wound up with a cracked rib. She was done crying. She felt sort of foolish; after all she knew she couldn't protect her children. Katan had literally tripped fallen hit his head and died. *Katan was doing nothing. No one was more careful than Katan and he is dead. Jestia has always been reckless and this should have killed her but it didn't. What is it the Katabull always say? It was their day to die, how many times I've heard that and only now I know what it means. If it is your time to die you will and nothing will stop it and if it isn't you will live against all odds.* Radkin handed her a handkerchief that had seen better days and Hestia used it anyway and didn't think about where it had been or what it had done. After all she was just making it dirtier.

# Chapter 14

*Jena threw some vegetables* into the pot hanging over the fire. Someone brought them a couple of fish, and Hared descaled and gutted them. Jena chopped them up and threw them in because by the time they ate in the evening after cooking all day the bones would go down as easy as the meat. She threw the heads in, too, stirred the soup threw in some garlic and herbs stirred it again and put the lid on it. She threw some more wood on the fire and she was done cooking.

She took the kids and went to the showers. When she got back home she put on her favorite dress, a short blue and green wrap around with short sleeves. It was cool and comfortable, but beyond that she knew she looked good in it. Tarius loved her in it. It gave for a little kick of confidence and she needed all the help she could get right then because she was feeling raw and tired of having to put on a brave face.

"Do you need some help?" She hadn't heard Kaden come up and she jumped. "Sorry."

"No one's fault." She did a quick check on Diana and remembered with a smile that the cub had company. Arvon was in the cradle with her and the cubs were curled up together, sound asleep. "Hared milked the goat and took care of the chickens. The only help I might need is if these babies wake up at the same time and are in foul moods."

Darian and Pete were happily playing with a wooden top Rimmy carved for them, "We will watch Arvon, Mama." Darian said.

"Yes well you can help an adult watch him and do not ask if you may wake him again."

"Is Kasiria sleeping?"

"Yes, she got next to no sleep last night and just hit a wall about an hour ago. I told her to lie down and I'd watch the cub."

"I can watch them both if you want to go lay down Jena,"

Kaden offered.

"Hared has offered the same. Do I look that bad?"

"You look that tired."

"I really could not sleep right now and I need to have my cubs around me to remind me of why I'm not in Montero with my mate. While we're on the subject, I'm afraid I was way too busy berating him to thank Riglid for helping—probably even saving Tarius."

"You're allowed to be upset, Jena. Your household has been hit a mighty blow by a catastrophe which most of the nation didn't feel only because of your family's sacrifice."

Jena smiled.

"What?"

"I can see why you are a bard. How is Riglid?"

"Exhausted, but he couldn't even think to go to sleep until he told me all that he'd done and seen. I think it will take me about a week to actually understand all of it."

"Is he angry with me?"

"No, he understands why you were mad and that you weren't really mad at him. At least I think he does. I only really understand him about half the time, yet we supposedly speak the same language."

Jena laughed then sat down in the Katabull throne which was next to the cradle. In Tarius's absence the throne seemed to be following her around. Since Jena was used to having it always in her space she didn't even realize it was odd until Hared pointed out that it normally follows the leader.

"Kaden, would it be too much to ask that you tell me what Riglid told you, taking into consideration that there are cubs about who are obviously listening? I really have no idea at all what has happened to Tarius or what Jestia needed her for."

"Madra is like a funnel," Darian said, not looking up from what he was doing.

Jena smiled at Kaden. "I think you see what I mean about the cubs."

**"Running way off course** then hit by a massive wave that splintered our boat yet obviously we are landing in the capital," Persius said, looking at the massive wall that wove along the coast till it went out of sight on both sides. There was a large natural harbor and three huge docks jetted out into it.

"The capital sits in the middle of the island," Hellibolt reminded. "That is not the capital."

"But that wall! It's massive; it is some fort then."

"It is the Katabull compound," Thomas said. To the look of doubt on Persius's face he said. "I am a sailing man and have made trade with the Katabull many times. There is nothing else that looks like the Katabull compound."

"Yes that is what I thought. Tarius said she had her people build a Great Wall," Hellibolt said.

"You have done this on purpose, old man!" Persius bellowed.

Hellibolt laughed. "I only dream of having that kind of power. I did a spell to take us to the nearest land. I had no idea where we would end up. In matters concerning you and her, the universe has always made it impossible to calculate. This is good news, Persius. We aren't landing on some deserted stretch of beach with no idea where we are, without food or shelter. Kasiria is here, she will help us...."

"The Katabull hate me."

"Which is why I'm sure only a handful of people know that Kasiria is your daughter. You will not tell them who you are, and none of the people who know will tell. You will say you're Kasiria's father that your name is William...."

"I don't like that name. I always wanted to be Fredrick."

"Then you are Fredrick." Hellibolt took in what Persius was wearing; he waved his hand in the air and said, "Clothes too rich for a poor sailing man make them look as rugged as any ole man's can."

Persius was soon wearing clothes not much different than what the sailors were wearing, which from the look on Thomas's face just made his whole day.

"Must I be a sailor? Could I not be a sword master at least?"

"What's wrong with being a sailor?" the helmsman—whose name he still did not know—said, so apparently insubordination was contagious.

"Exactly," Hellibolt said.

"What of you wizard?" Persius said. "What disguise will you use?"

"None. The Katabull love me. Without magic none of you would have survived that wave, so it makes things easier to explain not harder. I will say I was coming to visit my old friends when our ship was caught in the tidal wave," Hellibolt explained. "It is exactly the sort of thing I would do, so no one will think a thing of it.... Fred."

The sailors chuckled and Persius cut them a look that would spoil cheese. Still he could find nothing wrong with the plan. If they were to wind up in the Katabull compound he would happily be Fredrick the sailor. Anything was better than being Persius, King of the Jethrik, who put an arrow into the belly of the Katabull's Great Leader.

***Jena stirred the soup*** then reached down and picked up the screaming cub. Surprisingly, his squalling hadn't even made Diana turn over. He quit crying, but Jena knew he'd need to eat soon and since he was a biter.... "Kaden, could you go and get Kasiria?"

He nodded and took off.

Kasiria showed up just as Arvon started to fuss. She took her cub, flopped on the Katabull throne and started to feed him.

*Yep she no longer gives a rat's ass who sees her feed her cub, and he's only two and a half months old so she beat me. Jabone was six months old before I would feed him in front of anyone but Tarius, and after what happened with Darian.... I almost go out of my way not to feed Diana if I'm alone. So Kaden told me everything Riglid knew and I really still have no idea how bad Tarius is. I'm tired of people asking me things they would normally ask her and the cubs all miss her and it feels like forever and.... Arvon and Dustan. Darian said they are dead, and if Radkin couldn't find them then they are. My dear friends, my family, they saved me in more ways than one. Without them I would not have this life. Without them I would have been hanged for killing my husband. But.... They have not really been part of our lives for the last few years and while I loved them and I'm sure the loss will hit me at some strange time and I will cry my heart out, for now in this moment it feels like it was something that was meant to happen. Have I lived with the Katabull so long that I now hear things like "they died together in a horrible hunting accident" and am immediately comforted? Or is it just that I am too worried about Tarius to care about anyone else, or that so much has gone into my head that I just can't really deal with this loss properly?*

"Are you alright, Jena?" Kasiria asked.

Jena smiled. "Tarius has taken a dislike to that question of late. She says that we could write the story of our lives by just stringing that question together with the answers. She says what we really mean is, "Are you bleeding? Is anything broken? Are you going to die? I am not bleeding, nothing is broken, I am not going to die, and I'm not alright, but I will be as soon as Tarius gets home."

"And they find Arvon and Dustan," Kasiria said. It was obvious that Kasiria thought they would find them. Jena wasn't about to be the one to tell her that they were dead. Like most people who knew them, Kasiria liked Dustan but dearly loved Arvon. Until little Arvon was born Kasiria and Arvon were the only blond Katabull on the island. Add to that the fact that neither of them had really known they were the Katabull till they were adult, and they had a great deal in common. Losing Arvon was going to leave a bigger hole in Kasiria's life than it would most of theirs because he understood her in a way the rest of them didn't.

*Poor Dustan, such a love, a great friend and father, he gave up so much for us over the years and never complained. But he wasn't Arvon. Arvon was like Tarius—bigger than life. We will all miss Dustan, but the loss of him will be over shadowed by the loss of Arvon just as being always with Arvon overshadowed him in life, and he never cared. He never had any need to be as big or as bright as Arvon. He was happy to just be and.... Maybe that's what I should say at their memorial.*

Kasiria read her silence correctly and said, "You will see Jena, Jabone will find them."

*I hope he doesn't find them because I know they are dead. If anyone finds them let it be someone who didn't know them well and please Nameless One don't let it be my son. Don't let my son find his fathers dead.*

"Great Leader's wife," a Katabull said, skidding in the mud in front of her and stopping just inches from her. At that moment she was happy for the interruption because it kept her from having to lie and tell her daughter-in-law that she was sure they would find them alive or tell her the truth that she was sure they were dead and ruin what was left of a pretty crappy day. The Katabull caught her breath and said again, "Great Leader's wife."

*And now I know why Tarius fought so hard against them calling her Great Leader. It is annoying to become something instead of just you.* "Yes, Vony?"

"There is a boat with strangers rowing up to the dock. They ask that you come immediately."

"Why?"

She looked some confused by her question. "Because the Great Leader isn't here."

Jena sighed and checked the cradle. Her cub was still asleep. She looked around and Hared was nowhere in sight.

"We can watch the cubs Jena," Kasiria said.

"Can you also grow me Katabull legs? For I have walked more in the last two days than I have in my life till now." She started to follow Vony but didn't get two steps when Darian hopped up from where he was playing.

"No mama no!" he said. "Me go, me go." Mama was a term that came with her from the Jethrik; it wasn't Kartik. Jabone had called her mama, on occasion he still did, and both the little boys did it but oddly not as much when Tarius was there as if they thought the term might confuse her.

"Darian, I am not your madra. I cannot carry you." And there was no way he could walk all the way to the docks and back by himself.

"If you sit on the throne I'll let you hold Arvon," Kasiria said patting the seat beside her. "As soon as he's done eating."

Darian forgot all about her leaving ran over and crawled up on the throne beside Kasiria.

"Can I go, mama?" Pete asked. Jena nodded, hoping now to get away without Darian noticing that Pete was leaving, too. She took Pete's hand and started following Vony. "You having a bad day, mama?"

Jena squeezed his hand and smiled down at him. "Sort of Pete."

"I will sing you a song." He started singing her the whale song that Yri had sung them earlier that day except he didn't know the words and he just sort of strung words together. Occasionally he yelled out the word "whale" very loud.

When he finally finished his rather long rendition of the song, Vony turned around and smiled at him then at Jena.

"You know I think I like his version better."

They reached the docks just as the visitors were tying off the boat. When Jena saw who was in it she looked down at Pete and said, "You better start singing that whale song again, Pete. This day just managed to get even worse."

**Hellibolt had nearly** knocked him down to get off the boat first. He ran to Jena and embraced her, and the thick frown she'd been wearing and the eyes nearly glowing with hatred were replaced with joy. The wizard hugged her and she hugged him and kissed his cheek. Hellibolt whispered something to her she whispered something back and nodded.

"Great Leader's wife," one of the women said. "What should we do?"

"Help them off the boat. These men were hit by the tidal wave." She glared at Persius, no doubt just to remind him that she hated him more than anything or anyone else on the planet and that she now held his life in her hands. "This," she said with a wave of one of those hands in the wizard's direction, "Is the Great Leader's dear friend the wizard, Hellibolt."

And then the people who were working to repair the docks and those who were working on the shore cleaning up the beach and even those that were supposed to be helping them off the boat were cheering in a way that made a great roar.

Persius could not remember a time in his life when he had received such respect from his own people as these foreigners gave the wizard. *He is a great hero to them, and I know why because years after the fact he told me what all of these people know, that it is only because of Hellibolt and Robert that Tarius lived. As a youth I would have said they betrayed me. Now older and wiser I know that by saving Tarius they saved me and the whole of my kingdom. I know humility is a virtue, yet it is still so hard for me to be humble.*

"Where is Tarius?" Hellibolt asked.

"She is not here," Jena said simply. "This man...." Jena said, pointing at him. For a minute his blood ran cold. "Is Fredrick; he is Kasiria's father." She then looked at them all and said, "Come with me; I will take you back to our camp."

She kept a good pace. The child who held her hand looked back at him and frowned then turned back around. "Pete, sing that whale song son," Jena said. The child started to sing the most absurd song about a whale. Jena was talking to Hellibolt, and Persius realized why she had the child sing. The Katabull could hear a pin drop in a crowded bar. It wasn't for his benefit; unless Hellibolt had told her already that he'd changed his Jethrik to Kartik she probably thought he couldn't understand her anyway. So she was talking about him but was trying to hide his identity from the Katabull.

**"Seriously, Hellibolt, just** when I think the day couldn't possibly get any worse I look up and there is Persius," Jena said in disbelief. "What did I do to so piss off the Nameless One?"

"Where is Tarius?" Hellibolt asked in a whisper as they walked.

"She is in Montero; Jestia took her when the volcano erupted."

"Volcano!"

"It is a long story that someone else will tell better. She is going to live, but apparently both she and Jestia are in pretty bad shape. Can you bring Tarius here or go to her there?"

"Bring her here? I'm afraid not even on a good day. The young witch must be even more powerful than I knew. I couldn't even astral project there right now. It was all I could do to save any of us when that wave hit, and I am spent."

"Which is apparently what is wrong with Tarius and Jestia," Jena said. Then she turned and stared daggers at Persius. "What the hell is he doing here?"

Hellibolt laughed. "It was not his intention to wind up here at all. He was headed for the capital. He was finally doing something for all the right reasons when suddenly we were caught in a tidal wave. He thinks I brought him here on purpose, some pretense. In fact, he has been thinking a lot of absurd things ever since he wound up floating in the sea. We were coming to speak with Hestia because there are Amalites hiding in the Jethrik...."

"You're kidding me."

"I wish I were. He kept having these nightmares...."

"Good," Jena hissed.

Hellibolt grinned. "You really do hang onto a grudge, don't you?"

"Every time I lay with Tarius and see the scar I am reminded of how he tried to destroy us. Maybe worse I am reminded of the part I played in nearly destroying her. It is hard to let go of something when one has a constant reminder."

"I can see where it would be, yes.... Anyway he was having these nightmares and they reminded me of a Kartik prophecy. Then Kasiria sent word that she had a son...."

"She told him about Arvon?" Jena was surprised.

"Yes and at nearly the same time we found proof that the Amalite cult was once again hiding in our midst. I said we must go and he went and.... We didn't even send word first that we were coming and then we were hit by a giant tidal wave and wound up here." He looked at Pete. "So who is the budding bard?"

Jena smiled down at Pete who was still just singing his little heart out. "Our foster son, Pete."

"And how is the child Tarius saved from the cave floor?"

"Tarius doesn't allow anyone to say he isn't ours just so you know. Darian is fine...." And now was when the emotion over their deaths decided to hit her, and why? Why then? Because she was talking to an old friend that knew them, too and thinking about her little boy's tears. In a whisper she said, "My son's fathers are gone; Arvon and Dustan are dead. Jabone has gone to look for them, but they are dead. Kasiria thinks Jabone will go and find them but he will not. If he should he will find them dead which I do not want for him." And then she just started crying and she walked even faster as if walking faster might leave her grief behind her. She felt Pete's hand change in hers and she looked down; he had shifted.

"I was tired, mama." She stopped, bent down and kissed his cheek.

"I am sorry, son. I should not have walked so fast."

Seeing the child had shifted the Jethriks behind them gasped. She turned on them and said in their language as much to hide what she was saying from her son as so they would understand her. "How dare you! Where do you think you are? This is the Katabull compound. This is our home; you are here as our guests. My child has had a hard day, he is tired, and he shifted. We have all had a very hard day, not just you." She glared at Persius with meaning. "We will have none of your petty prejudices here. Women are equal to men and the Katabull are equal to humans—that is the land you are in now. If you have a problem with that, I will have Vony march you through the compound out the gates and put you on the road pointed away from us."

"Persius can't understand you," Hellibolt whispered in her ear. "I changed his Jethrik to Kartik. I have, however, already had this talk with him and I will remind him later." He took her arm and started her walking again. He looked around her at Pete who had dropped her hand and was now running ahead of them. "Pete is an odd name for a Katabull."

"His real name is Petrid which they all tell me is worse. We tried to change his name to Tweed but it didn't stick."

"Is it normal for them to be able to shift so young?"

Jena sniffled and Hellibolt handed her a handkerchief which stopped her from wiping her nose on her arm then her arm on her dress. "Tarius puts a sword in our cub's hands as soon as they can waddle and teaches them to shift as soon as they can run without bumping into things. She has never said, but I think it is because she didn't know how to shift when her pack was attacked. I think she believes that if she could have shifted she could have at least protected herself. So she teaches our cubs to shift way before they really know what to do with all that power because she wants them to be safe."

"I can tell looking at you that Tarius has given you half her years. You know I wouldn't cast the spell...."

"Unless she would ask me first. Yes, I know. Neither would Jazel but Jestia.... Well Jestia would have dived into the lava head first if Tarius told her to. Half her years is nothing, wait till you see what else she gave me." Jena smiled and she was able to once again push her grief away.

"Pete, leave that monkey alone!"

**When they went through** the gates Persius's breath caught in his chest. It was almost exactly like it was in his dream except he had clothes on and.... *So much more color. Flowers everywhere and fruit hanging in trees, each set of huts has its own gardens its own trees. And there are so many of them in every direction and the wall.... Everywhere I look.* He shut his eyes for a minute. In the dream there was a lake, and close to the lake vast pasture lands. He turned opened his eyes and there it was—a huge lake barely visible through a line of trees beyond pastures. *There is no horse shit in the streets, no smell of human waste, just the smell of ocean and flowers and that is what Kasiria told me. But I have seen this place in my dreams. If I had drawn a picture of one of these huts it would have been exactly what I'm seeing up to and including the rain barrels everywhere I look. It's all very primitive and yet it's not at all, it is an illusion. These people have a very complex society and choose to live simply. A huge tidal wave hit less than two days ago and they are already repairing the damage and.... Their leader isn't even here. She has set this place up so that it runs itself.*

"Pete, I said leave the monkeys alone!" Jena yelled at the boy Katabull who was half way up a tree. "Get back down here. If you must run off some steam, go and find your fadra and bring him back to our fire." The boy climbed down and took off in the direction of the lake. "Pete, do NOT go into the water."

"I won't, Mama."

A young man came running up to her with a monkey on his shoulder. "Jena, Jillest is having her cub...."

"Can Elise...."

"Elise is up to her elbows in a mare turning a foal."

"I must go to the Great Hall and deliver a baby. Vony, come with me. Laz, please take these men to our fire pour some milk into the soup and get them all something to eat. I will be there as soon as I can." Laz nodded and Jena and Vony took off at a brisk pace.

"I'm going to talk to Tarius about this whole not using horses in the compound thing. These last two days have nearly killed me," Jena mumbled. Her legs were burning. "Of course there are only about a dozen humans left in the whole compound, and you Katabull don't have any problem walking everywhere back and forth, back and forth...."

"Jena, the Great Leader did say in emergencies we could use horses, and I'm pretty sure all of today and yesterday would count as an emergency," Vony said.

Jena smacked herself in the head with her palm. "Of course. If we get there and they have brought an extra pair of hands for me, would you kindly go to my huts and have Laz or Hared saddle my horse to ride and bring her to the Great Hall?"

"I will." Vony smiled and looked at her feet.

"What?" Jena asked.

"Even with your coloring and your size I think most of us forget you are not Katabull."

"Thank you, Vony." Jena was actually very touched. When they had first moved to what was then called the Valley of the Katabull, the Marching Night had been pretty evenly split between humans and Katabull. But that was a long time ago and humans aged so much faster than Katabull. As the human members of the Marching Night reached ages where they could no longer fight they moved out of the compound and not too surprisingly their children left with them. They went back to where they had extended family. It had happened slowly over time till after the battle in the cave. After that nearly all of the remaining human members of the Marching Night had decided they were too old to fight. It was a horrific battle that had tested them all and.... Many had to admit they didn't have the speed or the agility needed to continue to fight with the Marching Night.

She still missed some of them, but most days Jena, too, forgot she wasn't the Katabull.

***Laz kept looking back at*** him as he led the way. Laz looked familiar to Persius. He moved up beside him and whispered, "You know who I am, don't you?" The monkey looked down at him before the Katabull did, and it was a bit off putting, but the boy smiled at him.

"I have met you briefly, and since Jabone is my step brother I know who Kasiria's father is. I hold you no grudge. The Great Leader tells a wonderful story in which it is only your bravery that saves her and my mother and father—really all of the Marching Night. My fadra died in the battle, and it is only because of you that I have my mother and father—and Tarius. However you should know that neither Jena nor Harris will stay when she tells that story. They hate you as do most of the Katabull in the compound in spite of it—which is why only a handful of us know you are Kasiria's father."

Persius nodded. "Where is Tarius?"

"In Montero," he said simply.

"And Jena is in charge?"

The Katabull smiled. "She normally is; she just lets Tarius

pretend to be."

Hellibolt laughed and slapped the boy on the back, upsetting the monkey. "How are your mother and father, Laz?" Hellibolt asked.

"They are well." He looked at Persius. "They can tell you more when they see you."

Persius got the idea that even though the boy didn't hold him any grudge he also didn't want to talk about his family in front of him.

Laz smiled and pointed. "I see that Kasiria is at the Great Leader's fire."

In the distance he could just make out a blond head.

"And Jabone?"

Laz frowned. "He also has gone to Montero."

Persius was relieved he would get to see his daughter and his grandson without the constant scowl of his huge Katabull son-in-law.

**Kasiria stirred the soup** and looked over to make sure Darian wasn't trying to take off with her son. He wasn't; he was just holding him in his lap rocking him to and fro. The cub was chuffing, so he was happy.

"I thought you weren't allowed to cook," Kaden said with a laugh. He was holding Diana who had woken up in a mood. She was wet so he changed her, she was hungry so Kasiria fed her, and now she seemed more than happy to let Kaden hold her.

"I'm not cooking I'm stirring, and well I don't think I'm that bad a cook. I just think they are all that good. That is the worst thing about the pack of the Marching Night. They are all so good at everything," Kasiria said. She put the spoon down on the small table which sat next to the fire pit and put the lid back on the pot. Something made her look down the road. She started to go right back to talking to Kaden but then realized what she was seeing—many white heads bobbing along, which wasn't normal at all for the Kartik. She focused then brought up her Katabull eyes and then she could clearly see what simply could not be. "That.... That is my father and the wizard."

Kaden turned to look where she was looking. No doubt all he could see were bobbing white heads. "What would the king be doing here?"

"I'm sure I don't know, but it rather explains the dead Sword Masters all over the beach." Kasiria looked at her son and suddenly panicked. "Kaden, give me Diana."

"Alright but hold her head you know how mad Jena gets...."

"Just hand her here. Take Darian and Arvon and go to the cubs' room."

Kaden walked over to her but didn't move to hand her the baby. "Kasiria, what are you doing?"

"Just give me the cub and take my cub...."

"Kasiria, he's going to find out. Jena is never...."

"Jena is delivering a baby she could be gone hours."

"Kasiria...."

"Just give me that cub and go. I don't want my son judged by him or anyone else." Kaden finally handed her Diana.

"This is a very bad idea, Kasiria. I don't care what he or anyone else thinks of Arvon, you shouldn't either. You know that Jabone will not understand what you're doing at all...."

"Just take him and Darian and go inside, please Kaden."

He nodded walked over and said to Darian, "Let's take Arvon into your room to play."

Darian nodded and Kaden took Arvon and followed Darian into the house, but not before giving her a look that would boil mud.

Diana fussed at her no doubt because she didn't like the way she was being held. She was a very picky baby. Kasiria looked at her sister-in-law. She was very pretty, but not so pretty that she couldn't be a boy.

# Chapter 15

**Jabone got to Jazel's** before the others. He jumped off his poor horse and ran in. He saw Jazel sitting at a back table nursing a cup of tea, she didn't look well.

"Jazel...."

"Your madra is sitting by the spring in the sun."

"Thanks." He ran past her and all the way down the hall. The springs were all fenced and could only be reached by going through the inns around them. He reached the door to the spring and stopped. He tried to compose himself; he didn't want to show his madra his belly. She would need him to be strong. He took in a deep breath and opened the door. Her back was to him. Radkin was with her, and so were the Queen, Jestia and Ufalla. Ufalla saw him and came running to him. She hugged him and he happily hugged her back.

"They are going to live, but steel yourself, for neither of them look like themselves," she whispered in his ear. Then she started to cry.

He held her tight and whispered in her ear, "Is there any word about my fathers?"

She shook her head no and cried harder. Jabone held her and walked towards the others carrying her with him. He knew it must look ridiculous when he saw Radkin smile at him, but he didn't care. Ufalla needed him, but right then probably not as much as he needed her.

"I smell my son," his madra said, and she turned her head which seemed like it was too much of an effort for her. "What are you doing here?"

Jabone looked at her in confusion, and Radkin caught his eye and shook her head.

He looked at his madra and fought his own tears. She looked as if she'd taken a beating; her eyes were swollen and bruised looking, her skin ashen.

"Mother asked me to come and check on you, to come get

you. They would not let her come and bring your cubs."

"My cubs should not be here, *you* should not be here. Your little brother should not be here for sure. Your mother sure as the Nameless One hates the pompous should not be here to see me like this."

Jabone put Ufalla down and Ufalla untangled herself from him. He walked over in front of his madra fell to his knees and then hugged her. She hugged him back. "I will be fine; I just need rest. In the morning if I no longer look like walking death you will take me back to your mother."

"My mother doesn't care what you look like. She wants you to come home. She wanted to go to you, and Radkin would not allow it."

His madra took his chin in her hand and forced him to look at her even as Rimmy and Harris joined them and Ufalla did to her father what she had done to him only moments before. Tarius looked at them briefly and then back at him.

"Has everyone abandoned your mother and the compound to come after me? What is going on?"

Jabone could see the moment in which his madra figured out what was wrong even before she spoke, for she looked around and appeared to count heads. "Where are Arvon and Dustan? They live here; they would have come.... Is that what everyone has been whispering about? Where are they?"

"They went up the mountain to hunt yesterday morning," Radkin said.

"You.... That's why you were so far behind Hestia. That's who you were looking for, and if you didn't find them...." His madra took in a deep breath and let it out.

Jabone moved his head till it was on her shoulder. He could neither bear to look at her face or contain his own pain. He started to cry to spite of his best efforts and his madra patted his back.

"Rimmy and Jabone and I will go look for them," Harris said.

"I will go with you so that you don't look anywhere I have already looked," Radkin offered.

"Do you want to go?" his madra whispered in his ear so low only he could hear.

He turned his head so that he could whisper to her, "Madra, if I don't go I will always wonder, but I am sure they are gone."

He cried all the harder, and his madra hugged him tighter to her, but it didn't feel like her because her strength was not there.

"Then go, and when you get done no matter the hour bring me home to your mother."

He sniffled, let go of her and stood up. He wiped his nose on his sleeve and started to leave. Ufalla handed him a towel and he took it.

He got a look at Jestia who was laying on a lounge, and if anything she looked worse than his madra did.

"Jestia, you look like ass," he croaked out.

She smiled at him. "You've always wanted to say that and have it be true, haven't you? Ufalla go with them."

"But Jestia...."

"Go with them, please. I'm fine and I'd like to have a few minutes without you looking at me as if I'm going to die at any moment."

"And she knows I need you," Jabone whispered to Ufalla.

Ufalla nodded and they left.

**Tarius worked at getting** to her feet took her robe off and got back into the spring. She dipped her face in the water brought it out and left it dripping. She could still barely walk; she needed to rebuild herself and how could she do that if Arvon and Dustan were dead? *They died together in a horrible hunting accident at least there is that. But my son and my friends and my family are going to look all over that mountain, and if they were alive they would be here with me, and if they could be found Radkin would have already found them. So they are either under the mountain or under the lava and either way they are dead. Last night nearly killed Jestia and I, and we didn't save Arvon and Dustan. We saved the people of Montero and possibly a handful of other villages, but we nearly killed ourselves, and my loved ones would have been safer if I'd been in the compound, and part of my family are dead. My sons have lost their fathers and it will be easy for Darian to just replace them with Rimmy and Hared; in all ways that matter he already has. But Arvon was Jabone's Fadra. His blood and mine run through our son and our grandson, and Dustan was his father who loved him and who he loved and he will not be able to replace them any more than I ever* *found a replacement for my father. Though Jena's father came close.... You know till he begged the king to put an arrow in me for dirtying his daughter in unnatural ways.*

Jestia slid into the spring with Hestia's help and said, "You know this will not work, right?"

"What?"

"No matter how much we soak and will it to be we are not going to heal instantly."

Tarius grinned. "No matter how much I need to?"

"Nope, sorry." Jestia moved to the side of the pool and laid her head back against the edge of it. Hestia went back to the small table she was sitting at and appeared to go back to work. "I can barely hold my head up, how about you?"

"Not for long stretches of time. Jestia, do you know are they dead?"

"I think you know as well as I do." Jestia sighed. "When Jabone named the cub Arvon I had a vision, and in it Arvon and Dustan tried to follow you but their way was cut off, and then they weren't there anymore."

Tarius wished she could say she had no idea what that meant but it made perfect sense. Hestia was being awful quiet, which meant she'd known since early that morning that Arvon and Dustan were missing and probably dead. "I can barely move. I hurt everywhere, and what am I supposed to do with the knowledge that they are dead? Dustan was my good friend, my protégé, but Arvon was like a brother to me."

"And the only man you ever did it with, am I right?" Jestia asked with a grin.

"Jestia, for the gods' sake," Hestia scolded from where she was obviously only pretending to look at a map one of her people had brought her.

"Don't act like you don't want to know, Mother." Jestia looked at Tarius and said, "Well?"

"You are right," Tarius said.

"And what was that like?" Jestia asked.

"Gods and spiders, Jestia, the man is missing presumed dead," Hestia said.

"And I'm thinking of him as I should be." Jestia looked at Tarius again. "Well?"

Tarius shrugged. "Arvon thought it was like this magical moment, but the whole time I was just wishing he would hurry up and finish so that I could get a bath and go to bed." She grinned then. "I guess it was kind of magic because I got pregnant with Jabone and only had to suffer through it once.

"That is how I've always found sex with men to be," Hestia said and chuckled.

"So were you always queer, Mother?" Jestia asked.

"Daughter, is there no question you will not ask at any time?" Hestia asked, shaking her head in disbelief, but she was smiling no doubt because Jestia was starting to act like Jestia again.

"I feel like crap. I don't want to be all sad and think about people we all loved who are now dead. I'd rather talk about anything else. I'd especially like to talk about your sexuality as I've wondered ever since I caught you up to your wrist in Radkin."

"Jestia that.... Isn't even true."

"Oh that's right she was getting ready to go down on you."

Tarius laughed. Hestia glared at her and Tarius smiled and shrugged. "I'm trying to heal completely in however long it's going to take them to come back and tell us what we already know. Anything at all that takes me away from the picture of Arvon and Dustan burning to death in a river of lava is fine with me."

"So come on, Mother, were you always queer or did someone turn you the way Ufalla turned me?"

Tarius laughed and shook her head. "The way I heard the story you asked her to have sex with you."

"No, I asked if she wanted to have it with me. There is a big difference," Jestia said with a smile. "Then she was so good at it that I never wanted to even look at a man again."

Hestia laughed. "I don't think that means she made you queer, Jestia."

"If she'd done a bad job I wouldn't be with her, so.... What about you?"

Tarius looked at Hestia expectantly and Hestia actually blushed.

"From the first time I was old enough to fantasize about sex it was always with women, but I knew that wasn't going to be allowed. I got caught with one of the servant girls in my room when I was thirteen doing...things. My parents made it clear that I was the heir to the throne and that wasn't going to be allowed. Besides, I was already betrothed to Dirk. As punishment they had a servant who enjoyed the chore much too much beat me. When I became queen one of the first things I did was have that man killed; he was an obvious pervert. After the beating my parents told me if they caught me again they would put a guard on me. They caught me again and they put a guard on me and I slept with her for quite a while till they caught me and sent her away. I was broken hearted. Then my father died and they rushed my marriage to Dirk and sat me on the throne at sixteen. I was the queen and I had all these crushing responsibilities and the best way to do the job was just to not feel the way my mother and father never felt anything. I just turned off the part of myself that wanted anything for myself...." She looked at Tarius. "Dirk thought the sex was wonderful and I was mostly thinking, 'Are you done yet? Get off of me.' But I had a duty to do and I did it. Then you walked into my throne room...."

"Don't blame Tarius for making you queer. You'd already been banging half the staff." Jestia laughed.

"Three girls is hardly half the staff. Are you going to let me tell my story or not?"

"Sorry. Though now I think about it Tarius obviously made Jena queer."

"Really Jestia? Because every time Jena was with a man she was completely creeped out which I don't think a straight woman would be. Let your mother tell her story."

"Tarius walked in and she was fantastic as she still is, and immediately I started to think things I had worked hard at not thinking. I made myself not think it. At the time there were important, urgent things that needed my attention. The next morning I was walking in the garden trying to clear my head and unthink all the dreams I'd had that night and who should I run into but Jena? I asked her how someone like her wound up with someone like you; at the time she was still new to our land and thought I meant it as some insult against you. But the truth is that—while I meant no insult to her—I wondered how such an ordinary woman like Jena—and of course I hadn't known her long enough to know there is nothing at all ordinary about her—wound up completely capturing the heart of someone as fabulous as you."

"So you crushed on Tarius like every queer woman on the island," Jestia said.

"Let your mother tell her story," Tarius said, and splashed Jestia in the face.

"Jena told me your whole story and when she did two things became clear: I needed to do something I wanted to do; and I needed to make things work with Dirk."

"But.... That doesn't make any sense at all," Jestia said.

"Yes it does because of the stupid thing you said earlier. Jena was with me because she thought I was a man, but even when she knew I wasn't a man she came to me because she loved me. Your mother thought I made Jena queer, and if I could make her queer then she thought she could 'unqueer' herself."

"Oh," Jestia said. Tarius splashed her again, and this time Jestia splashed her back. "I will try to restrain myself. Do go on, Mother."

"Now I had seen Radkin and thought her very attractive, but I was working hard at not having those feelings. Then as we were going to the Great War, well.... On a ship quarters are close and I was walking past her one day and got a whiff of her. As I'm sure you have noticed, the Katabull smell fantastic. I was aroused as I'd never been before. From that moment on she was all I could think about and I used every excuse to be close to her. We became friends; we would talk and have these wonderful conversations, and.... If my parents so wanted me to be straight then why did they pick someone as boring as Dirk for me? At the end of the day if any man were capable of 'unqueering' me, he had none of the qualities that could have done it. Him I couldn't stand talking to; his very demeanor annoyed me. Radkin and I could just talk for hours, still can. Anyway one day Radkin and I wound up alone and we kissed and she pushed me away and took off. After that I stayed away from her because I had a duty I couldn't perform if I were with her, and I knew her so well by then I knew she loved her wife and that I could never really have her. That being the case.... It was easy to go home and have kids and run the country and just not think about it anymore. So to answer your question, yes, I have always been a lover of women."

"What about you, Tarius?" Jestia asked.

"What about me?" Tarius didn't understand the question, and she would die with the secret that the only reason she called for Radkin that day was that she saw her getting ready to bang the queen. Had Tarius not stopped them it would have destroyed Irvana and Radkin's whole family and Jestia wouldn't be here at all. Ultimately Hestia and Radkin would have wound up hating each other. It really was all about timing.

"When did you know?"

"Jestia, I am third sex."

Jestia shrugged, obviously not knowing why it mattered.

"I have always known, Jestia. You of all people should know that my soul is as much male as it is female. My father used to tell a story that he knew when I was less than two because I kept trying to stand to pee." She smiled. "Ufalla did, too, but I don't think she is third sex, just butch. I think she did it because after all Tarius and Jabone did and she always had to do everything they did."

"Are you really going back to the compound today?" Jestia asked Tarius.

"Yes, if nothing else I will have to plan Arvon and Dustan's memorial."

**Persius nearly ran the** last few feet. Kasiria smiled at him, he looked at the baby in her arms and hugged her baby and all. She kissed his cheek.

"Father, what a surprise and how good it is to see you alive and all."

He stepped back and looked at the baby. "So this is my grandson." He beamed a huge smile and took a finger and brushed some of the black hair off the baby's face.

"Arvon," Kasiria said. Behind her father Laz gave her a look that would peel a winter squash.

"He is very dark but look at those blue, blue eyes." Her father laughed. "He has Tarius's scowl."

Hellibolt walked up beside her and whispered in her ear so close for a minute he might have been a Kartik and said, "That baby is neither male nor your child."

"Shut up, old man," Kasiria hissed.

"Hellibolt, don't torment Kasiria."

"I'm going to put milk in the soup like Jena told me to," Laz said out loud, then mouthed the words, "You really are crazy" in Kasiria's direction. He went into the house and came out with a jar of milk. He looked at the number of men and dumped the whole thing in and started to stir it. "You there." he pointed to one of the men and the man nodded. "Please stir this so it doesn't scorch. Kasiria why don't you help me get the bowls?"

Kasiria started to follow him in and Persius put his hand on her shoulder.

"Kasiria, could I hold my grandson?"

Kasiria saw Laz shaking his head violently no and she said quickly, "He really doesn't like strangers."

"Just for a minute while you go inside." Kasiria handed Diana to her father and of all days Diana picked that one not to be upset by strangers at all. "See he knows I'm not a stranger." Then he started to sit on the Katabull throne.

"Do not sit there!" Laz boomed. "That is the Great Leader's throne."

Persius nodded and moved to one of the other chairs and sat down. Kasiria followed Laz into the house where he took her by the shoulders, shook her till her teeth rattled and whispered, "What the hell is wrong with you?" To make matters worse the monkey was chattering at her, too. "You are pretending Jena and Hared and Tarius's baby girl is your son? You are crazier than I thought you were. Where is your son?"

"In the boys' bedroom with Darian and Kaden," she whispered back.

"It's not bad enough that you deny your own cub, Jabone's cub, but you have stuck Jena's only blood child in the arms of the man she hates most in this world. She will kill you. She will kill me for allowing it."

"I can't believe you are this afraid of Jena," Kasiria said, looking for and finding all the bowls and spoons in the house.

"First, Jena can be really mean when she is pissed off. Second, what is the sense of this? You cannot hide Arvon for.... How long? How long do you think he will be here? Is he leaving in the next few minutes? Do you think he will leave before Jabone returns with Tarius? Before Hared gets back from the lake and asks why some stranger is holding his daughter? Will he be gone before Jena gets done birthing Jillest's baby...."

"Jillest is having her cub! That's nice...."

"Don't change the subject, Kasiria. Can you not see that you have done this horrible thing for nothing?"

"Why is it such a horrible thing?" Kasiria asked.

"Where would you like me to start?" Laz said. He took the bowls and spoons from her and went outside. By the time she got there he was scoping out soup for everyone. The men with her father and the wizard had already found seats around the fire and were happily eating. No doubt noticing that he'd dropped a fish head into one of the bowls Laz announced, "It is our custom that the person who gets a fish head will have a lucky day." Kasiria cut him a look and he whispered at her, "If you can make up shit so can I."

Kasiria looked up and saw Hared coming, Pete all catted-out by his side. She was busy trying to think of some reason to get rid of him before he could reach them when Vony ran over to Hared and the next thing Kasiria knew he and Pete were on their way to the pasture. She sighed with relief.

Her father smiled at her from where he sat. "He has fallen to sleep."

"You can lay him in his cradle."

"That's alright I just want to hold him for a while."

"Of course he does," Laz hissed at her.

"He's a stout lad," Persius said.

"I'm sure the Great Leader would love to know that," Laz whispered in her ear, but apparently he was in no hurry to tell the truth.

*He's right, what am I doing? I can't hide my son from him, it's just wrong. And handing him Jena's baby? Laz is right; Jena will kill me.* One of the men had finished his soup and was almost asleep. She knew how she could hold off on the truth at least for a while longer. "You must all be exhausted. When you have finished eating Laz will show you the communal latrines, the showers, and a hut where you can sleep."

"I will?"

"Yes, Laz, you will. I know you know which houses are now vacant."

"You know, if I don't have to be here when Jena gets back that's fine with me." Laz looked at them all expectantly.

"Let me have the baby and you can get something to eat, and then go get some rest. You look exhausted," Kasiria said to her father.

"I have been sick most of the day and could not even think of eating. As for being tired I find that holding my grandson has revitalized me. That and seeing you my dear girl. How I have missed you."

"Surely you could use some rest, Father after your ordeal."

"Come on let's go if you're going," Laz said, hustling the men to get up. When Kasiria saw Hared leading Pete on Jena's horse in the direction of the Great Hall she knew why. They were bringing Jena her horse. Which meant she could be home in seconds after the cub was born. The men all seemed ready to get a shower and a bed. Except her father who just sat there beaming over her sister-in-law, and Hellibolt who just sat there giving her a knowing smile and shaking his head.

Laz gathered up the sailors and beat a hasty retreat.

Hellibolt got up went to the fire and ladled himself out another bowl of soup. "I must say Kartik cooks have a fantastic sense of how to use spice. This is a simple fish and vegetable chowder yet it is exquisite."

"The food is very good here," Kasiria said nervously looking at her father. "I'll be back in a second; I'm just going to take Darian a bowl of soup." Kasiria ladled out a bowl. She ran into the house and ran back to Darian and Pete's room. Arvon was lying in the middle of Darian's bed. Darian was sitting beside him holding his hand above the cubs face and jiggling his fingers the cub was chuffing and trying to grab Darian's chubby little fingers. "Darian I brought you some soup."

"Mama says no food in here."

"It will be fine for today."

Darian got up and took the bowl of soup from Kasiria. He made a face. "There is a head in my soup."

"What a lucky day for you. Laz said whoever gets a fish head will have a good day."

"Do I have to eat the fish head to get the luck?" Darian asked.

"No, you do not," Kasiria said, and Darian sat down on the little chair Tarius had made for him that looked just like a miniature version of the Katabull throne.

Kaden was sitting on Pete's bed watching them and he turned to give her a disapproving look the three-year-old could have read. "Oh, Kaden, you were right. What have I done?"

"You mean besides deny your son? Oh, I don't know what about the crass irony of telling your father that Tarius's daughter is your son." Kasiria didn't understand what he meant. "Are you really that dense, Kasiria? Tarius hid as a man in your father's army, a crime for which he nearly killed her..."

"And now I have told him Diana is a boy. Tell me how to fix it."

"Kasiria!" Jena boomed.

Kaden shook his head. "I think it may be a little late."

*Jena jumped off her* horse ran over and demanded of him, "Hand me my cub at once!"

Persius stood and handed her the sleeping baby.

Jena hugged the infant to her as if she'd saved him from some horrid death.

"Jena, I know how you feel about me and why, but surely we can share our grandson," Persius said.

"Grandson! Persius, this is not Arvon. Kasiria!" Jena looked at him and shook her head. "This is my child, Persius, mine! My daughter in fact."

Hared ran up with Pete then. "Is something wrong?"

"He was holding our child," Jena said. "He almost killed Tarius and he was holding our child."

"That was a long time ago. He also saved her, Jena, he saved you all," Hared said gently. "I can tell he meant our child no harm."

"Kasiria told him Diana was Arvon," Jena said, and Persius tread carefully because he could tell Jena was hot and the child's father was huge. Besides if he pissed off Jena he pissed of Tarius by default, and he was standing in the middle of a camp full of Katabull who hated him. If he'd ever felt more vulnerable he couldn't draw the where or why of it to mind.

"I am sorry. I thought I saw Tarius in the infant's face," Persius said, "and I don't understand why Kasiria would lie."

Kasiria walked out of the house then carrying a baby wrapped in a blanket though it was hardly cool enough to warrant it. "That baby looks like Tarius because she is Tarius and Jena...and Hared's cub. She has all three of their bloods coursing through her. I am so sorry, Jena. So sorry on all counts. I lied because I am the worst kind of coward. My son also looks like Tarius and Jabone and me, but not when we are human. He looks like us when we are Katabull. Because our son, mine and Jabone's, has a Katabull primary form."

She uncovered him then and Persius didn't have to ask what she meant. The baby was a perfect little Katabull. He looked from the baby to Pete and back again. The only difference was that the baby was covered in blond fur and was smaller. The cub looked at Persius and flashed him an infectious grin. Persius laughed walked over and took the baby from Kasiria. He kissed Kasiria on the forehead and then he kissed the baby on his cheek. He looked at her and sniffled. "He is perfect, Kasiria, just perfect." He looked at Jena and smiled. "When she told me your baby was my grandson I have to admit I thought he was too pretty. She is a beautiful baby, Jena, but this, this is a real boy!"

**There wasn't even a hint** of wildlife on the mountain, not a squirrel not a bird not even a tiny monkey. Nothing alive— everything had left, and if his fathers had been alive they would have left, too.

After Radkin had explained where she had already looked they had split up but two hours had passed and they would now all be working their way back to town.

Ufalla rode up beside him. "They died together in a horrible hunting accident," she reminded him.

He nodded silently. "They will never get to see my son grow up. I will never get to talk to them again, and when last I saw them I rushed the visit because I had things I thought were more important to do...."

"Jabone, if we knew the day we would die we would make sure that we were doing that which we most loved. We know they died hunting. Perhaps yesterday was the best day of their lives, maybe they rose early made love had a wonderful breakfast then had an amazing ride up the mountain in the morning. You know what that's like; most of the world is asleep and it's just you and the jungle and the sun is starting to rise but you can still see the moons and you can tell something is about to happen. And then *boom!* and the mountain falls on them and they're dead. It is quick but story-worthy, and neither has to live without the other. We are only sad for ourselves because we will miss them."

"You are right."

"I am? Are you sure because I have lived with Jestia so long now that I'm unaccustomed to ever being right."

Jabone laughed. "I didn't know what she had done; I didn't understand why they were both so wrecked till I saw that trench full of hardened lava. That kind of power.... When I think what those three witches did."

"Four Jabone, four witches. That's why Jestia took your madra; she could not have done it without her. I find I am jealous of this connection between them more than I would be if they were banging all crap out of each other."

"You don't mean that, Ufalla, and you shouldn't have said that because now I have an ugly picture of my madra and your wife." Jabone made a face.

"Funny it's not an ugly picture in my head." Ufalla looked at him with a crooked grin. "If they were having an affair, that I'd know how to deal with. If it was just a question of physical attraction I would just work a little harder and win my woman's affection back. I'd get my ass kicked trying to kick Tarius's and even though I lost it would all blow over because I know Jestia loves me. But this thing between them, it's not something I can do anything about. It's like I'm on the outside. It's something they have that I can never be part of. Does it not bother your mother?"

"Not even when Jestia spirited my madra away and left mother to run the compound. Even then she recognized that Jestia wouldn't have taken her unless she needed her. Because of Jestia my mother has the baby she always wanted. I don't think she sees their connection as any sort of threat at all, and do you know why Ufalla?"

Ufalla shook her head.

"Because even though she no longer looks it, my mother is older than we are and wiser. Maybe when you get worried about this thing that's what you should remember that my mother is older and wiser and she isn't bothered by it at all. Believe me, my mother is a very, very jealous woman. She accepted long ago that my madra was different from her and that because of it there were things she did and said that she was never going to understand. And my madra is only a Katabull; your Jestia is a powerful magic user and heir to the Kartik throne. Just accept what is true—that she loves you with all her heart, and that there are things she will say and things she will do that you will never understand. That sometimes you will feel left out but just when you are sure she doesn't need you she will come and grab you and try to explain to you things you just don't get."

Ufalla nodded turned to him and said, "I should be cheering you up."

"We are cheering each other up. You loved my fathers, too and Jestia almost killed herself, and our beautiful Great Mountain has been cut off and what is left is covered in ash. And I will never be Great Leader and do you know why?"

"No."

"Because I want to be. I *want* to be Great Leader or at least I thought I wanted to be. It wasn't till I left today that I realized everyone probably expected that I should step up and lead in my madra's absence. They probably thought that when Jestia took my madra I would take control and make sure things got done. But no I just followed. I had no ideas; I froze. I let my mother, Harris, Kasiria, Rimmy, Waden and basically everyone but me step up and run things. I didn't have the will to be responsible for anything. I want them to follow me around with a throne and call me Great Leader, but I don't want to do the work and you know what?" Jabone sniffed a bit and wiped at his eye. "My fadra said I got that from him and now he's gone. Whenever my stupid pride rears its ugly head it will remind me of him, and I will put it down but not feel bad about it."

**They were all sitting** around Jazel's dining room picking at the excellent meal Helen had prepared for them. Tarius was done pretending to eat and ready to go home. If they left right that minute they would be getting there after dark. She knew what they were doing; they were purposely stalling her so that she would wait till morning. "I'm going home. Pour my tired ass into a wagon and let's go already."

"Madra, you can hardly walk and as you said we will get there in the dark. That being the case why not leave in the morning when you've had another good night's sleep?"

"Because I want to go home." She thought for a minute tried to shift and couldn't. "Dammit all, as the Katabull I could do it just fine; ride my own horse be there in half the time."

"What about a half a bottle of rum?" Harris said under his breath with a smile.

She looked at him.

"Now wait a minute, Tarius, I was just remembering something and.... None of us want to deal with a drunk Katabull all the way back to the compound, and there will be singing and none of us want that, do we?"

"Here." Jazel handed her a bottle of rum. Harris gave Jazel a dirty look. "You know she's going to do it anyway. I'm tired; I'm ready for all of you people to go. You lot go to the compound and Jestia and Ufalla can take Eerin and Hestia and Radkin to their own inn. My dining room can stop being the kingdom base of operations for this disaster, and I can finally get some rest."

Harris tried to grab the bottle out of Tarius's hand but she just moved and downed half of it. He looked at her and shook his head. "Don't say I didn't warn you."

**They got fresh horses** saddled up and took off—Jabone, Harris, Rimmy, and his madra. He had never seen her drunk. He'd been drunk many times, but he'd never seen his madra drunk. The biggest trouble they had getting her on her horse was that she wouldn't quit hugging *everyone*, she even hugged Eerin and told him she loved him, and she hugged Helen and for reasons known only to his madra apologized for several minutes for never shagging her.

Now she was riding just fine but too fast for how obviously drunk she was and as Harris had warned them there was singing. His madra didn't sing, never had, and now he knew why. She was awful. No doubt for the same reason her voice was so deep. She'd had her throat cut when she was only a child; it had changed her voice and made it impossible to hit certain notes. Unfortunately it didn't stop her trying. To make matters worse the songs she sang were absurd Kartik sea shanties.

"And up went her pantaloons right up the mast, down came the captain flat on his ass, dancing on the kegs of ale without any pants."

"Yes there it is," Harris said where he road beside him. "That's the one my lovely wife knows as well that they sang the last time I saw her drunk when she was mostly trying to die from the arrow your father-in-law put in her side."

"A hell of a night, a hell of a night, both the moons were burning bright. The sky above the earth below someone stepped on the helmsman's toe he spilt his rum all over me went right between the crack ah my ass and looked jus' like I'd pissed ma pants," she sang, and to his amusement Rimmy then joined her in the chorus.

"And up went her pantaloons right up the mast and down came the captain flat on his ass, dancing on the kegs of ale without any pants."

Jabone laughed in spite of himself. "And to think I thought this trip home was going to be very somber."

"You know what, son? Neither of your father's would have wanted that for any of us."

**Persius and Hellibolt** had finally eaten and then allowed Laz to show them first to the public latrine and then to the showers. Persius couldn't help but be impressed. The public latrine was clean, and while it didn't smell good it did not smell bad. There were apparently a hundred of them spaced at regular intervals around the compound. Each unit had ten separate stalls. Pipes made of timber bamboo ran up the back to about ten feet above the roof apparently carting off part of the stink. Kasiria had explained that they used the leaves for wiping and then tossed them down the hole, and there was a bucket of ash in each stall. She explained that the natives got very angry when people didn't cover with the ash and wash their hands in the basins provided. Apparently covering was another reason it didn't smell as bad.

The showers were sheer genius. They were two stories tall, and the top story was all water barrels which filled with water caught off the roof. The first floor was all showers. The only down side for him was that it was not only communal but both sexes showered there and a gorgeous Katabull woman came in and showered while he and Hellibolt were showering and he got wood. Hellibolt had laughed at him, but the woman hadn't even noticed which made him feel worse than if she had. Then two Katabull men came in to shower and it was obvious why the woman hadn't even noticed him and he quickly threw a towel around his waist so as not to be judged and found wanting.

Laz then led them to a hut the rest of the men were apparently already staying in, which was in fact right next door to Kasiria's. "I don't know your ways, but we don't like to be separated from our kin when we are away from home, so I have put you next to Kasiria and Jabone in a hut like the Great Leaders. It was owned by a cross-paired family who had four cubs, so there are just enough beds."

Apparently the young Katabull's idea of "just enough beds" had two of the sailors sharing a double bed and him sharing one with Hellibolt. The huts were very primitive; the walls were made of mud and sticks and the floors were poured concrete. If he had to share, at least the bed was a good size. The frame was made of logs. Rope was stretched back and forth and woven and then a simple mattress with a cotton cloth cover stuffed with what he could only guess at lay on top of the rope.

"It is very comfortable," Hellibolt said.

"Could you not turn it into two beds, wizard?" Persius asked.

"Not till after I've had a good night sleep." The wizard looked at the blue and yellow striped tunic they had given Persius to wear with bright yellow pants that made him feel like a court jester. Then he looked down at the long blue and green striped tunic they'd given him and said, "You know I think I like all the color. They are awfully good hosts these Katabull. I mean they feed us they give us clean clothes and a place to sleep.... Let you hold the Great Leader's baby."

Persius ran his hands down his face. "Did you see the look on Jena's face? You know I think that's as close as I've come to death since I outed Tarius in front of Jena."

Hellibolt stretched out. He was a tall man, but the bed was obviously built for Katabull because it was way longer than even Hellibolt needed. The wizard patted the bed beside him. "Go ahead; lay down. I think it's stuffed with raw cotton balls, quite nice. And you don't have to worry; I am not a cuddler."

Persius lay down. It was very comfortable, and he smiled as he looked at the ceiling.

"My grandson is a Katabull and I have been shipwrecked in a land filled with giants who hate me so tell me why is it that instead of feeling cursed I feel blessed."

"Because we should have died at sea and we didn't,"

Hellibolt suggested. "There is no way we should have ended up here; it cannot be random chance. It is meant to be. And Arvon is a beautiful baby. He is everything you have ever wanted to be from the moment you saw your first Katabull in that form."

"Yes," Persius said, "yes, I think you are right. What an adventure. I am sorry that my Sword Masters have died and that so many sailors died as well, but what a grand adventure and what was it that Tarius always used to say?" He thought for a minute then smiled broadly. "And if I die, I die. Only now do I know what that truly means."

**It had been a very long,** very weird day. Jena looked up the road one more time then went in her hut. Tarius wasn't coming home tonight. She was still carrying Diana just because she wanted her close. Darian had gone right to sleep as soon as Kasiria had taken Arvon from him. His nap had been cut short that day, and he was just exhausted. It was a big day for her, and it was for sure a big day for her three year old. Jena had left Hared to deal with Pete who first had to be talked out of his Katabull form and then had to run off some steam before he could even think of sleeping. In fact as she lay down in her bed with her cub she could hear Pete and Hared still talking sitting out by their fire. Hared knew Rimmy was alright, but part of her thought Hared might be waiting up to see if he was going to come home. Since Pete was up anyway it was as good an excuse as any to sit by the fire watching the road.

Jena looked at her cub for a few more minutes then rolled over and blew out the light. *How silly am I sleeping with my baby because I don't want to sleep alone. I should be glad Tarius isn't coming home tonight, glad that she's staying in Montero another day healing and resting. It's what makes the most sense, but I'm tired and I don't want to be Great Leader's wife, I want to go back to just being Jena. Persius is here and she's not and volcanos and tidal waves and whales on the beach and dead Sword Masters and I need her here with me. They need her. This baby needs her mother. She will be like Darian; she will call Tarius Madra and me Mother and Mamu and never get it right. While I didn't give birth to Darian and don't care what he calls me, I did give birth to Diana yet I find I still don't care what she calls me. Darian is right, though it doesn't match the story she made up for him, Tarius is his madra because he was really born when she picked him up off the cave floor.* Jena looked, saw the moonlight coming in the open shudders, then got up went to the boys room got Darian and moved him into bed with her, too. He didn't even stir till she lay down between him and Diana. Then he rolled over and patted her shoulder with his little hand.

"Thank you, Mama."

"What for baby?"

"Being my mama."

"Thank you for being my son." She kissed him on the forehead and he was out again…if he'd ever really been awake. She dried the tears out of her eyes and in seconds she was asleep.

She was aware of someone shaking her gently. "Jena, the guard on the tower just yelled. The Great Leader is coming home," he whispered, "Your horse is still saddled outside and…."

Jena moved from between her babies and jumped up. She was already dressed so she just threw on her boots and started for the door.

"I will watch the cubs," Hared said with a laugh at her back.

Jena nearly forgot to untie her horse from the hitching pole. When she had she jumped on the horse and spurred her into a hard run through the compound towards the gate. As she rode through the gate she could just make them out across the freshly-covered lava field. She could tell it was them and there was an awful noise coming from them that sounded like someone beating a dog. She rode towards them and when she got closer in the moonlight she could tell that Tarius was the Katabull. At first she thought this was good news because if Tarius could shift she must be better and just shifting would help her heal. Then she could tell that the ungodly sound she heard was Tarius attempting to sing.

When she got closer Tarius locked eyes with her and then Tarius jumped off her horse, nearly fell and Rimmy had to pull his horse to the left hard to keep from hitting her. Jena jumped off her horse and ran to meet her, and when she got close Tarius grabbed her and hugged her to her in a way that made it hard for her to breathe and she could smell the liquor on

Tarius's breath. "Jena, my love, my life, every song I sing, I sing to thee...."

"Madra, please stop singing. If you love my mother half as much as I think you do, you will *not* sing to her," Jabone said. He got off his horse and caught both she and Tarius's horses up.

Jena wrestled her head free enough that she could breathe and looked up at her mate. Now in all the time they had been together Tarius had only been drunk twice, and Jena had not seen her on either occasion, yet she knew that Tarius was snockered. She kissed her lips and Tarius kissed her back.

"She is drunk off her ass," Rimmy said. "I blame Harris."

Jena caught and held Tarius's eyes. "I don't care; she is home."

"It was the only way I could shift and they wouldn't let me go home, but do you know who says the word no to a drunken Katabull?" She kissed Jena in a way Jena would rather not be kissed in front of her brother and her grown son, then said. "Only a mad man tells a drunk Katabull no. Come take me home and have your way with me for I am consumed completely with my desire for you."

"Really? Because you are near crushing me already." Jena laughed. "And while I always have desire for you and though you will think me mad, tonight I will say no to you."

Tarius laughed, and pushed her to arm's length. She looked down at her and said, "I would take a bath. We could both take a bath; we could do it together."

"The only thing you are doing after torturing us all night with your singing and going off the trail six times and making us chase after you is drinking a tube of blood and going to bed," Rimmy said. "We are all tired, and you are not yet well."

"But you will stay with me right, Jena?" Tarius swayed on her feet. "You will stay with me?"

"Always, my love, always; I will stay with you." Jena dried her tears on the back of her hand.

Her son patted her back with his free hand and told her. "She has been mostly very funny, singing stupid songs and telling funny stories, but in between she talked of nothing but you and how she loves you, and frankly, Mother, it was very embarrassing." He chuckled, kissed her cheek and then moved over to Rimmy and started talking about how they were going to get Tarius back on her horse since apparently she was both too drunk to walk straight and stay upright for long and too weak to really be even standing. In her Katabull form and with nothing but moonlight Jena couldn't tell looking at her how bad she might be hurt.

Harris rode up closer to them. He had been born with a club foot—something that they all forgot about on most days including him, but he didn't do up and down on the horse well and kept it to a minimum for that reason. "I can see that you have no idea what Jabone just said."

"She doesn't care that I talked of how I love her; it is a beautiful thing," Tarius said releasing her and slinging her arms around in huge arcs. She almost fell and Jena grabbed and steadied her.

Jena looked at Harris; she didn't understand what his point was.

"Emphasis on *how* she loves you, Jena," Rimmy said.

"I feel I need a shower," Harris added, smiling down at her.

"I love you so much, Jena," Tarius hugged her again even as Jena blushed hot enough she probably glowed in the dark.

"And apparently very often," Harris said.

"And in many different positions," Rimmy added.

"Come on guys, please," Jabone said. "As it is I will never be able to lay my son on their bed again."

"Or on the Katabull throne, or the kitchen table, or the deck of any ship in the fleet or on the dock," Rimmy added helpfully.

"Tarius, for the love of the Nameless One, is nothing sacred?" Jena said.

Tarius bent down and kissed Jena's throat and she could feel Tarius's canines gently brush her skin. Then Tarius whispered in her ear, "You are sacred, every inch of you an altar on which I happily sacrifice myself."

And then Jena was the one kissing Tarius in a way that just a few moments ago had been embarrassing in front of her son and her brother.

**It had taken all of them** to get Tarius on her horse. And now they were leading the horse because Tarius wanted to go in different directions to check on different things. Jena just wanted to get her home and into bed before she woke the whole camp, and they were so close.

Tarius suddenly stiffened in her saddle and sniffed the air. "Oh no!" Jena sighed.

"What?" Harris asked.

"I had forgotten and well you are not going to believe what happened after you left...."

"I smell...." Tarius sniffed the air again. "...old friends." She slid off her horse though he was still moving and made a b-line for the huts they had put Persius and Hellibolt and the others in. "How did they get here?"

Jabone jumped off his horse and beat her to Tarius's side.

Jena ran to catch up, and said more to her son then her mate, "The tidal wave tore their ship apart and they wound up here in a lifeboat."

"Who?" Jabone asked.

"My dear old friends," Tarius said.

"Tarius, they are asleep. Why don't we take you home and you may see them in the morning."

"Nonsense I've not seen them in years, they will not mind." And of course Jabone just helped Tarius to walk in the direction she wanted to go instead of the way Jena was pulling her because he still hadn't learned how not to do his madra's bidding. Not too surprisingly the wizard was just inside the door as Tarius slammed it open. "Ah ha! You see he is waiting for me." She moved to hug him, and he gleefully hugged her back.

"Huge Kartik thug, let me go or you will break me," Hellibolt laughed.

Jabone apparently thought he had to explain his madra's condition to the wizard. "She was too weak to travel or shift on her own, so...."

"She is in her cups. Yes, I can see that."

Tarius smelled the air again. "I would know that smell anywhere. My dear friend."

Then she pushed away from Hellibolt and stumbled through the house towards the fathers hut.

Jena tried to stop her but missed and the hall was such that two Katabull could not walk down it together so Jabone was mostly following behind her with the back of her shirt balled up in his hand making sure she didn't go through a wall.

By the time Jena got there Tarius had already crawled into bed with the very startled king. Persius had apparently been sound asleep till a huge drunken Katabull crawled into bed with him and started hugging him. The look on his face said he thought he was about to be killed.

"It is Tarius," Hellibolt told him quickly, which calmed Persius not at all.

"My dear friend Persius!" She was cupping his head in her huge hands, and she kissed him on the forehead and then buried his face in her cleavage. "I love you so much. I do not know why we ever fought."

"He shot you with an arrow and had you dragged behind a horse," Hellibolt reminded helpfully.

"But that was so long ago, and I am fine now," Tarius said. She patted his head. The terrified look on Persius's face brought Jena great joy.

"What the hell is he doing here?" Jabone asked.

"That's what I said." Jena sighed. "Tarius, can we please go home now?"

"I want to visit with my friends."

Rimmy showed up and she knew Jabone and Rimmy could handle Tarius, still she was sure there was one thing that would get Tarius up and moving in the direction she wanted her to go. "If you come home with me right now I'll give you a little."

"Mother!" Jabone gasped.

But Tarius was off Persius and out of the bed and on her arm in seconds.

Jena just looked at Jabone and smiled.

"Much easier than wrestling her." She looked back at Hellibolt. "Sorry for the intrusion."

When they reached their fire Pete and Hared were anxiously waiting. Tarius grinned as soon as she saw the boy. "Pete, you should not be up so late."

"I waited for you, Madra."

"I am blessed to have the best cubs in the world," Tarius said, Jena helped her sit on her throne and then she sat beside her. Any energy Jena had left was just gone. Pete walked over to Tarius and Tarius picked him up and sat him in her lap. "Jabone came and got me, and you waited up for me."

"Madra, Mama took us to see a whale and they saved him and put him back in the water. We all got to pet him even sister. I learned a song you want to hear it?" Jena was surprised; that was more than Pete normally talked in a week.

"Sure but first let me teach you a song...."

"Madra, no!" Jabone said sternly. "He is only a child."

Tarius laughed wildly.

"Here," Rimmy handed Tarius a vial of blood and she glared at him and shook her head. "Come on, Tarius."

"I will feel like crap again if I'm human," Tarius said.

"Tarius, we are all tired and no one can handle you like this. We all just want to go to bed, and you know you will stay like this till you are sober anyway," Harris said. It was only then that Jena even saw he was there and she realized that he had put their horses away. She smiled at him and he smiled back. *Good ole Harris he is always here for us.*

"Drink it, Madra," Pete said. "It is for your own good."

Tarius laughed. "Cheeky cub, feed me my own words." She kissed his cheek, took the vial and emptied it. "Happy?"

"I will be happier when you are in bed," Jena said.

"Or in the shower," Harris laughed.

"Or behind it," Rimmy added.

"Or in Jazel's spring," Harris said.

"Pete, I said you could wait for your madra and father. Now go to bed," Hared said.

"I will take you." Rimmy walked over and took Pete from Tarius and carried him inside as Pete sang him his whale song.

"Harris and I would like to go to our wives our cubs and our beds, so please let us help you to bed," Jabone pleaded.

Rimmy walked back out then and said, "Hared and Jena and I can take care of Tarius. You two go home you've both been through enough.... You know, Tarius's singing, her sex stories...."

Jena stood up walked over and hugged Harris. "Thank you for everything, Harris."

"There is no place else I would have been and nothing else I would have done." He patted her back and walked away.

She hugged her son and whispered in his ear, "I know. I am not saying because I can't without crying, but I know and

I grieve with you. I love you my son. I have other cubs but none are any dearer to me than you; you were my first."

He bent down and whispered in her ear, "She didn't just sing stupid songs and tell sex stories. Mother, over and over she said she couldn't live a day without you. I thought at first that she was saying it to make me feel better about my fathers because they died together. Then I realized that she was very drunk, beyond the point of worrying about me or thinking about them. She kept saying it because it's true. I am Katabull and so I assume I understand things you admit you don't, and today I realized that you only really understand the meaning of these things when age brings wisdom. When she says she wouldn't live a day without you she doesn't mean she would curl up her toes and die from her grief, nor does she mean she isn't a whole person all by herself or that you aren't. What it means is that she isn't the same person without you, and who she is with you would be gone if you were, and I have seen her without you and it is true. And my fathers? If one had died the one that was left wouldn't be the person I knew. Like Radkin wasn't Radkin when Irvana died and isn't the same with Hestia as she was when she was with Irvana. Neither of them has to go through the pain of losing the one they loved and then losing themselves. And while we could argue all day that Radkin's life is better now than it ever was, since all the wishing in the world will not bring them back and they are dead, the fact they died doing something they loved and together brings me comfort."

"I'm afraid that what I have learned is that pain brings wisdom," Jena said.

He kissed her on the cheek and released her and she him. He walked over and kissed his madra on the forehead and she grabbed him and pulled him into her lap and held him. "My cub, you make me proud every day.... Well not every day, but most.... Well not most but many.... My cub many days you make me proud."

Jabone laughed and shook his head.

"I am tired, what do you want, Madra?" he said, but Jena noticed with a smile that he made no attempt to get away.

"I just want to hold my cub." She kissed his cheek then said, "You can never lose your family, son, never. You carry them with you in here." She put her fist over his heart. Then she put her fist over her own heart. "This is where I carry you and where I carry them. In here you will always be together."

Jabone looked at Jena then back at Tarius. He whispered something that Jena couldn't hear in Tarius's ear. She smiled, kissed him again, and then she released him and he got up and went home.

"Alright woman, take me to bed," Tarius said.

Jena went to get her and Rimmy helped, Hared opened the doors for them. But of course when they got to the bedroom their bed was full of babies.

"The rest of my cubs," Tarius said, and then it looked like she was about to cry. She sat down in the rocking chair and just looked at them. Jena noticed someone had lit their light, and she was glad. It could be hard to live in a village, in a house filled with people who could see in the dark. Often it left her to fumble in the dark looking for a match. "Dammit," Tarius whispered. Or at least thought she was whispering.

"What?" Jena asked.

Tarius sighed. "I'm starting to lose my buzz."

Rimmy picked Darian up and started to take him back to his room. "Rimmy, please bring me my son." Rimmy walked over and put Darian into Tarius's arms. "Hey little man," she whispered, tears glistening in her eyes. Darian woke up looked at her and moved to throw his arms around her neck. She hugged him tight but not too much so, and kissed his whole face.

"I missed you; did you miss me?" Darian said.

"You know I did. I hear you petted a whale today."

He nodded. He looked up at Jena and smiled at her, and she reached out and brushed the hair out of his eyes.

"The Great Wall rumbled."

"I know," Tarius said.

"And the mountain spit fire and you were nowhere, but I found you."

"I thought I felt you there."

He let go of her neck and sat back to look at her. He stroked the fur on her cheek with his hand. "I got a fish head in my soup, so it was a lucky day for me, and I knew you would come home."

Tarius looked at Jena and Jena shrugged. She had no idea what he was talking about. "You go back to sleep now.

You can tell me all about everything in the morning. I love you."

She kissed him and then Rimmy took him from her and Hared followed them out leaving them alone.

Jena picked Diana up and moved to put her in her cradle. "Jena, please let me see our baby, please."

"Why would I not let you see our baby?"

"Because now I'm starting to lose my buzz I know I'm drunker than a goat. I don't trust myself to hold her; I just need to see her."

Jena brought her over. Tarius looked at her then looked at Jena and smiled. "She looks more like you every day."

"And see I think she looks more like you every day." Jena took the cub and put her in her cradle. Then she started to undress Tarius.

"So you didn't just say you'd give me sex to get me home?"

"Yes I did," Jena kissed her. "I don't mind at all making love to you when you are Katabull, but though it is tempting, I'm not sure I'm up for drunk *and* Katabull. I undress you only to put you to bed."

"But.... You'll stay with me Jena," Tarius said at last helping her to undress her, making Jena's life easier.

"Of course I will stay with you, Tarius. Why do you keep saying that?" Jena laughed and took Tarius's face between her hands and kissed her again. "I'm not afraid of you. I never have been. Mad at you, yes, afraid of you never."

Tarius nodded silently got up and crawled into bed. Jena got undressed herself then blew out the light and crawled into bed beside Tarius. She pulled a sheet over them then moved up till her back was against Tarius's front. Tarius pulled her against her and kissed the side of her neck. Jena took Tarius's huge Katabull hand and held it in hers. It was different, Tarius was bigger as the Katabull and covered in fur but as much as she physically felt different the way Jena felt when Tarius held her was exactly the same—safe, cherished.

"Does it ever bother you, Jena?" Tarius asked in a whisper.

"What?"

"This, this... what I am now... does it bother you?"

"It does not, Tarius, must I wake my tired ass up and make love with you admittedly as drunk as a goat to prove it to you?" She let go of Tarius's hand and stroked her arm.

"No, I just want to hold you and.... Well Riglid said something. I can't remember if it was today or yesterday or if it was all day or no day at all but.... I am not what you signed up for, Jena."

"You know that I do not have the gift for words that you do, but we all like clams. We shuck them and eat them, but every once in a while you open one and there is a beautiful pearl inside. You are like that clam. I thought you were one thing, but when I opened you up you were so much more wonderful than I thought you were. You are *better* than what I signed up for."

Tarius giggled in a very un-Tarius way. "I'm a clam? You do know that's another word for...."

Jena smiled. "Then it works on more than one level. Now quit spewing your rum breath on me and go to sleep."

"Or you'll spank me?"

Jena sighed. "I suppose you told them about that as well."

# Chapter 16

**Persius woke and at first** thought it had all been an elaborate dream. But when he opened his eyes and looked around, it was obvious that it was all real. Hellibolt was standing in a corner which looked odd, so maybe he was still asleep. Then Persius's feet hit the cool concrete floor and he knew he was awake. But surely there was at least one thing he had dreamed.

"Hellibolt, did Tarius the Black...."

"In Katabull form come and jump into bed with you? Yes she did, and quite drunk, too." He turned and seemed to be adjusting his junk.

"Did you.... Did you just pee in the corner?" Persius asked in disbelief.

Hellibolt stepped back and pointed to a funnel with a piece of bamboo on the end of it that went out the wall. "These people are geniuses," Hellibolt said. "We are sleeping in what would have been the fathers' room, so...." He waved his hand in the contraption's direction. "And did you notice that outside the latrines there were basins in which to wash your hands and right next to this thing is a pitcher and basin. I imagine when you get done washing your hands you dump it down the pee place."

"Move aside; I could use that," Persius said. He walked over to the funnel and peed. "When we get home I will put one of these in my room."

When he turned Hellibolt had already left. When he had finished washing and drying his hands he dumped the water down the funnel. "Genius," he said with a smile and walked down the hallway through the main room and out the front door. There stood Hellibolt just watching. Persius didn't have to ask what he was looking at; everywhere he looked Katabull were doing some strange, slow motion dance, and there was a quiet you didn't expect in such a populated place. "What are they doing?"

"It is Simbala, the Kartik martial arts. This is a morning exercise all Kartiks do for their health and for balancing their energy. I had read about it but don't think I understood the implications."

"I know I will be sorry I asked, but what implications?"

"Not all of them, mind you, because if you look around you can see that they aren't all doing the same thing at the same time. Some are finishing as others are just getting started, and yet thousands of them here and all across the island are doing the same thing at the same time. It probably goes on in shifts over the first few hours of the day, which means the country as a whole starts out every day with huge amounts of the population at peace and present, balancing energy. There was a major disaster not two full days ago, and without knowing they are doing it they are helping to fix all that damage."

Persius went over what the wizard said then smiled. "I was right; I should not have asked. You know what I was thinking watching them? That these people do this without being told. I can't get mine to not turn to worshiping the Amalite gods, but Hestia's people get up as a country and do this every morning for their health. Hell, the Katabull are doing it." He remembered something he had thought of even as he fell asleep the night before. "Speaking of my people, I need to send someone to the nearest port with the news that I am well or Amual will start to redecorate my castle. We could ask Tarius to send a runner to the nearest port with a missive."

"All the near ports have been sacked by the storm." Persius jumped then turned to look up at the young man with the monkey on his shoulder.

"The Katabull move like air," Hellibolt said with a chuckle, no doubt at the look on Persius's face.

"It would be a two, most likely three-day ride to the nearest port that could send a ship, and my guess would be that Hestia will be using any close ships to send aid and troops to the villages damaged by the tidal wave. The Katabull ships should be back in port in about nine days I think." The boy looked at Hellibolt. "Do you have a bird spell?"

"Bird spell?"

"Jestia and Jazel have this bird spell they use where they enchant a bird and send messages with it," he said.

"Even over the sea?" Hellibolt asked.

"Yes, when we went to the territories to get Jestia and Ufalla.... It is a long story that someone else will tell better.... The witches were sending little birds back and forth across the sea with notes to and from the Great Leader."

"I have no such spell," Hellibolt said, and he sounded a bit put out by the fact.

The boy shrugged. "The Great Leader will know what to do when she wakes up. Kasiria asked that I lead you and your fellows down to the Great Hall where breakfast has been prepared for you. Don't worry; Kasiria did not cook."

**The baby wasn't fussing yet,** but she would be soon, for now she was just telling Jena she was awake and hungry. Jena looked down and the arms around her were human again. She slid out of Tarius's embrace and went to the cradle. The baby smiled up at her and started pawing the air in front of her. Jena reached down and picked her up, carried her to the end of the bed and changed her wet diaper then she brought the cub to bed with her covering them with the sheet as she put the cub between her and Tarius. Diana started to feed greedily. Nothing had been right or regular for the last two days, and all things considered she'd been a really good cub, but Jena was sure Diana was as ready as she was to return to some sort of normal routine.

In the morning light streaming in the window she could clearly see Tarius for the first time since she got home. She looked as rough as Jena had ever seen her look. *I wonder if I will ever know what really happened to you. If you even know.* She reached out and ran her hand over Tarius's hair; it was a mess filled with tangles and knots, dirt and indigenous plant life. It had probably been wet many times and no doubt it hadn't been so much as combed since the night before the world shook. Jena always took care of Tarius's hair for her, not that Tarius wouldn't, just that Jena liked to do it and Tarius enjoyed the attention. Tarius started to open her eyes and Jena quickly stopped petting her; it wasn't her intention to wake Tarius up, she just wanted to be touching her.

"I am sorry," Tarius said, but didn't open her eyes and Diana forgot all about eating and turned to face Tarius. Then she was grabbing at Tarius's face and chuffing. Tarius opened her eyes and when she saw the baby her smile lit her whole face. "There's my bright girl, there you are." She moved and kissed the baby's cheek then ran her hand over her head of dark curls. The cub just chuffed more and Tarius chuffed right back at her.

"What are you sorry for?" Jena asked.

Tarius looked at her and smiled. "Mostly right now I'm sorry that I can't honestly say that I don't remember anything I did or said last night because what I do remember is that among those things I'm afraid I told our adult son, Harris and Rimmy things about our coupling that only you and I should know."

"Yes, I know." Jena smiled at her. "They have already been teasing me about it, but you know what I'm not ashamed of what we do, Tarius and.... well you were drunk and you were only drunk so that you could get home. I wanted you home, so you are forgiven."

Tarius laughed. "Damndest thing. I could have sworn I jumped into bed with Persius that I saw Hellibolt...."

"That really happened, too. They are here."

"How did they get here?"

"I will tell you about my day here only when you tell me exactly what happened to you."

Tarius kissed their baby again and then turned the baby back towards Jena and put her back on her breast. Jena smiled and shook her head. Tarius moved to lie down on her back and look at the ceiling. "Well for any of it to make sense you must first understand something. Remember how Jabone beat himself up because he could not catch the arrow that nearly killed Kasiria because after all I jumped off a running horse and caught one? The many things I have done in my life that I should not have been able to do were always because of the magic I trailed with me from my last life...."

**It was a huge stone and** mortar building with thick wood shutters set in the wall at about waist height every few feet. It was a warm day and most of the shutters were open revealing latticework made of what he assumed was reinforced concrete. It had a red tile roof. The building's design and its construction clashed with the huts all around it. Like the wall it showed a sophistication that was unexpected. It was smack in the middle of the Katabull compound.

When they walked in they were led to a huge table near the back that was spread with smoked fish and a dozen different kinds of fruit. Jabone was already sitting at the table with the cub cradled in one arm. Persius expected him to look up at him and scowl, but instead he smiled at him and nodded. Two other men already sat at the table with Jabone. The one fellow he had met the night before, he didn't remember his name but remembered that he was human.

Kasiria met them. She hugged him and said, "Sit wherever you like. Laz, have breakfast with us. We will bring what's left over to your father and Tarius's house when we are done."

The boy nodded, flopped down and started filling his plate.

"They are a people without pretense," Hellibolt whispered in his ear.

Kasiria sat between Jabone and the man who wasn't the human. "You met Kaden last night, this is his mate Riglid. Riglid is Tarius's runner and he is Jabone's step brother."

The door opened and a small blond man and a tall Jethrikian girl walked in. "This is...."

"Harris's son," Persius said, happy he remembered. "He is named for the Great Leader."

"And his wife, Eric," Kasiria announced.

This Tarius took a seat as far away from him as he could and looked at him with the same disdain Harris had always had for him. His wife smiled but didn't bow or even nod.

*Because to do so would offend every Katabull in this room. This girl hid as a man in my Sword Masters academy; she has no doubt unlearned everything she knew there except how to sling steal. She left everything she knew and came here and doesn't care to return, and I need to find out why when Jethrik girls come here they never want to come home again.*

"Introduce yourselves, men," Persius told the sailors and they did. Then all started filling their plates.

The fish was insanely good and every piece of fruit he ate was better than the one he ate before. When he was fuller than he wanted to be he looked at Jabone. "Could I hold him?" Jabone didn't hesitate just stood up walked over and handed him the baby. The cub looked at him and smiled that infectious smile, and he smiled right back and wondered why Jabone didn't hate him anymore.

"He was born on the same day as my mothers' cub," Jabone

said.

Hellibolt's head shot up from where he'd been stuffing his face. "What did you say?"

"My son and my sister were born less than an hour apart," Jabone said.

"Twins," Hellibolt said, looking at Persius with meaning. "They might as well have been twins."

"My fadra said they were like twins, too. He said they are both half human and have a quarter of my madra's blood and her scowl." Jabone looked pensive, but beside him Kasiria started crying. Jabone put his arms around her and patted her back.

"His fadra was killed in the volcano," Hellibolt whispered in Persius's ear.

"I am so sorry for your loss," Persius said.

"I have had more time to get used to it than Kasiria has," Jabone said. "She and Fadra had much in common. My father died with him and they were hunting, but I'm afraid those things do not comfort Kasiria."

**The baby had gone back** to sleep between them and Jena wasn't far behind her, so Tarius went back to sleep, too. When she woke up Darian was sitting on her stomach looking down at her expectantly. "What son what?" she asked with a laugh.

"They said wake you up for breakfast."

"That is not what Fadra said," Pete whispered from the door, shaking his head. "He said to check to see if you were awake."

"Same thing," Darian said.

"It really isn't," Jena told him.

Tarius watched as Jena snagged her clothes and started dressing under the sheet.

Tarius sat up, causing Darian to nearly roll to the floor and he laughed when she caught him. She sat him back on her knees and reached over and picked Diana up. When she did she held her close to her. "Pete, come here." She cradled the still-sleeping baby in her arm and patted the bed beside her. Pete trotted over and crawled up on the bed. Jena was dressed and she started to get out of bed. "No, stay Jena. I just need you all here with me for a minute. Just a minute, and then we will go and eat because I feel like I could eat a whale but.... Did my people get me a whale to eat? No, they put him back in the sea which is a better place for a whale than in my belly I suppose." The boys laughed at her and she smiled.

"He said thank you when he swam away," Darian said.

"I'm sure he did." Tarius just wanted to pretend like everything was the same as it had been before the wall rumbled just her and her cubs and Jena. When she walked out of her bedroom today everyone would have questions and problems and she had to prepare a memorial for her sons' fathers and everyone was sad and things weren't the same at all, and if that weren't enough Persius was there.

And she was still weak, she still felt hollowed out. She wished she could just take Jena and her cubs and go to the beach and play in the surf and forget all about it, but she imagined the beach would just remind her that everything wasn't the same. *The lake then.*

"Just sit with me a few minutes. Here where I only belong to you before I have to go out there where I belong to everyone."

*Jena watched with relief* as Tarius sat at their table on her throne, Diana in one hand and eating with the other the way the Katabull normally did—like it was their first and last meal.

"How do you feel really?"

"Really I feel better by the minute," she said around a mouthful of mango. She stuck most of a smoked sardine in her mouth, leaving the head hanging out on one side and the tail on the other. She growled till the boys looked at her and then they cracked up.

Pete was alright with it being her trick; Darian of course had to do it himself. He sat there growling sounding like he normally did when he chuffed or growled—like a human trying to make an unhuman sound—and then he sounded just like Tarius.

Jena looked at him in shock.

Darian looked nearly as surprised. He quickly spit the fish out and did it again, and this time it was so close to a Katabull growl that it made the hair stand up on the back of Jena's neck.

Tarius laughed and pointed at his plate. "Do not waste

your fish." She looked at Jena and smiled. "Our magic cub does magic way before he should, and while you can blame me for training our cubs to shift too soon, who do you think has taught him that?"

"You," Jena said with a smile.

"Woman, you cut me to the quick!"

"You are always growling; he just wants to be like you."

Tarius smiled at Darian. "She doesn't have to make it sound like it is some curse, does she son?"

"Not a curse woman," Darian said.

"Enough of your mouth, Darian," Jena scolded, shaking her head.

Darian put the fish back in his mouth the tail and head sticking out and once again started growling in an entirely too close to grown Katabull way.

"Eat your food and don't play with it. Tarius, why do you have to teach them things like that?" But she had to look at her plate so that the boys couldn't see her grinning.

Pete had finished eating he turned to Tarius. "Madra, can I sing you the whale song I learned from Yri yesterday?"

"Sure, son."

He started singing his song, and Jena noticed then that it never had the same words twice. And he still yelled out the word "whale" loudly every few stanzas and this time Darian started to sing along with him. Pete let him for a minute then got very frustrated and told him, "Darian you don't know how the song goes."

"I do. *You* don't know how it goes." Then Darian started singing it and Jena realized that Darian actually knew the song nearly word for word the way Yri had sung it to them.

Tarius obviously knew the song because she looked at Jena and shook her head then said to Darian, "Son, let your brother sing *his* song."

Darian nodded and was silent and Pete kept singing, but Darian who was sitting next to Jena stood up in his chair and whispered in her ear, "You know that's not how the song goes, Mama."

She turned and whispered in his ear, "I know I want you to stay a baby longer, my little man."

He nodded, kissed her cheek, sat back down and continued to eat.

**Tarius walked outside.** Diana woke up and Tarius moved her to her shoulder where the cub raised her head looked towards the tree that hung over their hut and smiled. "This cub loves trees, Jena."

"That tree is her big brother's tree," Jena reminded Tarius.

"So it is and right next to Darian's tree, and then there's Diana's tree. See? It's that little one right there. That's your little tree, yes it is. It will grow huge and strong like brothers'."

Two Katabull appeared as if out of thin air and moved the throne from their house to the spot Tarius liked to sit by their fire pit, a place where she had a clear view of the lake down one of the many trails that led to it. She sat down and moved the cub so she could continue to look at the trees. There was a little breeze in the limbs. Diana chuffed and grabbed and hung onto one of the braids that hung on either side of Tarius's face. It had taken Jena a good long time to comb all the tangles and knots from her hair. Before she was done Tarius had said she was going to cut it all off like it had been when she was in the Sword Master's academy. Jena had suggested she might do that over her dead body.

"Did you have a good breakfast?" Tarius asked.

Hellibolt walked around in front of her. "I never could sneak up on you," he said.

"Nor should you want to." Tarius laughed.

"Yes, I'm reminded that trying once nearly got me killed." He sat in a chair across from her. "I cast a spell so that I could hear you as soon as you walked outside. I wish to talk to you and to get away from Persius for a while. I find I can only tolerate him in short bursts before he gets annoying. My spell kicked in just as you were talking like an imbecile, and I thought at first you'd lost your mind, but apparently you just want your child to think you have. So tell me about that?" he said, pointing at Diana. No doubt he knew she was special.

"Don't call my daughter a 'that,' and I'm sure you know. This is mine and Jena's child.... Well and Hared's."

"The young witch has power such as I have never seen or heard tell of. You do realize to do that she had to weave together many spells."

"I do."

"And what will be the fate of a child conceived in

enchantment...?

"Hellibolt, please do not make any predictions concerning my children. Any of my children, but especially not my daughter," Jena said, putting her hand on Tarius's shoulder.

"I would never do that, Jena. As the Great Leader knows prophecy negates freewill...."

"And yet you all do it and she made a prophecy about our youngest son," Jena said. "So please Hellibolt..."

"I said maybe, Jena, maybe," Tarius said. She looked at Hellibolt. "I had a vision, and no I did not repeat it."

"No she said pieces of things and even the pieces of things she said I did not like so please...."

"Warlords should not have visions!" Hellibolt said, looking worried.

"That is exactly what Jestia said!" Jena's grip on Tarius's shoulder tightened.

"Jena, calm down," Tarius pleaded. She waved her hand towards herself asking Hellibolt to come closer, and he leaned towards her. "In my last life I was a very powerful wizard."

Hellibolt nodded and stood back up. "That explains a lot actually."

"And again that is exactly what Jestia said," Jena said.

"The only prediction I would make about your beautiful baby is that she will grow to be as striking as Jena, as wise and strong as Tarius.... and this fellow Hared whoever he is." He grinned.

Tarius looked over to where Pete and Darian were picking the mint out of her herb garden and chewing on it. "Boys." They jumped and she laughed. "I do not care if you take some leaves, but don't damage the plants and do *not* take more than you will eat."

"I met Pete yesterday, but even if I hadn't it would be clear which one is Darian," Hellibolt said.

"Without question," Jena said, "because he is the one who acts more like her than the one she gave birth to."

"Have you not met Darian?"

"Not yet," Hellibolt said.

"Honey, take our little girl for a minute." Tarius handed the baby off to Jena. "Darian, come here son."

Darian came running over with an entire stem of mint. Tarius sighed. She should never have showed the boys that the mint was good to eat right out of the bed. This particular mint had a sweetness to it which made it hard for them to resist. He climbed up in her lap and stuck the mint in her face. "Want a bite?" he asked. She didn't, but she took one anyway.

Jena sat down next to her with the baby and looked at Hellibolt. "And that right there is an example of why we have the most spoiled cubs in the whole of the compound."

"Bite, Mama?" He held the stem out towards Jena.

"No I don't want a bite, and I think you know that when your madra told you not to take more than you could eat she meant don't take a whole plant," Jena said.

And of course that was an example of why their cubs weren't the most spoiled in the compound because Jena kept a tight rein on them.

"It was an accident, Mama," he said. "Want a bite?" Darian asked Hellibolt and their eyes met. Hellibolt smiled and Darian smiled brightly back at him. "You are like me."

Hellibolt looked at Tarius and Tarius smiled.

"Go ahead, growl for him," Tarius prompted.

Darian did and Jena shook her head. "That is creeping me right out."

Hellibolt laughed, took the offered mint and ate it. "Tarius, your son is...."

"Filled with magic yes we know," Jena said, "and still my baby and please don't teach him anything. I already have a six-year-old who can shift. I don't need that one to do any more than what he does right now."

"I was going to say he must be the boy in Persius's dream," Hellibolt said.

"Darian this is my old friend Hellibolt," Tarius told her son. Darian looked at the old wizard and then back at her.

"I know him," Darian told her. Tarius guessed they were all waiting for him to give them some magic answer as to how and why. "From the stories."

Tarius could hear Jena's sigh of relief. "Yes exactly, from the stories."

"You are a good friend," Darian said. Because of course in stories the Katabull told about Hellibolt it was more important that he was a good and true friend than that he was a powerful wizard.

"Yes he is," Tarius said.

Darian hugged her neck which was his way of saying he wanted down to go play with his brother.

Tarius set him on the ground. "Find someplace to play and something else to do besides tearing up our garden. If you tear up our garden you will have to eat rocks."

Darian made a face. "We can't eat rocks."

"Exactly."

He nodded and took off. When he reached Pete he took his hand and whispered something to him that he thought she couldn't hear.

"No, I did not say you could go to the lake. Why don't you go to the play area and play with the other cubs for a while?"

"Tarius I don't know...."

"Jena, they are old enough. The big one will watch the little one, and I can hear them from here if they get into any trouble."

Jena looked not at her but at Hellibolt. "I worry about the other cubs."

**Hellibolt watched them** walk away, the bigger one slowing his stride for the little one. "Do you suppose they knew he was magic that's why he was a sacrifice?"

"No they could not have known. They sacrificed him only because there were too many of them and they found babies to be a tasty treat. They were filthy Amalites," Tarius spit on the ground. "Don't pretend that they use reason or logic. They do only what their twisted priests tell them to do. We didn't even know until his eyes changed color at six months...."

"His eyes changed color; they didn't start green that means...."

"He comes from the Kartik royal line, yes we know." Tarius suddenly looked far off and she said more to Jena than him. "His magic comes from the same well as mine."

"How could that be?"

"I will tell you if you will tell me about this dream of Persius's. Because I'm sure when I know the nature of this dream I will know why he is here."

**So she told Hellibolt all** about how the Kartik royal line had been fouled by the Amalite curse there was a lot of spitting and cussing and when she had finished he told her about Persius's dream.

Tarius looked pensive then said, "It could mean only one thing, that he must deal with the Amalite menace in his country and not leave it for my son to deal with."

"That is what I thought, but why now? Why were we sent in the middle of all of this? It is obvious that the universe means it for some purpose, but what?"

A sudden cloud washed across the Great Leader's already worn and ashen features, "What did Persius say when he saw my grandson?"

"Oh, now there is a story." Jena got up and turned her back to him and started to feed the infant who had gotten fussy. "You will not believe what your daughter-in-law did."

Tarius smiled. "I assume since she is my daughter-in-law it must have been bad."

"I was busy birthing Jillest's baby, and she told her father that our daughter was her son."

"Well that's twistedly ironic," Tarius said, making a face.

"Yes, that's what I thought, but then when Kasiria showed the old shithead our grandson... Well he was almost as silly about him as Jestia is in that I-was-not-expecting-it-at-all way," Jena said.

Tarius looked at him and Hellibolt nodded. "He just wants to hold him, and the only one of his children he didn't ignore completely was Kasiria. As far as I know he has not seen all much less held any of his other grandchildren."

"How long did crazy Kasiria think she could keep that going?" Tarius asked, no doubt having had a minute to think on it.

"You know Kasiria; I don't think she thought about it at all. I think she looked up saw him coming didn't want to explain Arvon, so she just had Kaden take him in to play with Darian and presented our child as hers. Just so you know she has already apologized and obviously feels really bad."

"I do not think we should tell our son," Tarius said. Then after a moment's thought added, "Or the witch for that matter."

Jena nodded and looked at Hellibolt. "Please I'm a wizard. All I know how to keep are secrets." He smiled at Tarius. "So all those years ago when you kept so many secrets did you ever in a million years think this would be your life? The woman you love and always have still at your side. Four children, one in which both of your blood flows. A grandchild who is seen as a good omen among your people. And all of this you have only because Persius put an arrow in you."

"Now see here wizard...." Jena spun on him so quickly she barely had her breast covered, and her baby made unhappy noises that didn't sound like a human baby at all. "What crap is this? Do not spin this so he is some great hero."

"But it's true Jena," Tarius said. "If he hadn't shot me I would have brought you here whether you wanted to come or not. You would have had the child of a man you hated. You would have always resented me. I wouldn't be who I am; you wouldn't be who you are, and who knows if I ever would have had a child, or who the father of your next cub would have been or if you could even stand me much less stay with me. Arvon and Dustan brought you here because you *wanted* to come. You wanted to come because you didn't have a choice. Harris brought me here to save me and he met Elise on the boat. They have four children that never would have been. We all have a life together because Persius tried to kill me. I learned long ago that when you pull at just one thread you soon ruin your whole shirt."

"I refuse to see him nearly killing you as some sort of blessing." Jena stood up. "I suppose next you will weave some tale in which Tragon is somehow a hero!" She gave them both a dirty look and then stomped into the house with her infant.

Tarius looked at Hellibolt and grinned. "Well that went better than I expected."

Jena stomped back out of the house and walked in the direction the boys had gone.

"She just has to go check on the cubs, though she knows they are perfectly safe. She didn't worry this much about Jabone, but then Jabone was never kidnapped, nor did he have people threatening Jena that they would kill him in horrible ways."

"I am sorry to pull the scab off an old wound. I know she still hates him, and I know why for she told me only yesterday," Hellibolt said. "It was hard for me to forgive him...."

"But you could because you knew it was the only way out of the corner I had willingly backed into. You understand that The Everything is always looking for balance and that sometimes a horrible thing has to happen to create that balance. The Katabull understand that, I do most days, but like most humans Jena does not," Tarius said.

"I am trying to rush something that I shouldn't," Hellibolt said. "In my old age I grow impatient."

Tarius smiled. "While I have always been impatient but have always known that somethings take time. I think maybe Persius came to the island to learn how to get rid of the Amalites, but I think maybe you ended up here because Persius needs to make peace with Jena."

# Chapter 17

**They were walking back** from the Great Hall heading back to Kasiria's hut when a small voice called out, "Brother, let Arvon play with us."

"You know Arvon is too small to play," Jabone said.

To the left of the trail on its own mound was an area obviously set up for children. There was a small hut built in a tree planted right in the middle of the mound, a seesaw made of planks and a structure made out of log ladders lashed together. There were about a dozen cubs playing and several parents of both sexes were sitting on benches that were set around the outside edge of the mound talking as the children played. Some had brought vegetables or fruit and were cutting and preparing them. Others had brought nets and were mending them or sewing up clothes.

"What is this?"

"Madra got the idea from the Kartiks actually. It's a play area," Jabone said. "There are twelve of them set up around the compound so they are easily accessible to everyone."

Suddenly Persius realized what was missing from this civilization there was literally *no* class system. Everyone had equal access to everything. Tarius lived exactly the same way her subjects did.

"It keeps the cubs fit," Jabone said. "It's a place for the cubs to play safely while their parents get things done and visit with each other." He smiled. "I can't believe my brothers have been allowed to come by themselves. Mother usually doesn't let them come unless one of the parents goes with them."

Persius saw the blond head among all the dark ones and smiled. "I assume that one belongs to your mother."

"And Dustan, they are his birth parents," Jabone said. "His name is Darian for my grandfather. We have to watch him very carefully or he takes off with our cub."

As if the child knew they were talking about him he turned and walked towards them, and as he got closer Persius's blood ran cold. "Is your little brother magic, Jabone?"

"Oh yes." Kasiria answered instead of Jabone. "He said for weeks that the Great Wall was going to rumble and he told us the sex of both babies when Jena and I were barely pregnant—even though we didn't want to know."

Jabone was holding Arvon and he squatted down no doubt so the child could see the baby. The older boy he'd met before dropped out of the tree and for a minute looked around in a panic. Then when he saw his brother he calmed immediately and ran over. *He feels responsible for his little brother, yet they are really not related. I don't think any of my children really know each other much less care about each other. I don't think one of my sons wouldn't stab all his brothers to be the next king.*

The little wizard bent down and kissed the baby's cheek then looked up at Jabone. "Pete climbed to the top of the tree."

Jabone looked at the older boy. "You know you would not have been allowed to do that if Mother or Hared were here," Jabone scolded. The boy looked at his feet and nodded.

"Madra lets him," Darian said.

"Well she shouldn't, and she only does because she could catch him if he fell," Jabone said.

"I'm sure she could." Persius laughed out.

Darian looked up at him and Persius flinched inwardly as he waited for the boy to tell him in that un-boy-like voice, "Do not leave me to do it alone." Instead he said, "Who are you?"

"This is my father," Kasiria said.

The child nodded then he seemed to forget all about Persius and looked at Jabone. "Can I hold him? Kasiria lets me hold him."

"My child is neither a monkey nor a toy," Jabone said. He turned to glare at Kasiria, who just shrugged.

"He just wants to play with him. The cub loves him; I don't see the harm."

Darian then turned back on Persius and he found the boy completely unnerved him. "Do you like monkeys?"

"I suppose so," Persius said. He really wasn't used to interacting with children.

"Arvon is my little monkey," Darian said.

"Now dammit Darian, how many times have I told you not to call him that?" Jabone stood up removing the baby from Darian and Arvon started to cry in a way that sounded nothing like a baby.

"He wants to play with me," the toddler said, and it was obvious he was seconds from crying himself. "I don't know why everyone has to be so mean."

Jabone growled at the child, which was enough to make the hair stand on the back of Persius's neck, but then the child stood as tall as he could and growled back, and he sounded exactly like his brother. Jabone looked startled and then he laughed and said, "Don't you growl at me."

"He started doing it this morning," Pete said. "Mother said it creeps her out."

Persius decided there was something he agreed with Jena on.

"You growled at me first," Darian said.

"Yes I did, and I'm sorry, but I have asked you to quit calling Arvon a monkey."

"I not say he's a monkey."

"Yes you did."

He shook his head. "No I call him my little monkey. Like mama calls me her little turd."

Persius and Jabone both cracked up, and Kasiria ignored them and said to Darian, "So it's a pet name?"

Darian shook his head. "No because he is my brother's cub not a pet."

The baby was still crying and obviously unhappy. "I wonder what he will look like in his human form?" Persius said it before he thought about it.

Before either Kasiria or Jabone could say anything or just kill him and get it over with, the toddler looked at Jabone and said, "He will look just like father."

Jabone's eyes started to tear up and he said in a voice choked with emotion, "Will he really Darian?"

Darian nodded. "Yes, just like him."

Beside Persius Kasiria started to cry, and then he was holding his daughter and comforting her as Jabone sat down on a bench and said, "Sit down, and I will let you hold your little monkey."

"Are the boys...?"

"They are fine, Mother," Jabone said, addressing Jena who managed to make running with a baby in her arms look easy. Only when she could clearly see all of her children did she stop running. She gave him a *go to hell* look for good measure then looked from Kasiria to her grown son and her silence said she knew why Kasiria was upset even before Jabone told her. "Darian said Arvon will look like Fadra when he is in his human form."

"Will he?" Jena asked Darian.

"Yes, just like father." He just nodded and smiled. "My fadra told me." And he just went right on playing with Arvon. The baby was chuffing at him and he chuffed right back, sounding just like any Katabull cub.

Jena took in a deep breath and let it out. He was talking about Dustan because while he had swapped out she and Tarius's titles so that they didn't match the story, he had always gotten his fathers right because of course just as Tarius had metaphorically given birth to him Dustan was the one who had gladly and proudly said he fathered him.

Only in their family could the three-year-old tell you he was talking to his dead Fadra and you didn't even think for a minute that he might be just making something up. As if to prove the point he pointed up at a bird with blue plumage and said, "Jestia is coming."

**Seeing the bird Tarius** held her arm up. The bird landed on it. She started to take the note off the bird's leg.

"What sort of bird is that, Tarius?" Hellibolt asked.

"Clearly it is a blue bird," Tarius said, and reading the note let the bird go.

Hellibolt laughed. "We have 'blue birds,' at home and that is not what we call a blue bird. That bird is larger and our blue bird has a rust-colored head and belly...."

"Then why do you call it a blue bird?" Tarius asked with a grin.

"Because it is mostly blue and.... I didn't name it. Do you know what kind of bird it is or not?"

"I do not, nor do I know why it matters so much to you, but Jestia and Jazel will be here before nightfall. They can tell you what you need to know." She looked around first to make sure he wasn't in striking distance before she called out. "Riglid!"

In minutes Riglid was there a towel around his waist and still wet. She laughed and shook her head. "Son, you could have finished showering."

"What if it was urgent?" Riglid asked.

"Then I would have called out like this," she cupped her mouth and yelled, "Riglid come at once it is urgent."

He nodded and with the hand that wasn't holding the towel up pushed the wet hair out of his face. "Well I am here now."

"The queen and your mother, all the witches, and Ufalla are on their way. They will be here before dusk. I see no reason to put off the memorial. We will need tables inside and out of the Great Hall. We need music, we need dancers. It should be as grand a celebration as there has ever been as we say good bye to my brothers. Finish your shower then spread the word immediately."

"Who will do the choosing? You know all will want to play and sing and all will want to dance."

"I am too weak and I don't think Jena, Kasiria or my son could stand it. If he is up for the task let Harris do it."

"Where are my father and Hared?" Riglid asked, no doubt thinking they could help Harris. Because Riglid was right; all who played an instrument anyone who sang or danced was going to want to do so at Arvon and Dustan's memorial. They were well loved throughout the nation.

"They have taken the king's lifeboat and gone to set out crab pots," Tarius said. Because of course crab was the traditional meal served at memorials, but all their big ships were across the ocean and all of their small boats had been destroyed out right or damaged in the storm. "See if Yri or Vony can help Harris. When we left Montero yesterday Hestia said they would come today if Jestia was able to. Hestia has ten soldiers with her, so they will need to be put into a couple of the empty houses, and I will want them watched the whole time they are here. But I do not want them to know they are being watched. That is the soldiers should be watched of course, not Hestia."

"Why do you want the soldiers watched?" Hellibolt asked.

"For the same reason I'm sure Jena had the sailors and

Persius watched." She looked at Riglid and he nodded. "There are crimes humans commit that Katabull don't even think of. No Katabull would molest a child, or rape someone, it is not in our nature. And no human will do one of those things to each other and certainly not to a Katabull on my watch in the compound. You save yourself a war when you don't allow brothers to fight."

"Oh, I like that. You save yourself a war when you don't allow brothers to fight," Hellibolt said.

"And I save myself an explanation of why I don't trust Hestia's people or Persius's when I don't let them know they are being watched. It is not so much that I don't trust them as it is that I don't want to *have* to trust them. I once trusted a man I should not have, but worse than that when years later I revisited that time I realized that I had never trusted him at all but I let first need and then sentimentality for a relationship that never really existed keep me from killing him. I have not made that mistake since and hope to never make it again. I would rather be prepared and have nothing happen than be unprepared and have to deal with what happened because of it."

Hellibolt smiled and shook his head.

"What?" Tarius asked.

"I can tell looking at you that you have just been through hell. Even your humming sounds labored, yet even in this state wisdom spills from your mouth and I find myself wondering for the hundredth time how old is your soul."

"Right now it's a question of how tired is this soul." Tarius grinned. "I have made as many mistakes as I have lived days, so I have had many lessons, yet I still think wisdom eludes me." She laughed. "I came home so drunk I crawled into bed with Persius and I told things that should have been private to possibly the last people Jena wanted to hear them, all because I wanted to be with my wife and cubs. That is not wisdom, Hellibolt. To let desire overrule good sense is foolish. We have been friends a long time and there is little you don't know about me if anything and much that I don't know about you. I know you are very old, hundreds of years, because I know how witches age, or don't, and you look to be in your seventies which means you are probably nearly seven-hundred years old."

"Nearly to the day," he said with a smile.

"Have you ever been in love?"

"Many times, though nothing lasting more than a few months."

"Do you have any children?"

"No."

"Have you ever had them?"

"No. I never had any desire to."

"That my friend is wisdom. A life without crushing responsibility and constant worry allows you to pursue pure knowledge. I love my wife and I couldn't live a day without her, and I love all my children the one I bore, the one I picked up off a cave floor, the one whose parents died and who we wound up unintentionally mothering, and I love the baby girl that is a miracle that allowed Jena and I to have a baby that is part of both of us. I love my grandson in who mine and Persius's blood flows together, and who always wears his Katabull face. There isn't one of them I would part with or one of them whose loss would not nearly kill me, and because of that I never really sleep. Only when I practice my Simbala in the morning is my brain ever quiet, and most of the time even then through the motions and the breathing there is a wrestling match going on in my head where I am trying oh so hard not to think and my thoughts keep coming in and breaking my silence. If there is nothing at all to worry about with my family, then there are my friends and my people and…. Though I love them all and wouldn't trade them, there are days when I wish I'd had the wisdom to follow the path I first started to blaze for myself where I didn't want to care for anyone and wanted no one to care for me…."

"Ah, but my friend, that path led you right to her. Because you were hell bent on doing what you wanted and damn what anyone else thought or the 'rules' you wound up in the Sword Master's academy. It was not wisdom that made me choose a solitary life. All those many centuries ago I had a younger sister, human of course, and I loved her and she me. When I buried my parents who were old when they died and my older siblings it was sad but seemed natural even though I looked like a youth of twenty and did for the first two hundred years of my life. But when my little sister died of old age it was more than I could bear, and I knew that the worst thing I could do for my sanity—you know what little a wizard has—would be to fall in love or worse yet have children. So it isn't wisdom, it is fear, and as I'm sure you know fear is the opposite of wisdom. Certainly being on the outside always looking in on something I don't have has not made me wise, and it certainly hasn't made me happy. Your wisdom comes from never letting fear rule you. Knowing how painful it can be, you never ran from love, no quite the opposite you have embraced love in all its forms. It is a lot to bear the load you carry, too much at times I'm sure. But all these many different things have made you very wise. To have great joy you must walk through a river of pain. Like you said, The Everything is always looking for balance."

**"I don't think you should be** riding yet," Ufalla said on her horse beside her. "You can hardly sit; we should have put you in a wagon."

"Yes being bounced around in the back of a wagon would be sooo much better. I am fine; I told you I'm fine! Why will you not listen when I tell you to shut up?" Jestia yelled back.

Her mother who was riding in front of her, Radkin by her side, turned to look at her. Then seeing that Jestia was only fighting with Ufalla, Hestia turned around, no doubt hoping to steer clear of Jestia's anger which had been erupting every few minutes for the last hour at any available target. At one point she had even accused a monkey of looking at her.

"You are the one who won't listen, Jestia," Ufalla said in a hissed whisper, no doubt so her mother couldn't hear. "You wouldn't listen then and you aren't listening now."

"You do know whispering is a wasted effort. Radkin can still hear you, and she will tell Mother everything either of us say as soon as Mother asks, and she will ask because Mother is extremely nosey. I had thought that having her own life would make her mind her own business, but no she still just has to know everything I'm doing and...."

"Shut up, Jestia!" Radkin shouted. She turned around and looked not at Jestia but at Ufalla. "We didn't put her in a wagon. We didn't bring one with us, and we aren't going back to get it, so quit bitching at her about it now. Do you not realize you are only adding fuel to the fire of she's-pissed-off-at-everyone-right-now? How bad could she really feel? She has done nothing but bitch at us in turn since we left." Radkin turned back to look at the road.

Behind Jestia Eerin snickered. Jestia turned to face him and from the way he cringed it was obvious that he wished he'd been able to stop his laughter. "I do not know why you are even going with us."

"Because they were my friends, too," Eerin said, and now looked close to tears. Arvon and Dustan had been giving him sword lessons which he badly needed because—much as he had been with his magic before Jazel's tutorage—he was a danger to himself and others with a sword in his hand. They had been nice to him, especially Dustan.

"It's alright boy," Jazel said. Eerin was much older than Jestia was, yet Jazel always addressed him as boy while she rarely called Jestia a girl anymore. "She's not really mad at any of us; she's just upset and you're an easy target."

Jestia neither thought she was being that big a bitch nor that it was because they were riding to go to Arvon and Dustan's memorial. She loved them, they were gone, she couldn't bring them back, and that was all. She had already dealt with it. She felt like boiled crap and she probably should have allowed them to put her happy ass in a wagon. Ufalla reminding her every three seconds was just bugging the living piss out of her, and.... *Everyone is hurting and everyone is tired and my pain and need is no greater or worse than theirs. I just need to shut up and leave them alone but they are all getting on absolutely my last damn nerve.*

"Ufalla, please let me ride in front of you and you hold me," Jestia said. They stopped just long enough for Radkin to pick her up and put her on the saddle in front of Ufalla. She leaned against Ufalla and Ufalla held her with one hand and her reins with the other. "I'm sorry," she said softly.

"I don't mind riding double with you at all." Ufalla kissed the side of her face.

"I meant I'm sorry I was talking crap to everyone," Jestia said.

Proving that she really could hear every word they said Radkin said without turning, "You know you saved Montcro, several smaller towns as well as whole sections of jungle, and the gods alone know how many people. I think you get a pass today for being a bitch. Tomorrow is another story."

"I don't know what's wrong with me; I'm just so pissed off at everything," Jestia told Ufalla.

Jestia allowed her weight to rest on Ufalla. Just having her hold her made Jestia feel better physically, but her soul hurt, too. She had been nearly dead. It was impossible for any of them to understand what she had been through. What Tarius had done to save her. What it had cost her. Why everything she had didn't seem to balance what she'd lost. *He's gone to me just like she is gone to Tarius, yet we are still here and we are in each other's lives. It's not what it was for them, though, and it never will be. But I have Ufalla and my mother and…. No one but Tarius comes close to really understanding me. Ufalla knows me and loves me but doesn't really understand me. My mother now loves me but neither really knows nor understands me. It was better not knowing, but if we weren't supposed to know The Everything never would have let us step on that place. But why must we know, what good is it? Without that knowledge I would not have known how to save Montero. We are both still alive, but we are not the same. She isn't and certainly I'm not. While Tarius seems to be alright to just be a key that is used to open the door of the will of Everything, I am too selfish to be happy to be just a vessel for The Everything to fill with the need of many. I'm just so tired of doing anything at all that I don't want to do. What about me? Why does nothing ever ask me what I want? Is it really necessary to make me give up being me? What is so wrong with me?*

"There is nothing at all wrong with you," Ufalla whispered in her ear.

Jestia's heart nearly stopped for a second. Did she speak out loud? She knew she didn't.

"I'm sorry. Radkin was right bitching about the wagon at this time is pointless. And when I thought about it I realized that I was doing it in part because I'd rather deal with mad Jestia than sad Jestia, but you have all the right in the world to be sad. Just as everyone has always done to Tarius they expect you to do the impossible at their whim, and like her because most of the time you can do it, they just keep asking. And my love, selfishly I care not a rat's ass about everyone else. I only care about you, but I can't protect you, not from you."

***Having seen her the night*** before in her terrifying Katabull form, Persius thought as they walked down the road towards where she was sitting on her throne that she looked so much smaller today. Yet he knew it was her because she was talking to the old wizard and Hellibolt was listening intently. The only person he'd ever seen the wizard actually listen to was Tarius the Black.

It was just him, Kasiria, Jabone and the baby, and Persius was carrying the baby because he wanted to. Jena had said she would stay at the park with her boys and let them play. He got the distinct impression that she would do just about anything to keep him away from her and her children.

They walked up to where Tarius and the wizard were sitting and she looked up at all of them and smiled. It was clear from her color that she wasn't well. Beside him he saw Kasiria flinch at the sight of her.

"Hello again," Tarius said to Persius, and in his arms the baby twisted towards her voice and started making that odd sound Kasiria told him was called chuffing. "Hello my bright boy." He was a tiny baby not even three months old yet Persius didn't have to wonder if he wanted to go to his grandmother he obviously did. She held out her arms and he gave her the baby. She put her hands under the baby's arms and stood him on his feet standing on her knees. "Did no one let you walk around? Did they make you lie down the whole time? Did you not tell them...." She roared then, a sound that sent a shiver down Persius's spine, but made the baby laugh. "...I am the Katabull. Do not make me lay around like a cub." The baby started chuffing even more and jumping with his knees.

Persius looked at Kasiria who just smiled and shrugged.

"Madra, he is a tiny....

"Katabull baby, yes he is, he is." Tarius picked him up above her head then brought him down and kissed his nose.

"You are too rough, Madra, and so is Kasiria," Jabone said with the air of someone who has held their tounge as long as they can.

Too rough? All Persius had noticed was that Tarius the Black, the most celebrated warlord in the known world was talking baby talk.

"I have not broken a cub yet," Tarius said and put the cub

on her shoulder where he proceeded to bury his face in her long hair. "Have I Arvon, have I? No, I haven't."

Kasiria must have noticed the look on his face because she said with a grin. "You should only hear how she talks to her daughter."

"I have," Hellibolt laughed. "It was most distressing."

"Ha, ha," Tarius said, and he noticed she held the baby a little closer. She rubbed her head on his face and he grabbed her hair and hung on. If it hurt or bothered her at all it didn't show as she just held him suddenly looking like she had forgotten all about all of them.

*And she has. Right now we are not even here. For her at this moment there is only our grandson, and that is why he wanted her as soon as he heard her voice because he knows her love.*

Kasiria found a chair around the dead fire pit and sat down. "I am not too rough with him," she told Persius.

"You are and so is Madra, and she does not handle Diana the way she handled me or my brother or our son," Jabone accused and sat beside Kasiria

"So am I really too rough with Arvon or do you just want me to rough your sister up a bit?" Tarius said, a twinkle in her eye that defied the tattered way her features looked.

"I just don't know why it's different is all," Jabone mumbled.

Tarius turned to look at Persius. "So I hear you were hit by a tidal wave and then had to deal with my wife."

"All things considered I think the tidal wave wished me less harm."

**Jena had started to walk** back home with the boys, but as she got closer she could see Persius was there.

*And she's just going to talk to him as if he isn't the lowest of slime. As if he didn't nearly kill her and me with her. Just because he led a charge that saved her.... That doesn't make them even, not to me. Not when the very war we were fighting at the time was his fault because he wouldn't listen to her in the first place.*

"What's wrong, Mama?" Pete asked.

"Nothing.... would you boys like to go to the lake?" she might as well have asked them if they wanted honey-coated sugar cane. She followed them right past their huts down the trail to the lake. She turned just in time to give Tarius a look that clearly said get *rid of him* and to give Persius a *go straight to hell* look. When she tried to look at Jabone he looked quickly away.

When she reached the water's edge the boys had their clothes off and were in before she had time to tell them they could. She had neither the strength nor the desire to argue with them, so she just picked up their discarded loincloths and told them not to go past the rope. Tarius had roped off an area for the cubs to play in by using rope with glass net floats. Every few feet the rope was tied to rocks under the surface of the water. The water level was already back to normal, and the water was nearly clear. She found a bench close to the water's edge and sat down. She set Diana on her lap in front of her leaning her against her stomach so that the cub could watch her brothers play.

"So how's that working out for you?" he said from just behind her. She jumped a bit but didn't turn to look at the old wizard. Hellibolt flopped on the bench beside her, making Diana jump, too. "So?"

"So, what?" Jena asked, unable to mask her frustration or anger.

"How's that working out for you?"

"What?"

"The whole staying mad forever thing? Hate is a lot of work, Jena."

"Hellibolt, for the love of the Nameless One I told you...."

"And I listened and heard you and still don't see how staying mad serves you."

Her attention was yanked away. "Do not even get close to that rope or I will make you get out at once," Jena said, seeing that both boys were eyeing the rope.

"Can they both swim?" Hellibolt asked.

"Yes, Tarius taught them. Pete when he first came here and Darian before he could walk," Jena said, smiling at the memory. Darian had learned to swim in Jazel's spring. The minute his face came out of the water the startled expression had immediately turned to bliss. All her cubs liked the water, but Darian loved it. "They are strong swimmers."

"Yet you don't take your eyes off them, why?"

"Because...." She stopped. Did he really know so little about children or was it one of those questions that she was going to wish she either didn't answer or answered in some other way. Finally she just answered, "Because they are just children and don't think things through before they do them."

"They act impulsively and do things that could hurt them or others without knowing it's not safe until they do it."

"That's right," Jena said carefully. "And sometimes they can be doing nothing at all wrong and something happens and you only have seconds to act."

"Because you can't trust that nothing will go wrong."

"Of course not... Just two days ago the earth shook, a volcano erupted, there was a tidal wave, Tarius and Jestia nearly died, and Arvon and Dustan did. For the love of all there was a huge whale on our beach and you sailed into our harbor in a dingy with Persius. Nothing is sure!" Diana fussed and she put her on her shoulder and started to pat her back. "Hellibolt, please just get to the point."

"There are things you can do things about, Jena, and things you cannot. This burning hate you have for Persius does you more harm than it has ever done him. You don't have to worry about Persius. Even if he still wished to hurt Tarius, which I promise you he does not, how would he do it? He is alone without guards, without wealth or clothes or sword, and his title is worth nothing here. He is completely stripped bare. The universe has laid him at your feet bare."

"Why do you care so much about him, Hellibolt?"

"Because he and his fathers before him are as close as I've ever come to having children. They are born they grow old and die, but there is always a new one and this one for reasons I can't fully explain has a special place in my heart. Perhaps because he is such a mess, so much trouble. The one who will rule after him, Amual.... I care for him not at all and will not stay to 'serve' him. When Persius is no more I will abandon the Jethrik throne. Persius does not deserve your hate; it is a gift he doesn't want and that you cannot afford to give."

Jena nodded silently. She knew he was right and most of the time she just didn't think about it. It wasn't like she'd stayed up nights for the last twenty-eight years thinking of ways to get back at him. She didn't. But any time she was near Persius.... She just really wanted to kill him.

# Chapter 18

**Persius didn't know what** he expected, but it wasn't this. No two tables matched, and few of the chairs. It was obvious that the tables and chairs came from the Katabull's own homes. The huge table they had eaten at that morning had been brought outside and on it was set out all the food. It seemed that each "pack" brought a meal and set it out on the big table. He thought he was seeing enough seating and tables for all of the Katabull Nation, but Kasiria told him that was not the case.

"They all helped bring chairs and cooked, but most attending are the Marching Night and Arvon and Dustan's closest friends."

"I was worried about my clothing, but...."

"I should warn you that not only are bright colors appropriate, but they will wear as little as possible and some of them will wear no clothes at all because in death all are the same," Kasiria said.

"I'm afraid I don't understand," Persius said.

"That's alright neither do I," Kasiria grinned at him.

"Where is the baby?"

"No children under twelve are allowed to come to a memorial. The Katabull believe that the collective sadness which is the undertone at a memorial will imprint on the cubs and make them associate death with sadness and then they will fear death. Since the Katabull don't fear death.... Most days I just nod and pretend I know what they mean. One of the other packs is watching all the babies, and that is where Arvon is. Jena and Tarius's cubs threw a near fit till they saw Arvon was staying. He and Diana are so cute. They will just spoon each other when they nap and if one is fussy if you put them together they are just fine. And of course Darian would just keep Arvon if we'd let him. The baby loves Darian, too, and he obviously trusts him so I don't know why Jabone gets so freaked out when Darian wants to play with him."

Persius started to explain that maybe Jabone had a point then remembered what the child was. "How did Tarius and Jena wind up with a magic child?" Persius asked.

"So asks the man who has a Katabull daughter," Kasiria said with a laugh.

"My father had a latent magic ability," Jabone said, appearing out of nowhere dressed in nothing but a loincloth. "Kasiria, Harris asks if you will be speaking...." She shook her head and tears glinted in her eyes. Jabone nodded leaned down and kissed her gently on her lips. "Though I feel a coward I am not speaking either." He turned and was gone.

"Eulogies?" Persius asked.

"No, they will tell stories about them. In none of them will they mention they are dead because we already know that. If nothing else I would hate to try to tell a story among them. There are no better bards than Katabull and no greater Katabull bards than in the Marching Night, and in the Marching Night the greatest bard is Tarius the Black."

"Tarius?" Persius was shocked.

"Oh yes even back during the war she could tell a story," Hellibolt said. Persius hadn't seen him come up at all, and when he looked at him the wizard already had a bowl of food.

Persius looked quickly around. "What are you doing? The feast has not yet started."

"Do you not understand, Fred? I am a great hero here and was a good friend to both of the deceased. I told you these are a people without pretense. The only way they would get mad at my eating a little before them is if I left nothing, and there is plenty of food."

Kasiria nodded.

"I never knew you were such a glutton," Persius said in disgust.

"The food here is really good," Kasiria said, giving the wizard a knowing smile.

Persius lowered his voice still more and looked up at the wizard. "Certainly a little propriety is in order. My daughter's husband's fathers are dead."

"Say that three times very fast," Hellibolt challenged.

He heard a bit of commotion and when he looked up he saw Hestia. "I see the queen and the princess have entered with their guards, please Hellibolt try to pretend that you have some court manners," Persius pleaded.

"Do not bow or the Katabull will thump you," Kasiria said quickly. "I once bowed to Tarius and you would have thought *I* shoot her with an arrow."

**Kasiria turned to see** Hestia and Jestia, smiled and shook her head.

"I suppose they wear so little clothing because of Katabull custom," Persius said.

"They wear so little clothing because they are Kartik and it is a hot day," Kasiria told him. "And that is not Jestia's guard that is her wife, and that is not the queen's guard, that is Laz and Riglid's mother Radkin."

"And is Radkin then banging the queen?" Hellibolt asked, nearly glowing at the scandal of it.

"It's supposed to be a secret, but it isn't a very good one." Kasiria grinned.

"Is everyone on this island queer?" Persius hissed, looking at his feet.

"No, though more Katabull are than aren't, the rest of the island is just like the Jethrik. These people just don't hide it like they do at home.... Except the queen, and like I said she isn't doing a very good job of it." Kasiria waved at them. "I need to go check on Jestia."

She walked quickly towards them. When she got close she could see that Jestia didn't look much better than Tarius did, and no doubt Jestia was working at looking better much harder than Tarius was. "How are you?"

"Worse than I thought unless your father and his wizard arc here," Jestia said.

"They are," Kasiria said, and Jestia looked relieved.

"What the hell is he doing here?" Hestia asked.

"All manner of stupid things I imagine," Jestia said, rolling her eyes. "Kasiria, I need to sit." Kasiria took hold of the arm Ufalla didn't have and took Jestia to what would serve as the head table. It was actually the dining table out of Tarius and Jena's house coupled with the one from Radkin's house. Jestia sat down then looked expectantly at Kasiria.

"What?" Kasiria shrugged.

"Where is my godson?"

Ufalla took a deep breath and let it out. "Jestia, I told you babies aren't allowed...."

"It hasn't started yet," Jestia said. "Go and get him."

"She has been a total bitch all day," Radkin supplied.

"So it must be a day on which the sun rose," Kasiria said with a grin.

"Kasiria, what is your father doing here?" Hestia asked again, looking over at where he was standing having some sort of argument with Hellibolt.

"I don't give a shit. I want to see Arvon," Jestia ordered.

"Jestia, for the love of the Nameless One, can you just stop being...*you* for a minute!" Ufalla snapped. She looked at Kasiria. "Where is the cub? Radkin and I will carry her over there so no one else has to deal with her mouth."

Jestia gave Ufalla a look that if she had been in better shape would have had Kasiria pleading for Ufalla's life. "Seriously, Ufalla who do you think you're talking to?"

"Right now a screaming, willful brat," Ufalla said.

Kasiria quickly told her where the cub was and then Radkin and Ufalla picked Jestia up and more carried than led her away.

"That child wasn't out of her comma a full day when she made us wonder why we so wanted her to wake up." Hestia smiled at Kasiria. "So.... Why is your father here?"

"He was on his way to talk to you about some problem when he got hit by a tidal wave and wound up here."

"I had no idea he was coming. I received no such message...."

"He didn't send one ahead. It's a long story someone else will tell better. We are calling him Fredrick."

Hestia started to make her way towards her father and Hellibolt, and Kasiria followed. "Please remember that he is a Jethrikian man and they are by nature pretty stupid."

"You forget that I have not only dealt with Jethrikian men before, but I have dealt with your father before," Hestia said.

"Yes, but last time you had a man by your side."

Hestia turned to her and smiled. "Lovely girl, Radkin is a hundred times more masculine than Dirk was, and much more likely to kill Persius if he disrespects me."

"Yes, that's kind of what I was worried about."

***Hestia walked right up*** to the king and held out her hand. "Fredrick I presume?" He took her hand and she brought their elbows together. If she could shake the way they did when she was in his country, he could shake like her in hers.

"Queen Hestia." She put her hand on his shoulder as he started to bow, and he nodded knowing she'd saved him a beating. "I meant to meet with you with a full retinue and proper attire, but I'm afraid fate had other plans for me."

"The last few days fate has had different plans for us all. I do not wish to talk of kingdom business at this time, not yours and not mine. My dear friends have died and I have done nothing but worry that I was about to lose my only child for two days as I tried to take care of the damages done to my country by an earthquake, a volcano and a tidal wave. I wish to be allowed to grieve with my friends. I hope what you need from me can wait till tomorrow."

"It can; I understand. Since it is my son-in-law's father who has died...."

"Fathers," Hestia corrected with a sigh. Persius wasn't the monster Jena painted him to be, but certainly he was one of the biggest dumbasses she'd ever known.

"Of course. What I meant to say is I know this is not a time for business."

Hellibolt caught her eye and smiled a knowing smile. Most days she forgot she was young again especially days like the last few. She walked over and hugged him. She kissed his cheek and he smiled even bigger.

"So how is the huge Katabull woman in the sack?"

"Hellibolt, for the love of the gods..."

"She's fantastic," Hestia said with a smile as she released him.

Hellibolt nodded. "So was the little witch...."

"Throwing a fit? Yes she was. We're all lucky she can't access her power right now or I don't think any of us would have made it here alive. She is in a horrible mood, even for Jestia. Jazel, Helen and Eerin are with us, but do you see them? No, because as soon as we put our horses in the pasture they made up an excuse to get away from her."

She realized Persius was looking at her like she had a cat growing out of her head. She smiled at him then gently patted the side of his face, which made him flinch. "I removed the stick from my ass, and I feel so much better. You should really try it."

She took Hellibolt's arm. "Come; help me find the Great Leader. Maybe she can do something with Jestia."

**And just like that Persius** was alone with Kasiria again. Kasiria just looked at him and shrugged.

"The Kartik queen has a Katabull lover?"

"They are more than lovers," Kasiria said a hint of aggravation in her voice. "They love each other, and you'd better not be rude to the queen because Radkin will beat you to a pulp. I am remembering Jestia and Ufalla's wedding where Dirk showed up only to get his ass kicked."

"Are you mad at me?" Persius asked, confused.

"I'm not mad at you really. I just don't understand why you have to make an issue out of who people love. Because of the stupid way I was raised I still find myself thinking of people I've come to love as somehow beneath me. I'm normal and they aren't and.... It's all such absolute crap. Here, in this place, because we are attracted to the opposite sex we aren't 'normal' they are. Yet they don't treat Jabone and I any different. Our cub is Katabull prime and far from treating him like some sort of freak they all think he's a good omen. Do you know why my first instinct when I looked up and saw you was to hide my son?"

Personally Persius could think of a dozen reasons, none of which he felt safe repeating, so he just shrugged.

"Because you people judge everyone and find them wanting. I didn't want my son judged by you. I don't want him judged by *anyone*. The Katabull don't look at someone and judge them. They judge them only on their deeds, not by how they look or where they come from, and certainly they don't judge them by who they love. Hestia is Queen of the Kartik; she loves a woman who happens to be Katabull. You are King of the Jethrik; you loved a woman who happened to be Katabull, so you have a great deal in common."

Then Kasiria stomped off saying she had something to do and he was alone.... Except for the Katabull who were starting to fill the area. He found a chair, sat down and decided to just stay out of the way. The sailors weren't invited because the only people who could come to the memorial were people who actually knew the people who had died. He of course had, as had Hellibolt. He suddenly felt like a big, raw wound.

*"You people." My own daughter called me "you people." She has severed all connections with us, and if she hadn't done so already she would have done it the minute her son was born with a Katabull face. Because she's right; here he has acceptance and there they would have already killed him and no one would be prosecuted for the crime. I would have allowed him to be killed; hell, if he'd been born like that in my castle I probably would have ordered it done myself. Yet when I hold him I have a love for him that I only ever had for his mother, a sense of ownership in another spirit. What does it all mean? Why am I here in this place at this time?*

"Are you alright, Persius?" He looked up and there stood Jabone.

"I.... I'm fine. Kasiria just told me off, but I think I needed to hear what she said, so.... I am fine." Jabone started to walk away. "Jabone wait...." Jabone turned to face him and walked closer. "Why do you not hate me anymore?"

"I never hated you; I hated what you did," Jabone said. Persius was still pretty sure that was the same thing. "My fathers just died. You are Kasiria's father. I have no fathers, but she does."

And there would be one of those things that Katabull understood that no one else did.

"When Kasiria and I first married we moved to Montero. I didn't want to be around my madra, for she shines brighter than the sun. I thought I would never make a name for myself if I was always in her shadow. Then my mother and little brother were kidnaped from within the walls of Hestia's own palace. My madra was in a state; as long as my mother was missing, my madra was both dangerously crazy and broken inside. My mother and brother were saved, the culprits were killed in the hundreds, all deserved death.

"Yet I cannot help but believe that if Kasiria and I had been with my mothers, it never would have happened. I left my family's belly open only for my pride. For a long time after everyone was home and safe I was ashamed of myself. Then I heard my madra tell a story that only she will tell. No other Katabull or Kartik bard has ever told it, for it is her story alone to tell. All my life my mother would take my hand and take me away when Madra started to tell the story, but after the battle of Sedrik's keep was over and we were home she told it, and being a grown man I stayed and listened. She calls it The Redemption of Persius. It is a wonderful story and though Mother pointed out that battle and that war never would have happened had you but listened to my madra in the first place.... I understand how pride can blind you.

"When I saw you holding my son, though he is different from all but a handful of people on this world, the love you have for him was obvious. I thought, this is the man who put his own safety aside to save my madra and fadra and my pack, this is not the man who shot my madra through with an arrow."

"Thank you Jabone."

**If he didn't know it was** a memorial service, he never would have guessed it. There were no servers; if you wanted food you took your plate or bowl went to the table and got it. There was no real order. When people got there they just took the plates or bowls they'd brought with them and went and got food. There was also no alcohol. There was fruit juice though, a huge pitcher sat in the middle of their table, and Persius felt like he could make a meal out of just it.

Kasiria hadn't been wrong; no one was wearing nearly as much clothing as he was, and several Katabull wore no clothes at all. It made it sort of hard for him to decide where to look.

Tarius and Jena had come in a little late, and beside him he heard Kasiria sigh and tell Jabone, "Thank the gods your mother got Tarius to wear a shirt." It wasn't much of a shirt; it had no sleeves and tied at the waist leaving very little to the imagination. It was blue to match the loincloth she wore. He was mostly glad because he didn't want to see the scar he'd made on her body.

"They were arguing about it, but I'm pretty sure that is not why they are late. They apparently just do it all the time and just about anywhere," Jabone said with a wry smile.

When Persius realized what the boy meant he blushed.

They had butted another table up to the one they sat at, no doubt to make the table long enough to accommodate their whole rather large extended family, and it didn't escape

Persius's attention that Jena and Tarius sat as far away from him as they could. Two men set her throne down and then she sat down.

"There used to be four porters for the throne," Kasiria whispered in his ear. "But Tarius immediately thought the whole practice silly and said certainly four was just a waste of man power. So now there are only two. The funny thing is she never calls for the chair because it doesn't make any sense to her, but they have gotten really good at showing up with it just when she starts to sit. One day she spent the whole day just pretending to be about to sit so that they had to run around after her carrying it, setting it down, and then picking it back up again."

Persius smiled. "She always did have a twisted sense of humor. She once had our latrines placed over a stream that ran through the Amalites' camp."

"That's nothing. At Sedrik's keep she had Jestia set all the shit pits on fire to smoke them out," Jabone said.

"They are chimneys," everyone on their end of the table said at once, and then they started to laugh, so it was apparently some inside joke.

He smiled just because their laughter was sort of contagious. *This is basically a funeral, yet when I look around I do not see the undertone of sadness they are afraid will make their children fear death.*

Beside him the wizard turned and whispered in his ear. "They do not believe in doing things to make themselves or each other sadder. They have a loss, they feel it, but they don't wish to. They will honor their dead by celebrating their lives. They will not at any time focus on the fact they are gone; they already know that. They remember their dead by actively living, by bringing together all that knew Arvon and Dustan and having a party in their name."

Persius nodded but couldn't say he understood at all.

Hellibolt sighed and shook his head. "Must you be taken by the hand and led through everything, Persius? Can you discover nothing for yourself? How does wearing dark, dreary clothing, crying aloud, and wallowing in loss help anyone?"

"It shows you miss the person, that they mattered...."

"Shows who, Persius? The dead don't know they're dead; they certainly don't know what you do because they are dead.

A funeral, a memorial, it doesn't serve the one who is dead; it only serves those who live on. That being the case what better serves the living? Is it beating themselves with a stick of agony, guilt and regret, or is it this—a giant reaffirmation that life goes on, that those who have passed still remain in our hearts and in our memory? But they cannot, should not, be as important to us as the living."

Now when Persius nodded he almost understood. He smiled at the wizard. "Thank the gods you take me by the hand and lead me." He lowered his voice and moved to whisper in Hellibolt's ear. "And I just figured out what Hestia meant by the stick in her butt because right now I realized that here I'm not King, not really. Even those who know who I am do not care even one bit about my title. Every fraction of every second I find myself a little more relaxed... and the more relaxed I get, the more my brain is not bombarded by all that I must do or that must be done, what I should or should not wear or what I should or should not do, the more I embrace the fact that at this moment I have nothing... the more I'm beginning to see things clearly that have always eluded me. Please do not pick this time my old friend to lose all patience with me."

**Kaden found himself** sitting between Riglid and the wizard Hellibolt. Across from him Eerin was sitting beside Helen who sat beside Jazel. The old witch was deep in conversation with Hestia. Though he couldn't hear them he guessed it concerned Jestia who was not yet there. Eerin was funny; he was doing everything but standing on his head trying to get the old wizard's attention without actually speaking to him. Kaden whispered as much in Riglid's ear.

Riglid watched Eerin for a second and smiled. He leaned down and whispered in Kaden's ear, "I cannot tell if he is attracted to him or in awe."

"It could always be both. I was both attracted and in awe when I first met you," Kaden said.

Riglid kissed him quickly but then turned to Eerin. "Eerin, have you met the wizard Hellibolt?"

Eerin shook his head.

Riglid sighed and rolled his eyes. "Hellibolt, Eerin is a weather wizard."

Hellibolt looked at the young wizard, smiled graciously,

and said, "I have been drenched by your work."

"I.... I'm very sorry about that," Eerin said. "It is a great honor to meet you."

"Is it then?" Hellibolt laughed.

"Yes, I have heard of your great power...."

"Son, is Jestia not your cousin?"

"Second cousin."

"At my strongest I cannot do a tenth of what Jestia does with a flick of her wrist," the wizard said.

Eerin lowered his voice, turned to see that Jazel was still busy talking to the queen, and said, "But she will not teach me. I train with Jazel...."

"Who is a fine teacher," Hellibolt said. "She and I have traded spells many times through the years."

"I.... I would love to trade spells...."

Kaden couldn't be sure, but it was starting to sound like maybe Eerin was trying to flirt with Hellibolt. Kaden took a covert look at the old wizard; he wasn't bad looking he supposed, but he was really old. Hellibolt turned to look at Kaden who looked quickly away.

The wizard laughed and said to Kaden in a voice loud enough that Eerin and the whole middle of the table could hear it, "What he flirts for is to be my apprentice, not to lie under or on top of me. What he doesn't know is that I have yet to kill a lover and have killed not one but two apprentices."

"I know why you killed the last one, but what about the one before that?" Helen asked.

Eerin looked like he was three seconds from climbing under the table.

"He used a spell I taught him to steal another man's home, his land and his wife."

"You were right to kill him," Eerin said.

Kaden's curiosity was piqued. "Why did you kill the last one?"

"Because the last one helped the king to capture Tarius the Black while she slept. He used the knowledge I had taught him to bring harm to my dearest friend, and to put her blood on Persius's hands. Persius knew better than to ask me to do it because he knew in his heart that what he was doing was wrong and he knew that was what I would tell him. People never want to hear that they are wrong when they already know it. He went to my apprentice because the man was a dumbass who wanted more power than magic could give him. By the time I knew what was going on it was way too late to stop it." Hellibolt picked up a pear and took a huge bite then said around the fruit in his mouth, "He died slowly and not well." Then he swallowed and smiled in a way that made the hair stand on Kaden's arms.

**Jena brought Tarius a** plate of food as soon as they arrived, and she had already finished everything on the plate.

Jena looked at her and smiled. "Would you like some more food?" Jena asked.

Tarius nodded and did not even pretend that she felt well enough to get up and get it herself. Although she was feeling pretty good at the moment, it was mostly an illusion. She was by no means well and while making love with Jena had helped fill the hollow spot inside her it probably had not helped her physically.

**Shortly after Jena had** taken the cubs to where they would be staying during the memorial, Hestia and Hellibolt had found Tarius sitting outside her huts where she had spent most of the day answering this question or that about the memorial or the work on the docks and beach. Every so often Jena would run them all off, telling them that Tarius needed some rest, but then they would slowly trickle back again.

Hestia explained that Jestia was in a state and that she hoped Tarius might be able to do something with her.

"It is a bit of a walk," Tarius said. "And I don't have much strength."

"I'm up for a strength spell," Hellibolt said. So the wizard cast it with the most horrid incantation to date, and then they walked over just in time for Jena to meet them halfway and yell at her.

"What are you doing up?" Jena demanded.

"I'm sorry, Jena that is my fault," Hestia said. "Jestia is on the way to see Jabone's cub and well she is in a mood...."

"Jestia in a mood, what is it, a day on which the sun rose?" Jena asked with a smile. She moved to take Tarius's arm.

"Apparently she is in a mood even for Jestia," Tarius said. "While I will gladly let you hold my arm into eternity, you do not need to work to prop me up. Hellibolt put a strength spell on me and I feel fine at the moment."

By the time they had reached the house of the parents who were watching the cubs for the Marching Night, Jestia was already sitting with Arvon in her lap. She looked up at Tarius and when their eyes met Tarius could see the glint of tears in the girl's eyes.

"What have you got there, little sister?" Tarius asked with a smile.

"I...." She couldn't speak. Beside her Ufalla was just hovering in a near panic, and if anything the look on her face was worse than the one of Jestia's. *She has no idea what to do. She doesn't know whether to slap Jestia or hug her. She wants to help but cannot. She feels useless. Exactly the way I felt when they took Jena and my son.*

"Do you love him, Jestia?" Tarius asked.

Jestia just nodded.

"And he loves you, doesn't he?"

Jestia nodded again.

"He doesn't care that you are being a flaming bitch, does he?"

Jestia shook her head.

Tarius smiled. "And neither do I."

"I haven't been a bitch to you yet," Jestia said. Her voice was filled with unshed tears.

"Today."

Jestia looked at Tarius and smiled. "You look better."

That was when it dawned on Tarius and she turned to Hellibolt. "Do you have enough energy to do a strength spell on Jestia?"

"I do, but you both know the nature of the spell is that it will wear off in a few hours, and if you overdo...."

"A few hours will get us through the memorial," Tarius said.

And so Hellibolt did the spell on Jestia. Jestia made a face but said nothing, so she was too grateful to have some strength back for even just a few hours to make a snide remark over the really ugly incantation. So she really wasn't herself at all.

Tarius motioned for Ufalla to follow her outside even as Darian realized she and Jena were there and came running from the cub's room where he had been playing with the other children. He wanted up, so she picked him up and took him with her. He kissed her cheek and then laid his head on her shoulder. He wasn't tired; he was just her cub and she'd been gone for a couple of days and now he was being left with other people. He just wanted to be close to her.

"What?" Ufalla snipped.

Tarius gave her a look that would boil mud. "Child, who do you think you are talking to?"

"I'm sorry, but she's done nothing but bitch at me all day and find new and interesting ways to call me an idiot. I'm worried sick about her; I have no idea what to do.... Then you she doesn't so much as tell to shut up and.... Well how would you like it if your woman listened to every word someone else said but just blew you completely off?"

"I would not like it, but I dear child did not marry the heir to the Kartik throne and the most powerful witch in our world. She needs to know that you are like that cub, that you love her even when she is showing her whole entire ass."

"I do."

"No you don't. That's the bull crap we say, but when the one we love is treating us like crap we really don't love them at all in that moment. We feel hurt and put out, but this is not about you. Something horrible that you cannot imagine has happened to her and she needs to know that you love her no matter what. Don't you get it? It's a stupid test and you are failing it." Tarius sighed. "She should be dead. Having danced with death she is now pulled between the life she had and the one she has now. We were Nowhere. do you have any idea what it feels like to be Nowhere?"

"I do," Darian said.

"Yes, I'm sure you do, son."

"And then you picked me up," Darian said and hugged her tighter.

Ufalla looked a little shocked. Tarius just shrugged and kissed her son's cheek. "Jestia needs to be reminded that this life is not only as good as the last; it is better. Part of her knows that; that's why she wants to hold my grandson. In that last life neither of us lived long enough to have anything like him or what I have with Jena or she has with you. We were barely in our twenties and completely sheltered from the outside world until it killed us...."

"So you remember it, too."

"I do."

"And why are you not spinning out of control...."

"First, I am the Katabull, not a witch. She bore the brunt of what she did. Second, in this life I have nearly thirty years on her. Though when we're young we never believe it, with age comes wisdom. No part of me would trade that life for this one." Tarius smiled knowing then what Ufalla was so put out about. "That's the problem isn't it; that it doesn't have anything to do with you?"

"Why am I not enough?" Ufalla sighed. "Why would she test me? Why can she not just forget that life like you do?"

"Oh, Ufalla, can you not stop thinking about yourself for even a second? You need to take that woman and remind her of why she'd much rather be here with you."

"How?"

"How? Child, you slay me. How else? We are talking about Jestia; take her somewhere and bang her till she sings like a drum."

"Like a drum," Darian said and giggled.

Ufalla smiled at her then. "I can do that."

"And do it now while the strength spell is at its peak."

Tarius then turned on her heel and walked back in. She put Darian down, kissed his cheek and told him, "Go play with your brother."

Then she turned to Jestia. "Jestia, give my grandson to Naoma and go with your woman at once, and yes that is an order. Hestia and Hellibolt, could you go to the Great Hall please and make sure everything is going as it should? Jena..." Tarius took her arm in her hand. "...come with me."

Jena smiled at her, no doubt seeing the look in her eyes and followed her out.

She had always been a strong believer in following her own advice, and she saw no use at all in wasting a perfectly good strength spell.

**It was getting late and** Tarius was starting to worry that maybe she had given Ufalla the wrong advice. After all what was wrong with Jestia was pretty complex, and wasn't it sort of stupid to think that sex could fix it? She hoped they weren't fighting. *But I feel better about everything and it's not just the* *strength spell.*

Jena set a plate of food in front of her, sat down beside her, and ran her hand over Tarius's thigh. *Maybe I should have taken longer. I mean it isn't often we don't have babies to work around and the house all to ourselves. But.... They know I will not start without them and surely if everything were alright with them they would be here by now. Unless they are just showing off.*

Then she looked up and Ufalla and Jestia were headed towards them. Ufalla was grinning in a smug, satisfied way, and Jestia looked just like herself again; no features of her past life on her face, just her. Jestia caught Tarius's eyes, smiled and winked. *Because I was right and good sex can fix just about anything.* She smiled back and nodded.

Ufalla whispered something to Jestia and Jestia nodded as Ufalla went to obviously get them food. Jestia found the chair they had saved for her and sat down across from Tarius. She then looked at Hellibolt. "I'm afraid I didn't thank you for the spell," she said.

Hellibolt nodded and grinned, "You are more than welcome."

Jestia grinned wickedly at Tarius and said, "So, Jena, did she bang you like a drum till you sang?"

Jena just shook her head and laughed but didn't bother to answer.

Down the table her son said, "Jestia, for the love of the Nameless One I have heard quite enough about my mothers' coupling to last a life time."

"Everywhere," Rimmy said.

"All the time," Harris added helpfully.

"In every conceivable position," Rimmy added.

"Sounds like a great story," Jestia said with a grin.

"No it really wasn't," Jabone assured her, making a face. "Suffice it to say that when Madra is drunk she likes to brag about having sex with my mother.

"Everywhere," Harris said.

"All the time," Rimmy said.

"In every conceivable position," Harris finished.

Jena shook her head and looked into her plate, but then moved till her lips were nearly on Tarius's ear and whispered, "I do not care. They may tease me all they like. As much as they think they know the one thing they can never know is how I feel when you touch me."

Tarius turned and whispered in Jena's ear, "I am ashamed to say that I would rather spend what is left of this spell alone with you than remembering my brothers."

**As soon as no one was** going back for more food it was taken away and the table was cleaned. Kaden had never been to a Katabull memorial and had no idea what to expect, so he watched with interest. Torches were lit around the whole area, seven torches in all. Not really enough light for a human to see well, but more than enough for the Katabull. He watched as the Marching Night started to mill around moving from table to table talking to each other, and he wondered if that was it. But most everyone was still sitting. Laz had moved to flirt with some woman at another table, and Radkin had moved to hunker down behind Harris's chair. They were in deep conversation, but Kaden could not even guess about what. Near the very end of the table young Tarius was talking to his wife and looked very nervous. She was obviously reassuring him.

Kaden remembered that Riglid had said there would be dancers and singers, but he wondered if maybe that idea had been scrapped. This crowd looked less like a group of people starting to do something and more like a group getting ready to dismiss themselves and go home. Then Tarius the Black stood up, and without a single spoken word from her they started to take their seats and there was silence. She looked down the table at young Tarius, nodded and sat down.

Now Kaden knew why young Tarius had looked so nervous all day. He was to speak first. Young Tarius walked up and jumped on top of the table, so apparently they hadn't just used it as a stage in an emergency; they used it for that all the time. It explained the sturdy construction that meant it needed ten Katabull to move it.

The young bard paced back and forth for a second and then he didn't give a eulogy, he told a story. A wonderful story about how Arvon had taken him, Ufalla and Jabone out hiking one day when they were too little to even have swords. Arvon had walked around the jungle till they had no idea where they were and then he had slipped away from them unnoticed, leaving them alone with nothing but the clothes on their backs and their belt knives. He had then apparently hidden and watched as they panicked and then started to work on finding and following their trail out. He did such a good job telling it that once again Kanden found he was jealous of the man's talent, and he was glad he hadn't known them well enough to get up and tell a story.

Then Harris told a story, though not as well as his son, he was quite good. He actually told a story about Dustan and when they both used to ride at the heels of Tarius the Black.

Jena went next. She told the story of how they had saved her and brought her here. She was no bard, but the story she told had the whole group in tears. Oddly the part of the story that brought even the strongest Katabull to tears was when Dustan had sold his beloved horse to pay for their passage to the Kartik.

Rimmy went next telling a story of when he had first met Arvon and Dustan, Tarius and Jena. He was with Tweed, but they were very young and had not partnered with Radkin and Irvana yet. When he asked Riglid about it he said simply that they had met them only after they joined the Marching Night. In the story they were all in a bar looking for the same thing, word on any Amalites anyone might have seen, because they were all selling Amalite scalps to the kingdom for money. Tweed had been drunk and was Katabull as was Arvon. Tweed just kept staring at Tarius till finally not Tarius but Arvon swung on him and said, "What are you looking at!" assuming he was staring at him since after all he was the only blond Katabull on the island.

"Not you," Tweed had said. "Her. I know her."

"Of course you do, that is Tarius the Black," Arvon had said.

As the story unfolded Tweed and Arvon nearly came to blows, with Rimmy trying to calm Tweed and Tarius and Dustan trying to calm Arvon. Rimmy did a good job and it was a funny story. It turned out that Tweed was from the same pack as Tarius, and just as she'd been fostered out so had he; she had been six and he'd been three. Rimmy finished the story and as they all clapped Kaden turned to Riglid.

"I didn't know your fadra was part of Tarius's original pack."

"Yes they were both part of the Pack of the Morning Star," Riglid said.

"Were your fadra and Tarius related?"

"We don't know." Riglid shrugged. "They were too young to remember. My fadra didn't even know his birth parents' names. Since they didn't know one way or the other, Tarius said we were family. Our family and theirs were always close even before my father's husband impregnated the Great Leader's wife."

Kaden didn't think they had any idea how some of the things they said might sound to the outside world, but by now he also knew they didn't care.

Waden took the stage. Like all the rest he paced back and forth and Kaden suddenly realized why. *They are pushing all other thought from their heads and completely setting the story up in their minds before they start. The physical movement helps them do this.* Of course Waden was fantastic. His story was about a battle where he had fought beside Arvon and Dustan about how Dustan had caught a blow that would have taken his head. It was brilliantly told though personally Kaden could have lived without the line, "though he was only a tiny, weak human man...."

Radkin was next, and as Kaden already knew, Radkin was an amazing bard.

"I tell the tale of Persius's Redemption." As if they were only one organism, the whole of the Marching Night gasped.

Beside him Riglid said quickly, "That is a story only Tarius the Black tells."

"I have permission," Radkin said with a laugh at their dismay, and they all seemed to calm right down.

Down the table he saw Jena start to rise, but Tarius grabbed her arm and pulled her back into her seat. Jena hissed something in Tarius's ear that he couldn't hear, and then Tarius said something that he could. "You will not leave our brothers' memorial."

There was a second when it looked like Jena was going to just go ahead and make a huge scene then she just nodded, but he noticed she looked down the table and gave Persius a *go to hell* look.

The tale was wonderful. He laughed, he cried, he cheered. What had it taken for Tarius to send everyone else away while she stood there alone to face the Amalite horde, and how much loyalty and love did those who stood with her have to disobey her order and stand to fight with her? What did Radkin say Jena's father had said? *"She was going to die to save you; I could not let my devotion to you be any less."* *How beautiful. Riglid's birth father died that day. How must that have been for Tarius, to find a member of her pack only to lose him? Then to have them all saved by the very man who had tried to kill her.*

As Radkin finished the tale, Kaden took a covert look at both Jena and Persius. They were both crying, and.... *The expressions on their faces are very nearly the same. As if they have both gotten answers to questions they didn't ask.*

Radkin jumped off the table and helped Tarius to stand on it. Tarius took three huge paces down the length of the table to the right then came back to center, took a deep breath and took three to the left and stopped. She was doing more than collecting her thoughts; she was trying to compose herself.

"She should not have gone last," Riglid said in a whisper.

"She is last?"

"Yes, only seven stories. And that last one.... Well she normally sheds tears when she tells it, and though I may be biased I believe my mother told it better than she does."

Tarius moved her head to look at Jena and Jena smiled and nodded. Tarius nodded back, took a deep breath and walked to the middle of the table and.... *Well that is why she has gone last because no one would want to follow her.*

She told the story of Rorik's Keep. It was profound and amazing. While she glossed over the horrors they found under it, there was no one who didn't get a chill. She said more with fewer words than any bard he'd ever heard. He wondered at first why she had chosen the story because while it was brilliant Arvon, and especially Dustan, were just side notes. The reason became clear when she came to the end of it.

She had paused for effect. "Now during this battle Arvon was leading the left flank as he so often did over the years, and our son was on one side and Dustan was on his other. But in all truth Arvon should not have been in that fight at all. He was addicted to powders, his judgement was impaired, and he was hard to deal with. His health was failing him for an injury in his youth had forced him to age like a human not a Katabull.

"Arvon called a charge and they were making short work of

the children of the breeding program, for all of them had been poorly trained and Rorik had hidden them so that they didn't go into military service. They were easy to kill, but there were very many of them, and we all know Kasiria is blood thirsty."

All of the Katabull said aye and nodded. Kaden noticed Kasiria turned her head glaring in all directions.

"Crazy Kasiria jumped off her horse, broke ranks, and took off into the battle. Jabone looked and saw she was surrounded, and also being braver than he is wise, he went to save her. Then Arvon, who was old enough to know better, took off after his son.

"This left Dustan alone. There were many of these things, and though they could barely hold their swords if you stand on an ant hill long enough you will get bitten. He was mowing them down, but a sword blow hit him in the shoulder. Now Dustan had never had such a bad blow in his whole life, for as he pointed out he had at first been my friend Gudgeon's page and he rode behind him, when I inherited him from Gudgin he rode behind me and Harris, and then he rode behind Arvon. So maybe because he was an amazing swordsman surrounded by those who were even better, he had never once had a bad blow hit him.

"Though most will never admit it, the first time a weapon gives you a bad wound you think you will probably die, and this is what happened to Dustan. Though he whined about it for weeks, he was only really scared those first few moments after he was hit because Dustan, you see, was no faint heart. He was a fighter, a man of prowess, a strong man, but above all of that he was a man who loved with his whole heart. He loved our sons. He loved his friends, but above all of that he loved Arvon. Dustan knew that Arvon needed to stop fighting or he was going to get himself or someone else killed. Arvon needed to stop fighting so that he could quit taking so many powders. So Dustan let everyone think he was a simpering coward in an attempt to stop Arvon from getting killed.

"We taunted and teased him and he didn't care because Arvon *did* quit fighting and he stopped using the powders and was himself again. Dustan would have sacrificed everything to save any of us. That was the nature of Dustan's love."

And she did it all without shedding a tear, yet there wasn't another dry eye on the island he was sure.

Riglid leaned over to him even as he was still clapping and said, "That's not why Arvon quit fighting. He only quit because Tarius made him."

Kaden nodded then turned to look at him and said, "The story Tarius told is a much better story."

**Persius had barely known** them till he heard these people tell stories about them, and now he felt their loss as much as all those there and he finally felt that undertone of sadness he hadn't really felt before. *And who would have thought that the great warlord, the killer of people, would have the best bardic voice I have ever heard. Of course who would have thought Tarius the Black would hold and coddle an infant. All who really know her love her. Her people adore her because she lives amongst them and they know her. Of course her people are not as numerous as mine. There are not so many, I could never know all of mine.... But I know none of them, none save the nobility and a handful of Sword Masters.... No wait I know only the nobility, for all the Sword Masters I knew well drown in the tidal wave. And how well did I really know them? Not really for there is not one of them I could stand and tell even one story about. They were buried here somewhere by the Katabull, and I have really given them no thought at all till this moment.*

Instruments were placed on the table and the musicians now climbed onto it. The princess Jestia was helped onto the table by the woman she was married to. *I don't think I could ever get so used to the whole "she and she" or the "he and he" thing as my daughter has.*

The musicians started to play.... It was a sound like he had never heard. It was loud and wild and filled with drums and the rhythm of it mimicked the sound of your heart beating in your ears. Seven dancers started to dance in the clear area in front of the table. They gyrated and moved with the music, fast and furious, it was beautiful and then.... Then the instruments played softer and the young witch started to sing. Her voice seemed as magical as she was. Loud and powerful, the words of the song talked of life and living and having a good time and.... *I bet it's a common pub song.*

"It was Arvon's favorite song!" Kasiria yelled in his ear.

He nodded.

Then Jabone was tugging on Kasiria and then.... Well his daughter was dancing with her husband in as wild and provocative a way as the other dancers and then most of them were getting up and dancing.

Another singer sang after the witch and then another until there were seven in all, and the whole time the team of dancers danced, and so did everyone else. He noticed even Hellibolt had gotten up to dance with the young wizard and he found himself wondering if maybe the reason Hellibolt had no woman was because he just wasn't interested in them.

For a second he was so swept up he seriously considered getting up and trying to dance himself, but it looked like a lot of work and he was too hot just sitting there.

Suddenly it hit him and he understood exactly what the wizard had said. *They can do nothing about their loved ones' deaths, so they celebrate their lives. They celebrate these men's lives by going on with their own. Everything about what they have done tonight is about them moving on from their grief and finding the joy in their own lives.*

"So?"

The voice behind him startled him. He turned and there stood the witch Jazel, her woman wrapped all around her. Again he thought it was something he was never going to get used to.

"Excuse me?" Persius asked.

"Helen, for the love of the Nameless One, it is hotter than the hubs of hell. Get off me for just a second," Jazel said. The woman unhanded her and far from pouting turned and started to follow some young Katabull woman. "Such a slut. So, Hellibolt said you need a spell from me?"

Persius couldn't think of what she was talking about for a minute.

"He said you needed to get word back to your kingdom...."

"Oh, yes, yes. I need a note sent to the kingdom with my seal...." He held up his ring, literally the only thing of his kinghood that he hadn't lost in the sea. "...to tell them that I am alive and fine and when I will return. I don't want word of the tsunami to hit my country before word that I am well does."

She nodded. "We will meet first thing in the morning and I will do the spell." She smiled a knowing smile. "You've never seen anything like this have you?"

He shook his head in answer.

"Mind you a Kartik memorial is a little more, somber but not much. You could learn much here, Persius, if you will open your mind."

"I am beginning to see why all women who come here stay. The longer I am here the smaller the gap between women and men I see. If you were a woman, any woman, why would you give up being treated like this to go back to a land where you would always be limited?"

Jazel smiled. "You will not be able to change your country overnight or even in a generation, but you could make a start. Like the one you made when you allowed women into the Sword Master's academy. Such a man who starts such a drastic change will not be remembered in books or stories as the one who changed the world; the credit will go to the one who simply finishes the work. But the soul needs no credit for doing a good deed, and it will know what it has done—all that it has done."

Then the witch just walked away, not giving him a chance to say anything in return. When he thought about it he realized that he would have really had to work to find words. *She knew that. It is why she walked away.*

# Chapter 19

**Tarius woke late**. She knew it was late because there was no one in bed with her at all. Jena must have gotten up with the baby and then intercepted the boys so that Tarius could sleep. Her moment of loneliness was pushed away by the fact they all cared enough about her to let her get the rest she needed.

The strength spell had worn off even before she'd crawled into bed last night, but as she stretched she felt almost, but not quite, like her old self again. Of course it helped to have the memorial behind her. She smiled when she remembered what her son had whispered in her ear the night he'd brought her home. She got up, threw on a loincloth and most of a shirt and headed for the outhouse. She wasn't too surprised to find her family sitting at their table outside. Again the thoughtfulness of it warmed her heart. She smiled and nodded at them and headed for the privy.

When she got back she walked over and kissed Jena and then each one of her cubs. Then she started to do her Simbala set. As she went through the motions and the breathing she was able to think absolutely nothing at least twice for several seconds each time. When she finished she sat on her throne at the table, reached over and took her daughter from Jena.

"Tarius, you should eat something," Jena said, but let her have the baby anyway.

"I will. I will eat this little cub." Tarius picked the baby up and started blowing on her belly. The cub laughed and chuffed.

"Madra, don't eat sister, eat me," Darian said in a put-out voice, no doubt because it was a game she played with him, too.

"I will eat you later," Tarius said.

Jena shoved a plate full of food in front of her.

"Quit eating our children and eat your breakfast. You look better; do you feel better?"

"I do, I feel good."

"Hestia has more or less taken over the Great Hall," Rimmy said. "She asks to see you, if you are well, as soon as possible."

"You don't feel that good," Jena told her.

"I do. Jena you know Hestia would not ask for me if she didn't need my help. The country has been hit a mighty blow and all that has happened must be dealt with. Many have died, more have lost their homes, and.... I know exactly what she wants to ask me. I don't know why I didn't think of it before...."

"Because a witch emptied your brain to build a trench," Jena mumbled.

Tarius smiled but ignored her. "Rimmy. could you run to the Great Hall and tell Hestia that of course they can move the refugees into our empty homes until theirs can be rebuilt."

Rimmy was finished with his breakfast and he took off. It was technically Riglid's job now, but it seemed foolish to call for Riglid when Rimmy was sitting right there.

Jena shook her head but said nothing.

"What?" Tarius asked.

"That is an obvious solution I never would have thought of," Jena said. She stood up and kissed Tarius on the top of her head. "I find that I am still in awe of you on most days."

"Only most?" Tarius asked.

"Face it, my love, some days you do nothing but fish." Jena started clearing the table, humming the same tune Jestia had sung the night before. It reminded Tarius of Arvon, but didn't make her sad at all.

"Can you not be in awe of my superior fishing?" Tarius said.

Down the table Hared laughed. Tarius glared at him in jest; she knew why he laughed. Tarius didn't have the patience to be good at fishing; in fact, Hared called what she did *casting* and not *fishing* at all. If she caught nothing she would often get frustrated, jump in the lake with her sword, and kill a fish that way.

"Your problem is that you want always to be doing something," Jena said. "You need to learn to slow down, not a lot but just a little, at least when you don't feel well."

Tarius nodded. Jena loved Tarius, so she worried about her. It could be a royal pain in the ass when it stopped Tarius from doing something she wanted to do, but it wasn't a bad thing to have someone who actually cared what happened to you. Not when so many couldn't be bothered to care if it meant you weren't going to be able to do what they wanted you to do when they wanted you to do it.

She stuck the cub in the crook of her arm and started to eat her breakfast. She started to give the cub some food and Jena slapped her.

"Do not feed that cub food yet or you can walk the floor when she cannot sleep."

"And change her diaper," Hared added with meaning, because of course Tarius had already given the baby some food that didn't sit right with her and the result was not great. But of course as much as Tarius did not want to nurse a baby that was how much she wanted to feed her because otherwise what did she do? *I hold her and play with her and change a diaper or two. But that's important too, isn't it? I love her that's important. Dammit I'm important, too.*

Jena moved till she was mere inches from Tarius's face she smiled. "Now what is that look for?"

"Woman, I'm allowed to have a private thought."

"But not a negative one Tarius, not now, that will not help you heal."

Tarius nodded and she started eating again. When both Hared and Jena had gone inside Tarius whispered in her daughter's ear, "I'm more important than Hared at least, right?" The baby chuffed at her and she said, "That is what I thought."

"I love you more than anyone," Darian said and moved into the chair to her right.

"You do, do you? More than Mama?"

He thought for a minute. "No, not more than Mama."

"More than Pete then?"

Darian looked over at Pete and Pete stacked the deck by smiling at the toddler. "No, not more than Pete."

"Surely you love me more than Arvon?"

"Madra!" He laughed and shook his head. "You know I can't love you more than my little monkey." He grinned impishly. "I love you more than sister."

Tarius shook her head and sighed. "Poor little cub."

"Alright, not more than sister, but I do love you more than Jabone."

Jena walked out and kissed the top of the boy's head but looked at Tarius as she said, "Love is not a competition, Darian. Were your Madra fully well she would tell you that herself."

**Persius stood at a** distance hidden in the shade behind a rain barrel beside Jabone and Kasiria's huts. Tarius was sitting on her throne with her baby in one arm eating her breakfast as she talked to and played with her other children. Jena filled her plate and gave it to her and then walked around cleaning up from breakfast and one of the men who lived with them helped her.

Tarius was the reigning monarch of the Katabull, yet here she sat with her children and her wife eating outside with the dirt for a floor and... *Her wife and her children are the most important things in her life. She doesn't really care about her title, not as Great Leader, not as war lord. This is all she really cares about, and she only does those other things to protect them to make sure they are safe.*

"What are you doing, Father?" Kasiria asked in a worried tone at his shoulder.

He turned and saw her standing there with the cub. He started to make up a story then sighed. "I was watching her."

"Father you must not want her..."

"That is not it, and now I don't think it ever was. But there is something that stirs inside me whenever I see her that I think I mistook for love or even lust when I was younger."

Kasiria sighed. "Please do not let them catch you watching her no matter what the reason, it would not be taken well."

He nodded; she was right.

"Where is the wizard?" Kasiria asked.

"He has gone off with Jazel and that other wizard. Jazel sent my message with an enthralled bird. It would have probably been done much quicker if Hellibolt would have quit asking questions—mostly about the bird of all things."

"It has to be a bird capable of flying across the ocean, and there are only a few that can."

He jumped and turned to see the princess Jestia. She looked him up and down and over. When she had finished he no longer felt that he had a single thought that was his own.

"The bird is the most important part of the spell. Without the right bird you can't cast the spell." Then she just reached over, plucked the cub out of Kasiria's arms and left with him.

"It's alright; she is one of his godmothers," Kasiria told Persius.

He watched as Jestia sat on the other side of Tarius across from the baby wizard. The blond-headed child immediately crawled onto the table and started across it.

"Darian, get off the table!" Jena bellowed. The child quickly scooted across it to sit beside Jestia. "Tarius, do not let them walk on the table," Jena said and took Tarius's empty plate.

"Why do you not just go join them? It would be less conspicuous than hanging around our rain barrel just peeking out at them, which is sort of creepy, Father."

"Daughter, can you not see the way Jena looks at me?"

Kasiria nodded. "Yes, and she can be really mean, too. She once got mad at Jabone and said such horrible things to him that he cried."

**Hestia had already sent** runners to collect all the refugees when Tarius and Jestia arrived. Jestia looked bored but well. Riglid was not far behind the Great Leader. He was carrying a chest which Hestia soon learned was where Tarius kept all her important papers concerning the Katabull compound. Soon maps of the compound and the shore were laid before them on the Great Table which was back inside in its usual spot. In fact, if Hestia didn't know better she would have sworn there could not have been a massive feast there just the night before. Every single table, every chair, every bowl and plate were gone from the area, and everything had been cleaned.

"We have ten ports and towns in the affected area," Hestia explained to Tarius. "Only three have sustained such severe damage that people cannot live there. We will have to assess the situation and decided whether it is safe to build back and where. Of course the biggest town hit was Russet which is our most important port. And if you laugh I will kill you but I am thinking of building a wall between Russet and the sea. It was sacked in a hurricane not ten years ago and again now. While the damage to the port is extensive its location is too ideal to just scrap it. I believe it would be better to repair what is there and add a sea wall than to try to relocate all who live there, and.... What?"

Tarius shrugged, "I said nothing and I certainly did not

laugh."

"Yoland is completely gone," Hestia said, shaking her head. "I don't think a single soul escaped, no ships, no boats, no buildings are left. Even the piers are in pieces no bigger than an oar. I have two hundred men there doing nothing but stacking debris and bodies on the beach and burning them."

"Roughly how many people are coming here?" Tarius asked. "If you will bring them food and supply them with firewood we can easily accommodate as many as two thousand. After that it will start to get tight."

"Sadly, I think we are talking about less than a thousand. Tarius, this disaster is monumental. Thousands have died...."

"The dust cloud alone would have killed three times again as many as have died, and several towns were in the path of the lava besides Montero. Were it not for the rain thousands of acres of jungle would have burned as well. The earth itself attacked us," Radkin said. "We must not dwell on those who died, not when so many lived." She caught Hestia's eye and then nodded her head first towards Jestia and then Tarius.

Hestia nodded and ran her hands down her face. She was exhausted and brain tired; that was her only excuse for being so insensitive. "Of course, of course, I mean were it not for all of you things would be far worse." *And what the hell was that? Why are my words always so clumsy? I might as well have a burning ember in my mouth. When I talk to advisors and council and even great groups of my people, I do not make such mistakes. But among the people I love best I simply can never seem to say the right thing at the right time.*

"Less than a thousand will be no trouble at all, but they must follow our rules while they stay here," Tarius said. "That means they always pick up their own messes, and if they break any of our laws we will kill them."

"That's fair," Hestia said. "And I suppose you will have them watched even as you've had my own people watched."

"Well of course."

**Hestia, Tarius, Radkin,** Rimmy and Harris spent most of the day deciding what would be fixed, how, when and with what. Jestia got bored after only an hour and left. Hestia wondered how the child ever thought she was going to learn to be queen, but she supposed Jestia had plenty of time to learn, and maybe at some point she would learn patience as well. Though that might be asking a lot of only one hundred and twenty years.

Hestia remembered the day one of the nobles had accused her of giving the Katabull too much power; he had of course been talking about Tarius the Black. As Hestia looked around the table she realized that she was letting three Katabull and a Jethrik help her make decisions that affected the kingdom without one Kartik advisor. Fortunately she'd had Radkin kill that man who accused her of Katabull favoritism and none had said anything about it since.

They had just finished tackling the last of the problems caused by the earthquake, volcano and tidal wave. Hestia looked up and said, "Tarius?"

The Great Leader looked at her, and it was obvious she was still weak and mostly as tired of thinking as Hestia was. "Radkin and I have been talking, and...." She gave Radkin a pleading look.

Radkin nodded and continued for her, "I was thinking about Arvon and Dustan's school. Tarius, you studied at the Jethrikian Sword Masters' academy as did your father. Such places train excellent sword slingers. Hestia wants to build a sword school in Arvon and Dustan's names in Montero."

Tarius looked at Hestia and Hestia nodded.

Tarius's eyes filled with tears she didn't shed. "I think that's a fitting tribute," Tarius said. "In case I haven't told you in a while, Hestia, you are not only a great queen but the best of friends."

"Thank you, Tarius. I think we could all use a break from all of this."

And Hestia had been about to start for the door herself when Persius and Hellibolt walked in. Hestia sighed. She just wanted to go home with Radkin lie around and not have to think at all, but he had been coming to the island to speak with her when he was nearly killed and she supposed she might as well get it over with.

The look on Radkin's face said she'd rather chew broken glass than spend even one more minute talking about any kingdom's problems.

Hestia stood on her tiptoes and whispered in Radkin's ear, "Go on. I've got this." Hestia kissed her on the cheek.

"Are you sure?" Radkin asked.

"I am."

There were a few moments at the door when hellos and goodbyes were exchanged, and she watched with a smile as the Katabull throne followed the Great Leader out. Hestia motioned to chairs even as she herself continued to stand. "If you don't mind, I need to stretch a bit. So why did you nearly get yourselves killed coming here?" Hestia asked and smiled at Laz who showed up and took up a stance near the door. Obviously Radkin had sent the boy to "protect" her. It was unnecessary but sweet.

Persius sat and looked at the papers and such Riglid was gathering to put back into the Great Leader's chest. Papers that had been made specifically for Hestia to keep he had already stacked in a neat pile. "I'm sorry, I can both see and imagine that you have been very busy all day."

Hellibolt had not sat down; in fact, he had gone back to the kitchen area and when he came back he was carrying some sort of meat on a small stick. The kitchen in the Great Hall was being used to prepare meals ever since the disaster in order to serve the many Katabull who were working at the docks and cleaning the beach, so that they didn't have to worry about feeding themselves or their families while they worked for the compound. These were civil duties for which none of them would be paid, and they worked in shifts so that they could get their normal work done as well. The Great Leader made sure they didn't have to worry about feeding themselves and their families, too. The people working the kitchen and those gathering the food were being paid.

Such things as these were why Hestia always listened to Tarius's council. Tarius was, above all else, a thoughtful, fair and caring leader.

"I was wondering," Hellibolt said, holding up the stick now nearly bare of meat. "Everywhere I look the Katabull are using wood, yet it is poisonous to them. Is it only if they are pierced with it?"

"Hellibolt, must you waste the queen's time with such...?"

"Yes," Hestia answered the wizard. "I had wondered the same thing. Turns out it has to make a pretty large wound and with a large piece of wood big enough to get into their blood stream. However you should see how everything grinds to a halt if one of them gets even a splinter. I have seen Radkin take her knife and make a huge cut in her finger just to get out a splinter so tiny my eyes couldn't see it. Yet Jazel has told me that a splinter wouldn't do much more damage to them than it does to us if any."

"This can wait till you have rested...."

"Persius, I am queen of a country that was hit by an earthquake, a volcano and a tidal wave as fast as I just said it. It will be months before I am able to really rest, and I have put you off once so.... How can I help you?"

Persius took in a deep breath then let it out. "I find I am suddenly ashamed to admit that we have evidence that the Amalite cult has new members in our country."

"While distressing, there is no reason for you to feel shame. I sent word to you that we had to put down the Amalite cult here. I didn't elaborate and I don't know how much of the story has reached your shores, but here my own brother and other members of the royal family had joined the cult even as I fought in the Great War." Persius looked shocked, so she guessed they hadn't heard much about it in the Jethrik. "Rorik started a breeding program and was eating the children he didn't like while he kept a basement filled with Amalite women he and his fellows raped on a regular basis. His plot had him kidnapping Jena and Darian in order to force Tarius to kill me so that he could take the throne and drive the army to kill every Katabull on the island for the glory of the Amalite gods. Then he was going to force the Kartiks to join the cult or die. My brother was a great imbecile with a stupid plan that could never have worked—unless we were as stupid as he was. We killed him quickly and all he loved. But I would not now be in a position to judge you."

"Jabone told me Jena was kidnapped, but I had no idea the two things were related. We have heard only a small part of what happened here and mostly only what you sent in your report on the matter," Persius said.

"To have let such a thing fester and been none the wiser— it was not a proud moment for me or my kingdom. While I wanted you to know that the Amalites are still a problem, I didn't wish to show my complete incompetence." She smiled. "As the Katabull say, I didn't want to show you my belly."

"I have heard nothing that implies you were incompetent.

I know you have implemented policy to stop them coming back which appears to be working here and in the territories. That is what I need to know, Hestia, I need to know just exactly what you are doing so that we may copy it."

"I pay a large number of people—most of whom were once beggars and now only pretend to be—to watch everyone and everything. Thousands of spies both here and in the territories, all paid by the crown, do nothing all day but insinuate themselves into situations, watch and listen. If they hear or see anything the least suspicious they watch closely, and only when they are sure something is wrong do we investigate. If the suspect is indeed a believer in the Amalite gods we kill him."

"He, do you not check women?"

"Of course, but women.... No Kartik woman is going to willingly follow the cult. Do you know why your country has always had so much trouble with the Amalite's curse?"

"Because we share a border...."

"You have not shared a border with them since the end of the Great War. They have always easily infiltrated your country because you are not that much different than they are, not just in coloring but in your ways. You have similar rules. Your customs are nearly the same. You allow witches, Katabull and queers to live but not as equals. When someone already thinks he is better than another person.... Do you have any idea how easily that can be turned to hate? You treat your women nearly the same as they do. Your class system is the same kind of mess; if you change the word 'priests' to 'the nobility' it is exactly the same. There is a gaping hole between those who have and those who don't in your country."

"I noticed almost as soon as I got off the boat that the Katabull have *no* class system at all. Are you saying it doesn't exist in the rest of your kingdom as well?"

Hestia smiled. "Do not for one minute think that the Katabull come under my rule. They are a sovereign nation within ours. We do have a class system, but it is not as all or nothing as yours. In truth, though it may shock you, if I had my way I would never leave the Katabull compound. I am happiest when I am here for the complexities of life in the rest of my kingdom do not exist here." She paused to regroup her thoughts.

"Here is the problem with having a handful of rich people basically all but owning everyone else. The poor, their dreams are simple and yet even those they cannot achieve because the rich are never happy to have *most* they must have *all*. The wealthy dam off the river, keep all the water, and allow the plants downstream to get just enough water to exist but not to thrive. There is no reason for the poor to believe a word you say. You say the Amalite gods are evil, but the priests tell them that these gods will give them whatever their hearts desire. The poor have nothing to lose because they have nothing. The priests tell them that if they kill you they will be rewarded. Again, what have they got to lose? So then they kill a bunch of 'non-believers' and take their stuff, and lo and behold! Things are better for them. They started out thinking that artists, magic users, Katabull and queers were something to fear, so it's easy to push them over into seeing these people as the enemy because they are so different. The more people they kill the more stuff there is for them until one day the priests come and tell them they must give up all that they have gained, and by then it is way too late to stop them. You, my friend, are ripe for a takeover."

"My head swims. I have more problems than there are answers for," Persius said.

"Do not tax the rich with the same ruler you use for everyone else. Tax your rich more than you tax the poor and your coffers will fill quickly. Take the money and put people to work building and repairing the country's roads, schools and ports, and the gap between the rich and poor slowly closes.

"Do what we did. The poorest of the poor, the beggars and infirm make the best spies for two reasons. First, when you take them from abject poverty to a living wage they are fiercely loyal to you. Second, everyone ignores them on purpose. No one makes eye contact with them. They are like shadows. Oh, and I almost forgot. We use a lot of barkeepers and whores for spies as well because people tell them everything."

Hellibolt smiled at her and smacked Persius on the back, splattering his shirt with the grease off the food he'd just finished. "And that is something she has learned from Tarius. To do one thing to solve numerous problems. Don't you see, Persius? By making those people spies, the people the priests are most likely to recruit first are already gone to them. Better than that, when the Amalites approach them they are the very people who will turn them in. By spreading the wealth a bit people have less reason to follow the cult in the first place. She is right; in the Jethrik the rich have grown fat on the backs of the poor and working classes. The system works for them; they should have to pay for it. If they do not like it, kill *them,* and then there will be more for everyone."

"My cousin Joran came up with the system to recruit spies and he runs most of our operation here. I could send him to your country as an advisor for a while when we get things settled here. He likes to travel, but a word to the wise—he is very shrewd and will probably talk you into selling him mineral rights."

**It wasn't much under a** thousand if it was, and they came not in waves but all at once. The Katabull had stopped them at the gates and were processing them. Laz sat at the gate with Riglid, carefully taking down the names of the people as they arrived. When there were twenty people, Riglid gave them a Katabull guide, handed the Katabull the hut numbers for the group and sent them on as Laz wrote the hut numbers by the names of the people who would be staying there. Then Riglid crossed off the used hut numbers from the list that Tarius had her people prepare and started on the next group of twenty.

And why were they doing all the numbering and name taking? Because almost every family he talked to was missing someone. This way if someone should come later looking for their family they could tell them right where their family was. Frankly, Laz was way ready to have someone come and relieve them. He was exhausted, and the whole thing was making him a little heart sick. Also he was tired of everyone touching his monkey.

These people had nothing. A few had burlap bags with everything they had salvaged, and most of these were still dripping with water. They were missing children or parents or lovers or friends. Their homes were gone and everything of the life they knew demolished. If the Great Leader had not had them build a giant wall around their homes and land they would be in the same shape. It was only while processing these people that he began to understand just how close they had all come to disaster.

Riglid got quickly to his feet, and Laz thought they were finally going to be done but Riglid yelled out, "You old man stop!" The group just kept moving as a whole, so Riglid ordered, "Everyone stop, please."

Then Laz saw what Riglid had, and he stood up as well as the flesh rose on his arms.

His brother turned to face him and said what Laz already knew, "His finger is in his sword."

"He is Katabull," Laz said. They waded through the people till they caught up to him.

"Old man?"

He looked up at them and hissed, "What is it boys?"

"Is that your sword?" Laz asked.

"Of all the bloody cheek, of course it's my sword."

"Are you from the Pack of the Morning Star?" Riglid asked, his voice shaking only so much that Laz would notice it.

"I was. My pack was killed out. I live a solitary life wanting no part of this," he said, swinging his hand around at the people surrounding him.

"Riglid, go and get Tarius at once," Laz said, and Riglid took off.

"What is going on? Laz, you are holding up the whole process," Halda said.

"Look at his sword," Laz told her.

Halda looked, took a step back and nodded. "Take this group over there out of the road and we can keep going. I will get someone to take you and your brother's place."

"What is going on?" the old man grumbled. "I told them leave me where I am I will sleep on the sand, but they wouldn't listen and...."

"Our fadra, mine and my brother's, was from the Pack of the Morning Star."

The old man's features softened. He thought for a minute and then smiled. "Then you must be either Jabone's son, or there was a young boy named...." He thought for a moment then nodded. "Tweed. I am the only other male who lived."

"Tweed was our fadra." Laz looked up and saw her coming with Riglid by her side. "And that is Jabone's daughter, Tarius. She is the Katabull's Great Leader."

"She lived then!" Tears came to his eyes as he looked

down the road at Tarius. "When Elise pulled her from between the bodies I thought her mad."

"How could you not have heard of Tarius the Black?" Laz asked.

"He is a crazy hermit," one of the humans in his group said.

Taking immediate offense, Laz said to the Katabull who was to guide them, "You may take the rest of them to their huts."

"I'm not crazy," the old man told him, "but I do keep to myself."

Tarius and Riglid reached them and Tarius was out of breath which was proof that she still wasn't quite herself. She looked from the man to his sword and back, searching for any familiarity in his features. The old man reached out and touched her throat and she flinched a bit. He smiled at her brightly.

"All these years I thought I was the only one."

Tarius embraced him and patted his back.

"Elvin," Tarius said quickly as she pushed away from him.

He smiled and nodded silently, tears glinting in his eyes.

"I recognized your voice. These are Tweed's sons."

"That one has already told me," he said, pointing at Laz with a smile.

"Do you know.... Who were Tweed's parents?"

"Do you not know?"

"I do not. I was only six and many memories of that time are vague. I only remembered your name because my madra loved you so and she would tell me a story of when she was a child and you carried her on your back the way you did me."

"Shadra was not just my little sister, she was my dearest friend." His tears fell then, and he quickly wiped them away.

"Tweed was only three and he remembered nothing of his life with our pack. I know my father had older children, who had children, who had children and we always wondered...."

"These fine boys are your...." He counted on his hand as Laz held his breath. "...third nephews."

Tarius smiled and hugged both Laz and his brother in turn then said, "See? I told you so." Then she was helping Elvin towards her hut and they followed. "You will stay with us, Elvin. We have a new pack, a huge pack. I personally have four cubs, two in which my blood flows, and a grandson who always wears his Katabull face."

"Such a good omen," Elvin said.

Laz looked at his brother and smiled. "What?" Riglid asked.

"It is not just you and me, Riglid. We share blood with Tarius and Jabone and Arvon and Diana, but...." He lowered his voice to a bare whisper and said, "I will still always love you best."

Riglid smiled and nodded. "As I will you, my brother. As I will you."

# Chapter 21

**Hellibolt did a spell, and** soon he was at Jazel's side as she was walking beside the lake with Helen hand in hand. She didn't so much as flinch, no doubt because she had felt his spell before he reached her.

"So what exactly is it you want?" she asked with a smile.

He fell into step beside her and noted that she must be feeling much better because she was keeping a pretty good pace. "We came here mostly because of a dream Persius just kept having which was obviously prophetic. But also because it immediately reminded me of a prophecy written by a Kartik wizard. There were many elements from Persius's dream that coincided with the prophecy, and when I learned Kasiria's baby was born on the night the moons converged...."

"Arvon was not born on a night the moons converged, not here anyway," Jazel said.

Hellibolt ran his hands down his face. "Of course not. If the moons converged in the Jethrik it would be days before they did here. Well then the prophecy confounds me even more."

"Let's hear this prophecy then," Jazel said. She and Helen moved to sit on a bench placed just off the trail near the water's edge. Hellibolt moved to stand in front of her.

"When the twins converge on the well of power and shine with the same light and the one bathed twice in blood walks with his royal Katabull brother through the valley of the Katabull and the Great Wall rumbles, those who do not rise against the Amalite gods shall perish by the sword of the Nameless One."

Jazel nodded.

"Well?"

"This place used to be called the Valley of the Katabull. The wall rumbled. When the twins converge they always shine with one light, so I don't understand that part at all."

"I thought perhaps it meant Arvon and Diana. Arvon is a royal Katabull...."

"Hellibolt, you said the prophecy was written by a Kartik wizard. He would not think Kasiria's son was royal. Nor do I think he would refer to Diana and Arvon as twins, and who then is the one bathed twice in blood?

"I thought Tarius."

"Tarius had been covered in blood more than twice by the time she was ten."

"You aren't helping, only confounding me more."

"Sorry," Jazel laughed. "It's a Kartik prophecy and I am a Jethrikian witch. If you want the answer to a Kartik prophecy I suggest you talk to a Kartik witch."

"The boy?" Hellibolt asked hopefully.

Jazel shook her head. "Hellibolt, Jestia has forgotten more than that boy will ever know."

Hellibolt sighed. "I was afraid you were going to say that."

"Don't tell me you are afraid of Jestia?"

"I am not, but Jestia is very blunt and if it means something awful I would prefer to have that news spoon-fed to me."

**He found Jestia sitting** in the sun on a bench outside one of the huts not far from where he and Persius and the sailors were staying. Of course his great smoking door of fire entrance was completely wasted on the young witch. She patted the bench beside her and he walked over and sat down like a trained dog.

"What do you think of our new house?" Jestia asked.

"I think it is in a good spot; the energy is very good."

"Ufalla gets bored in Montero and we need to spend more time here. *I* need to spend more time here." She turned to look at him and smiled a knowing smile. "So, what can I do for you?"

"I'm sure Tarius and your mother have told you what we are doing here."

"Persius was having a prophetic dream that included Darian and you have an Amalite problem.... again." Jestia said. "That is not all though, am I right?"

"His dream has elements from an old Kartik prophecy laced all through it."

"Well let's hear it," Jestia said. "So far I can't read minds."

"When the twins converge on the well of power and shine with the same light and the one bathed twice in blood walks with his royal Katabull brother through the valley of the Katabull and the Great Wall rumbles, those who do not rise against the Amalite gods shall perish by the sword of the Nameless One."

The young witch jumped to her feet and paced back and forth in front of him. Then she stopped, looked down on him and demanded, "Who wrote that prophecy?"

"Bentone your, great-grand...."

"Here is the meaning of the prophecy." Jestia started not waiting for him to finish. "Tarius and I were twins in our last lives, Bentone's twins to be exact. When we fought the battle at Sedrik's Keep we all stepped on an energy well. All of the Katabull glowed blue, but Tarius and I glowed white." She turned suddenly to point at where Tarius's two youngest sons were playing in the dirt outside their huts. "Darian has been twice bathed in blood, once during the battle in the cave, and once when we rescued he and Jena from Rorik's Keep. Pete's mother was Katabull, but his father was my mother's dead cousin. While he lives with the Katabull, Mother has made sure he has retained his title. He is literally a royal Katabull. The compound used to be called the Valley of the Katabull. I think we all know that the Great Wall rumbled, and when we were at Sedrik's Keep, Tarius called *me* the sword of the Nameless One. I can promise you this, Hellibolt. If Persius once again lets the Amalites breed and rise up in his land, if I and all whom I love have to go there to fight them again, I will not just lay waste to the Amalites, but I will take control of his kingdom as well."

Hellibolt smiled and nodded, that all made perfect sense. "Well then I guess it is a good thing we came exactly when we did."

**The whole of the Katabull** Armada had returned from the territories just the day before. When they went to the docks Persius noticed there were already half a dozen small boats docked at the piers which had all been repaired. The new timbers on repairs stood out among the weathered wood, but other than that no one would look at this harbor and guess it had been decimated by a huge tsunami less than two weeks ago.

The sailors who had been stranded with he and Hellibolt seemed in no more hurry than they were to board the ship, though it was hard to say whether it was because the last time they'd been at sea they'd all nearly died or because they hated to leave the beauty of the Kartik. He looked down at the cub in his arms then at Kasiria.

"I find myself wishing that I had not sent that message, that I had just let them call me dead so that I could stay here and continue to be Fredrick. He is a much happier fellow than I am."

"It is not such a voyage that you cannot make it again soon," Tarius said.

She had come with Jabone and Kasiria to see them off and had brought both of her little boys with her. Jena had not come with them. In fact she had successfully avoided him most of the time he'd been there, though he knew she'd spoken with Hellibolt many times and had even taken him on a tour of the compound. Persius didn't blame Jena, but it did make things more difficult and had him leaving feeling that things he should have gotten done there he had not.

He kissed Arvon's furry forehead and then handed him to Jabone. He turned to Kasiria. "I will come back." He hugged her and she him, and he was not ashamed to shed a tear.

When he finally let her go Tarius embraced him, holding him almost too tight, and whispered in his ear her lips nearly touching him, "Do not stay too long gone. Cubs grow quickly."

Persius nodded, finding no words.

Tarius released him and then turned and grabbed Hellibolt and hugged him. They exchanged not a single word, and yet Persius got the feeling that they carried on an entire conversation. When they parted the old wizard looked down at the blond toddler and nodded.

"Do not leave me to do it alone," Darian said in a voice that didn't sound like a child at all.

Persius jumped and started to sweat then Tarius and Hellibolt looked at each other and laughed like huge, ridiculous children.

"That! That was *not* funny."

This of course made them laugh all the harder.

Persius ignored them. He got down on one knee and locked

eyes with the child who was smiling at him. "Mark my words, Darian, and remember them. These cackling fools aside, I will *not* leave you to do it alone."

"I know," the boy said. He reached out and patted the side of Persius's cheek.

Persius rose to his full height. "I cannot thank you or your people enough, Tarius. Once again in my hour of need you were there. Though I know she will not care, please extend my thanks to your good wife as well."

"I will," Tarius said.

*Jena laid her sleeping* cub down in her cradle. Persius was finally leaving and—a thousand refuges aside—life could get back to normal. So why didn't she feel better about it? Why did something feel undone? She walked out of the bedroom down the hall into the main room just as Hared walked in the door carrying a bucket of clams. She remembered what she had said to Tarius regarding clams and smiled. Then she frowned.

"She wasn't what I signed up for," she said out loud.

"What?" Hared asked.

"She wasn't what I signed up for. Oh, Hared, I have to go." She started for the door. "The baby is asleep in our room."

She took off at a run hoping she wasn't too late.

*Persius had just started* up the gangplank when he heard someone call his name. He was more than a little surprised when he turned and saw Jena running towards the dock. He came down and walked towards the others. When she reached them she held up her hand then moved to put her hands on her knees and was obviously trying to catch her breath.

Tarius looked concerned, "Jena, are you...."

"Alright? Yes for the love of the gods I am all right. Everyone and everything is alright. Please let me catch my breath." She took a few slow, deep breaths. Finally she straightened. "I need to talk to Persius."

She took hold of his arm and dragged him much further away from the others than he thought was really necessary. As if reading his mind she said, "The Katabull can hear a frog farting in a rainstorm. I cannot let you leave without settling this thing between us. I need to forgive you...."

"I don't expect you to...."

"*I* need it. Not forgiving you has left a dark spot on my life. Hellibolt said—and he is right—hating you is a lot of work. You think I cannot let go of my hate for you because you shot her with an arrow, but that is not it at all. Did Tarius beg you for her life? Even once, did she beg you not to kill her?"

"She did not. She asked that I kill her quickly."

"What did she beg you for, Persius? What is the only thing she begged you for? The thing you denied her?"

He thought about it, he did, but nothing came to mind. He was about to admit he could think of nothing and then he remembered who he was talking to and it all became clear. "She begged me to let her tell you herself."

"And maybe if you had I wouldn't own part of her scar. Maybe, just maybe, I would have said that none of it mattered and instead of nearly asking for her death myself she and I would have gotten away together. We both know if I'd gone with her that night, you wouldn't have been able to stop her. I wasn't there for her—when she most needed me I was not there for her—because she wasn't what I signed up for." She wiped her tears quickly away.

"Dear lady, if I could but go back in time and undo one thing it would be what I did to Tarius and to you. I cannot change the past. There is no excuse for a pride that would have you kill a friend because you felt they had made you look stupid. You do not own any part of her scar, no part of it. I own it all. If you cannot forgive me, no one would blame you, but I cannot bear it if you blame yourself. I am not the man I was, Jena. I'm not even the man I was two weeks ago. And you are not the woman you were then, so why hold yourself at fault?"

"I realized that I can't forgive myself as long as I can't forgive you."

She hugged his neck and he hugged her and held her till it was almost embarrassing, and then she pushed away from him.

"I still think you're a bastard."

Persius laughed and nodded. "I expected no less."

**As the ship pulled away** from the pier, Persius stood at the stern with Hellibolt, waving to them all. He watched as Tarius stooped to pick her little one up then straightening with him on her hip she put her arm around Jena. Persius laughed then sighed.

"She forgave you." Hellibolt said.

"She did," Persius answered. "I have a lightness of spirit I have not had since I was a boy. But beyond that, watching Tarius just now with her children and her woman I realized something profound."

"Please share," Hellibolt said impatiently.

"I just realized it was never about wanting Tarius. It was always about wanting to be her. To be more like her, and…. That has always been in my power, hasn't it?"

"Yes." Hellibolt laughed and he slapped Persius on the back hard enough to rock him. "And you aren't nearly dead yet, so there is still time."

*Jabone and Kasiria had* taken a walk down the beach with the baby. Tarius guessed it was probably so that Kasiria could watch her father till she could no longer see the ship.

She and Jena started for home the boys running on ahead of them as they often did.

"Do you want to talk about it?" Tarius asked Jena as she took her hand.

Jena smiled up at her. "Not just yet. Right now I just want to enjoy the way I feel and not think it to death."

"I know exactly what you mean." Tarius looked down the beach to where Jabone was walking with his wife and baby. "He is quite the man our boy."

"Yes he is," Jena said proudly. "Tarius, I had almost forgotten, when you came home drunk, before Jabone left he whispered something in your ear. What did he say?"

Tarius smiled and held Jena's hand tighter. "He said he loved and will miss his fathers, but that you and I are now and always have been all the parents he needs."

# End

# About the Author

*I started writing at twelve* as an escape. The situations I have lived through are the stuff of which my fiction is born. My relationships with the many and varied people I have come into contact with over the years is a catalogue of characters from which I pull.

I am Jewish but consider myself spiritual not religious. I have studied every form of spirituality and try to live a spiritual life. I don't always succeed, but I do try.

My wife of nearly twenty-five years and I own a small farm where I raise milk goats, rabbits, chickens and a garden. I raise—depending on the weather and bugs—between forty and sixty percent of our food mostly organically. By "mostly" I mean if it looks like I will lose an animal I will do what I think is necessary. We make no trash; we use or recycle everything.

I lived for fourteen years of my life without electricity or running water. I had my only son naturally with no drugs. Though I was married off at sixteen (in an attempt to keep me from being gay) to a thirty-four-year-old man who immediately took me to New York and stuck me in a drug den for a month, I have smoked a total of five joints in my life. I have never done any other drugs.

My son was a prescription drug addict for nine years.

I have worked every shit job you can imagine from pulling car parts in a junk yard and cleaning rich people's houses to home health care. I ran an industrial plane and have logged timber using a team of mules. I have worked at saw mills, framed houses, and poured slabs. I am a carpenter and a rock mason. I can run (install) electricity, and I can plumb (I hate plumbing). I have also built more than one house using only hand tools and a chain saw. I like to hike and cave, and I love the ocean.

I fought heavy weapons (and trained other fighters) with the SCA (The Society for Creative Anachronism) for about twelve years. During that time I broke several bones (mosty mine), and I have a seven-inch plate and eight screws in my left arm as a result of a bastard sword blow. Elizabeth Moon talked me into fencing many years ago and I still do that, but I sold all my armor and heavy weapons a few years ago. Erin Grey talked me into trying Tai Chi to help with my CFS, so I have now been doing a mixture of Tai Chi and Chi Gung every day for the last five years.

Mercedes Lackey helped me get my first short story sale in *Marion Zimmer Bradley's Fantasy Magazine*. That sale opened the door for other sales to MZB, one of which was included in a German-language anthology, and the royalties came in steadily for many years.

CJ Cherryh line edited the first two chapters of *Chains of Freedom* and taught me more about writing doing that than I had learned to that point.

I'm not just name-dropping here; I'm giving credit to people who helped me who certainly didn't have to. Over the years I've come to know many very famous people, and here's what I know for sure—we are ALL the same.

In the writing community the person who is the most famous and makes the most money is often the least talented or deserving—not always, but often. In our business who makes it and who doesn't is often determined by nothing in the world but dumb-ass luck. That being the case, the near worship we see of the "famous" is something I just don't get at all.

The truth is I always think bios are sort of a waste. Anyone who reads my work knows more about the real me than I could ever put in a bio. If you want to talk to me, find me on Facebook. If you see me somewhere, come right up and talk to me. I am just like you. Luckily, I have a job I love, and the reason I have this great job is that people like you let me.

Friend me on Facebook, or if you prefer you can contact me through my personal website www.selinarosen.com, or Email me at selinarosen@cox.net.

# About the Cover Artist

**John Kaufmann has over** twenty years of experience in the commercial field where he enjoys creating art for the education and advertising markets. He is an avid reader and loves creating Astronomical, Sci/Fi, and Fantasy art for art shows and publishing. John's work appears on numerous fiction book covers1 and has received top honors at art shows and conventions in the US and Canada.

**NOTE FROM THE EDITOR:** John's Yard Dog Press covers include *The Burden of the Crown, Leopard's Daughter* (by Lee Killough), *Gods and Other Children* (by Bill Allen), *The Guardians* (by Lynn Abbey), and this cover. He has also created covers for Dragon Moon Publishing in Canada, including the covers for *Sword Masters* and *Jabone's Sword*, fantasy novels by Selina Rosen.

# Yard Dog Press Titles As Of This Print Date

*The Guardians,* Lynn Abbey
*Hammer Town,* Selina Rosen
*The Happiness Box,* Beverly A. Hale
*The Host Series: The Host, Fright Eater, Gang Approval,* Selina Rosen
*Houston, We've Got Bubbas!,* Edited by Selina Rosen
*How I Spent the Apocolypse,* Selina Rosen
*I Didn't Quite Make It To Oz,* Edited by Selina Rosen
*I Should Have Stayed In Oz,* Edited by Selina Rosen
*In the Shadows,* Bradley H. Sinor
*International House of Bubbas,* Edited by Selina Rosen
*It's the Great Bumpkin, Cletus Brown!,* Katherine A. Turski
*The Killswitch Review,* Steven-Elliot Altman & Diane DeKelb-Rittenhouse
*The Leopard's Daughter,* Lee Killough
*The Lightning Horse,* John Moore
*The Logic of Departure,* Mark W. Tiedemann
*The Long, Cold Walk To Mars,* Jeffrey Turner
*Marking the Signs and Other Tales Of Mischief,* Laura J. Underwood
*Material Things,* Selina Rosen
*Medieval Misfits: Renaissance Rejects,* Tracy S. Morris
*Mirror Images,* Susan Satterfield
*Mirror, Mirror and Other Reflections,* James K. Burk
*More Stories That Won't Make Your Parents Hurl,* Edited by Selina Rosen
*Music for Four Hands,* Louis Antonelli & Edward Morris
*My Life with Geeks and Freaks,* Claudia Christian
*The Necronomicrap: A Guide To Your Horoooscope,* Tim Frayser
*Playing With Secrets,* Bradley H & Sue P. Sinor
*Redheads In Love,* Linda L. Donahue, Rhonda Eudaly, Julia S. Mandala, & Dusty Rainbolt
*Reruns,* Selina Rosen
*Rock 'n' Roll Universe,* Ken Rand
*Shadows In Green,* Richard Dansky
*Stories That Won't Make Your Parents Hurl,* Edited by Selina Rosen
*Tales from Keltora,* Laura J. Underwood
*Tales Of the Lucky Nickel Saloon, Second Ave., Laramie, Wyoming, U S of A,* Ken Rand
*Tarbox Station,* Rhonda Eudaly
*Texistani: Indo-Pak Food From A Texas Kitchen,* Beverly A. Hale
*That's All Folks,* J. F. Gonzalez
*Through Wyoming Eyes,* Ken Rand
*Turn Left to Tomorrow,* Robin Wayne Bailey
*The Twins,* Selina Rosen

*Wandering Lark,* Laura J. Underwood
*Wings of Morning,* Katharine Eliska Kimbriel
*Zombies In Oz and Other Undead Musings,* Robin Wayne Bailey

# Double Dog
## *(A YDP Imprint):*

#1:
*Of Stars & Shadows,*
Mark W. Tiedemann
*This Instance Of Me,*
Jeffrey Turner

#2:
*Gods and Other Children,*
Bill D. Allen
*Tranquility,*
Tracy Morris

#3:
*Home Is the Hunter,*
James K. Burk
*Farstep Station,*
Lazette Gifford

#4:
*Sabre Dance,*
Melanie Fletcher
*The Lunari Mask,*
Laura J. Underwood

#5:
*House of Doors,*
Julia Mandala
*Jaguar Moon,*
Linda A. Donahue

## *Just Cause*
### *(A YDP Imprint):*

*Death Under the Crescent Moon*
Dusty Rainbolt

*The Ghost Writer*
Selina Rosen

*It's Not Rocket Science: Spirituality for the Working-Class Soul*
Selina Rosen

*Meditations of a Hoarder*
Melinda LaFevers

*Not My Life*
Selina Rosen

*The Pit*
Selina Rosen

*Plots and Protagonists: A Reference Guide for Writers*
Mel. White

*Vanishing Fame*
Selina Rosen

### *Non-YDP titles we distribute:*

*Chains of Freedom*
*Chains of Destruction*
*Jabone's Sword*
*Queen of Denial*
*Recycled*
*Strange Robby*
*Sword Masters*
Selina Rosen

# *Three Ways to Order:*

1.  Write us a letter telling us what you want, then send it along with your check or money order (made payable to Yard Dog Press) to: Yard Dog Press, 710 W. Redbud Lane, Alma, AR 72921-7247

2.  Use selinarosen@cox.net or lynnstran@cox.net to contact us and place your order. Then send your check or money order to the address above. *This has the advantage of allowing you to check on the availability of short-stock items such as T-shirts and back-issues of Yard Dog Comics.*

3.  Contact us as in #1 or #2 above and pay with a credit card or by debit from your checking account. Either give us the credit card information in your letter/Email/phone call, or go to our website and use our shopping carts. If you send us your information, please include your name as it appears on the card, your credit card number, the expiration date, and the 3 or 4-digit security code after your signature on the back (CVV). Please remember that we will include media rate (minimum $3.00) S/H for mailing in the lower 48 states.

*Watch our website at*
*www.yarddogpress.com*
*for news of upcoming projects*
*and new titles!!*

# *A Note to Our Readers*

We at Yard Dog Press understand that many people buy used books because they simply can't afford new ones. That said, and understanding that not everyone is made of money, we'd like you to know something that you may not have realized. Writers only make money on new books that sell. At the big houses a writer's entire future can hinge on the number of books they sell. While this isn't the case at Yard Dog Press, the honest truth is that when you sell or trade your book or let many people read it, the writer and the publishing house aren't making any money.

As much as we'd all like to believe that we can exist on love and sweet potato pie, the truth is we all need money to buy the things essential to our daily lives. Writers and publishers are no different.

We realize that these "freebies" and cheap books often turn people on to new writers and books that they wouldn't otherwise read. However we hope that you will reconsider selling your copy, and that if you trade it or let your friends borrow it, you also pass on the information that if they really like the author's work they should consider buying one of their books at full price sometime so that the writer can afford to continue to write work that entertains you.

We appreciate all our readers and *depend* upon their support.

Thanks,
The Editorial Staff
Yard Dog Press

PS – Please note that "used" books without covers have, in most cases, been stolen. Neither the author nor the publisher has made any money on these books because they were supposed to be pulped for lack of sales.

Please do not purchase books without covers.